GIVE US
BARABBAS

*For Sandy and Marianne
Holy Spirit gifts
to the church of
Airdrie. Blessings!
Thom.*

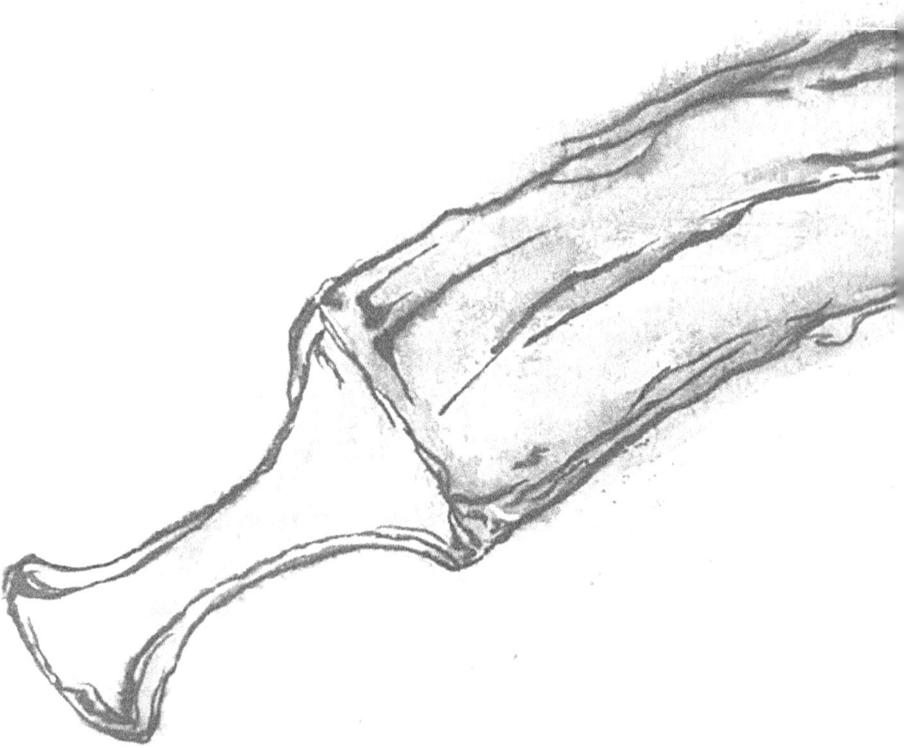

GIVE US BARABBAS
A REDEMPTION STORY

BY
THOM KOOP

XULON PRESS ELITE

Xulon Press
2301 Lucien Way #415
Maitland, FL 32751
407.339.4217
www.xulonpress.com

Exulon ELITE

Give Us Barabbas: A Redemption Story
© 2020 by Thom Koop

Author Photo: Hannah Koop

Cover Art: Meaghan Blane

All rights reserved solely by the author. The author guarantees all contents are original and do not infringe upon the legal rights of any other person or work. No part of this book may be reproduced in any form without the permission of the author. The views expressed in this book are not necessarily those of the publisher. For permission requests, contact the author: thom@thomkoop.com

Unless otherwise indicated, Scripture quotations are taken from the Holy Bible, New International Version (NIV). Copyright © 1973, 1978, 1984, 2011 by Biblica, Inc.™. Used by permission. All rights reserved.

Scripture quotations marked NASB are taken from the New American Standard Bible ©, Copyright © 1960, 1962, 1963, 1968, 1971, 1972, 1973, 1975, 1977, 1995 by the Lockman Foundation. Used by permission. (www.Lockman.org)

* Note: Scripture quotations that contain the designations "God," or "the LORD," have most often been modified, in keeping with the author's criteria as spelled out in the Introduction. Pronouns referring to Him or the Holy Spirit have also been capitalized, and pronouns referring to Jesus have been capitalized in those places where He was recognized by the character in the story as Divine.

Printed in the United States of America.

ISBN-13: 978-1-6312-9460-0

Dedicated to

My wife, Mary Jane.

Other than God giving Himself to me,
she was and is each day
the very best gift I ever received.

And to the three persons we co-created with Him:
Benjamin, Hannah, and Meaghan.

These amazing people
— my family —
have loved, honored, respected
and encouraged me,
always and in everything.

Thank you!

TABLE OF CONTENTS

Introduction	ix
Prison	1
Galilee	8
Apprenticeship	18
Abraham	24
The Day	29
Murder	33
Ambush	39
Funeral	46
Moving On	55
Reconnection	64
Revelation	70
In Search of Destiny	82
Blood Bricks	89
Renewal	95
To Work	101
Homecoming	105
Zephaniah	110
Brotherhood	120
Reunion	125
Magdala	132
Meeting	140
Completion	149

Captivated	155
Ariah	161
Retrieval	174
Flight	183
Gamala	191
Connection	199
Harbor	206
Martyrs Monument	214
Committed	220
The Qanaim	227
Training	236
Active Status	248
Barabbas	256
A Crisis of Faith	262
Laying Low	274
The Uprising	279
Arrest	286
Imprisonment	291
Brought Out	297
Pontius Pilate	300
The Man	303
Condemned	308
Freedom	313
The Crowd	316
Golgotha	320
Next Steps	328
Beginning Again	333
Going Home	336
Visitation	340
Family Renewed	346
Joshua's Story	357
Home and Away	367
Ariah's Story	377

Clarity 386
Betrothed 390
Wedding 392
Jerusalem. 398
Pentecost 405
Bethany 415
Gethsemane 419
Simon. 425
The Community of the Called 438
Sent Out 446
To Rhages and Beyond 457
Before Kings 465
Under House Arrest 474

Afterword 479

Endnotes 481

INTRODUCTION

What you have before you is a piece of historical fiction, and as such, the majority of the content is admittedly and simply the product of my own imagination: a creative story, whose roots are at one and the same time planted in real people, real places, and real events. That being said, my dream is that I have done at least three things in its telling.

I hope, first of all, that I have done justice to the actual persons and the true history contained within the Biblical account.[1] At the same time, I trust that I have not taken excessive creative or artistic liberties in my picturing of what and who else might have been. Finally, I pray that I have crafted this historical tale in such a way that, not only are you enabled to enter into this distant world and its era, but also and of equal importance, that you, its reader, enjoy and benefit from the time you spend here.

As a lifelong student of Scripture who holds three theological degrees and is proficient in both Greek and Hebrew languages, I carefully researched every aspect of this story. In the process, I read everything I could get my hands on: history books including Josephus, Biblical encyclopedias, Bible dictionaries, scholarly articles, commentaries, and more, allowing all of it to inform my imagination and add to what I already knew. I have included a few notes at the end of the book, should you be so inclined. But I have left all of this backstage, for in the final analysis, this is a novel and I didn't want it to be bogged down in academia.

It was important to me that *Give Us Barabbas* remain a *story* rather than a study.

It must be acknowledged at the outset that we know very little about our main character. Secular history bears no record of him. Some have even suggested he was an invention of the biblical writers.[2] He is simply mentioned in each of the four gospel accounts as a criminal, imprisoned and slated to be executed for his crimes, whom Pontius Pilate then released to the crowd in Jesus's stead at the conclusion of His trial.

In Mark's version, and Luke says almost the same thing, we are told without elaboration that Barabbas was an individual, "in prison with the insurrectionists who had committed murder in the uprising" (Mark 15:7; Luke 23:19). John's gospel gives us some additional detail, calling him a *robber* or a *bandit* (John 18:40 NASB). Other translations have gone so far in their renditions of the word used here, as to brand him a *revolutionary* (NLT and others) or a *terrorist* (CEV). In his account, Matthew neglected to mention any uprising, murder, or thievery but simply said that, "At that time they were holding a *notorious* prisoner, called Barabbas" (Matthew 27:16 NASB).

Some manuscripts of Matthew's gospel however, a reading followed by almost all modern translations,[3] do contain one extra, very significant detail not found in the other gospels. We discover there that Barabbas actually had a first name, and that his full name was, "***Jesus*** Barabbas."[4]

Origen, an early third-century church father from Alexandria, was so bothered by the fact that some of his manuscripts of the gospel gave Barabbas this fuller name, he argued that some heretic must have added it. He felt it was inconceivable that such an evil man could have such a holy name.[5]

If we ask why the two-part name, *Jesus Barabbas,* is not in all manuscripts of Matthew, we simply don't know. It seems reasonable to assume that Matthew, as the most Jewish of all the gospels, saw fit to include his full name, while some scribes, most likely feeling the same way as Origen, did in fact *correct* their manuscripts of Matthew in this place so as to guard the honor of the One whom they too believed to be the good and the true Jesus. Possibly they felt justified in doing so since none of the other three gospels had included it.

In large part *because* of its challenges, I strongly believe that "Jesus Barabbas" *is* the preferred reading here, and that in reality, what Pilate did was to place before the gathered and largely Jewish crowd, an extremely significant choice, absolutely blatant in the way in which it placed the two men named opposite each other:

"Which one do you want me to release to you?
Jesus Barabbas, or **Jesus Christ**?"

In the ancient world and especially within Jewish culture, names were extremely important. Certainly, that is nowhere truer than here. We have two men standing next to each other, both of whom bear the name, *Jesus*. One is further identified as *Bar Abba(s)*, or "son of the father," while the other is described as "he who is called the Christ," *Messiah* or *Anointed One*, "Son of the Blessed One" (Mark 14:61), or "Son of the living God" (Matthew 16:16).

Those gathered were forced to decide between two individuals named *Jesus,* meaning savior or deliverer (Matthew 1:21), but who represent opposing and entirely different ways of bringing the salvation of Israel and indeed, that of all of humanity, into effect.

In history, then and now, there has always been this choice. Barabbas's way is that of power, violence, murder, and the political overthrow of secular, in this case, Roman rule; Christ's option is one of grace and peace, in a kingdom not of this world even though totally immersed in it. It is the will of heaven being done on earth, but worked out in such a truly powerful way that its servants do not need to fight with physical weapons to gain the desired outcome (John 18:36).

The two approaches could not be more opposite each other. One is fed by and grows out of hatred. The other one is moved by compassion. History records that, in this instance, the crowd chose Jesus Barabbas and clamored for the other Jesus to be crucified.

So that I don't have to interrupt the flow of my story later on, allow me to elaborate on the two parts of Jesus Barabbas's name here.

"Iesous" is the way his name would have been written in Greek—the language of the New Testament. And *"Iesus"* is the way it is written in Latin, from which we get the English name, *Jesus.* Greek and Latin were the two predominant languages of the Roman Empire.

Most Jewish people at this time spoke Aramaic, a linguistic relative of Hebrew. The fourth gospel tells us that the inscription on the cross, "Jesus of Nazareth, The King of the Jews," was written in these three languages: Latin, Greek and Aramaic (John 19:19-20).

Since Barabbas was a Jew, the actual Hebrew or Aramaic name he would have been given at birth was *Jehoshua,* meaning, "Yahweh is salvation," or "Yahweh is deliverance." This was the same name Moses had given to his successor, Hoshea, the leader who eventually brought the children of Israel into the Promised Land (Numbers 13:16).

Jehoshua or *Yehoshua,* sometimes written as *Yeshua,* then, would be Barabbas's proper name, and *Joshua,* the English equivalent of his Hebrew designation. This is what he would have likely been called in most situations among family and friends and in day-to-day life. In larger Roman society, he would have been called *Jesus.* And I have also imagined that his family lovingly altered his name to *Yoshi* when he was a boy, as a childhood endearment, in the way parents often do.

INTRODUCTION

Though some writers have suggested that *Barabbas,* coming from the Aramaic "bar Abba" or "bar Abbas," could mean that his father's given name was *Abba,* a proper name known in the first century, I chose rather to imagine that his father's name was actually *Abrahim,* and that Barabbas was born, "Jehoshua ben (son of) Abrahim." I have then suggested that *Barabbas* was a name he made up and took to himself as an alias, so that his family would not be connected to and negatively impacted by his life choice to align himself with the Jewish Zealot party.

One other thing on the subject of names: While *Elohim* is the basic Hebrew word that means "God," the four letters Y-H-W-H represent what is considered to be the most significant of all His names (Hebrew didn't originally have vowels). This holiest of all names comes from a verb meaning, "to be," or "to exist," and is the "I AM" name for God (Exodus 3:1-15). In most English Bibles, *YHWH* is written as "the LORD," in upper case letters, to parallel the four letters of His Hebrew name and possibly, in some way, to set it above all His other names, but also to distinguish it from *Adonai,* which actually means "Lord."

Starting somewhere in the third century BCE,[6] as a way of ensuring that they would never take the name of YHWH in vain (Exodus 20:7), most devout Jews would not pronounce this name aloud, silently to themselves, or even read transliterated forms of the word such as *Yahweh* or *Jehovah,* but when they saw YHWH, always spoke it simply as *Ha Shem*—"the Name," or substituted another one of the many names for God such as: *Adonai*—"the Lord," *El Shaddai*—"the Almighty God," or *Ha Kadosh*—"the Holy One," just to cite a few examples.

And so, since the characters in this story were Jewish, it made sense to me, not only to have them use their Hebrew names for God, but to substitute *Ha Shem, Adonai,* or one of His other names when they are actually referencing the name, *YHWH*. In Scripture quotations I have written it as YHWH, allowing you, the reader, the freedom to determine how *you* choose to refer to Him in those places.

The death and resurrection of Jesus, celebrated by the Church worldwide every Easter, is without doubt, the central, pivotal event of Christian history. What happened in those few days forever changed everything that followed and gave new and deeper meaning to all that had gone on before.

In truth, the Barabbas narrative is but one small piece of that Passion Week. But I can truly say that I have gained a much deeper appreciation of the whole, even as I riveted my attention on imagining out this minor character's *unknown* saga from within the larger and much more familiar story of Jesus's ultimate sacrifice.

My prayer is that you have a similar experience. I pray that you are impacted, encouraged, uplifted, and even challenged by the entirety of "the Good News to all people" even as you read my rendition of Barabbas's life and his one unique part in the salvation drama.

As I conclude this introduction, may I say one final thing: I have attempted to put flesh and blood on the enigmatic character of Jesus Barabbas and to weave a more complete story around his singular mention in the New Testament.

I pray that I have done it well.

Ultimately, eternity alone will reveal how closely my creativity aligns with what actually happened.

Chapter 1

PRISON

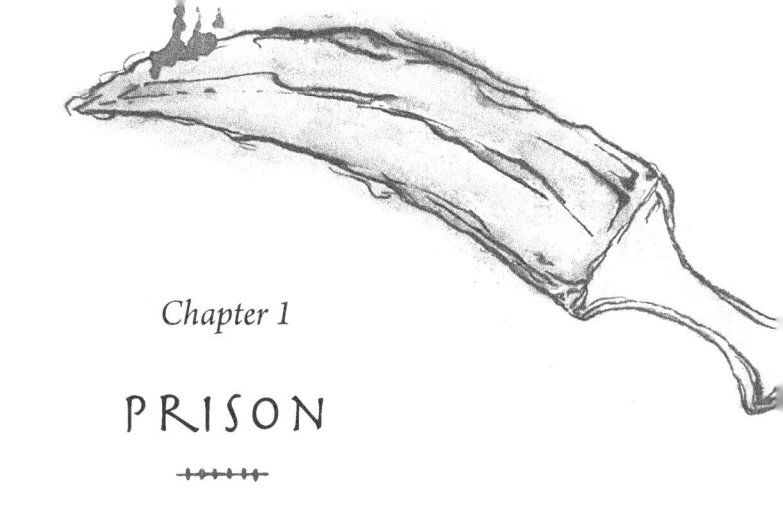

How long had he been, here in this dungeon; confined in this awful place? "And there was evening, and there was morning...*another* day." How many times had that happened?

At this very moment in the half-dark of early morning, jolted out of his fitful slumber by the unceremonious and noisy arrival of yet another inmate, Barabbas didn't know how long it had been. Not exactly, anyway. There was little sense of time here, though he thought it must surely be close to a month or so now. Had Passover come already?

He lay there, or more correctly half sat, fighting for even a little bit of sleep, leaning against the rough-hewn wall with his threadbare cloak pulled up around himself. He was grateful for the little bit of warmth it provided in his dank surroundings.

Why was it taking so long? Barabbas didn't know that either. Prisoners were given very little if any information. All he knew for certain right now was that he was starving and ill and that he was physically, emotionally, and even spiritually, the most miserable he had ever been.

The inmates received little or no food. Why did they need to be fed? They were after all, criminals, persons of little or no consequence. This was just a holding cell for those who were condemned to die anyway.

Barabbas remembered early on in his stay when Justus, a fellow brigand who knew where they had all been taken and detained, had bribed a guard and dropped provisions down through the grate after calling his name. On that occasion, Barabbas had managed to keep most of it for himself in the ensuing riot. On another occasion, he had helped himself to what had been brought for someone else. He had been healthier and stronger then.

Sometimes the guards held a lantern in the opening and threw their own lunch in for sport, just so they could watch the frenzy that would most certainly transpire below.

Fights over food or clothing or almost anything else for that matter were a daily occurrence.

Once or twice he had seen prisoners get so hungry, they had killed the ever-present rats that chose to make this nether world their home and had then eaten them raw. There were even stories of captives eating their fellow inmates who had died, and although Barabbas had never actually seen it nor did he want to, it did not seem like something outside the realm of possibility.

That would be an abomination to a Jew. Romans wouldn't look favorably upon it either. Barabbas had decided that he would rather starve than stoop to either level, for the time being anyway. As a result, it had been quite some time since he had eaten anything.

The only good in all of this he supposed, was that he was still alive, even though he knew it was a gross exaggeration to describe his present state of existence as *living*. His life had been far from easy or comfortable, especially for the last decade or so, but being imprisoned in a place like this despair came easily, and he had thought already many times that full-on death might be the preferable option.

Of the eight of them, all members of the Jewish Zealot faction known as "Q," who had been arrested and brought here after the most recent uprising, he was the only one still alive or at least, so he assumed. Given his condition, he might soon join them, he thought.

Abiathar, sadly, had died almost right away from injuries he'd sustained when they were cast into this abyss. Josiah and all of the others had been removed about a week later. Most likely, they had been crucified. The Romans loved to torture and kill Jewish nationalists within the immediate purview of their very own Holy City.

Barabbas had no idea why *he* had been spared the cross and singled out to die a secluded and secret death. It made no sense.

He cursed the Empire and all things Roman.

In the few days they had together initially, he had talked to the others. About the uprising in which they were arrested. About what had gone wrong. And about what they would do to the Romans if they managed to escape this place, if they somehow managed to escape death. Not that they were afraid of dying. They had all fully committed themselves to the cause.

Indeed, to die for the ideals of the Fourth Way was considered glorious.

Now, Barabbas couldn't remember the last time he had talked to anyone about anything.

"Silence is the language of the hopeless," he said.

This had surprised him, not realizing initially, that he had actually spoken it aloud. And he marveled that his own voice sounded strange, not having heard it other than in his own head for very many days.

Not that anyone was listening or that anyone cared. He was alone and forgotten.

Barabbas imagined that this was as close as any place could be to the earthly equivalent of *Sheol*, that shadowy place of the dying, or maybe more correctly, of the living dead.

Many of those who were cast into this hellhole died right here, even before they had the chance to be executed in public. It had happened already several times over, even in the short time Barabbas himself had been incarcerated. One of those men had been so kind as to *share* his clothing with Barabbas on his second day. Barabbas had fought off all of the others and *borrowed* the garments knowing that a dead man certainly wouldn't need them any longer. And once dead, the unfortunate ones were simply piled off to one side, to be unceremoniously removed, little by little and piece by piece, courtesy of the rot and the rats.

His mind broke free from this prison and ran at light speed to another place.

The place where life had started.

Would he ever…?

Or, was that too much to hope?

He was almost certain that those things and those people were lost to him and him to them forever.

Did *they* ever think of him? Or had they long ago resigned themselves to his eternal disappearance?

And then, what about when he was actually dead? It would most likely be soon, whether by execution, disease, or starvation.

He would simply cease to be.

Would *they* find out somehow? Would *anyone* mourn his passing?

Or, would he end up a nonentity? Left to rot away here, hidden in this dungeon? Or maybe brought out, but only to be crucified and then buried with all of the others, without significance, without connection, in the paupers' common grave?

What *had* he brought upon those close to him and upon his own family through all of this? Yes, he had distanced himself. Tried to protect them. But, what must they have still endured as a result of his life and actions, regardless of the fact that he had tried to spare them? At the time, there had seemed to be no other option.

A time and a place far away and long ago? He was amazed at how quickly and easily he could still go there in his thoughts.

Galilee...home.

He had been forced to leave and to flee for his life.

Barabbas knew that he had come to be part of the Jewish Zealot movement by choice in a way, but maybe more so through circumstances that had been beyond his control. He had simply been in the wrong place at the wrong time, or maybe the right place at the wrong time, or the wrong place at the right time...he wasn't sure how to best describe what had actually happened.

He *was* grateful that he had been there.

If for nothing or for no one else, then for *her* sake.

But maybe it could have all turned out differently.

If only.

Was it really destiny, or was it something less that had opened his way into the brotherhood of the Qanaim? They had taken him in and given him a semblance of family when he had lost everything.

Had he believed what they taught only because of what he received in return? No. It had made sense to him even before he joined. It still made sense to him. He did not doubt the ideals of the Fourth Way.

But what about the methods used to achieve these ideals? This, above all, had been the one thing dogging him lately. He had given thought to that almost nonstop over the past few days and weeks, and truth be told, a fair bit even before he had been imprisoned.

Indeed, did all of the bloodshed, all of the violence, really accomplish the goal?

Was this really the way that Adonai intended to bring about His kingdom, His reign on the earth?

Barabbas's biggest question was whether He, Elohim Himself, was pleased?

Was this a crisis of faith he was experiencing?

Or did he just not have the stomach for this way of life anymore?

His thoughts seemed to be taking him all over the map. But here, now, Barabbas was forced to ask himself what each of us must ask ourselves at some point:

Has my life, my unique contribution within history, in any way made a positive difference in the world?

And on an even more personal note:

Have I myself *mattered* to anyone?

That last question cut deeper than any *sicae*, the small curved dagger that was their weapon of choice, ever could.

He knew that people were far more important than any ideology.

People matter. Relationships are paramount. Especially family.

Was that simply age, wisdom, and experience, speaking?

As he reminisced, Jesus Barabbas was surprised at how real and fresh all of it actually was, surprised by the raw emotion that rose up from some place deep within the pit of his stomach, overwhelming even the very real physical ache that lodged there. Confusion and a host of even less clearly defined feelings now threatened to completely undo him.

Profound sadness and pain surfaced, bubbling up from the center of everything that was churning inside. And yet there was some kind of striking clarity.

In the past, Barabbas had most often forced those hurts and life-size questions way down deep inside, inviting anger and hatred to take their place. Those emotions seemed easier to control… to channel.

It made him feel less vulnerable…more powerful.

But maybe he didn't need or want to respond that way any longer.

Where had anger and hate taken him?

Nowhere good it seemed.

But was change an impossibility? Was it, as they say, "too little, too late"?

He didn't know.

Tears were streaming down Barabbas's face. He made no effort to stop them. In fact, he welcomed them.

And then, a thought, a revelation, appeared from some forgotten, or maybe from some brand-new place within him.

Hope wrestling to be born.

"Adonai," Barabbas began, and then somewhat tentatively declared, "David said that even if I make my bed in *Sheol,* You are there, and that even the darkness will not be dark to You. That Your light will shine!"

He surveyed his surroundings momentarily, his hands reaching out for something, or maybe…

…for Some One.

"Are You really…are *You* actually…*here?*"

"If You are, then I beg You, shine Your light and find me please…Abba!"

Barabbas gasped at that last word. It had escaped his lips before he had thought about or could stop it.

But it was the one thing he knew he craved.

And he was now keenly aware that he was a man who had little to lose.

Or maybe, more correctly, that he was at the core of his being, simply and once more…a desperate and lonely child.

Chapter 2

GALILEE

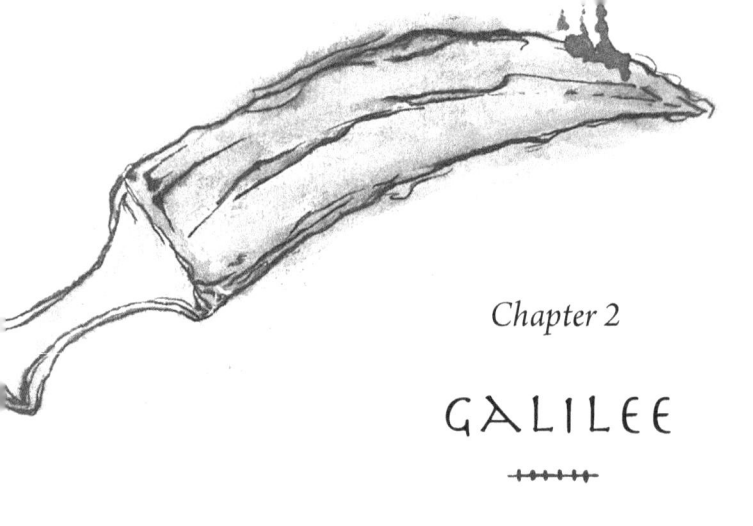

As a youngster, Yoshi was sure that Galilee was the best place on earth. Not that he had lived anywhere else or that he knew much of the rest of the world. In fact, other than Jerusalem and a few neighboring towns, he rarely travelled beyond its borders.

He had been born here, in the rather small town of Rakkath, in lower Galilee, and had so far lived out all of his days in this area of northeastern Israel.

The townsite itself was on a hill along the western shore of the Sea of Galilee, the body of water known in Hebrew as *Yam Ha-Kinnereth*. Rakkath itself was an old Israelite town strategically located along the ancient east-west road leading between the urban centers of Damascus and Acre.

The population was predominantly Jewish and had long been here, Rakkath having been one of nineteen fortified cities in northern Israel given to the tribe of Naphtali after the conquest of the Land of Promise by the leader who shared Yoshi's given name.

Recently however, a significant number of people had moved here, probably in part at least, due to the seventeen natural mineral hot springs that surrounded the town. People believed that their waters had healing properties.

This influx of people had meant there was a fair bit of construction and as a result, their family had a healthy market for his father's bricks and masonry skills. The city was expanding too, mostly toward the southeast, since there was no longer room within the old fortified section of the city up on the hill. This swell however now also included a fair number of Gentiles and a growing Roman presence, and while that too had meant more business, it came with an additional hidden cost. And, at least some longtime residents thought it much too high a price to pay.

As far as Yoshi knew, his parents had moved here about a year and a half or so after they had been married and almost immediately after his older brother Zephaniah had been born. He himself appeared on the scene a few years later. In time, his three other siblings had come along.

He had certainly heard them talk about having moved from Bethlehem and knew that Abrahim had apprenticed himself to a brick maker there. He assumed that family had brought them back here and had so far never had occasion or opportunity to ask them anything beyond that. Besides, those things were ancient history as far as Yoshi was concerned and, to this point at least, of little interest.

Of course, as devout Jewish parents, on his eighth day of life, they had taken him to the town synagogue, and the local *mohel*, the Jewish man trained in the art, had performed the *brit milah*, or covenant of circumcision. There, in the midst of blessings for his parents, prayers for his own personal eventual perception of and trust in Adonai, the one true God, along with petitions for the speedy coming of the Messiah, the return of the prophet Elijah and the re-establishment of David's reign, *Jehoshua ben Abrahim*, Joshua son of Abrahim, of the tribe of Judah, was welcomed into the lineage of Israel's children.

They had named him Jehoshua. "YHWH is salvation," or "YHWH is deliverance," his name meant. And even though they were not wealthy or of noble birth, alongside many other Jewish parents, they prayed, hoped, dreamed that they might be the favored ones to give birth to the Messiah, the Anointed One, the one who would restore the throne of David, would bring deliverance and salvation to Israel, and restore the fortunes and future of the people of Elohim.

"Yoshi," his father Abrahim had said to him many times, "your name, the name, *Jehoshua,* first and famously, was one given by Moses to his successor, Hoshea the son of Nun. That Joshua was the man who had not only been at Moses's side during our deliverance from Egypt; he was the one chosen by Adonai to lead His people into the Land of Promise. And who knows what great thing Adonai Elohim might want *you* to do some day?"

It always made Joshua proud to wear such a significant name. And indeed, what would he do one day, when he grew up?

Yoshi, the name he had answered to for as long as he could remember, had heard his people's history repeated often in their home. How, sadly, as a result of sin, of the original twelve tribes, only a remnant of the people of Elohim remained. And how, while they did still remain in the land, the greatest disappointment of their history was that the land itself, the land that Elohim had promised to Abraham, no longer actually belonged to them. Because of their half-hearted devotion, they had lost it to the Assyrians, the Babylonians, to the Medes and the Persians, and then to the Greeks. They won it back and then lost it again. It was the ongoing story. And for the last several generations at least, they had been under the iron hand of Rome, with the area of Galilee in which they lived, now ruled over by Herod Antipas, one of the four children among whom Herod the First's dynasty had been divided.

So it was that the nation of Israel asked: When would the yoke be removed and the throne of David, the promised eternal throne, be re-established?

Yoshi grew up hearing these prayers from his parents at home, in the synagogue, and in the homes of his relatives and friends. His father, Abrahim, for sure, and his mother as well, had often shared their failed history alongside this restoration hope with their family, even more so at the Passover and other festive times in the Jewish year.

On a more mundane level, Yoshi could remember playing along the seashore and running through the hills surrounding the Sea of Galilee. *Rakkath* means "shore" and, by extension, "town by the shore." Adults said the place was picturesque and idyllic. He simply knew it was a great place to be alive. There were just so many adventures to have and to create. There were fish to catch. There were stones to collect and pieces of driftwood that looked like and could become all kinds of things. There were forts and hideouts to build. He could skip smooth rocks across the water. Though he learned the hard way, that scared the fish away. There was mud to play in, especially at the hot springs where it was warm mud. That made it even more fun. There were trees to climb. There were trails to run barefoot along. The sky was blue and the sea was many different colors. The hills and the trees were every imaginable hue of green. The dirt was brown and red. The rocks were gray and black.

It was a colorful and wonderful world.

Growing up right next to the seashore, these were some of his earliest memories. And Yoshi had shared many such glorious days with his two closest friends, Jonathan and Caleb. They were most often inseparable and even their families had shared much together.

One of their favorite games was called, "spying out the land." He had heard this story from as far back as he could remember.

When they played this game, Yoshi, who made it clear that he was actually named Joshua, and Caleb got to be the spies, sent by Moses to check out the land. That meant that Jonathan got to be the Canaanites, which he didn't really mind because he could pretend and act as though he were a giant. He *was* the tallest of the three of them. Joshua and Caleb would try not to be seen by the evil Jonathan as they spied out the land. They would eventually *find* some grapes or other available produce to bring back and show their people how good the land was, but then of course, they had to eat all of the evidence. At this point in the game, conveniently, Jonathan got to change his identity and become an Israelite again so he could share in the "milk and honey" of the Promised Land.

One day recently, the three of them had returned home from a new adventure they had found, a little dirtier than usual, even though they had tried to wash themselves in the Galilean waters. Clay apparently didn't wash off as easily as good old mud did.

"Jehoshua ben Abrahim, come over here this instant," Yoshi's *ima,* his mother, said, eyeing the trio as they entered the yard.

"What's this I see in your hair? Looks remarkably similar to the clay from Abba's clay deposits. Yoshi, you shouldn't be playing in there. What were you thinking?"

Batiyah instantly grabbed a wet cloth from the basin in which she was washing dishes and ran it over his head of curly, dark hair, spit-bathing a few places on his face as well. Yoshi squirmed to get away, but it was fruitless. She was still bigger and stronger than he.

"Just wait until Abba gets home!" she said, shaking her finger in his direction, and then turning her cleansing efforts equally to Jonathan and Caleb. Joshua noted that his friends were both more respectful and compliant, however he knew that to do anything else with regards to someone else's parent, another adult, would have been unthinkable.

When Abrahim did eventually return home from the delivery of bricks he had been making that day, Batiyah wasted no time in relating the entire incident in living color. His father then gave him *the look,* and informed him they must have a *discussion* in the far corner of the yard. Yoshi had been a participant in those types of discussions before. He certainly did not relish another one. However, on this particular day, Abrahim had surprised his young son. He had waited until they were out of sight and then turned to face Yoshi, sitting down on a pile of bricks so as to be on the same level as his progeny.

"This was the first time you did this," Abrahim began, "so, I choose leniency. I know that you and your friends were not really thinking and got carried away. But please, Yoshi, I would so rather you stayed out of the clay that we use for making bricks. The more that you are in there, the more the clay is muddied and mixed with other things. It really would make my life so much easier if you stayed away from there."

Abrahim had hugged him and smiled at him, then shook his head and chuckled to himself as if he was remembering something from his own childhood. Yoshi did wonder what it was but he didn't ask. He was afraid it might spoil the fact that he had somehow not been punished.

"Because this is the first time, Yoshi, I will simply let it go. But understand something, whether I punish you or overlook your fault, either way, just know that I love you with all that is in me, and that I do what I do in each situation because I know and want only what's best for you. Adonai in heaven loves you that way too."

He paused, making sure he had his son's full attention.

"Please, Yoshi, just don't do *that* again, all right? Adonai Elohim has certainly created many other wonderful places where you can play."

Yoshi hugged his father and said he wouldn't.

On this day, Abrahim had shown himself true to one of the other possible meanings of his name, a "father of mercy," kind and compassionate.

Now, on other occasions and for different things, Yoshi had most certainly been disciplined severely, but his abba was always fair and just. And Yoshi did know, even in discipline, maybe because of discipline, that he was cherished.

Of course, there were many other memories of home. More time was actually spent here than anywhere else.

Everyone at home had chores to do. They all had to pitch in and do his or her part. Helping clean and tidy up the yard or the house. Maybe going to the market for daily supplies and food. There was always lots to do. An abundance of work was never very far away, it seemed.

Occasionally, Yoshi got to help his ima with the cooking. It didn't even matter to him that it was not really considered work for boys. He thoroughly enjoyed it. Especially preparing fish. Abrahim had taught him how to catch fish a while ago, how to deftly throw the net and then draw it in, and Yoshi proudly brought his bounty home to share. He had also been shown how to clean them, and his ima showed him how to properly roast the fruits of his labor over the fire. Now he enjoyed sharing all of what he had learned with the rest of his family.

And then there was extended family. Immediate family was never all there was. This had always been a part of their lives, especially since Abrahim's three brothers and their respective families all lived in their same town.

There was his uncle Joseph, his wife Milcah, and their six children: Judah, Ruth, Lemuel, Abel, Rebbah, and David. Then his uncle Johanan, his wife Abigail, and their children: Benjamin, Brachah, Beulah, and Boaz. And finally, his uncle Hazaiah, his wife Sharon, and their two little boys: Malachi and Japheth.

Of all his cousins, Judah and Benjamin were the ones he knew best, mostly due to the fact that they were fairly close to him age wise. Judah was slightly older, and Benjamin was a little younger. The reality was that none of his relatives, on his father's side at least, were strangers.

They would all get together often. It seemed that any occasion was a good excuse. Sometimes they would just decide to meet somewhere on a given evening after work. And of course, being together for the feasts of the Jewish calendar was nonnegotiable. When they were together, there was lots of conversation and noise. And there was always food. Lots of food. Abrahim said many times that Elohim invented feasts because He wanted us to be together, that He loved family and celebration and food.

Joshua did enjoy being together with all of his cousins even if it could get a bit overwhelming at times. He was extremely grateful for one thing however: that at least they didn't all live in one house together.

His mother, Batiyah, was from a devout family, from Gamala on the far side of the Sea of Galilee in the territory governed by Philip, one of Herod's other sons. But, other than that, he didn't know that much about his mother's family. It was not ever talked about. As a child, he had just always assumed that was the way that things were. Women got married and became part of a new family, that of their husband. He did sometimes wonder what her family was like though, and whether he would ever get to meet them. Maybe he had cousins and uncles and aunts somewhere else that he would appreciate even more.

His ima was hardworking and a wonderful cook. She was soft and caring but with a strong side as well. In fact, she never hesitated to discipline them, or even at times, to let Abrahim know when she thought that he needed to correct something. When she did the latter though especially, she was always honoring and respectful. Speaking with a twinkle in her eye, Abrahim would just know that her way was the way that things needed to be.

In fact, just the other day, Abrahim had asked for some more meat at supper. Batiyah had looked at him, put her hands on her hips and said, in a calm voice, "Not until your vegetables are gone, dear. And, how do you ask?"

Joshua knew that it was a teachable moment, meant more for their benefit than for his father.

Abrahim had rather quickly finished his lentils and beans, and then passed his bowl to her with a wink and a, "please?"

She smiled and gave him another piece of goat.

Lesson communicated…class dismissed.

Joshua grew up in a house where his parents loved each other. It was evident every day even if not often publicly displayed. He had seen them hug and kiss each other from time to time for sure. But he most often saw their affection in other things, in all of the little things that they did for and with each other each and every day. In the way that they honored and respected each other, always and in everything it seemed. The way that they were of one mind and heart. And then too, in the way that they simply looked at each other.

He watched the two of them esteem their children too, each one of them, though in ways as unique as their personalities. Every person was a treasure, Abrahim had taught him. Each individual was a precious child of Adonai Himself. Gifts of Elohim, all of them!

Joshua most assuredly looked up to Zephaniah, and not just because his elder sibling was taller than him; he thought he was the best older brother in the world, often imitating him and trying to be just like him. Most often, they got along pretty well. Zephaniah had often invited him to be part of what he was doing and had taken him along on his own adventures quite regularly in days gone by. Joshua liked that. While the others were younger than he—his brother Elijah, his sister Sarah and lastly, baby Seth—and he had probably not spent as much time with them as he had with Zephaniah, he enjoyed having them around and had definitely often played with them too. The fact that he was older and that they looked up to him made him feel superior to them in a way, and he had certainly used that to his advantage from time to time. But he knew and had been taught that he had to be careful about that and always treat each of them as he would want to be treated in return. He hoped that they felt the same way about their *older brother* as he genuinely felt about his.

Maybe in large part because of the name he had been given at his birth, Joshua himself grew up thinking that he was, in some way, more than most others, a child with a destiny, thinking of himself as a person with a special and unique call on his life.

It made him feel more responsible, like he needed to be significant, like he had something extraordinary to contribute beyond his immediate and even his extended family. That there was some important thing that he alone could do for Adonai and for His people.

Maybe even for the world!

He thought it was pretty certain that he was not *the* Messiah, but maybe he could and should live up to his name and at least do some saving or delivering, something truly heroic, somewhere or for someone.

Only time would reveal what that would be.

He wondered when he would know.

The sooner the better, he thought.

Chapter 3

APPRENTICESHIP

As Joshua grew older, approaching the age of twelve, time for play disappeared. His energy was now almost entirely dedicated to learning the family business. And his daily routine, always shared with his brother, Zephaniah, began by helping his father Abrahim collect clay from the special spot down by the water. When they all returned home, it was time to fill the seemingly endless rows of molds with a combination of clay and sand after it had been worked, at times mixed with straw, other things, or nothing at all, depending on what the bricks were being used for—Abrahim had come up with all kinds of *brick recipes.*

Still later, after a day or even several days, entirely dependent on the weather or season, they would then unmold them and lay the new bricks out in the sun to complete their drying. Some bricks were even baked in a special oven they had to make them extra durable, rather than just letting them dry naturally in the hot sun.

He knew that Zephaniah and he, and eventually Elijah too, would take over or at least take on Abrahim's trade. That was the way that things were. He guessed that one day, Seth would learn it all too, but since he was only a baby, he put that out of his mind for the time being. For now, he just had to concentrate and remember and learn how to do everything well, to do it all just like his father.

APPRENTICESHIP

There was much to learn.

One of Yoshi's favorite things in all of this was to sit nearby as his father negotiated the particular composition and then the price of bricks for some new construction project in the area. He liked *man talk*. It made him feel grown up. And then too, he very much enjoyed going with Abrahim to deliver those bricks to the particular building site for which they had been made. He was always allowed a little bit of time to wander around and to watch everything that was going on, providing he didn't get in the way. He enjoyed asking the builders questions about what they were doing and why. It was a nice break from the routine and always so fascinating discovering how buildings were constructed. He loved seeing how the bricks that he had helped to make became something.

Zephaniah had already been at this for some time since he was about three years older than Yoshi. Occasionally, he liked to rub in the fact that he knew more about masonry than Yoshi did and especially that he got to do some things that Yoshi didn't. One of those *excellent jobs,* because it was somewhat technical, was loading fresh, sometimes called "green," bricks into the oven. These bricks had spent some time in the sun drying already but were then extra-hardened by being fired in the kiln. There was an art to using the long tongs to stack them so that the super-heated air would evenly surround them. When that was done, a layer of already fired bricks was put on top to concentrate the heat. And all of this had to be done when the kiln was preheated and very hot.

One day, when Zephaniah was doing this very task, he glanced in Yoshi's direction. Yoshi had been assigned the *novice task* of stomping out the clay, not a job that was particularly fun or appealing. Zephaniah made a show of what *he* was doing and then mouthed a "ha-ha," while pointing at Yoshi. Without a moment's hesitation, Yoshi exited the clay pit and, with what was still clinging to his feet now flying in every direction, ran at Zephaniah and tackled him. Several bricks fell to the ground, ruining them. The two of them began rolling around in the dirt and pummeling each other.

Just then, Abrahim returned.

"That is enough!" he said sternly. "Stop it you two! Someone is going to get hurt and I can't afford to lose either of you. Our work will not get done this way. We work *together!*"

Abrahim strongly emphasized the last word.

He hadn't laid a hand on either of them. But they simply separated from each other. They knew better than to persist to the point where he had to physically break them apart. That never ended well.

"He was teasing me because he gets to load the oven and I am stuck treading out the clay. It's not fair!" Yoshi said, maybe a little more vehemently than was wise.

"All in time, Yoshi, all in time," Abrahim said calmly. "I will teach you everything eventually. Both of you. There are still many things that Zephaniah hasn't learned yet!"

Yoshi grinned at this and gave Zephaniah a condescending glance.

Abrahim stared Yoshi into retreat. Then, turning to the elder of the two brothers, now reprimanded him.

"Zephaniah, why do you have to tease your brother like that? Do I need to make you tread out the clay today?"

Zephaniah shook his head no and said sorry.

Abrahim paused.

"Wash your feet off, Yoshi. I do have another job for you," he said. "I want you to go across the street to Nathanael and ask him if he could make us some new brick molds. Could you do that for me please?"

Yoshi beamed and hurriedly washed the bits of remaining clay from his bare feet.

"Yes, Abba, I would very much love to do that for you!" he said.

He contemplated turning in Zephaniah's direction and sticking out his tongue for yet one more show of payback but thought better of it.

"Good," said Abrahim. "Take this one as the sample and tell Nathanael that we would like 500 of them made as soon as he can. Also, can you find out from him when they will be ready? Thank you, son."

Yoshi grabbed the sample and ran next door. He loved going to visit Nathanael. He was such a nice man and it always smelled so good at his place—the smell of fresh cut wood. So much better than stinky and sticky clay, Yoshi thought. And often, Nathanael's wife, Elizabeth, would bring the best sweet buns in the world out to the barn when he was there. Those were delicious.

He wondered why they didn't have any children but knew that it was impolite to ask. He wondered if they didn't want any but thought that couldn't possibly be true. He wondered to whom Nathanael would pass on *his* business.

Yoshi wondered why he wondered so much about so many things.

"Hi Abba Nathanael!" he said enthusiastically as he entered the yard minutes later. "Shalom! I hope you are having a good day. I am having a good day. Well, other than that Zephaniah and I had a fight. What are you making today? It sure smells good here! I have an order for you. My abba would like 500 new brick molds the same size as the one I have here. How soon do you think that you could have them done…?"

Nathanael broke into a broad smile and laughed out loud, now holding both hands up in the air so that Yoshi would stop and he would be able to get a word in edgewise.

Yoshi relented.

"Well, shalom to you too, Yoshi. Always good to see you! Shall I tell Mrs. Elizabeth that you are here? She may have something sweet to share with us workingmen! Let's see if I can remember all of what you said and then answer all of your questions."

"Oh yes, brick molds. Now, where's that sample?"

Yoshi handed it to Nathanael.

"Hmmm," he said turning the mold this way and that, inspecting it with his eyes, and using a special stick he had with lots of little marks on it to measure it in each direction.

"Five hundred, you say?" He mumbled to himself a list of other jobs he had to complete. "I think...maybe Wednesday of next week?"

Nathanael didn't have to call Elizabeth. She was already there, and she was holding a tray of wonderful warm goodness.

"Would you like one or two, Yoshi? You are a growing boy."

"Yes, please!" Yoshi said, as Elizabeth handed him one. He took a generous bite.

"Mmmm, these are so good!" he said, mouth still full.

"Here, have another," Elizabeth said smiling, handing him a second one, and a first one to Nathanael as well.

They both watched as Yoshi devoured his treats.

"Thank you, Ima," he said as he paused briefly between bites.

Nathanael and Elizabeth smiled and looked at each other and Yoshi now noticed tears in Elizabeth's eyes.

"Did I do something to make you sad?" he asked.

"No, child, it's fine," Elizabeth said. "Adonai knows."

Yoshi felt a little bit bothered by the fact that he had made Elizabeth cry even though he didn't know how or why. She had said she was okay, so maybe he didn't need to worry about it.

He finished eating the second of his treats, licked his fingers, said his goodbyes and then left the yard to return home.

Elizabeth gave him the rest of the buns to take and share with his family. He contemplated having a third one but didn't.

It was then that he realized she had teared up when he had called her "Ima."

He was just being respectful. He hadn't meant to hurt her with his words but could see now how that might cause her some pain.

"Why do you talk before you think?" he mumbled to himself.

And then, his own question having no real or immediate answer, he quietly prayed as he crossed the road.

"Adonai, would You please give Nathanael and Elizabeth children? Like You did for Abraham and Sarah and some others I can't remember right now. They are such nice people. It is a shame they don't have any children of their own. I think they would be a great abba and ima!"

Chapter 4

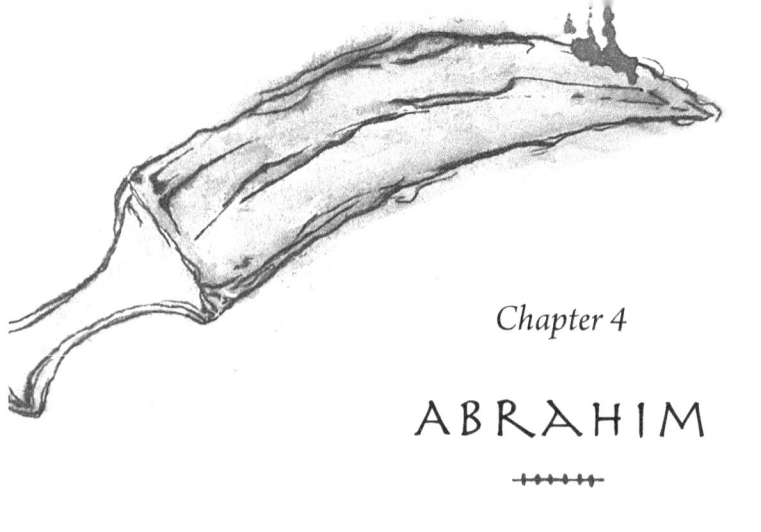

ABRAHIM

Masonry was far more challenging and much more complicated than he had thought growing up, and it was difficult just trying to grasp, let alone perfect all of the techniques and tricks that his father had spent a major part of his lifetime learning. Not to mention the fact that much of the time, it was just plain hard work. Some days Yoshi's head hurt from all of the things that he was trying to file there. Especially frustrating was when he couldn't remember something that he had been shown even just a few days before. He was glad that Abrahim was so patient.

"All in time," his father would just say over and over again, "all in time."

This seemed to be Abba's favorite thing to say.

And, while brick making had many interesting facets, in Yoshi's opinion, even more engaging were the discussions that happened to be a somewhat regular occurrence in their small yard. It seemed that his father Abrahim had come to be viewed by many in their village and the surrounding area as being a very wise and thoughtful man with a keen knowledge of the Holy Writings, an unofficial rabbi of sorts. As a result, many people would come, maybe also to order some bricks, or sometimes not, but simply to ask Abrahim's sage advice or to discuss matters of faith and practice. Yoshi also noticed that many of them, out of their respect for his zeal and devotion to sacred things, his wisdom, shortened his actual name—"father of multitudes" or "father of nations" it meant—and called him *Abba,* just as he most often did, though meant by them in this case as a term of honor.

Yoshi certainly thought his father was wise but often wondered where and how he had come to learn all of what just seemed to so readily flow out of him. One day he would ask, he thought.

He loved listening in on these conversations, but he longed for the day when he would be fully permitted to join in the discussion. What made it worse in a way was that Zephaniah was already free to do so since he was older.

Finally, *his* day came, the day of his *bar mitzvah,* the celebration of his becoming "a son of the commandment," and the occasion for yet another family get-together, complete with noise and food.

At one place in the ceremony, Abba prayed a prayer of blessing for him that was so touching that Yoshi, rather now, *Joshua,* thought he might cry. He didn't. He wouldn't allow himself to. He was now a man.

But finally, he could ask questions about the various topics that were being debated and discussed and even share his own opinion. How wonderful it was to actively learn even more about the ways of Adonai and the people that He had called unto Himself, the race of which *he* was a part. And, in the midst of all of this, Joshua was discovering a love of Scripture, the tenets of their faith, and indeed, of Elohim Himself!

For as long as he could remember, Yoshi had looked up to his older brother too. And while Zephaniah still occasionally made him mad and sometimes, they would fight, the anger never lasted very long. Things were quickly forgiven and forgotten. This was, after all, his brother, his *achi.*

Which is why it was extremely difficult when Abrahim told him that Zephaniah was going away to Jerusalem to study under one of the rabbis there, a certain Rabbi Shemai. Joshua knew that it *was* every young boy's dream, his too, to be the student of some famous teacher.

Fairly late in life, but Zephaniah had now been given this chance. Joshua was happy for him, but...

Two days later, Zephaniah left.

They had said goodbye. And yet somehow, Joshua knew that they had never really *said* it. If they actually did, he felt that it was the worst goodbye ever. They needed more time together. He was just getting to know his brother as an adult rather than as children. He was just coming to really like him.

Joshua cried some at night when he was alone. He missed having Zephaniah around. And working by himself only made it worse. He had thought in times past, especially on days when they didn't get along so well, that it would be better. But now that Zephaniah was actually gone, he was sure that it wasn't at all as great as he had thought it might be.

Over time however, being the only one who was there beside Abrahim became Joshua's new normal. And with each day, he did miss Zephaniah less and less. Eventually, he hardly thought of him at all. That saddened him a little, or maybe, a lot. When he did remember.

Abrahim had said a while back that he needed both of them to get everything done. With Zephaniah gone, Joshua's workload had definitely increased. But now, *he* got to learn and to do *all* the things that went into making the best bricks in the region. And over the next several years, he paid careful attention and learned as much as he could from his abba.

Far beyond all of that though, Joshua valued the interactions he and Abrahim now had as they worked elbow to elbow. He felt as though he was really getting to know *who* his father actually was. And, it was here, day in and day out, where he saw his father's character shine most clearly. It was in this place where he got to learn what was really important in life…and that it was far more than just making a living.

His abba truly was an amazing man.

Not that everything was serious.

Just recently they had been between two rather large orders and decided to take the day just to clean up around home. Joshua had been on one side of the yard and his father was on the other, both busying themselves with putting things back in order. Joshua had bent over to pick up a few loose bricks lying on the ground. As he stood and turned slightly, he heard his father's laughter from the other side of the yard. He was about to look over to see what was so funny when he was promptly smacked by a well-thrown and very moist pat of clay. It hit him squarely on the shoulder and bits of wet clay went flying in every direction.

"Aha! I got you!" his father Abrahim gleefully yelled from the other side of the yard.

Not to be outdone or to back away from a good fight, Joshua quickly ran to the nearby wagon and poured a pail of water over the contents that still remained there. He scooped up a large handful and flung it in his abba's direction. It was a direct hit!

For the next few minutes, the two lobbed clay back and forth at each other, hiding behind stacks of bricks, running for cover, and trying to get closer to each other with their attacks. Laughter and screaming filled the courtyard.

Their revelry was soon interrupted.

"What do the two of you think you're doing?" Batiyah asked in a stern albeit somewhat feigned voice, making her presence known. She looked at Joshua and then at Abrahim, both standing there with globs of moist clay in their hands and mud stains all over their clothes.

"We're cleaning up!" Joshua said, snickering loudly.

Batiyah quickly surveyed the yard.

"Obviously," she said. "It looks amazing!"

The three of them burst into laughter and Abrahim promptly moved in Batiyah's direction, now threatening her with his present handful of sloppy ammunition.

"Don't you dare!" she warned.

He ran to where she was standing, smeared some on her cheek and then added a giant and very muddy hug. She squirmed to free herself but with very minimal effort.

They all laughed.

"I think that many times we are all too serious for our own good," Abrahim said playfully.

"King Solomon said that laughter is like good medicine. I have taken a rather large dose of it today and must say that I feel great!"

The others nodded in agreement.

"Now Joshua, let's you and I actually clean up this yard!" Abrahim said, moving toward a pail of water to wash his hands.

"It sure needs it!" Joshua replied. "It's a mess!"

And they all burst into laughter again.

That night, as he climbed into bed and recited his prayers, Joshua thanked Elohim for his parents. He was sure that they were two of the most wonderful people in the world. He felt so blessed.

"Thank you, Adonai," he prayed. "You make it easy for me to honor my father and mother. Thank you for Ima. And for Abba."

Joshua was convinced that he wanted to grow up to be just like them, and especially…to be just like his dad. To be *that* kind of man!

He fell asleep smiling.

It had been a most excellent day!

Chapter 5

THE DAY

The next day began like all of the others before it.

Joshua awoke to the shrill call of their rooster, the one whom his little sister Sarah had named Hezekiah. The sun wasn't up quite yet but it was time to rise and shine. There was work to do.

He caught a whiff of smoke from the fire and within minutes, also smelled bread and meat being made ready for breakfast. He knew that Abrahim and Batiyah were already up and busy with first things of the day that needed to be done.

He put on his clothes and made his way down from the flat roof of their house where they often slept in the summertime since the evening breeze made it much cooler than being indoors. It was nice sleeping under the stars, he thought.

He greeted his ima and his abba and silently went to get more wood for the fire and water for cooking.

Today, they would start on the sizeable order of bricks they had received from one of the local merchants in town who was opening a new bakery and retail outlet. Abrahim had negotiated the contract with Jephthah just the other day. Joshua looked forward to doing something a little bit different. He knew that the project required several unique types of bricks for the various ovens and buildings being constructed. And that meant he would probably be learning some new things. That always made the day go by quickly.

They had their breakfast together and Abrahim and Joshua hitched Samson, their donkey, to his cart. That done, the three of them made their way to retrieve clay from the seaside, a job that always took up the early part of each day. They would return sometime slightly before mid-morning and begin the task of making whichever bricks Abrahim had scheduled for that particular day.

The sky was overcast but the day was pleasant and the walk to and from the Sea of Galilee was usually enjoyable, even more so when Samson cooperated. Today he seemed to be in a reasonable mood.

As they were finishing up at the clay pit, Abrahim had scooped up another handful and made as if he was going to throw it in Joshua's direction. He hesitated. Then let the lump of clay slide off of his hand and into the water with a splash.

"Better not," he said. "Ima might catch us!"

And they both laughed as they remembered their war in the yard the day before.

They moistened the canvas and draped it over the wagon. It would keep their cargo soft and pliable until they could transform it into the day's bricks. And now the three of them, cart in tow and loaded with moist and heavy clay, made their way back toward home.

Batiyah met them and related that she was taking the children to the market with her and would return sometime later on in the morning. This was all very routine, the cycle of many days before.

Abrahim and Joshua unloaded a portion of the clay and began stomping it out with their feet both to make it more workable and also to *discover* any large rocks that were contained in the raw material they had brought home. At this point, sand, part of all bricks, would be added to the mixture, as well as whatever else was needed for the particular order.

They would get a good start on putting the mixture into molds. And then on most days, while Abrahim completed the brick molding, setting them all out in the sun to dry for the next number of days, Joshua would leave to deliver finished orders to various customers in town.

But not today.

Those deliveries had all been completed the day before yesterday.

"Joshua, can you go up on the roof and get me the trowel?" Abrahim asked, and then added, "I think we left it up there the other day when we were making those repairs."

"Yes, Abba, I know exactly where it is," Joshua replied as he ran to the side of the house and up the stairs leading to the roof.

He bounded up the incline skipping every other one on his ascent.

Joshua had to look for a minute or two since the trowel wasn't where he thought it was. Eventually, he found it though, partially obscured from view under some blankets that had fallen down on top of it. He folded the blankets and carried them to the front of the house. A commotion on the street had caught his attention and he wondered what was going on. It was Nathanael, unloading a delivery of boards of various descriptions and lengths, and Joshua stood there watching for a minute or so. When he turned to make his way back to the stairs and the yard below, trowel in hand, he heard voices coming from the courtyard behind their house.

Who was here he wondered? They weren't expecting anyone this morning, not that he knew of anyway.

Maybe this would be one of those wonderful God conversations that happened from time to time.

As he approached the top of the stairs, Joshua was about to call out to his father, "I found it. I'll be right down."

He peered over the parapet of the roof.
And stopped dead in his tracks!
His words remained where they had begun...
...trapped inside.

Chapter 6

MURDER

✢✢✢✢✢

Every fiber of Joshua's being was screaming. And even though he was not purposely holding it in, no sound was nor would come out of his mouth. Somewhere, way down deep inside his very core, everything was in full boil, but without any way it seemed, for the steam to escape.

Maybe it was Providence's protection that had made him mute.

He had so desperately wanted to run and help. He wanted to do something, anything, immediately, but he simply could not move. He just stood, or more truthfully, crouched low, on the roof of the house overlooking the small yard.

Frozen.

Transfixed.

Terrified.

He watched as the four Roman soldiers quickly glanced around and then exited the courtyard behind the house. And then he let his eyes return to the place where his father was, face down now on the course of bricks that had just recently been unmolded and laid out in the sun to continue their slow dry. The bricks and wood on top of Abrahim partly obscured Joshua's view. But he could clearly see that blood flowing from his father's wounds was already turning the clay bricks in the area underneath him a much darker shade of red.

Joshua's mouth was as dry as old bricks. His heart was pounding in his chest, and it felt as though it might just burst forth and run away. Tears welled up behind the dam of his eyes and came cascading down his cheeks. He was sure that everything that made anything make sense had just come unglued.

What had just happened, and why?

"Abba?" he whispered, so quiet that he alone heard.

He shook his head and now angrily wiped the tears from his face with the back of his hand. What was he doing, he thought? Here he was acting like a little baby. Why was he just sitting here, crying?

He needed to get to his father.

He checked, waiting for another moment or two, but it seemed reasonable to assume that the soldiers had gone for good, so he picked himself up and ran, almost tripping and falling headlong, back down the stairs that now made their descent along the side of the house. He paused briefly at the bottom just to take another quick look around and then bolted across the yard and over to his wounded father.

Was he only wounded, or was it worse…Joshua thought to himself as he approached?

"Abba, Abba," he called out, more loudly now as he neared his father's side.

For a second or two, he just stood there, horrified at what assaulted his eyes: his abba lying there in a crumpled heap, face down, bleeding, unmoving, covered in bricks and broken bits of wood planking.

No longer hesitating, Joshua tossed aside the bricks and wood that covered his father so that he could get to him. He had only one thing on his mind, caring little whether he broke any more bricks in the process. They could make more later. His father needed help right now!

"Abba, are you okay?" he asked, even though he knew clearly that he was anything but okay.

There was no answer.

No movement.

No sound.

As soon as Joshua had removed enough of the debris to roll Abrahim over, his suspicion was terrifyingly confirmed. His abba was in grave trouble. His forehead was split wide open, his face mangled and covered in a mixture of dirt and brick dust and blood. Where a small sharp piece of wood had pierced his chest, blood oozed and was rather quickly turning that part of his cloak bright crimson.

Immediately and without invitation, fear rammed its way through the door of Joshua's soul and rushed in like an unwelcome stampede. Waves of terror threatened to overwhelm him. Anger lurked in the shadows waiting to pounce.

"Keep your head about you," he had to tell himself.

Was there still breath? Was there still life? He couldn't tell for sure. He had heard at synagogue just recently that the life was in the blood, and it seemed to him now that much of it was no longer in his father. That thought was terrifying.

"Help...help me!" he yelled into the air.

"Someone, anyone, please?" he called out, more loudly now, reaching down to touch his father.

"I'll help you," Joshua heard from very close behind him even though he had not noticed anyone come into the yard. He was about to whirl around to see who it was when he felt his hair being grabbed roughly from behind and the cold steel of a Roman knife on his throat.

"Don't move!" the soldier whispered hoarsely, so close that Joshua could feel the heat of his words on the back of his neck. "Don't move or I will kill you! And don't you dare say anything to anyone. Nothing! Ever! What happened here was an accident. You were not supposed to be here. Tell anyone, and we will—*I will*—find you and kill you for sure!"

"I thought that I had heard something. You were up on the roof, weren't you, boy? Good thing I dropped my glove and had to come back for it, or we would have never known."

The soldier slowly removed the knife and came around to face Joshua, still holding him tightly by his hair. He was only inches away, his hot and foul breath now assaulting Joshua's face.

"I should kill you now, just like I did your father! Maybe I will! Or maybe…I just don't feel like cleaning up the mess of another dead body. But know this. Say anything and, as sure as I am Cassius Maximus, you *will* die!" he growled, snarling and spitting as he spoke.

The soldier took his knife and lightly sliced Joshua's cheek with its blade. Joshua could feel the blood run. He then slapped Joshua's face with the glove he had retrieved, released his grip, and made his way out of the gate for the second time.

Joshua's face burned.

And something seemed now to turn like a twisted towel inside his stomach. His body began to shake and he was unable to make it stop. Hot tears erupted again and, like volcanic lava, flowed down his cheeks. The salt of his sorrow burned into the long angular cut on the one side. Waves of terror and fear warred with sadness and anguish for the supremacy of his mind. Thoughts raced between concern for his own safety and the present welfare of his father.

He decided that he could think about himself later.

"Is my, can my abba be…?" he wondered, though he could not bring himself to say the word.

The soldier had seemed pretty certain.

There were no words.

Just agonizing groans.

Joshua raised his bloody and bleeding hands toward the grey and cloudy sky above. The iron heavens seemed entirely oblivious to his pain. At the very least, they did not respond. All outside of himself was quiet.

"Ahhhhhhhhhhh!" he sighed, or more truthfully, bellowed at the top of his lungs.

It was a long, painful cry of lament.

"Adonai...what do I do?" he wailed.

His father lay still.

Unmoving.

Unbreathing.

Unblinking.

"Help!" Joshua called now, as loudly as he could.

Try as he might, he simply could not bring himself to leave his father's side, to go and look for someone, for help. He knew that he should, he supposed, but he was both too weak and too attached to move. Sitting on the ground in a heap himself, he held his father's beaten body in his lap and stroked his already ashen face.

And in that moment, Joshua noticed his father's hands. He did not know why exactly. Had they simply caught his eye? Or, was it that he could not bear to look at anything else? Rough, calloused hands that had held him, and disciplined him, taught him, and loved him, lying limp on the ground by his own feet. Tough but tender hands. Abraham's strong, now bloodied hands.

Joshua longed to feel the warmth of those hands again. Unconsciously, he pulled one of them to his own.

The gate opened and there stood their longtime neighbor Nathanael, who had appeared from across the street. A gasp escaped his lips and he dropped the armload of brick molds he was carrying to run to where Joshua sat cradling his father's body.

"What happened...?" Nathanael started to ask, but stopped mid-sentence because it was obvious.

"Oh, no! El Shaddai!" he said.

He rushed over and bent down next to Abrahim's limp and bloody frame, clumsily held by his already grieving son. Nathanael leaned his ear next to Abrahim's chest to listen for a heartbeat and then listened closely at his mouth for any sign of life breath. Everything was quiet except for his own heavy panting and Joshua's painful sobs.

"Oh Joshua!" Nathanael said, "May Elohim have mercy on us all. I am afraid your abba is...*dead!*"

Joshua had courted the suspicion that this was the truth, but those words...

...or more correctly, that *one—final—word* grabbed hold of his heart, refusing to release its mortifying grip.

"No, No, it cannot be!" Joshua sobbed.

"Please, no!"

Chapter 7

AMBUSH

Within seconds, Joshua's mind was a veritable battlefield. He had been totally unprepared for this surprise ambush. A legion of thoughts rushed in on him all at once from every direction. He felt as if he was in a war he could not possibly win. The enemy was just too strong.

At the center of it all was: *Why? Why* did this happen? *Why* did these Roman soldiers do what they did?

They had invaded the peace that was their home, assaulted his father, and killed him in cold blood. Yes, they had engineered it to look like an accident, but he knew and they knew that it was murder.

What in heaven's name had his father done that deserved such treatment? Was it all just some kind of mistake, some kind of misunderstanding gone horribly wrong? Or could it possibly be true? Joshua wished that this were just a very bad dream, a nightmare, from which he would soon awake.

Abraham had been busy putting clay into the molds, just like he did every day. Well, of course, every day except the Sabbath. At his father's request, Joshua had gone up onto the roof to get the trowel that had been left there when they had been doing some repairs a few days earlier. Dawdling and distracted, that's where he had been when he heard the small band of soldiers arrive. They had burst through the gate uninvited and almost immediately began verbally attacking his father.

"Abrahim son of Jehudah, we know that you are one of those… *Zealots!*" one of the soldiers had snarled.

Joshua knew that his father was not very fond of the Romans. In fact, they had been talking about those in power over them just the other day. Anti-Roman sentiment would be true of most Jews at the time. But, that Abrahim was in fact a freedom fighter? Joshua couldn't imagine that he wouldn't know this about his own father were it true!

"We were tipped off several days ago by some of your own Jewish leaders, and we have been tracking your movement ever since. How you managed to evade us is a mystery, but we know for certain that you did meet with Jacob and Simeon, the rebel sons of Judas the Gaulinite," the soldiers said. "They are on our most wanted list and because of that, so are you!"

"We suspect, rather, we *know* that you are sympathetic to them and their lot!"

"Jewish Zealots!" one soldier venomously said, and spit on the ground at Abrahim's feet. "Such an awful blight on the Peace of Rome!"

"The things you say against the Empire have not gone unnoticed."

"What things? What have I said?" Abrahim had asked, attempting to plead his case.

Joshua had wondered in the past about Jews who would turn on their own countrymen. He could think of few things more despicable. But he had come to realize that there were those of the ruling class, much too friendly with the present regime—"Some of your own," the soldiers had called them—who would do almost anything if it meant they could gain some personal political advantage. They were opportunists of the worst kind, willing to sell out their own brothers and sisters. "For the good of the many," they would say. For their own good, more like it, Joshua thought. And it would seem that these very people who claimed to be family, had in fact betrayed his father.

Then too, Joshua was curious about the *brothers* the soldiers had mentioned: Simeon and Jacob. Where had his father gone to meet them and why? Who were they? He had heard mention of the rebel leader Judah the Galilean once or twice in the past, but knew only sketchy details about him and his cause. Abrahim had never mentioned the two brothers or Judah. Joshua thought he had met most of his father's friends. Maybe these weren't really friends at all! It had certainly turned out to be a most unfortunate meeting.

"There are many otherwise law-abiding Jews who have a negative opinion about Roman occupation," his father had protested. "Is that a crime? Is the Empire that fragile?"

It was of little consequence. Nothing he could say would change anything. They had made their decision. Or maybe it had been made for them higher up, and they were simply carrying out orders. It mattered not. He had been sold out and offered up as a sacrifice.

The verdict had simply been announced: His father was a traitor and a threat to Roman peace. And the penalty must now follow.

They administered *justice* quickly and as quietly as possible. And, since Abrahim was not a Roman citizen, the law could be applied more freely. Every Jew was well aware of how the *rules* worked against those who were not insiders. They had neither the right to a trial or the ability to appeal, in reality at least if not in policy.

One of the soldiers had grabbed the *keffiyeh*, the piece of fabric most Jewish men wore to guard themselves against the sun, from Abrahim's head and wrapped it around his face. Joshua could hear his father trying to say something now, but he couldn't make out the words since it was almost completely muffled by the fabric jammed into his mouth. At the same time, another soldier, the one he had come to know as Cassius Maximus, had picked up a nearby brick and smashed it across the back of Abrahim's skull. Joshua heard it hit with a sickening thud. He heard his father groan as the masonry made contact. They slapped him and spit on him as they spun his head around to face them.

"That will teach you who is sovereign! Where is your god now, you silly Jew? Death to all rebels! You cannot kill us if we get to you first! Know that none but the Emperor is divine," Cassius had said.

Abrahim's body went limp as he lapsed into unconsciousness, and they simply let him fall headlong to the ground, kicking him a couple of times for good measure. They paused long enough to help themselves to the money pouch concealed in his cloak. Then they toppled a nearby stand of bricks on top of Abrahim's battered frame so that his death could appear an unfortunate accident.

They had looked around to see if there was any movement. They listened briefly for any sound. Cassius had inadvertently glanced in the direction of the rooftop. Had he heard something? Joshua was pretty sure they hadn't seen him. Had he been quiet enough?

It was now a moot point.

They quickly slipped out the gate they had entered only moments before. It had all happened in minutes even if it felt as though an eternity of time had passed. Every minute detail etched into Joshua's mind.

Why had he remained immobilized on the roof? Were there any loose bricks up there? He could have thrown them down onto the soldiers. And why hadn't he yelled? Would someone, anyone, have come to help them, a neighbor perhaps? He could have come running down himself. He could have hit them or something.

Why had he been so afraid?

There were four of them and only one of him, a mere boy, barely fifteen years of age. He berated himself, and said that he should have been more of a...man.

He was supposed to be a man!

Could he have stopped them?

Maybe they would have stopped. Maybe they would have left. Maybe his father would still...

Maybe his father would still...be.

Joshua cursed under his breath but immediately felt guilty for doing so. He knew he should not say things like that. But he was so angry. At Rome and at these specific soldiers for sure, but equally or more, he was mad at himself. Had it been cowardice or wisdom that had kept him transfixed on the rooftop? Hidden? Had it been Elohim? Right now, Joshua didn't have a clue. He questioned the wisdom of his choice.

He had thought initially that his presence had gone undetected. And in reality, it had. However, the soldier had returned for his missing glove, so whether Joshua had hidden well or not didn't matter at all. His presence had been discovered.

In his mind, that just made his decision to remain concealed in a way even worse. He should have at least tried to stop them. But then, maybe they would have killed *him* on the spot, just as they had his father.

Why hadn't Cassius killed him when he returned? That was a mystery. But, was that a blessing or a curse? Joshua wasn't sure.

And if it somehow was Elohim protecting him, why then hadn't He seen fit to protect his father?

The soldiers now knew that he had seen them and what they had done. However, did they really even care about that? Abraham was just one more Jew, a nobody really, a non-citizen, and from Galilee no less. They knew there would be no trouble. And Joshua? They were probably pretty sure he wouldn't say anything. Even if he did, no one important would be concerned. Any Jews who might have had some political power obviously didn't care. They were apparently in on it.

Joshua wondered in that instant whether he *would* say anything, to anyone, ever? Was it only an idle threat? The soldier who threatened him certainly seemed serious enough. And he certainly felt afraid. It was all so confusing...and terrifying. What should, what could he do? He noticed that his body was still trembling on the inside and there seemed to be little he could do to calm it.

Joshua remained lost somewhere, even as he sat there holding his precious abba's dead and bloody corpse. There had been, even just minutes ago, so much life and zeal in this man. They had been laughing and joking as they worked together that morning.

It had been so good.

Now, there was nothing.

It was all gone.

It was all wrong.

At fifteen, you are trying to make sense out of life and what is going on all around you and in you. That is hard at the best of times, and everyone needs those who will guide them through these dangerous waters. Who would, to whom could he go now?

He needed a father.

What had been taken from him threatened to undo everything that he had been working so hard to put together, to bring into alignment.

Joshua knew that.

Felt it.

All in that instant.

In that very moment.

Even if he could not put into any coherent sentence exactly what it was that he was feeling right then...

He knew that *he* too had been ambushed.

Had had the life taken out of him.

In the midst of this confusion, he felt hot anger arise again. Not even bothering to knock, but simply bursting through the door of his young and still malleable heart.

How dare they?

Joshua had experienced anger and hatred before, but this was a level far beyond anything he had ever known.

Justice screamed.

Anger invaded.

Hatred seethed.

And it felt good to allow it.

To let it in, to let it have its way.

It was comforting, empowering, and emboldening in a way, to this young man whose very world had been assaulted, turned upside-down and sideways, and would most assuredly never be the same again.

Chapter 8

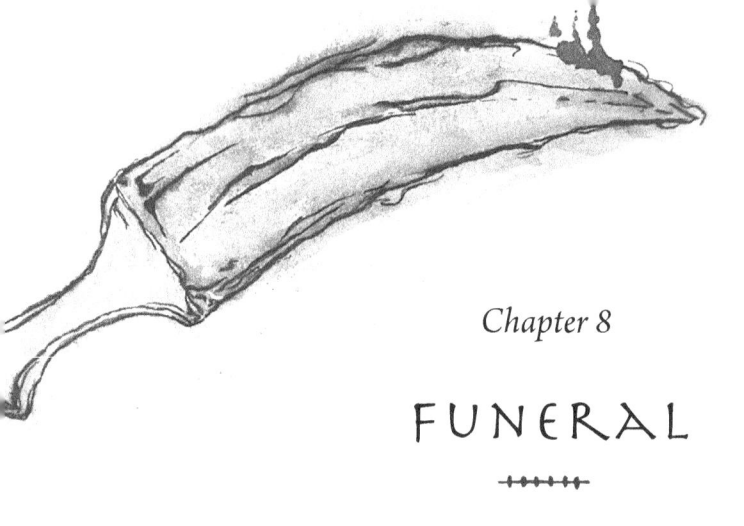

FUNERAL

THE REMAINDER OF THE DAY WAS AN ABSOLUTE BLUR. Joshua felt like he was wandering around in a dense fog.

Within the hour, and it certainly was not any longer than that, the house was filled to overflowing with family members who came to console them and to share their grief. Noise, albeit somewhat muted out of respect, and activity took over from the deathly stillness and aloneness that Joshua had found himself immersed in just moments before.

The busyness was in many ways a welcome distraction. It meant that all of the thoughts that raged in his head had to step to the rear, had to quiet themselves, at least for a little while.

Batiyah had returned from the market with the other younger children not long after the horrible events of that mid-morning. The soldiers obviously had studied and knew the family routine and had planned the attack while most of the family was gone. They had clearly thought that Joshua would be absent as well. And on any other day, he probably would have been.

She had screamed when she entered the yard and pieced together in her own mind what had happened. Joshua had seen tears in her eyes as she tore her garments, however, almost immediately all of that was stowed away somewhere inside and she became very matter-of-fact and strong. She had hugged him and asked if he was okay, and he had said that he was when he really wasn't at all. And then she had bit her lip and dried her tears with a torn piece of fabric. She paused just long enough to wipe Joshua's bloody cheek with the moist cloth. She gave him a questioning look but must have assumed he had cut it trying to uncover Abrahim's body. She didn't ask about it. And he didn't volunteer anything either. Better to just leave well enough alone.

Batiyah launched into what needed to be done.

"For my children, and for Abba," she had said out loud to no one in particular.

"Adonai, help me!" she whispered, and then added, "At least *my* children still have their mother."

Joshua wondered what she meant by that but didn't ask. He was trying to be strong too, for the others, and for Abba. How could his ima be so strong right now? Was this just something that all women were capable of? It didn't seem easy at all. She was broken-hearted, yet still rock-solid. Joshua thought he saw a hint of anger. And he wondered what force in life gave her such strength? Where did she find the ability to carry on no matter what? What didn't he know? Were there things he hadn't been told? About everything? About them? The last few hours showed there had been more to Abrahim than he had ever known.

The events of the day, as tragic as they were, had made him even more hungry to know everything he could about these people who had brought him into the world and raised him. He would ask her later after all of this was over. Maybe soon there would be opportunity. Just not today. Too many boxes of worms were crawling all over the place already.

Joshua supposed that Nathanael, their neighbor who had arrived on the scene, either in response to his call for help or more likely just because he happened to be delivering some new brick molds Abrahim had ordered, had immediately notified his uncle Joseph, who had then let all of the other relatives know what had happened. Many arrived within minutes, it seemed. They had already set about busying themselves with the noon meal while others were given the task of looking after his younger siblings, Elijah who was now eleven, Sarah, who was nine, and Seth who was five.

Joshua wondered if anyone had yet sent word to Zephaniah, around three years his senior, who was presently in Jerusalem studying under Rabbi Shemai? Surely someone had done that, even though the message would most certainly not get there soon enough for his older brother to make it home in time for the funeral. Zephaniah might not even find out about his father's passing for several days.

He caught his uncle Johanan's attention.

"Has anyone sent word to notify Zephaniah?"

"Yes, Joshua, sorry, I should have told you. I hired a messenger and dispatched him with the sad news right away," Uncle Johanan said. "Though, in any event, Zephaniah will surely not make it home in time for the funeral. Hopefully he will be here soon."

Joshua nodded.

Hopefully he would.

"Thank you for doing that," he said.

How long had Zephaniah been gone now? Two years, give or take? Joshua knew that he had only thought of him rarely in the last little while. That thought saddened him.

Joshua suddenly realized that he felt very alone. Maybe because he was already a son of the commandment, all grown up, no one thought he needed taking care of. And in a way, he didn't. Maybe everyone else was just busy with all that was going on.

But it would have been nice to have someone to talk to. He needed to talk right now. Maybe no one knew quite what to say.

There was so much that he needed to process. Or maybe he didn't want to talk at all? Maybe he had no idea what to say?

It was all so confusing.

What had happened? And why? The fact that he hadn't moved gnawed away at his very soul.

He felt very much like his ripped and torn clothing, like the garments he had customarily rent in the time following his realization that his father was indeed dead. His clothes were torn, exposing his skin in places, but his emotions, those ones that ebbed and flowed like a raging tide on the inside of him, hidden somewhere, those were torn to shreds. Far more than he even knew at the time.

Maybe almost beyond repair.

Later…he would have to deal with that later. There would be time for that another day.

And then, there was the soldier's threat and the secret that he now held under house arrest. What would he, what could he do with that? His body involuntarily shuddered as he rehearsed that interaction again in his thoughts, absentmindedly running his hand over the scar in its infancy now forming on his cheek.

The harsh reality was that the man that he had loved and admired and looked up to and was learning life from was…gone.

His corpse was there. First cleansed with oil, then bathed with water, anointed with sweet smelling spices, and finally wrapped in the shrouds of linen fabric that every Jewish family kept washed and ready in the anticipation of death. The mandatory candles had been lit and placed around the body. And an attendant, actually several of them, some of the relatives who had descended on them, had been appointed to stay with Abrahim's remains, since tradition held that there must be someone with the body at all times until it was placed in the tomb.

The body was there…well taken care of.

But what was the point of all of this?

That question cried out to be heard.

And answered.

Abba was gone. His abba.

Others had referred to him as Abba out of respect, but he was Joshua's true abba on every level. And now he was gone.

There were candles, but no light. There was a body, but no life. No wind. No breath. The spirit and soul of this robust and wonderful and passionate man were gone. Joshua's own spirit and soul seemed depleted. He felt as though it too had left, that his father had unintentionally taken it with him. And he was, or at least felt he was, even in this crowd of people, more alone than he had ever been before.

The body, cleansed, washed, anointed, and wrapped and now in its knitted covering called a *kliva*, was placed onto a large, empty brick pallet, covered with their best blanket and hastily repurposed as a funeral bier, to be carried to the family tomb. Joshua was at one of the leading corners, holding the end of one of the poles that supported the platform as they walked to lay his father to rest. Abrahim's three brothers, Joseph, Johanan, and Hazaiah were stationed at the other three corners. Batiyah and the children, the rest of their extended family, and then other relatives and friends walked behind them—the slow walk of the funerary procession.

People paused as they passed, bowing their heads and paying their respects. The pipers who had been hired played and the mourners lamented and wailed.

But Joshua saw and heard very little of it. It was as if he was in another world, another place. His mind at least would not remain focused, refused for the most part to be present.

What was going on inside of him was strange. Very strange indeed. He was sad for sure but there was this other stronger sensation boiling directly beneath the surface. It had been gaining strength all day. Joshua felt it. Knew it. Was it not understandable given the events of the day? He wondered whether it had always been there. Sure, many of the people he knew seemed to harbor a kind of quiet hatred for the situation in which they all were imprisoned.

But this was different, more significant.

The blame for his father's death was to be laid squarely at the feet of an Empire whose government they all longed to escape and whose sovereignty was so wrong. They were supposed to mount up with wings as eagles, not be prey for the Roman eagle!

Joshua did not know what he could do with those feelings. And, it didn't matter what anyone else did or didn't do. He wanted to know, and sooner rather than later, what should *he* do?

Right now, inconvenient as it might be, there was no denying or silencing this other bolder, more passionate feeling. It was anger. Rage even. It was justice crying out to be given its due.

He felt hatred like he had never hated before. How dare they do this? Who do they think they are?

Borrowing the words of young David before he was king, Joshua whispered, to himself but in a stage-like whisper, "Who is this that they should defy the armies of Elohim Hayyim—the living God?"

Who indeed?

He wanted to slay the giant.

Somebody needed to.

The events of the present brought him back from his ruminations. The heavy stone was rolled away and the body was laid in the tomb where all of the other relatives who had died before had been placed, in the family tomb. But this was profoundly different. Those others had been old and ready to die, more distant relations, or newborns that they had not yet come to know as individuals.

This, well this, was just too personal and real. It flew in the face of everything that was good.

This was…

His Abba.

Was…

Past tense.

He had unjustly and too early been taken from him. It just wasn't right. It should not have been.

Some prayers were prayed and parts of the Torah were read. The mourning and dirge continued. People wept and whispered to each other. Many said kind things about his father. It was all very solemn and somber and sad. It felt more practiced and rehearsed than real.

"They don't know you at all, Abba!" Joshua screamed in his head. "You are, were, so much more than words!"

Finally, freed of his responsibility and the burden of carrying the funeral bier, all of a sudden, and without warning, Joshua was aware that he could stand this no longer. The dam had broken inside. He had to get away or he was going to explode. And so, as soon as it was possible to do so, when he thought that not many would notice, he touched his mother on the shoulder, out of respect and so she wouldn't worry, and his look posed this question: "Can I please get out of here?"

Batiyah looked back at him as if she knew exactly what he was feeling. She probably did. She gave a slight nod in his direction.

Joshua turned to begin making his quiet albeit hasty exit. And then, once he had fully eclipsed the tomb, he simply ran…and ran…and ran.

Tears streamed down his face, and the salt dried on his cheeks as he made his escape. He felt ashamed and silly and angry as people who did not really know him questioningly watched him go by. He could no longer pretend or keep up appearances. He wasn't strong.

Still, he kept it mostly in check until the town disappeared and he was truly alone out in the hills. There, in the solitary place, exhausted and out of breath, he fully opened his mouth and let the intense pain and profound anger come pouring out, wave upon wave, until his voice was hoarse and his energy was totally spent.

Deep moans and wails arose from some secret place. Screams and groans from the well of his soul. Feelings too deep for any words. Molten tears trickled down his face. He lay back against a rock, his body heaving in the throes of an agony he had never before experienced. Profound sadness. A mountain of pain.

The anger seemed not to disappear. The hatred had not in any way diminished. If anything, it would not stop growing.

"I hate them! I hate them! I curse all of them!" he yelled.

But now, at last, his anger having been given voice, his cry found its way into the wonderful place and healing power of lament, even though he did not know at the time that was what it was.

He was simply trying to cope. To survive.

"Why? El Shaddai? Why? Where is Your justice?"

"Come to my rescue. My Deliverer, I need You now more that I have ever needed You before," Joshua sobbed.

The words of the ninety-fourth poem in the *Tehillim* somehow sprang to mind.

YHWH is Elohim who avenges.
O Elohim who avenges, shine forth.
Rise up, Judge of the earth;
pay back to the proud what they deserve.

Joshua repeated the words as a prayer, the true nature of many of the psalms, their syllables summing up his own cry for justice.

And in these ancient words, *he* found some comfort.

He hoped and maybe even trusted that...

...Someone was listening, hearing his petition.

And then, suddenly, it seemed as if David, or more likely Adonai Himself, was asking the question found toward the end of this very psalm on which he was meditating.

Who will rise up for Me against the wicked?
Who will take a stand for Me against evildoers?

Joshua shook his head. Was he losing his mind?

Now he was hearing voices.

But no, it was real. It had to be real. He could not deny the power of the question that now demanded a response.

Joshua *had* wondered what it was that he was to be and to do for some time. Maybe *this* was *the thing* he was called to, even if he didn't know exactly what *it* was.

"Here am I, send me!" he breathed out slowly and deliberately, each word measured.

And he wondered: *Was the tragedy of Abba's murder now to be the pathway to his own destiny's door? Would this be a way some good could come out of it?*

He wasn't sure.

Maybe…

Joshua was completely worn out and utterly spent, but his soul and spirit seemed to vibrate now, trembling with both the gravity and the uncertainty of whatever it was to which he had just offered himself.

He lay there until all light was gone and the day, the most awful day he had ever known, had entirely exhausted itself.

Chapter 9

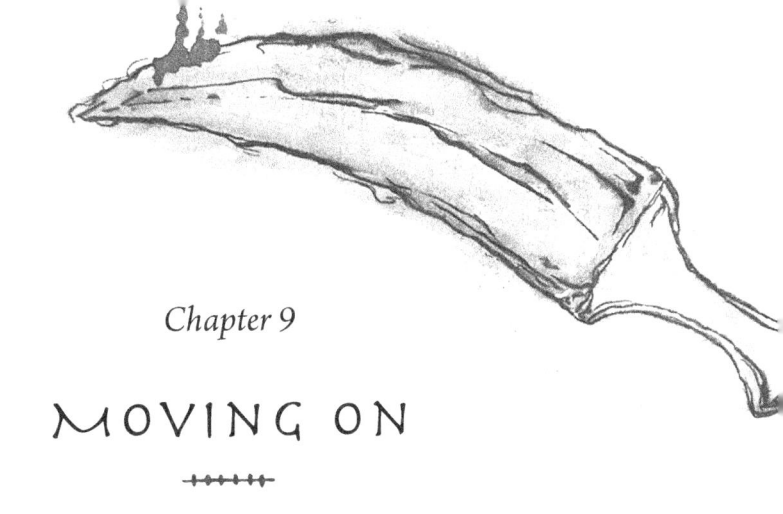

Moving On

The days immediately following Abba's death and the funeral were, to say the least, difficult. Sometimes it would be okay. Well, sort of. But at most other times, Joshua felt like reality now weighed on him like being crushed under a load of bricks.

Literally.

Grief was a very cruel taskmaster. It didn't really feel like life. And it wasn't. Death seemed to give birth to more death. Joshua knew that he was often just going through the motions of living. Breathing one more breath and then another. Another sunset. Another sunrise. Time marching, or rather more like, trudging on. Unrelenting.

He wondered if he would ever not feel like this.

He was now the man of the house. Not that he had been given a choice. He was now the one responsible for what happened… or didn't. And, while he was willing to rise to the occasion, he simply had to, that seemed at least at most times, a lot for a fifteen-year-old, for him to have to take on.

"Ima, do you think Zephaniah has received our message? And if he has, why isn't he home?" Joshua asked.

"What if something…?"

Batiyah shushed him.

"We must always pray and not give up hope," she said quietly.

They had now dispatched several couriers, knowing that for one reason or another, what was sent...didn't always get delivered.

Joshua had simply assumed that his older brother would return, would be home by now. But then, what would that be like after all these years? Would Zephaniah come back, to stay at least? Maybe he had changed, wasn't the same. Would he take over? Joshua wasn't sure he would welcome any of that. Or would he just come home briefly, only to quickly return to Jerusalem and to his Rabbi?

They hadn't heard from him. What if something *had* happened and he could not...?

A second tragedy seemed too much to even consider.

Galilee had been a great place to grow up. But with Abrahim's death, it seemed that everything had changed. What was picture perfect and idyllic before was no longer. Did the sun even shine anymore? The joy was most certainly gone. It was now just a place more confining than freeing. More deadly than life-giving. There seemed little cause for celebration and family get-togethers became a thing of the past. Abrahim had apparently been the glue that held their extended family together.

Everything Joshua knew had been called into question.

On a practical level, his uncle Hazaiah, the youngest of Abrahim's three brothers, was there each day to help out. There was still clay to fetch and bricks to make and orders to fill. They needed to carry on so that their family could continue to survive even if not thrive. Joshua's cousin, Johanan's son Benjamin, had also been volunteered to help out.

But the reality was that Hazaiah was married and had his own little family to look after. He couldn't really afford the time long-term. He was in the midst of working to establish his own life and business.

His cousin Benjamin was present somewhat begrudgingly.

They all anticipated Zephaniah's return.

And as time dragged on, the others gradually helped out less and less, making excuses as to why their own obligations wouldn't allow them to be present as much as they had at the beginning. As a result, Joshua and his immediate family found themselves more and more on their own with each passage of time.

Elijah, Joshua's younger brother, joined the workforce and even Batiyah pitched in as much as she could spare, but the burden now fell squarely on Joshua's shoulders and his days became interminable.

There was so much he wished he had learned, techniques to which he wished he had paid closer attention as Abraham had patiently taught him. But alas, that time was past. He now had to get on with what was at hand. Do the best he could.

There was no other option.

And unfortunately, he knew that it would amount to nothing if he erred on the part that involved finances. Abraham had not thought it necessary to share any of that. He shouldn't have needed to, not yet at least. Joshua agonized over the fact that it was an area he was totally unprepared for and felt himself far short of the task. He hoped all of his efforts and his best guesses would somehow end up being enough.

Joshua had very little time to think. He didn't really want to think. Most of his thoughts lately just drove him mad anyway. And yet it seemed, he could not do anything but think no matter how busy he kept himself. The most troubling reality was the rage inside. It was as if he was angry about everything and the littlest thing could set him off. He knew that he was far more angry than was healthy for anyone. It was understandable, in part, due to recent circumstances, particularly his father's death. But, he really disliked feeling like this. He saw how it often hurt those around him, those near him. It was just that it was near impossible to keep it all stuffed down inside, to pretend that everything was fine…

…when it wasn't.

Neither avoidance nor distraction nor even hard work seemed to come to his aid.

Peace had hidden itself somewhere far away and was not about to be found.

Each day, he rose very early in the morning. He had to. There was much to do. After having a little bit to eat, he would drive Samson, and the cart he dutifully pulled, the short distance down to the seashore and the rich deposit of clay just to the east of town. Most mornings, he was already there when the sun came up over the hills on the other side of the Sea of Galilee. He was grateful for the fact that they would not lack raw materials for quite some time. He wondered where he would even begin to look if their supply ran out.

Joshua shoveled the wet and slimy material into the cart and then made his way back through the streets as daylight fully asserted itself over Rakkath. When he arrived home, the clay was unloaded into a large trough and stomped with bare feet to remove some of the water and to make it more workable. Impurities were discovered and removed. Sand was worked in and straw or other materials, things like volcanic rock powder, all based on the customer's needs, were then added to give the particular order its necessary qualities. After the finished material was scooped, pounded, and leveled into the wooden molds waiting to receive the next round of bricks, he would often fit in a few deliveries. Then, it was usually time for a little lunch, inhaled in the moments of the ride home after dropping off any completed orders.

Following that, and as difficult as it was in the heat of the day, it was the best time to unmold the bricks that had spent some time drying in that same unrelenting sun. Joshua would stack those bricks in courses of 100 to complete their drying, and to await shipment to some location in the city or one of the cities or villages nearby. Sometimes, bricks were loaded into the kiln to be fired when they needed to be extra strong for some project. At times, there were more deliveries to be made. When he returned from those, the bricks that had been made the day before were turned over so they could dry evenly making them less prone to cracking. Fully dry bricks were stacked. Maybe some clean up.

The sun would disappear at the conclusion of another day. Joshua would have some late supper, often eating alone or with Batiyah as his only company, though he most often felt too tired to talk. He would fall into bed totally spent. And then, only minutes later it often seemed, Hezekiah would crow and it would begin all over again.

The only reprieve in this endless routine was once a week when *Shabbat* rolled around. He would finish earlier on Friday, for the Sabbath started as soon as the sun went down. It was the one time in the week that they all ate the evening meal together as a family. And then, in the morning, they would go to synagogue together, though Joshua's energy level lately seemed to seriously hinder listening or paying careful heed to what was being taught.

"Six days you shall labor and do all your work," had been the text they had studied just recently. This had caught Joshua's attention.

As devout Jews, there was no *work* done on the Sabbath, but to Joshua, at least lately, it never felt like a day of rest either. Or rather, not *enough* of a rest. He knew that he himself was never at rest, and Joshua often questioned whether Adonai meant they were to work, "every available moment of every day, except the seventh," or whether that part of it was mankind's fatal addition and interpretation, an awful misreading of the commandment?

His family was doing as much as they could—doing the best they knew how—to help ease the load. He didn't feel as though he had the time, knew he hadn't made time to teach Elijah anything. He gave him only simple tasks so he wouldn't have to explain much. And as a result, there was, for Joshua at least, never an escape from work.

"Hard work? It's our own fault. Us sinners!" he remembered Abrahim used to joke. "Part of the curse that we brought on ourselves!"

Cursed indeed, Joshua thought.

How long would it take for life to be normal, to make sense again?

Would it ever?

Probably not, he thought.

Every once in a while, he remembered the secret. And, truth be told, he simply wasn't sure what to do with that. He so wished that he did not have to keep it tightly locked up inside. Wished it would disappear. It haunted him.

Why had he not said anything? Would they really find out and hunt him down? Could he risk it?

He was pretty sure that he could not.

In fact, several weeks after the murder, he had been in town making a delivery when he saw *him,* the very same soldier who had come back for the glove. They had locked eyes and Cassius Maximus had grinned wickedly in Joshua's direction, grabbed the handle of his knife, rubbed his own cheek exaggeratedly with his gloved hand and then made a slow chopping motion across his neck.

Could the message be any clearer?

"Don't you dare say anything…unless you have a death wish!"

At the time, Joshua had easily convinced himself that if he did tell someone, anyone, the soldiers would surely find out somehow. And then, they would come and kill him.

And that would most assuredly guarantee the death of his family.

They were depending on him.

They needed him.

He felt he simply could not risk it.

While everyone close to him assumed it had been an accident, Joshua knew that his father's death had been anything but accidental.

His mother, and his uncles as well had eventually asked him about that day. They obviously wanted more details.

Did they suspect anything? Who knew? Joshua didn't think so. He did wonder though whether somehow Batiyah saw through his charade.

He had simply repeated the story he had rehearsed in his mind:

"I was up on the roof retrieving a trowel we had left there, and then I heard a crash. When I came down, I found Abba lying face down on the ground covered in bricks and wood."

It was true, insofar as this sketch of the story went. But it was most certainly not the whole truth. And it pained him, destroying him just that much more on the inside, each time he told only a part of what really happened. It was especially painful to keep the true circumstances of his father's death from his ima. She had a right to know the truth.

Did she know he was lying?

Keeping something from her?

He had often thought of telling someone the *more* to the story. But really, even if he got away with it, what good would it do? What could be done about it now? Especially after so much time had passed. Cassius had said that there would be no fuss, and that had always been Joshua's experience. They did not make trouble for their Roman overlords. Mostly, they simply complied with whatever they were told whether they liked it or not. They might complain to each other, but nothing ever came of it.

Such was the plight of the Jewish people under Roman rule.

With each passing day, the events of that fateful day were put further into the past, more into a place of forgetfulness. Which was good and bad. Good because not remembering made carrying on easier, but bad because it would never totally go away. And then, when he did think about it, he would feel guilty for forgetting.

Joshua lifted his arms up to the heavens in a questioning gesture, briefly noting the fact that the color of his clay-stained hands almost matched the sky on this rather dreary day.

His mind went to one particular time in the distant past, when as a young man he had tried to imagine what Adonai might have planned for him and what it was that he was called to be and to do.

He had asked his father about it, but Abrahim had steered him in this other, heavenly direction.

"Joshua, I am not the person that you need to be asking. Adonai Himself will show you when the time is right—in His time. He is the One to ask," his father had said on that occasion.

Now, Adonai was indeed the only one he could ask.

Had Abrahim's death brought even more urgency to his question? It had certainly exacerbated the process.

So far, however, there was no answer. Nothing specific anyway. No response even to the *commitment* that Joshua himself had made to Adonai out there in the hills immediately following the funeral.

Chalk it up to youthful impertinence, but he had actually expected the El Shaddai to audibly answer.

So far, there was nothing. Just prayers prayed, and...still little sense of even what *it* was.

Joshua wondered some days if *it* actually existed?

This just added to his anger and frustration.

In the midst of all of the day-to-day busyness, not having the luxury to just stop and sit and think, Joshua would ask himself whether this was all there was to life?

Was there no wonder?

No adventure or excitement?

No joy?

What *was* his purpose? His calling?

Would he spend the rest of his life...

...making bricks?

That certainly couldn't be *the thing* that Adonai had for him.

It was so unfulfilling and so...not significant.

Only fifteen years of age, he had been forced to grow up so fast. Before he was ready.

And it was completely maddening that his present reality was so far from any dream he had ever had of how his life would be.

The writer of Ecclesiastes had said that, "there was nothing new under the sun and that all was meaningless and empty."

King Solomon had said that.

The wise man who had everything.

Joshua, who felt he had so little and had been forced into rather than chosen his life at this point, was convinced that he felt it and thought it, on most days, even more so than Solomon ever could have.

Meaningless...Empty...Routine...

He would carry on for his family whom he loved, he supposed.

But deep down, he knew with an intense passion that he hated his life, this life that he had in no way chosen, but had been forced to live.

Chapter 10

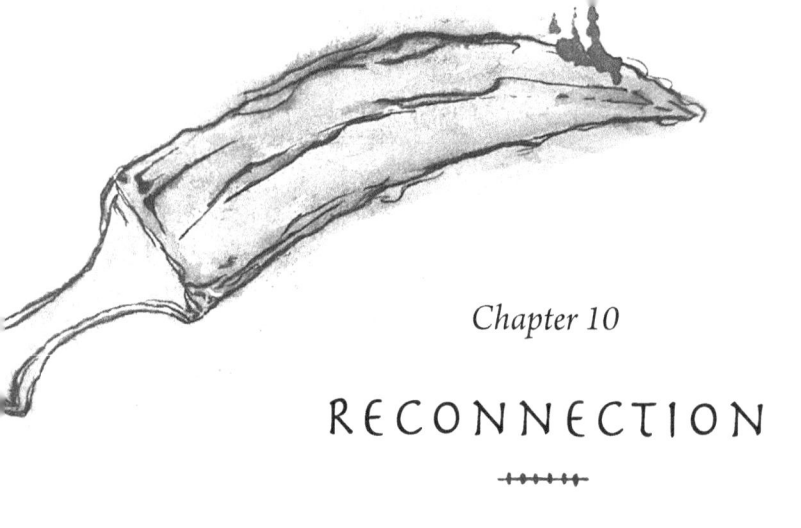

RECONNECTION

Several months had gone by now and life, more out of obligation than anything else, had taken on a kind of normality, even though it was not an agreeable one. There simply was no other option than to carry on with the new and unpleasant reality that had forced itself upon all of them. The younger children probably felt something, but were mostly oblivious to the very real struggle that faced their little family, now devoid of its leader: the struggle just to survive day to day.

As the oldest, or at least the oldest child at home, Joshua very strongly felt the weight of trying to make up for what was missing, if such a thing could even be possible.

It was a struggle just to keep going some days.

He was doing okay he thought. Doing the best he knew how.

Would it be enough?

Why hadn't Zephaniah, his older brother, come home yet he wondered? They had not heard anything from him at all. Not even a word to say that he was on the way or coming soon. If only he were here to relieve the burden, or at least to share it, things could maybe be a little better. Abba would still be missing for sure, there was no going back from that, but then at least there would be only one empty place.

What if what he feared most had happened to his brother too?

And what would happen to them if their family were called upon to handle yet one more tragedy? Not knowing one way or the other kept that at bay, for the time being anyway.

Every so often, even though she tried her best to keep it all tightly locked up, Joshua was sure he noticed something on his ima's face that revealed the ache down deep inside. Some days he thought she did not look well at all, as if she was physically ill. Joshua wondered whether he should be even more concerned about her than he already was.

Then again, what must it be like, he thought, to lose the one that you love and with whom you have spent the majority of your life? How does one carry on after that?

He knew what it felt like to him.

It was awful!

It was painful at first, and then what followed was the knowledge that you could do nothing that would ever ease that pain.

As time passed, he grew to accept that this was simply the way that things would be from now on. Death had come calling and the attempt to go on living would never be anything but miserable.

Joshua thought about mortality often.

Death was so final!

There seemed to be no way back.

Many nights since that fateful day, he had cried himself to sleep, quietly though so as not to disturb anyone else. He certainly did not want the others to know what he was doing and he felt angry and ashamed at his supposed weakness.

He too, like his mother had said on the day of the funeral, wanted to be brave for his family and for his abba.

But, could he? Be the man that was needed? Stand in the gap for them all? He really wasn't sure. In a way it didn't matter, his family needed him to somehow hold it all together. He simply must.

Strangely, or maybe not, he found himself praying, more now than ever before, that *El Jireh* would provide for them, that comfort would not be a stranger, that they would make it somehow, even that Messiah would appear. He was sure that it was all beyond his capabilities. He knew that he, Joshua, could do nothing to really make a difference, could not change anything, but that Adonai, the El Shaddai, might see fit to come and rescue them.

Rescue him.

He also knew that he needed desperately to do something with all of the anger that seemed to be ever-present, sometimes more and sometimes less, but always boiling directly beneath the surface, like a volcano…

…waiting to erupt.

And then there was the loneliness he profoundly felt. It had started when Zephaniah went away and Joshua was left on his own. Later, when Abba was stolen from him, desolation had poisoned his soul with a sickness from which he wasn't sure he would ever recover.

Family, the remainder of it anyway, was still present, but it just didn't seem to be enough.

Praying did seem to help; to calm what quietly and ceaselessly raged inside.

"Please, Adonai," he prayed, begged even, "Maranatha! Come!"

And although he wasn't exactly certain how it was happening, he did sense that Adonai was closer, maybe more personal.

One evening, as Joshua was falling asleep himself, he thought that he heard soft weeping coming from his mother's bed. He was pretty sure he had heard it at least once before during the past several weeks, but on this occasion, he climbed out of his bed, wrapped his cloak around himself and tiptoed over to his ima's bedside. He stopped short and listened for a moment.

She was crying sure enough.

But she was praying in the midst of her sobs. Quietly reciting one of the *Tehillim*:

Hallelujah—Praise YHWH—O my soul;
all my inmost being, praise His Holy Name.
Hallelujah—Praise YHWH—O my soul,
and forget not all His benefits—
Who forgives all your sins
and heals all your diseases…

Joshua did not really want to interrupt. He considered going back to bed and just leaving her to her prayers. But she paused… maybe because she sensed that he was there.

"Ima?" Joshua ventured softly.

"Yes, son," Batiyah replied sitting up, "Come here."

"Do you miss Abba?" Joshua asked, the answer being obvious.

"Most certainly!" Batiyah said, wiping her tears.

"I do too!" Joshua replied without being asked.

"Why did he have to die? Why did this have to happen?" Joshua said, a little louder than he wanted to.

It appeared for a moment as if Batiyah was going to take his hand and pull him closer to herself. She hesitated.

"I don't know, Yoshi," she said quietly.

She hadn't called him that for years. It was strange, but welcome.

Joshua moved toward her, kneeling at her bedside.

She held up her hand forcing him to stop.

"I am ceremonially unclean right now, son," Batiyah said. "You probably shouldn't…"

"I don't really understand or care about any of that stuff!" Joshua said, moving to her side. "Besides, there's no one here to see us anyway!"

Batiyah dropped her guard.

They embraced each other.

Joshua was fifteen, almost sixteen years old, and a *man*, but in this moment, he allowed himself to be a child again, held close by a loving mother. It felt wonderful.

Sacred in a way.

He choked back the tears.

But then somehow, there was no holding them in. There seemed to be no sense in keeping them at bay.

He let them come pouring out.

Batiyah's tears flowed unhindered as well, as she allowed herself freedom in the comfort of her young son, a young man who in so very many ways, reminded her of the man that had gone missing from her life.

And, for what felt like an extremely long and very precious time, even though it was probably only several minutes, they simply held each other in this soggy embrace and quietly wept together.

Reaching through some kind of veil and entering a most holy place.

Joshua wondered briefly about Elohim's Torah and all of its uncleanness legislation, and especially why women in particular were so often forced to hide themselves away.

It seemed only to bring separation when He clearly wanted us to be together. He hoped that maybe someday, he would understand it all.

It was night but the moon cast enough light through the window that, as they pulled away from each other ever so slightly, both could see the smile that now lit up the other's face. They laughed a little.

Feeling a little silly but also more wonderful than either had felt in some time.

This was the thing that would make carrying on possible. They had both just experienced it.

Love.

And they knew, as everyone really does, that it was the only thing that could conquer even death.

Unclean or not, whatever all of that fuss was about, Joshua thought his mother looked lovely.

Time had clearly etched lines in her face. The sun had weathered her skin. But she was a beautiful lady. Here in the moonlight, her brown hair flowing down her back, and her dark eyes shining as the tears that filled them glistened in the light, beauty seemed to radiate out from her, rising up from some deep place inside.

Joshua knew why Abba must have loved her. He knew that he too had always loved her, even if he hadn't paid much attention to it as of late. Circumstance had led him, or simply allowed him, to forget what was really most important.

How wonderful to have it reappear.

"Would you like a cup of tea?" Batiyah asked.

"Maybe we could…talk?"

"I would like that very much!" Joshua replied.

Chapter 11

REVELATION

JOSHUA AND BATIYAH QUIETLY MADE THEIR WAY out of the house so as not to wake the rest of their sleeping family. Once they were in the yard, Batiyah stirred the embers in the fire pit and carefully placed some kindling and dry wood. Skillfully blowing at the base of the pile, flames almost immediately appeared. Joshua returned shortly with some more wood and a cooking pot containing enough water for several cups of tea. He hung it over the fire that was now making its way into the night air. All of this happened without a word.

"Abba and I talked about telling you what I would like to share for quite a while, Joshua," Batiyah opened, hesitating slightly. "I'm not sure how we never got around to it...before. Waiting for just the right time? Who knows? But I suppose that tonight's circumstance has finally created the opportunity, though now it would appear it's up to me alone to tell it."

Joshua thought this sounded somewhat ominous but sensed only mild apprehension in Batiyah's voice. He dismissed it as simply due to the fact that Abba was no longer present by her side.

"I'm listening," he said. "What is it that you neglected to tell me?"

"How it is that you came to be named Jehoshua," she replied.

"You don't have to tell me *that!*" Joshua interrupted. "Abba told me *that* often! You named me Jehoshua because you were looking forward to the arrival of Adonai's Anointed One and you hoped and prayed that the child born to you would be the one to bring His deliverance to Israel! I *know* why you named me Joshua! You wanted me to be *the One!*"

Batiyah slowly raised her finger to her lips.

Joshua was caught up short, immediately realizing he had already broken his promise…to listen.

"Sorry, Ima," he said apologetically.

She waved her hand over her shoulder to let him know his indiscretion was already forgiven and forgotten.

"All of what you say is most definitely true, Joshua," Batiyah said slowly, now measuring each of her words…

"But there is actually *much* more to it than just that!"

Joshua rather quickly drew in his breath at this, almost choking on it. And he instantly thought of *the much more* of another story, which *he* had not yet told his mother: the whole truth surrounding Abba's death.

He cringed inside once more at the fact that he was withholding. But even as he had done many times already, he simply remained mute. Besides, he was eager to hear this new thing Batiyah had to share with him and wasn't sure he was ready to reciprocate yet.

Someday.

Maybe…soon?

Or…

…maybe not ever!

She poured the water, added some honey to each, stirred his cup and then hers and finally, pushing his tea toward him, started in.

"Let's see, where do I begin?" Batiyah asked herself.

"After Abba and I were married here in Rakkath, we moved in with his uncle Jeremias, who had made a place in his home for

Abba's mother Salome, and for Abba and his brothers. He was a wonderful man who had felt honored and obliged to take them all in after Abba's father Jehudah died, I think when Abba was maybe about eleven or so. He now made room for me and us as well."

"Uncle Jeremias's wife had died a long time before, only several years after they had been married. They had not had any children and he had never remarried. He said often that he actually loved having Salome and her family around and had welcomed them all with open arms. I guess it made his home feel less lonely. He was a potter by trade, and had also taught all of the boys what he knew, as they each came of age. That's why all of your uncles are potters, Joshua."

"Well, less than a year, maybe nine months later, Abba's mother Salome passed away. It was a very sad and difficult time for all of us, but she had been ill for several months so it was in some ways a blessing too."

"At about the same time, a request had come from one of Abrahim's other relatives in Bethlehem. Abba's third cousin Enoch was a brick maker there who found himself with more business than he could handle and who desperately needed someone to come alongside, since his own children were still too young to help out."

"Oh, did I say that Uncle Jeremias was a potter? Yes, I'm pretty sure I did, but did I *also* say that he liked to make bricks on the side! I don't think so...but he did, and since he was already very familiar working with clay, it made sense. That's important to the story!"

"We weren't sure what to do. Abrahim did actually enjoy brick making a lot more than pottery and thought that he would rather do that. This seemed like a perfect opportunity! But then too, with his mother's passing and our recent marriage, he now felt very responsible for his brothers, especially since he had been gone from home for quite some time and we had just recently returned."

"Your great-uncle Jeremias told us not to worry and said he didn't mind looking after Joseph, Johanan, and Hazaiah. He reminded us that he had been doing that for years already anyway! He strongly encouraged us to go!"

"I think he had seen the way that Abba enjoyed making bricks!"

"By the way, do you remember Uncle Jeremias? He probably died when you were about seven or so," Batiyah interjected.

"I think so," Joshua said.

He didn't really. Uncle Jeremias was likely one of those relatives they had buried in the family tomb whom he didn't know that well at all.

"Have you heard any of this before?" Batiyah queried, pausing.

"Some, yes, I suppose," Joshua said. "But I'm okay with hearing things again. Besides, I do want to know the whole story!"

"Of course, you know that we are of the tribe of Judah, but did you know that Abba's family was originally from the town of David, from Bethlehem? That's why we still had some relatives there."

"His forefathers were *from* there?" Joshua replied. "I just always thought they lived here in Rakkath forever. I knew that you and Abba had been in Bethlehem for a bit because he was learning to make bricks, but our family is from there…? Interesting!"

"I wish I knew more of the history of Abrahim's family line way back, well…besides the fact that they *were* from Bethlehem," Batiyah said.

"I do know that his father Jehudah had moved his little family here to Rakkath when Abba was very young, before any of your other uncles had been born. But as to why exactly they left Bethlehem to come here, I'm afraid I don't know that either."

"*We* left Bethlehem for reasons far more significant than just being done learning or to be back here with family, as nice as that was," Batiyah now revealed. "That's the part of the story that I am getting to, and your name, Jehoshua, is all bound up in *that* part of the story!"

She hesitated.

They both took a sip of their tea.

And Batiyah paused again, now drawing in a very deep breath.

Joshua wanted desperately to pursue even just a few of the myriad of questions that had come to *his* mind. He always had so many questions. At the same time, he knew that all of his interruptions would only hinder his mother's unfolding of whatever this new Bethlehem revelation was. He wondered how it specifically related to his name.

He decided to hold his tongue, decided to just listen, as he had promised he would.

"Let's see, where was I?" Batiyah asked herself.

"Oh yes, our challenging and wonderful journey from Bethlehem. But I guess I have to actually get us *to* Bethlehem before I can bring us back!"

She laughed at that.

"We obviously did say yes to Enoch's request and Abba apprenticed himself to his brick making relative. And it all fell into place quite well, even though it meant that we now had to move away from what was familiar, the people that I was just getting to know and particularly from Abba's family here in Rakkath. We knew that Enoch's invitation *was* a really great opportunity and a wise move for us. But that did not in any way minimize its difficulty!"

"Abba and I had been married for about a year at the time. We were excited for the opportunity and looked forward to the challenges of a new life, but it was a difficult journey especially because I was about five months pregnant at the time. It is only a journey of about thirty-five miles, but the road to Jericho is very narrow and switches back and forth as it moves its way south along the west bank of the Jordan River. It was not the middle of summer thankfully, but it was still very warm. And then too, the road up from Jericho to Jerusalem and on to Bethlehem is very steep and all uphill. Because we had to stop often and because it is safest to travel during the day, it took us almost a full week to complete our journey. We had scraped together a little money and bought an old donkey so that I wouldn't have to walk the whole way. But whether that sped up our journey or slowed us down, who knows? Your father wasn't sure whether the beast was a blessing or a curse!"

Batiyah smiled and laughed a little as she remembered.

"We were never happier to see a final destination than when we knocked on the gate and saw Enoch's broad smile welcoming us *home*. He invited us in and his wife, Hannah, put warm food in front of us and made us comfortable. Nothing ever felt more wonderful or tasted better than the bread and meat, vegetables, and fruit they shared with us that very first evening. It was so encouraging to finally meet them and feel like we were still part of a family, even though our surroundings were new and unfamiliar and we were far from everything and everyone we knew."

"After supper, Hannah showed us to a smaller house, which didn't look like much on the outside but was quite nice really, at the back of the yard out behind the main house in which they lived. She said that this was the place that *they* had moved into after Enoch and her were married. Later, when Enoch's father had passed away, they had moved into the main house since it had more room for their growing family. She told me how much they had enjoyed their time in this little house and said that both Enoch and she hoped and prayed that we would too."

"'We are just so glad that you are here! An answer to our prayers,' Hannah had said, 'Enoch will really appreciate the help. He has been so busy lately. And I think, I hope, we will get along like sisters'!"

Batiyah stared off for a bit, lost in the moments from days gone by. She closed her eyes contentedly.

Maybe she was wishing that life could return to a place like that!

"And it *was* wonderful! An answer to *our* prayers," Batiyah said after a moment, now looking directly at Joshua.

"Abrahim and Enoch got along famously. The business was doing great. And Abba was learning so much. Of course, they talked often about work, but more about family and about faith, all things that your father would come and share with me in the evening. Life was very good and we were grateful for every one of Elohim's many blessings!"

"We grew to love them all so very much and I really did treasure the time with Hannah. It was a great way to prepare for having our own family, an event that was getting closer with each passing day. Helping with household chores, cooking and cleaning, and looking after their three small children, Samuel, Rebekah...and Jonathan... who had been born only shortly before we had arrived."

Joshua was sure he saw something dark pass over his ima's face as she completed that last sentence and he questioned himself as to what that was about.

Batiyah paused briefly once more.

She took a deep breath and pressed on.

"One night after we had been there about four months, in fact only days after your brother had been born, we were awakened by loud voices, screams, shrieks, and commotion coming from outside. We thought it might be a robbery or disturbance of some sort, but we were not at all prepared for what was actually going on. No one was!"

Joshua watched as tears filled his ima's eyes. She tried in vain to sniff them back but pushed on nevertheless.

"Herodian guards came without any warning in the middle of the night and broke down the door of Enoch and Hannah's house.

They grabbed young Jonathan out of his crib and killed him, bludgeoning him to death on the floor, right there in front of Enoch and Hannah…"

At this last sentence, Batiyah's voice broke completely and she was forced to stop.

"Oh, Ima!" Joshua interjected as he reached out to grab her hand. "That must have been dreadful!"

Joshua immediately thought of another murderous attack on an innocent person by Imperial soldiers. The one *he* had witnessed. His own anger and sense of injustice almost immediately rose up again. How dare they, he thought!

He knew exactly how dreadful it could be.

He forced it down inside once again and after a moment Batiyah continued with her story even though the raw emotion that now welled up in her made it extremely difficult.

"It was, Yoshi. Beyond imagining! Hannah and Enoch were beside themselves wondering why they were being singled out for such harsh and seemingly unjust treatment. Sobbing, Hannah could do nothing but cradle their little Jonathan's bloody and lifeless body. Enoch's arms surrounded them both, inconsolable in his own grief and shock. Abba and I just held each other and wept. It was unbelievably painful to watch. We felt helpless, not knowing what if anything we could do!"

"And if that wasn't bad enough, it quickly became apparent that this was not an isolated event! In fact, as the sun rose, we discovered that the guards had carried out a similar task in every one of the homes in the little town that night!"

"Apparently, King Herod believed that the Messiah, the King of the Jewish people, had just recently been born in Bethlehem and was making sure that he would not survive. He could not have anyone jeopardize or threaten his reign. The Herodian guards had in fact barged into each house in Bethlehem looking for any male children that seemed to them to be about two years old or less. They had taken and killed each one, most often right in front of their horrified parents. In all, I think twenty-seven or so young boys had been murdered within the small town. Later we heard it was not just Bethlehem but the entire surrounding area. Who knows how many little ones were lost that night?"

"How they didn't come and break into the little house where we were staying and kill your brother, I don't know," Batiyah said. "Maybe they didn't think that anyone was living there. It was kind of hidden in the back of the yard behind all of the stacks of bricks. From the outside I guess it looked more like a tool shed than a place where anyone would live."

"We were extremely grateful to Elohim but knew for certain that we dare not stay any longer. To do so was far too dangerous! And so, we hid inside all of the next day, at least I did, making sure to keep our baby very quiet. Abrahim didn't do any work that day but rather quickly put together a few supplies. We said a hasty goodbye to Enoch and Hannah, so sad to leave them in their hour of grief, and then very cautiously made our own way out of town after night fell, making certain that we were not seen by anyone."

"I thought that the journey *to* Bethlehem had been rough. Our flight was far worse, though for very different reasons. Now there were three of us and we had to walk the whole way. Did I say *walk*? We actually ran much of the time, especially in those first few days. We wanted to put as much distance between ourselves and the horror of that little town as quickly as we could."

"By far however, the worst part of the journey was the terror that I felt. It threatened to overwhelm us, me for sure, at times. At the same time, I was so sad as I thought of Enoch and Hannah and Jonathan and their remaining children. All of those other families too! Bethlehem was no longer quiet and peaceful! Every family had in some way been violated!"

"We travelled only by night for the first few days, for fear of being seen and apprehended, which would have certainly meant the death of Zephaniah, until we were out of Herod's jurisdiction, or at least out of Judea, heading north again, back to where we had come from only a few months earlier."

"What would happen now, we wondered? Life was going so well. And now we would have to start over. All over once more! I didn't know if we could, if I could do it! Would we be safe anywhere ever again?"

"*That* is what brought *us* back to Rakkath!"

Batiyah paused.

"Oh my goodness, Joshua. That is actually a very gruesome tale!" she said, now rehearsing the details, running them over in her mind, as she was finishing.

"I guess that's maybe why we didn't tell you sooner. I suppose we were waiting until you were old enough!"

Joshua had listened to this last part of the story with rapt attention, no interruptions, only nodding or maybe inserting a brief response here or there.

This was a riveting tale.

Missing pieces of a puzzle for sure.

Another question came almost immediately to mind.

"Does Zephaniah know all of this?" Joshua asked. "Or did he?" he added, rather awkwardly.

"Yes, most certainly," Batiyah said, "Abba and I told him the whole story in the days just before he left for Jerusalem. It is in fact why we named *him* Zephaniah. We chose it on the way as we fled Judea. *His* name means, 'YHWH has hidden'!"

"And, that is why, to bring this rather long story around to its point, when you were born several years after our return to Rakkath, we named *you* Jehoshua. We were just so grateful for

Adonai's deliverance. We knew that we had most assuredly been saved and delivered!"

"And so, maybe even more so because of what happened, we continue to pray for Adonai's complete rescue, His ultimate deliverance of our entire nation from the ungodly and despicably evil reign of Rome."

Batiyah paused once more, now looking intently at her son.

"*That* is why we named you, Jehoshua!"

"And, while you may not be *the* Messiah, Joshua, I believe and have always believed that you are nevertheless a child of destiny! That you are someone who will champion others!"

"Exactly what that will look like, I know not. But I do know that Adonai Elohim will most assuredly reveal exactly what it is that you are especially destined to become and to do!"

"What did Abrahim always say? 'All in time'?"

Joshua smiled and nodded.

That was what his abba always said.

Joshua longed for Adonai's complete revelation.

"Wow, Ima! That *is* quite the story!" he responded finally, replaying the details, working to absorb, just trying to put this all together with everything else that he knew and had experienced.

Joshua suddenly thought of something else.

"Ima, since you are in the mood for sharing, I remember you saying, on the day that Abba was…on the day that Abba…died, that, 'at least your children still had their mother.'"

"What exactly did you mean by that?"

Batiyah just stared at him.

Eventually, she replied.

"Oh Joshua…*that* is a very long and involved story. Haven't *you* had enough for one day? It is extremely late and I simply don't know that I have the energy to go into all of that right now. Could we please just save *that* revelation for another day?"

Joshua wasn't sure he wanted to wait, but he had been given no other choice.

The two of them quietly returned to the house.

Morning was due to arrive in a few hours.

"Come to think of it now, there are many things we never shared with all of you!" Batiyah whispered quietly to herself as they both made their way back to their beds.

Chapter 12

IN SEARCH OF DESTINY

Today marked exactly one year since Abba had been murdered. Twelve moons or this year at least, in the Jewish calendar, 354 times the same thing, day after day.

It had been a particularly difficult one. Joshua felt he had not accomplished much; his thoughts had continued their assault on his peace.

He had kept the secret zealously guarded. And unfortunately, he and Batiyah had somehow never quite returned to the place of that one precious evening.

Joshua told himself that life was just too busy, that it was understandable given their present circumstance. Maybe he just knew that more revelation on Batiyah's part might necessitate him having to come clean as well.

Deeper relationship—*love*—gives much, but also demands much from each of its participants.

Zephaniah had not returned home. They had heard nothing from him. And they all feared the worst even though no one ever said anything about that possibility.

Had they just about given up hope?

Recently, the one thing they had discovered was that he had apparently left Rabbi Shemai in Jerusalem, but no one knew where he had gone or what had happened to him after that. And so far, everything they had done to try and chase down the possibilities that had been suggested had only resulted in dead ends.

Life moved on.

That only added to the pain that all of them felt.

No one wanted it to move on. They wanted it to return to the way that it had been.

It had been good once.

Joshua had gotten better at it, not at the living part, but at least at most aspects of brick making. In a way, he had even grown to appreciate the daily routine.

And the business was doing fairly well, all things considered, especially now, with the ancient town of Rakkath overflowing the confines of the walled city on the hill. It was even more than rumored that there were plans to build a new Imperial garrison just to the south or southwest of Rakkath. Everywhere there was a lot more construction and activity.

They were surviving, financially at least, and all probably seemed well to the outside observer.

But something monumental continued to eat away at Joshua's insides. Maybe even more so now as the Roman presence grew ever larger.

Rakkath had been a Jewish town. Now it was clearly not that. At least not as it had been in the past.

And, while it made sense in a way, while it even meant money in their belts, each increase of the Roman Imperial invasion of the Holy Land was an assault on his growing knowledge of what Adonai's Chosen people were meant to be and what He had intended for them.

It was good for business but Joshua hated it.

Things were changing but not all for the better.

"We are to be the head and not the tail," Moses had written.

Joshua repeated it often, probably more to himself than to anybody in particular.

"We are to serve Adonai and Him alone."

"We are to serve no other gods, Roman or otherwise."

Each day for as long as he could remember, Joshua had recited these words from Moses's fifth scroll:

"*Shema,* O Israel—*Hear,* O Israel: YHWH is our God, YHWH is One. Love YHWH Elohim with all your heart and with all your soul and with all your strength."

The commandment was simple.

All-encompassing.

It was a command to love Him. Only.

The One and Only.

With everything in you.

Had the love of many grown cold?

It seemed that many had much too strong an appreciation for the Empire, the *Pax Romana*—the "Peace of Rome"—and all that it brought with it.

But they were the people of Adonai, not Romans. They were the people set apart for, holy unto, Elohim, not to bow down to Caesar. The commands, the instructions of Ha Shem, were to be in their hearts, not the laws of Rome.

Joshua knew and loved all the stories of faith from times past. But he wondered, was the faith of the fathers no longer important to Israel's children of today?

They were to impress the things of Adonai on their offspring. They were to talk about them: when you sit at home and when you walk along the road, and when you lie down and when you get up.

Joshua knew that this was the one thing that Abrahim had done so well, and one of the things that *he* now dearly missed.

Abrahim had believed in and lived out teaching his children about Adonai, the commandments, and how to live wisely in this world, in every conversation, everywhere, every day.

Joshua longed to hear his father's words again. But in a way, he still was, he thought with a smile.

It was called the *Shema* after the first word in this command.

"*Shema,* O Israel—*Hear,* O Israel..."

"Was Israel still listening?" he asked.

"Or just repeating empty words?"

They were supposed to, and many Pharisees literally did, tie those commandments on their hands and on their foreheads and write them on the doorframes of their houses and on the gates of their land. But it was not enough just to decorate your doorposts.

Moses had sternly warned the people that, "When YHWH Elohim brings you into the land He swore to your fathers, to Abraham, Isaac, and Jacob, to give you—a land with large, flourishing cities you did not build, houses filled with all kinds of good things you did not provide, wells you did not dig, and vineyards and olive groves you did not plant—then when you eat and are satisfied, be careful that you do not forget YHWH, who brought you out of Egypt, out of the land of slavery."

Were they not hearing? Was the danger spoken of in this prophetic warning coming true?

Joshua thought that many had forgotten their Adonai, maybe not totally, but certainly as far as Him being their singular or even primary focus. They seemed to him to be like seeds that had grown up well at first but were being choked out by all of the *weeds* around them that prosperity had brought.

In the very same place in the fifth scroll, Moses had encouraged, "Fear YHWH Elohim, serve Him only. Do not follow other gods, the gods of the peoples around you; *for YHWH Elohim, who is among you, is a jealous God*...Be sure to keep the commands of

YHWH Elohim and the stipulations and decrees He has given you. Do what is right and good in YHWH's sight, so that it may go well with you and you may go in and take over the good land YHWH promised on oath to your ancestors, thrusting out your enemies before you, as YHWH said."

It was this in particular that had arrested Joshua as of late: the fact that Adonai is a jealous God. And that, because of that, *they* were to do what was right and good, to keep His commands, stipulations, and decrees. The conclusion however, was even more far reaching: it was expected that they *take over* the land.

"Take over the land, the good land, that He had promised to the ancestors," Moses had told them.

They were to take it back. They were to thrust out their enemies before them. Don't become satisfied with your prosperity in a land that should be yours. Don't accommodate or give in to the enemy even if it means some kind of advantage for you.

For the last several months now, Joshua had felt this passion for the people of Adonai rising up in him. A passion for the Land. Things were good or at least okay but they were not as they should be. Was it not fundamentally wrong that Rome ruled over Israel and claimed the land promised to Abraham and his descendants as their own?

King Herod had been raised as and claimed to be Jewish, taking to himself the title, "King of the Jews," as he asserted himself from his beginnings as Roman-appointed governor of Galilee.

But he was actually an Idumean, an Edomite, a descendant of a people who had been forced to convert to Judaism, making their faith suspect to all true Jews. Was Herod a Jew?

Joshua was pretty certain he was not.

In reality, he was a tyrant and a most despicable man. He had done many good and great things but evil things as well. Even those of the Sadducees, known to be the most politically accommodating of the Jewish parties, had condemned his brutality.

Had he done more good or more evil?

Joshua thought once more of his mother Batiyah's story. Of what Herod had done in Bethlehem, history that they had experienced firsthand.

More evil for sure.

King Herod had died just before Joshua was born. Many Jews had actually celebrated his death. However, had anything improved in the decade and a half or so since then? Rome had divided the kingdom between Herod's three sons and his sister. Had they not simply carried on the legacy they had been handed?

Nothing had changed.

Joshua's own anger against Rome had been kindled the day they took his father's life. And his contempt for all enemies of the True One, no matter who they were, continued to gain strength.

Joshua had seen exactly what the enemy could and would do. It was not good. Only Elohim was good. And, while he had questioned His goodness a little at first, he had become convinced lately that He did indeed have their best in mind and would always provide.

Even though it had only been a year since he had been forced to stand on his own, Joshua knew that he was now truly a man. Then too, he was growing into the awareness that he was more than just that. As Batiyah had said to him a while ago, he was *a man of destiny!*

What that was or what that all meant, he still wasn't sure, but his prayer lately had been that Adonai would not only lead him into it but also empower him through His Spirit to accomplish whatever *that* was.

Like Abrahim had always told him, he believed that Elohim would reveal it to him in His perfect time.

He did wonder when and how he would know.

"Not by might nor by power but by My Spirit," Adonai El Shaddai had said to Zerubbabel.

Joshua had an idea. He knelt down in the dirt, reminiscent of a time exactly a year ago when he had done something very similar. He held out his hands, opening his palms to the heavens, and prayed:

"Spirit of Adonai, would You come upon me now as You came on Gideon and Samson and all of the others who put down the enemies of Your Chosen ones in the past. Empower me now to do Your will..."

It was almost the end of the day and the sky was getting dark but he remained in this posture for quite some time, quietly waiting.

His meditation was suddenly and rudely interrupted though, as he heard the gate swing open behind him.

He whirled around and sprang to his feet!

Two men now stood directly in front of him, their eyes darting back and forth on high alert as if they thought someone might be watching! They were men who Joshua had never seen before.

"Shalom, Jehoshua," one of the men said. "Sorry to interrupt your prayer. But time is not always our friend. We will get right to the point of our visit. Would you please honor us by allowing us to have some of the bricks stained with Abba's blood?"

Chapter 13

BLOOD BRICKS

"The what?" Joshua asked, even though he knew exactly what they had requested.

"Whatever are you talking about?"

"The blood bricks," the older looking one said. "The freshly made bricks on which your father fell when he was murdered by those Roman swine. The bricks that soaked up his precious martyr blood. The bricks you put carefully away in homage to your abba's memory. Those bricks."

Joshua's mouth hung open.

How did they know about the bricks? Or that he had hidden them away?

"Sorry, how impolite of us," the younger man said. "We failed to introduce ourselves. I am Simeon and this is my older brother Jacob. We are sons of Judah of Galilee. And you are Jehoshua ben Abraham? Your father told us about you."

Joshua's head was spinning and not just because he had stood up so fast.

He grabbed hold of a nearby stand of bricks to steady himself.

"Yes…umm, I am Jehoshua ben Abraham. But please, you can call me Joshua."

"Well then, Joshua, know that we too are zealous for Israel and believe that the blood of those murdered cries out to Adonai for vindication as it has throughout history ever since the blood of righteous Abel was shed by his evil brother," Jacob said.

It had taken a few moments, but thoughts now rather slowly assembled themselves in Joshua's mind.

He interrupted the two men.

"You are the rebels the soldiers accused Abba of meeting with! That is why he was..." Joshua said, his voice trailing off and the sentence remaining incomplete.

Joshua had simply let the words pour forth. He couldn't stop them. He hadn't thought of how accusing they might sound. He was about to say something about his rudeness, but they seemed not to care or be offended in any way.

"Yes, unfortunately what you say is most likely true. We never intended for that to be the outcome. We always tried to make our visits inconspicuous. Rome has eyes in many places though it seems. Your abba paid the ultimate price. We are truly sorry, for you and for your family," Jacob responded.

"We do know how you feel," Simeon continued, smiling at Joshua as he spoke. "Our father was killed by the Romans too, even though it was a little different circumstance. He was leading an uprising at the time, protesting governor Quirinius's wrongful taxation of Elohim's Chosen people."

Simeon placed his hand on Joshua's shoulder and Joshua felt that this stranger truly knew. He was caught up short as another sudden realization hit him, unsure of why it had taken him so long to hear all of what they had actually said.

"Wait! How did *you* know that my abba's death was murder and not an accident?" Joshua asked, somewhat overwhelmed at the thought that another person truly knew what had happened that morning.

"I was here," Simeon said. "I had come to meet briefly with your father when the soldiers arrived. I heard everything. I saw it all, though there was nothing that I could do. At the time anyway."

Joshua shook his head, now totally unsure of what to even ask.

"We have known your abba for many years and always appreciated him even if he was not an active part of our movement. He had a hard decision to make at the time and he chose what seemed best. We loved the fact that he supported our cause and we always enjoyed time spent with him when we would pass through here on our way from Gamala or other places to Jerusalem and back."

Joshua's eyes now welled up with tears at the thought that others not only knew, but also cared for the man who stood head and shoulders above everyone else in his mind.

His abba had been part of some rebel movement, or at least sympathetic to it? They had known Abrahim for a long time? They were from Gamala? His mother was from Gamala. Had his father been there too for a time? Who were these young men, older than he but still young nevertheless? Joshua was shocked to hear that they had met together with him often. When and where he wondered, and why had Abrahim kept these meetings a secret?

He had heard a little about Judas the Gaulilite, Judah the Galilean. Now, he longed to hear more.

And, in the middle of his own million questions, it *was* now intriguing to know that another individual had stood by and done nothing on that awful morning—someone who maybe could have done something.

"Unfortunately, we have little time," the younger brother said. "And we don't want to draw any attention to this place or to your family by our being here. We know now that was probably what implicated your father and got him killed. We only want some of the blood bricks so as to honor Abba's memory and to inspire others."

"But I have so many questions!" Joshua interjected. "There is so much I need...so much I want to know!"

"That will have to wait for another time," Simeon said. "We would love to sit with you and explain everything, but not right now and not here. It is far too dangerous! Please, Joshua, in honor of Abba's memory, can you simply take us to the bricks?"

Joshua led them to a small pile hidden in the lean-to against the back wall of the yard where they kept firewood. He pulled back the heavy blanket that had concealed them and picked one up. It had aged slightly but you could still see the dark red stain of Abba's blood on the brick that he held up in the twilight. He had not looked at them for quite some time. A wave rising up out of the depths threatened to overwhelm him as the dam of his soul again weakened at the sight. Things hastily buried and stowed away strained to escape. His body heaved. Tears flowed. And, as he looked up through blurred eyes, he noticed tears on both Simeon and Jacob's cheeks too. He knew that they knew. They had experienced the same kind of loss. Felt the pain. He saw the anger and sense of justice as well. There was much comfort in that.

"For a number of years now we have been creating a monument to the martyrs. That is why we want some of the bricks that captured your father's life. The life is in the blood, Moses taught us. We have one of the stones from the pavement where our father fell. And we have the stones and bricks from many places where our fathers and brothers, and our sisters and mothers, have fallen. Your relatives, Joshua. We raise this monument in their honor. We seek only to pay them respect. To never forget. We want a place to intercede for our nation and to be inspired by those who have gone before us. Those who have paid such a high price."

He handed them several of the bricks. They divided them into their bags. Joshua carefully covered the remainder with the blanket pausing for a brief moment to let his hand remain on the precious cache. The three of them stood in silence for a short time.

Joshua wondered about this movement they represented. He definitely needed to hear and find out more. His father had apparently been partial to it, even if at a distance.

He suddenly felt almost giddy.

Maybe *this* was part of his calling, the thing that he should be doing, his life's destiny?

"I know that you have to go. But, when can we talk more? Where can I find you?" Joshua entreated the two young brothers.

"We will find you," Jacob said. "We will come to you. Or at the very least, we will send someone to you. Somewhere. It is not safe for any of us otherwise. We are wanted men. But we will meet again. Soon. Oh, and one more thing Joshua, suffice it to say that none of those soldiers who attacked your father, assuredly not that one, will bother you now. They have all been, well, shall we just say…dispatched. Shalom, little brother."

And with that, pausing briefly at the gate to make sure no one was watching, the two of them disappeared into the night.

Joshua again dropped to his knees, this time because he no longer had the strength to stand. He remained for a few moments just staring at the gate they had gone through. His mind was racing.

But he had to smile.

Even though nothing made sense, this latest encounter had somehow brought at least the hope of sanity to everything.

"Shalom," they had said to him. And for the first time in a long time, it was as if even a few pieces of life were reassembling themselves. For the first time in a long time, he did feel some *peace* on the inside.

Not yet what it should be, but better than in ages.

Batiyah interrupted his thoughts.

"Was someone here? I thought that I heard voices."

She was looking at him strangely, wondering why on earth he was kneeling on the ground.

"Sorry, Ima. Just a couple of men who wanted some uh…bricks," Joshua said standing to his feet.

"Not to worry," he added, hoping it was all nothing that would bring any trouble.

She shook her head, trying to make sense of it all.

"So late in the day? Strange. Did they place an order? And…they are gone already?"

She was clearly confused but did not pursue it.

"What about you, are you almost done for today?" she asked.

"Yes, Ima. I will be up shortly," Joshua said.

When she left, he returned to the pile of bricks and their makeshift covering. He pulled the cover back once more to let his hand rest upon them and breathed a silent and wordless prayer of thankfulness, remaining there for several minutes, lost in this whole new world that was crying out to be explored.

Eventually, Joshua made his way up onto the roof and crawled into bed. But sleep was a long time coming.

There was just so much to consider, and his brain resisted being turned off.

He simply must know.

It was as if his entire universe had been turned upside down once more.

He wondered whether that meant that life might now, or at least very soon, be right side up again?

Chapter 14

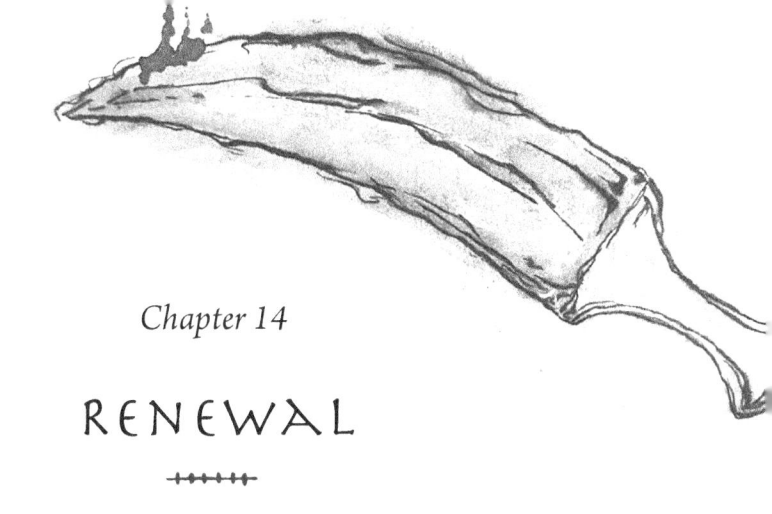

RENEWAL

THE NEXT DAY, JOSHUA WOKE WITH AN ENTHUSIASM that hadn't been present for quite some time. He felt as though he had a reason to continue, something significant in which to hope, that gave purpose to his life. Even some kind of reconnection with his abba, far beyond any bricks.

One of the biggest things was that the weight of *the secret* had been lifted from his shoulders. Or at the very least, that burden was now shared. There were at least two other human beings with whom he could and did carry the load.

He realized in a profound way how much of a millstone that had been hanging around his neck.

Freedom. He felt free!

Even if only a little.

And it was life-giving!

He did wonder when the brothers would contact him. Where and when would they meet again? They had said it would be soon, but how soon? Would it be soon enough? He didn't know how long he could wait. And he began to mentally list all of the questions that he needed to ask them. He felt so connected to them, even if he had only met them this once, and briefly at that. And the fact that they had some kind of connection with his abba in the past only intensified his attraction to them. They knew, they really knew, what he felt and thought. Or at least, so he imagined. And he was convinced that he simply must know more of what *they* were about. They seemed to be so wrapped up in all of that which Adonai imagined for His people, dreams that he too was discovering resonated somewhere inside.

He had scooped up his wagonload of clay almost before he knew it and was headed back toward home. Even Samson, their family donkey, seemed more eager to co-operate today.

It had struck him previously, but Joshua laughed out loud now at the fact that they or at least somebody had actually named their donkey Samson. He was a hairy beast to be sure. But, the strength part? That was probably just a wish. Maybe though, as far as donkeys went, he did pretty well.

Joshua smiled. And that felt good. He knew that he hadn't smiled very much in the last little while, in the last year. He had been too busy. And too angry.

On the way, actually just as he was nearing home, he wondered to himself what Simeon had meant when he said that the soldiers who had threatened him and Cassius in particular, would not be a problem, that they had been, *dispatched?* Did that mean what it seemed obvious it did? He would have to ask them that too. Just to be sure.

His thoughts were interrupted however, as he turned down the alley that made its way behind their yard. For there, just outside the gate were several Roman soldiers, directly in front of him, apparently awaiting his arrival and blocking his path.

A veritable tsunami of fear cascaded over him in that instant, threatening to undo every vestige of his peace. Maybe the brothers were mistaken and the problems had now come calling. Joshua knew that it was too late to turn around and run the other way. He tried hard not to let any of his apprehension show. Had someone seen him with the visitors the night before and reported him? The brothers had said that Rome had eyes and ears everywhere. Did they imagine he had told someone the truth about Abba's death? He wasn't sure of anything at this point but the cadre made no aggressive moves toward him so maybe it was nothing to be concerned about. Still, he wasn't taking anything for granted.

"Can I help you?" Joshua asked tentatively, keeping his voice as calm and steady as possible.

"Hello, ah..." one among the band of soldiers said, hesitating.

"Joshua," he said. "Or rather...Jesus."

"Yes, all right then, Jesus, is your father home?"

"No, he is...not. I have been left in charge."

"Do you know when he will be back?" they asked.

"My father is dead!" Joshua said rather bluntly, and then repeated with emphasis, *"He* will not be back. *I am* the one in charge!"

They looked at each other and one nodded.

"Well then, master Jesus, be it known that our commander, Octavius Rufus, has dispatched us here today to place an order for a building project slated to start very soon just to the south of Rakkath. We have been sent to procure a contract of approximately 500,000 of your family's bricks to be delivered over the next six months or so. I trust that that would not be a problem," the leading soldier stated matter-of-factly.

Joshua breathed a private sigh of relief, as they all made their way into the yard. Another part of him still felt terror, though now of another sort.

"We will be securing bricks from several of the masons in Rakkath," the soldier who was the spokesman for the group now explained. "And we have been told that your family's bricks are among the best in the area. We have been authorized to give you 100 denarii as an advance provided you feel you are able to fulfill this contract. The remainder of the money will be given to you in increments equal to the cost as the bricks are delivered. We trust those terms are agreeable to you?"

Joshua did some quick mental math in his head. 400 bricks sell for one denarius. 500,000…that would be 1,250 denarii! That was the equivalent of almost four years' wages. On his best day, he had made about 1500 bricks by himself. They wanted this in six months? Could they do it? Could they afford not to? He would definitely need more help. But, what could this mean for their family? For him?

"We can most certainly do that!" Joshua asserted, with more confidence than he actually felt. He didn't know at this exact moment *how* they would do it, but some way, he thought, somehow, he knew they simply had to.

He was very grateful for the business and even more grateful that they hadn't come for some other more sinister purpose. Still, their presence in the yard was unnerving.

They showed him the contract, went through the contents in detail, filled in a few blanks, and they each signed both copies. They left one with him and counted out the 100 denarii advance.

Just that alone was more money than Joshua had ever seen at one time in his life.

"We will expect your first installment of 25,000 bricks in exactly two weeks."

And just like that, they promptly disappeared.

As soon as they left, Joshua slumped to the ground. Once more, he simply had no strength left to stand.

In the past few minutes, he had experienced almost every emotion he had ever known. From initial fear, even terror, to relief. Disbelief. Joy. Happiness. Gratitude. And then, fear again though of a different kind, wondering how they would ever fulfill what he had just agreed to. He looked down at the money in his hand and started to tremble, knowing what this and also what was to come would mean for his family.

"Thank you, Adonai! Thank you, Elohim!" he prayed, almost shouting.

"Hallelujah! Adonai Jireh! Our provider. My provider!"

Tears of joy clouded his eyes.

As soon as he was able to pick himself up off the ground, Joshua ran screaming into the house.

"Ima, Ima! Look! Look!"

"What?" his mother asked in terror.

She whirled around; eyes wide to face him.

"What's wrong, Joshua?"

In a flash, all of the other children appeared at Batiyah's side from whatever corner of the house they were in.

"Nothing is wrong!" Joshua exclaimed.

"We just got our biggest order ever! We are going to be wealthy! Our worries are over! Not only will we survive, we are going to thrive!"

And with that he simply dumped the 100 denarii on the table.

The house erupted.

And the next half hour was a mixture of cheers and tears and hugs and so many things that had been strangers since Abba's death. It was undignified and unlike anything that had happened as of late, maybe unlike anything that had ever gone on in their home before. It just felt so wonderful to let the dam that had been holding everything back burst its bounds and wash them all in its flood.

It was new and clean and fresh.

Nobody really cared what it looked like.

It felt amazing!

Like a revival—a "coming back to life!"

When they all finally sat exhausted, just looking at each other and laughing, maybe feeling a little silly given what had just transpired, Batiyah finally brought herself to ask the question that begged asking.

"Joshua," she said, "How are we, how are you, going to be able to make all of those bricks? I don't think even your father ever made that many in so short a time!"

"I don't know exactly, Ima," Joshua replied with an optimistic smile. "We may actually have to hire some help. We could certainly afford it! I don't know. We will do it somehow! We must! Adonai will make a way. I hope. Pray that He does. In the meantime, we need to get to work! We will figure it out, I guess. Anyway, we have no other choice now! I said that we would!"

"It's probably too late to think! We can't afford the luxury of thinking!"

"It is time we get to work!"

Chapter 15

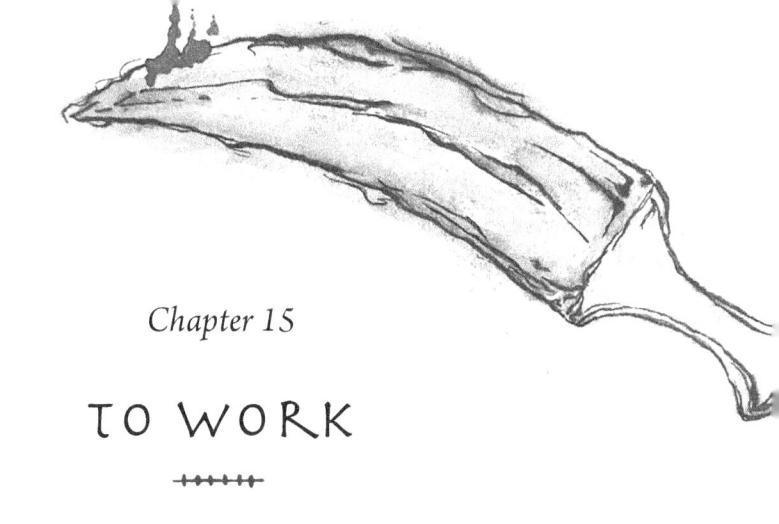

TO WORK

Batiyah and the children set to gathering up and counting all of the coins scattered atop the small table, finding quite a few on the floor as well. Joshua returned to the yard. The only sound was Samson chewing on some hay, the wagon sitting crookedly behind him as a result of his attempt to get through the gate and to his food trough with his burden still attached from their morning's trek to the seashore. The covering was lying off to one side. In all of the excitement, Joshua had totally forgotten about him.

He went over to the wagon. As he suspected, the contents having been unprotected, the late morning sun had soaked up much of the moisture. Joshua wondered how much of the clay would be useable anymore. At the very least, he would have to rid the load of the now crusty layer on top, maybe rehydrate it and get at what was still soft underneath. Which also meant that he might have to go to the seashore to get a second load today. After all, they had bricks to make: lots and lots of them.

He didn't really care. Not even the threat of extra work could upset him today. He couldn't stop smiling and shaking his head in disbelief.

Joshua made his way back into the house, took several stacks of the denarii and darted across the street to Nathanael's place.

"Shalom, Nathanael, I need to order I think about five thousand brick molds!"

A shocked Nathanael spun around to face him.

"Five thousand? Joshua, did I hear you right?" Nathanael queried.

"Five thousand? Why in the world would you ever need so many?"

"Well, we just got an order for five hundred thousand bricks over the next six months! The Romans are building a new garrison to the southwest of Rakkath and they want our bricks! This is the biggest order we have ever received! Adonai be praised!" Joshua replied excitedly.

"How soon do you think I could have them?" Joshua now asked.

"Well, if I get right on it and work some extra, I could have maybe a thousand of them done by the end of the week, and two thousand or so more by the end of next week?" Nathanael said, shaking his head. "The rest, ahh, sometime shortly after that, I guess? Is that okay? That is a tall order, Joshua!"

"That will have to be okay," Joshua replied, thinking out loud. "Thank you so much! Shalom to you, *Abba* Nathanael...and to your *family!*"

Joshua had exaggerated his use of the title "Abba" and strongly emphasized the last word of the sentence.

Just recently it had become obvious that Elizabeth was most assuredly "in the family way!"

"Shalom to you too," Nathanael replied, grinning from ear to ear.

"We are very excited about, well...*that!* And then too, thank you for the work! Thank you, Joshua, for including us in *your* blessing!"

"Oh, I almost forgot, here is a twenty-five denarii advance," Joshua said. "We will settle up later if that's okay. I have to get going. I have bricks to make!"

"That's too much," Nathanael protested. "Maybe even more than they will cost!"

"Not to worry," Joshua said. "Be blessed!"

The next few days were crazy.

Like always, Joshua rose early and he and Samson would go get a load of clay from their special spot along the seashore. Joshua however, would not dawdle even for a minute as he had on some days in the past. There was much to be done in a very little amount of time.

For the most part, Samson was cooperative. It was as if he knew how important this was. It seemed as though he was willing to pull a little harder as Joshua piled on more than he ever had, as much as the little wagon could carry, and then even a bit more.

Everyone at home pitched in as well. Batiyah was out in the yard for a good portion of every day. Elijah, now twelve and feeling much more like a man than a boy, was a big help. It was almost time for his *bar mitzvah*. They would have to talk about how and when that would happen. Joshua thought it may even fall to him to be the one to bless his younger brother, since his father was no longer alive and Zephaniah was…well, no one knew what had become of his older brother. Maybe the ceremony would have to wait until all of this was done, or at the very least, until it had become a little more routine.

Sarah, now ten, and Seth who was only six, tried to help out as well, but at most times, they seemed more of a hindrance than a help. Sarah made it her mission to ensure that they all had enough water to drink but always thought they should stop and partake of the pretend meal that she had also prepared.

They had talked about hiring his cousin Benjamin, but now actually paying him. Seeing as he had helped them at the beginning and knew a little bit about what he was doing, they thought he might be an asset. It was a good idea.

So far however, Joshua had neglected to ask him.

As the first week drew to a close, Joshua went out into the yard late one afternoon to do an actual physical tally of bricks and to assess the situation. He had a sense of how things were progressing, but wanted to be sure. He feared that they were significantly short and might not even be able to fulfill their first installment. He counted stack after stack and was just about to do a final tally when he heard a familiar and yet strange voice behind him.

"Hello, little brother, how are you?" someone said.

Joshua whirled around to see his older brother Zephaniah's broad smile, as he came through the gate and across the yard.

The bricks he was holding crashed to the ground and broke upon each other. His jaw dropped to the ground just like the bricks.

Chapter 16

HOMECOMING

Zephaniah had left boyhood behind and looked more like a grown man, a ruddy beard obscuring or maybe enhancing his facial features, but it was undeniably him.

Joshua couldn't believe his eyes.

"Whaaaa...?" he screamed, running, dodging, and jumping over the stacks of bricks that filled the yard, racing to embrace his older brother.

Then, almost right away, he took a step back and punched him in the chest, maybe a little harder than he had actually intended, tears somewhat obscuring his vision.

Zephaniah choked and sputtered. Tears came to his eyes too but for a variety of reasons.

"Where have you been?" Joshua lashed out. "I didn't think you would ever come home! I thought maybe you were dead! Or that you just didn't care about us anymore!"

"I set out the moment I got the news!" Zephaniah protested, still struggling to catch his breath.

"But it's been more than a year since Abba passed away!" Joshua fired back. "We didn't have any idea what had happened to you! And if you came as soon as you heard, then how come it took you so long to actually get here? Why didn't you let us know anything?"

"As far as I can make out..." Zephaniah began.

He didn't get to complete his response.

Joshua grabbed him and hugged him once more, tight and long this time.

"I don't care! Really, I don't care what happened! You are home!" Joshua exploded, weeping freely into his older brother's shoulder.

"I love you, Zephaniah, I love you!"

The moment seemed to give permission to all of the emotions that young men and old men too often hide from.

"I love you too," Zephaniah said. "And while it is wonderful to be home, why it took so long is important. I need to...explain. I want you to know."

Joshua moved back a bit, giving Zephaniah space.

"As far as I can make out..." Zephaniah began a second time.

But for a second time, he was not able to continue. Batiyah had heard the rather loud and animated voices in the yard and had come to see what was going on.

"*Ya tuv!*" she now screamed, running to embrace Zephaniah herself, tears streaming down her face.

"Welcome home, precious boy! We thought..." she sobbed.

"Oh, Ima!" Zephaniah managed to choke out, "I'm okay. I'm okay. I'm home. I'm finally home."

Batiyah hugged and held her oldest son for a long while. She was crying and laughing and smiling all at the same time. She would push Zephaniah away just far enough to look at him and then pull him close again for another embrace. Zephaniah was crying and laughing too.

So was Joshua. And Elijah and Sarah and even Seth. He had only been three years old when Zephaniah had left and now wasn't sure why there was so much fuss over this stranger that had invaded their home, but he didn't want to be left out.

It was awkward and messy and beautiful all at the same time. Each one lost in the other's embrace and the love of family. They were all laughing and crying and noisily carrying on.

Zephaniah was not dead! Or missing! He had returned. He was very much alive!

He was here, *home,* where he belonged.

In some way, this was similar to what had gone on in their house just a week earlier. Totally undignified but absolutely wonderful.

Finally, Zephaniah spoke again, a harsh reality now suddenly tempering his joy.

"Abba is really...?" he started.

His voice broke and wouldn't let him complete the question he had begun to ask.

Batiyah nodded.

Sorrow erupted and Zephaniah's body heaved.

Batiyah held him once more.

Profound sadness warring with overwhelming joy.

Family taken away and family restored.

It was hard to process all of the feelings at once.

Finally, after several minutes, Batiyah loosened her hold and took a step back.

"So, Zephaniah, what *did* happen? Why was it that your homecoming was so long delayed?" she asked.

Zephaniah dried his eyes and managed to regain a little of his composure.

"As far as I can make out..." he said for the third time, pausing momentarily just to see if there would be yet another interruption. No one stopped him.

"As far as I can make out...the first messenger you sent actually made it to Jerusalem within a couple of days of Abba's death. And later, other messengers had come with the same message! Rabbi Shemai told me that only a few days ago now, when I stopped in there ever so briefly on my way home to apologize for the way I left and to get a few of my things that I had left behind in my haste. They would have told me right away, but I was not there when the messages arrived."

"We did find that part out," Joshua interjected. "Rabbi Shemai eventually responded to one of our later messages and told us that you had left rather abruptly but that no one knew where you had gone."

"I know that I should have, but I hadn't told them exactly *where* I was going," Zephaniah continued. "I had left Jerusalem to go and live with the disciples in the community of Qumran on the west bank of the Dead Sea. By the way, I have a lot to tell you about all of that, and I will, later. And I did try to send a message home when I left to run away to Qumran in the middle of the night, but that message obviously did not make it here. My messenger apparently did not fare well."

"I only found out about Abba's death when the disciple of another rabbi, interestingly named Jehoshua just like you, brother, happened to see me in En Gedi. I knew him somewhat from my time in Jerusalem. He recognized me and then shared with me how they had been told that a messenger had shown up saying that my, our, father had died, and they were asked if anyone knew where I was. As soon as he told me, I made immediate plans to return home. If I had only known, I would surely have come a lot sooner. I would have come right away!"

"We just thought that you couldn't get away...or that something awful had happened," Joshua said.

"I didn't come only because I didn't know," Zephaniah replied quietly.

"And I'm so sorry," he continued. "Sorry that I wasn't here. Sorry about a whole lot of things. I was selfish and not a very honorable son."

"Well, I for one am grateful you are here now! It's wonderful to see you at last and to know that *you're* not dead!" Joshua said.

Joshua punched him once more for good measure but then hugged him again. His *achi* had come home.

Joshua suddenly thought of something else. There was now another body to help, someone who even knew what he was doing when it came to making bricks. Joshua had not even considered that in the first moments of Zephaniah's appearance.

But it was true.

Joshua had believed that Elohim would look after them and provide what they needed, and He had.

Adonai had made a way when there was no way.

They would be able to do what had seemed impossible even just hours before.

He breathed a silent prayer of thankfulness.

This homecoming day ended up stretching itself rather late into the night as each one shared with the other all of what had transpired over the past year or so, and even before that, all of the details of life and death that had been experienced independently but which were now, in the act of sharing, a common memory.

Some sadness for sure, but they were a family once again.

And *that* was something worth celebrating.

Chapter 17

ZEPHANIAH

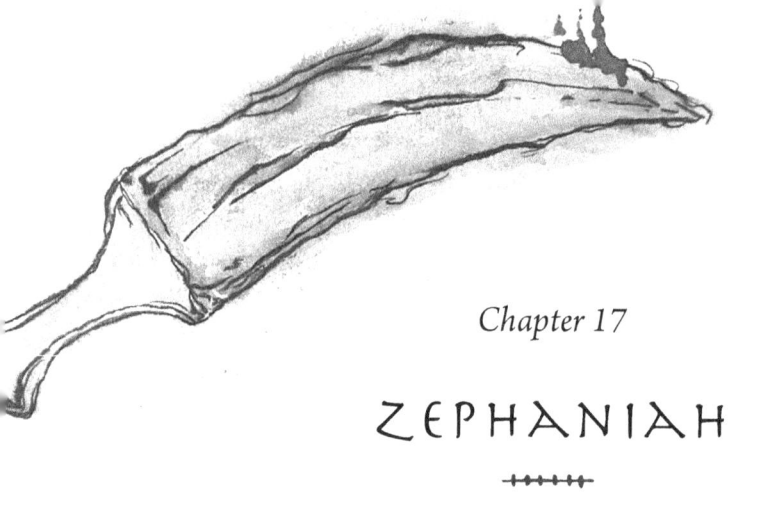

HAVING ZEPHANIAH HOME AGAIN WAS WONDERFUL.

Joshua noticed right away that not only were they more often sharing meals together, but also, that as a family, they were spending much more time just lingering around the table talking. That hadn't happened since the funeral. Doing things as a family had only been a painful reminder of all that was missing. Now, visibly, everyone was smiling again. Happiness was no longer a stranger in their home. And they were, even though Abba was still missing and profoundly missed, once more a family united, as whole as they could be, given what had happened.

It was such a blessing: healing even.

It was great working together as well. Zephaniah was a hard worker and Joshua saw that he had obviously learned the trade well, that is, before he left home for Jerusalem and the Rabbi and then Qumran and the community there. Joshua very much appreciated not having to be solely responsible for the family business. And then too, Zephaniah showed himself to be very adept at the business end of things, which was a huge relief to Joshua. There was such an ease to their working together. It seemed that as brothers, they didn't even have to speak at times. They could simply anticipate what the other was thinking needed to be done and do it even before being asked.

It became obvious after only a few days that they would now be able to fulfill the order that Joshua had said in faith they could. Not without a lot of hard work, mind you, but at least they would have no problem staying true to their word. Joshua couldn't help but thank Adonai for that. He had provided everything they needed, and more.

At the end of the second week, their family celebrated the completion of the first installment of bricks: all twenty-five thousand of them! And the next day, as Joshua and Zephaniah were unmolding bricks, now for their second delivery, a rather mindless even if somewhat delicate task, Zephaniah said he really wanted to tell Joshua the whole story—beyond the sketchy details he had shared with everyone on his first night back—of leaving home, going to Jerusalem, and his experiences there, but mostly, about the decision to leave the rabbinical school in Jerusalem to go be with the brothers at Qumran.

"Mostly I want you to know why. Why I did it all."

"I'm all ears!" Joshua replied.

Zephaniah started in on his story as he moved another armload of bricks onto a stack on the ground.

"I told Abba and Ima that I had grown to love the Scriptures. I wanted to be able to search them out, to know what Adonai's desire was for us, His people. I even wondered whether I might become a scribe eventually. My being invited by the Rabbi to come to Jerusalem was an open door. I told them I must go."

"Abba said he completely understood. He said that he himself had felt a similar pull to devote himself to Elohim's service, though in a different way from me, but somehow just never felt the timing was quite right for him. Still, as we both know, even as a common man, he was quite a student of the Holy Writings!"

Zephaniah paused, thinking through a few of the implications of what he had just voiced.

"Joshua, do you realize that we were disciples all along?" he said suddenly.

"We have been discipled! You and I. Each one of us. By Rabbi Abba! We were his disciples! He taught us everything that he had learned and continued learning, each and every day of our lives! Why did I think I had to go somewhere else? Hmmm. Interesting thought! And now that I think of it, we have been equally blessed by our ima too! Joshua, we have…or had…still have…I don't know the correct way to say it now that Abba is gone, but our parents were…are amazing! We have definitely been given a very rich heritage of faith!"

Joshua nodded.

He had recently thought the very same thing.

Zephaniah was shaking his head, still somewhat overwhelmed by what he had just realized, but he carried on.

"Well, although neither of them really wanted me to go away, they had kind of always thought that at some point I might, given the circumstances of my birth and near death in Bethlehem, which they shared with me that night. It is quite a story, Joshua!"

"I know!" Joshua interjected. "Ima told me about what happened there just a little while ago. It is pretty amazing, the way Adonai protected you!"

"Well, they both cried," Zephaniah continued. "Actually, we all did. But they still blessed me to go. They told me they had long believed that Adonai had some special plan for me, having hidden me away as He did. And Abba didn't even say anything about needing me to take over the family business eventually or anything. You know that matters of faith were always more important to him than anything else! I guess he just trusted Elohim to work everything out."

"He unhesitatingly laid his hands on my head and prayed for Adonai's blessing and guidance. I just know that I felt so encouraged! So blessed to pursue Elohim's call! And so, after a few days getting everything in order and packing up my few belongings, we found a caravan headed to Jerusalem and I joined it."

"I remember the day you left," Joshua said. "I knew that you were going to Jerusalem to pursue a religious education, studying under this Rabbi Shemai, but I know that I didn't fully understand *why* you had to leave. I was just so sad. I didn't want you to go. I was only thirteen years old and needed my older brother. I wanted more time with you. It was like Abba told me…and the next day you left! Did we really even say goodbye? It sure didn't feel like it, to me at least."

Joshua lowered his chin and turned away as he remembered how he had felt the day Zephaniah left.

Zephaniah moved over and gave his little brother a squeeze.

"As exciting as it was, it wasn't easy for me to leave either, but I had received an invitation and knew that I must go, hard as it was. This might be my only chance! I think that Abba and Ima understood that too, and that was probably another reason why they blessed me to go."

"Well, after several days of travel, we arrived in Jerusalem and I immediately went to the Temple. It was where it had been arranged that I was to meet Rabbi Shemai. And, there he was, waiting for me. We exchanged greetings and then walked to his home together with the other disciples that were following him and learning from him. There were fifteen in total, and almost all of them were younger than I. Some of them had been with him since they were six years old! I had lots to 'catch up' on, but I was just so grateful for the opportunity, especially since I was a bit older than most disciples a master takes on."

"We lived and ate and worked together, but each day we would also go for walks in and around Jerusalem. As we did, Rabbi Shemai would teach us about Jewish history and quote the Scriptures, giving their interpretation as had been handed down by all of the rabbis that had preceded him. I was learning so much about the Word of Adonai and the faith of our nation every day, sitting under this Rabbi, gleaning the wisdom of the sages throughout the years, reading and memorizing even more of the Torah, the law of Ha Shem. We would always pause for prayers too, at least three times a day and four on the Sabbath, reciting those passed down from David and others in the Writings."

"As a family, we had been to Jerusalem almost every year for a least one of the festivals, but it was so much different being in that environment every day. The Temple. And all of the places where our forefathers lived and walked and worshipped and heard from Adonai."

"It was amazing!"

"I had to pinch myself! I was *living* in Zion!"

"But, at the same time that it was so great being in Jerusalem, immersed in all of the history, learning to write and being exposed to the Word of Elohim like that each day, there was another side of Jerusalem culture that I found extremely troubling: the politics."

"The Sanhedrin, our religious leaders, have made and continue to make so many compromises with Rome just to keep and further their own power, that the faith of the fathers seemed, to me at least, to be in serious jeopardy! It was scary to what depths they would sink just to maintain their own prestige and control. It was not impossible to imagine they might even set aside the commands of Ha Kadosh for the sake of their beloved traditions!"

"I have thought the same things!" Joshua said, interrupting. "Just recently. And, it is so wrong when they do that!"

"Well, *we* saw it first hand, and you have to either be okay with it, ignore it, or at least tell yourself it doesn't really matter…"

"Or leave!"

"I wasn't sure what to do. I had felt such a draw to Jerusalem at first. It was just that the longer I was there, the more the Holy City felt so contrary to what I knew was Adonai's true nature and calling."

"Being at the Temple day after day, and seeing how it, or at least pretty much the entire court of the Gentiles for sure, had been turned into a noisy marketplace, was also very troubling. I don't think that Adonai would be pleased with that either! It was supposed to be a place of prayer and worship. But there was much that didn't feel right, that seemed anything but holy."

"Two things happened to me during this time of turmoil."

"A good part of each day, we would gather together and have the Scriptures read to us, word by word, sometimes letter by letter, while we each did our best to copy to a clean piece of parchment the words that Adonai had spoken. Making copies of the scrolls was one of the ways that Rabbi Shemai could afford to look after his own family and all of us as well. Abba had shared with us his love of the Scriptures, but I found my own deep appreciation there. And Joshua, I actually got to hold one of the ancient scrolls in my hands for the first time! To touch its letters, feeling how the ink had slightly raised the parchment beneath."

"It was beyond words!"

Joshua just stared at his brother, his mouth hanging open, imagining what it would be like to have one of those ancient scrolls in his own hands. To touch it and feel its letters as Zephaniah described.

He was a little, maybe a lot, jealous.

"We started to transcribe the scroll of Hosea, a very troubling book indeed. That the Holy One would call His prophet to marry a prostitute, even if to prove something true, had always bothered me. Adonai compared His own Chosen ones to Gomer but then, in spite of unfaithfulness, He showed His love to her—to them, to us—nonetheless. In one place however, I read, even as I copied the letters onto the fresh parchment, these very words of Adonai: *'Therefore I am now going to allure her; I will lead her into the wilderness and speak tenderly to her...I will betroth you to Me forever; I will betroth you in righteousness and justice, in love and compassion. I will betroth you in faithfulness, and you will acknowledge YHWH'.*"

"Joshua, I don't know how to describe it other than that I felt those words speaking to me. I felt as though *He* was calling *me*, calling me out of Jerusalem, away from Jerusalem, and into the wilderness to be with Him. It most certainly corresponded with the struggle that was going on in my own heart at the time with respect to the Holy City."

"But what? Was I just going to one day wander off into the wilderness? I wondered if I was going crazy. Maybe my interpretation of Scripture was far too literal. I didn't know what to do. I prayed a lot."

Joshua just stared at Zephaniah, his eyes wide, his heart burning within him.

What his brother was sharing had happened, was the very thing *he* so desperately craved, a personal and direct *call* of Adonai.

"Well, a few days later, as I wandered through the city alone—a very rare occurrence—still trying to make sense of this first thing I was feeling, I heard someone preaching on the street corner that Jerusalem, more specifically the Temple, was actually despised by Elohim. Like Ezekiel and Jeremiah had prophesied, he said that the glory of Ha Kadosh Baruch Hu had left the Temple, even if the people didn't know it. He preached with passion how Adonai contemplated a New Jerusalem, rebuilt as a Holy City with a new and holy Temple as its centerpiece."

"I could not tear myself away. I wondered how he could get away with saying such things! And when he finished speaking, I asked him privately about it. I wondered where he had received such teaching?"

"He told me about the community of brothers at Qumran, *in the desert,* on the west bank of the Salt Sea, disciples who poured over the Scriptures daily, seeking the Holy Spirit's revelation as to what Adonai had actually told His people to be and do, and who then attempted to live out those very commandments of Ha Shem within that same community."

"What he was saying spoke to something deep inside of me. It was so appealing. As if everything came together. The answer to my prayers? Was I going crazy? I simply knew that I had to go and see for myself. I felt compelled. By Adonai? Maybe. I wasn't sure at all and yet I was so very sure at the same time."

"So, without even packing up my few belongings, not wanting to disturb anyone, I left a brief note saying thank you to Rabbi Shemai for everything, and then, in the middle of the night, I ran away to Qumran. I know it was not the best way or the right way to leave, but in the moment, I couldn't think of a better way. I wasn't really thinking. I just knew that I had to go. I had to discover for myself. I had to take that leap of faith!"

"And when I got to Qumran, I found exactly what this man had shared with me! It was heaven on earth, or so it seemed to me!"

"By the way, the name of the preacher I had met on the streets of Jerusalem was Hosea! How's that for coincidence? Was it a sign? A confirmation? Who knows? I laughed!"

"I think that Elohim has a sense of humor!"

Zephaniah and Joshua smiled at that thought.

"And in that place," Zephaniah said, continuing, "I discovered a community of brothers that loved Adonai with all their heart, soul, mind, and strength. There was no compromise with the world.

Here was a group of disciples passionate about the kingdom and the Scriptures and finding Adonai's end-time vision for the world. It was irresistible! My heart had found a home! It all resonated with my spirit. So much so in fact that after only a few weeks there, I was baptized, and became a member of the community."

"And now, even more than I had been able to in Jerusalem, I could spend time making copies of the Scriptures and also, the other writings of the community. It was even better than I had imagined! Joshua, you wouldn't believe it! They had massive libraries of the Scriptures! Caches of scrolls in caves that no one outside of the community even knew existed. Scrolls numbering beyond imagination!"

Zephaniah stared off in the direction of Qumran for a moment. He knew that at least part of him was still there.

"I loved all of the brothers and I loved being there! Oh, Joshua, I will have to tell you so much more about all of it in the days to come!"

"I would really like that," Joshua replied grinning.

Zephaniah changed the direction of the conversation.

"I did think of you all often and even wanted to come home but there always seemed to be some reason that I could not leave right away. Always in the middle of something or another. I certainly should have written to at least let you all know where I was. But the community exists pretty isolated from the rest of the world. That is both its blessing and...its curse."

"When Jehoshua, the other young man that I told you about, the one that I knew from Jerusalem, saw me in the nearby town of En Gedi and gave me the very sad news that Abba had died, there was no question as to what I must do. I knew that I could stay no longer, that I shouldn't have cut myself off, that it had been selfish of me. I knew that I needed to come home!"

"Will I go back? I don't know. I want to. Maybe eventually. I am extremely grateful for the time that I was able to spend there.

And then again, maybe El Shaddai has other plans for me. For now, I know that this is where I need to be. For now, here at home is where I most want to be!"

"Maybe I will come back with you if you return!" Joshua said. "That kind of brotherhood sounds amazing!"

Joshua smiled at his older brother. He really was someone worthy of his adoration. And he loved hearing this, especially his passion and zeal. He reminded him of Abba. So much like him in so many ways. Having Zephaniah home actually made him miss Abba less. And more too, though in a very good way.

Joshua could not stop smiling.

Zephaniah was home.

This was good, very good indeed!

They would most assuredly need to have many more discussions on many more days. He looked forward to hearing even more about all the brothers and the activities at Qumran. And about Zephaniah's time in Jerusalem.

Then too, Joshua knew that he had some things of his own to share with Zephaniah. About all that had happened here in Rakkath during his absence.

Save that for another day, he thought. There was no rush really.

Time was again their friend...were it not for the fact that they had a lot of bricks to make. But now they would for sure be able to accomplish even that.

Zephaniah was home for good and Joshua's burden was shared. Not only was it shared; it was carried together with a true brother.

Chapter 18

BROTHERHOOD

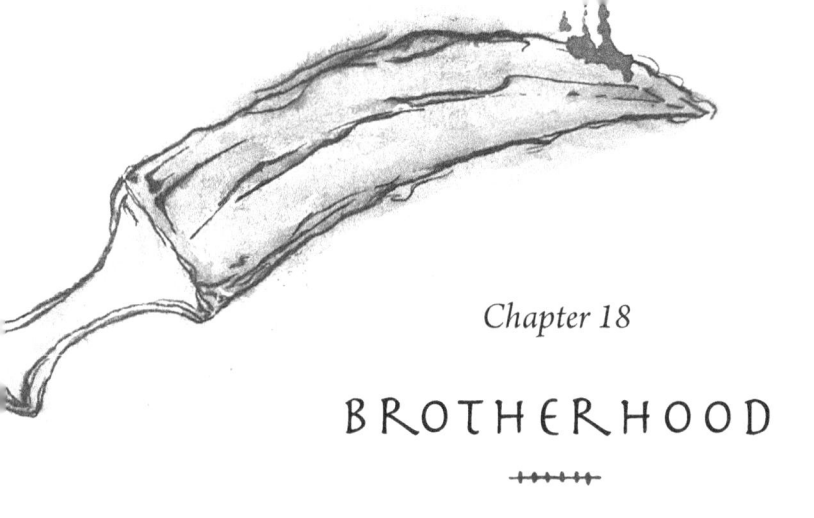

OVER THE NEXT NUMBER OF MONTHS, JOSHUA AND Zephaniah worked hard, extremely hard in fact. The rest of the family pitched in and helped, mostly just picking up all of the other tasks around home that the two brothers had little if any time for.

Life was hectic but good.

Benjamin, their cousin, Uncle Johanan's oldest son, who had helped Joshua right at first after Abba had died, had now been hired on to help out. He seemed to work much better and harder now that he was no longer *volunteering* his time and energy.

Elijah too was proving to be a great asset and was a quick learner, motivated in part by his recent move toward manhood, his own becoming "a son of the commandment." Joshua had wondered how they would make that happen, but with Zephaniah's return, Elijah's *bar mitzvah* turned out to be a joyous celebration—one that the whole family had attended.

Zephaniah had learned many things while he was in Jerusalem and then at Qumran and his prayer of blessing for his younger brother was absolutely beautiful. Heartfelt! It had brought tears to Ima's eyes. Zephaniah could be very eloquent when he wanted to. It reminded Joshua of his father's prayer at his own celebration.

As promised, Joshua and Zephaniah continued to have discussions about Qumran and the community there. They shared their own goals and ideals. About what Adonai wanted for His people and all of the different ways to go about achieving it. They would often ask questions of each other and quote Scriptures that they remembered, all the while trying to discern what Adonai's will might be in the present political environment. It was invigorating and made the work go by quickly. They were discipling each other and even Elijah got to join in.

Joshua thrived. Zephaniah too. They were brothers not just by blood but also in the faith. And they would often remind each other of something that Abrahim had taught them and remark how wise and learned their father had been. It felt as though he was still there with them, as they shared their memories of a time past and of growing up under his care, so many good memories. They knew that Abrahim had been a great father because of how he actually lived, not just because it is easy or popular to esteem people highly after they are gone.

Early on, Joshua had filled Zephaniah in on the events of the day that Abba died, being careful to omit the details that still remained a secret to everyone else. He told him simply where he had been when it happened and that he had run down and held him and called for help and about how Nathanael had showed up. Listening for breath.

He talked about when Ima returned home from the market with the other children. How it was when all the relatives showed up. The funeral. Some of his struggles. And how life had been since then. Just trying to maintain the business and keep the family going.

Joshua wanted desperately to tell him more but he still wasn't sure it was safe to divulge all of the facts, even as much as he trusted his older brother. He did not want to do anything to in any way jeopardize the good that now was.

Recently, Joshua had felt free to tell Zephaniah about the two visitors who had come late that one night sometime after Abba's death. Of their movement and the philosophy of the Fourth Way. He even shared how they somehow knew Abba and had met with him from time to time. He shared how their ideals seemed to make so much sense to him, at least what little he knew of them. And, in the flow of conversation, he went on to tell him of their request for some of the blood-stained bricks, and their desire to honor Abraham by including him in their monument...

Joshua knew right away that he had accidentally and inadvertently said too much.

But it was too late.

Words spoken cannot be recalled.

And it had only taken a moment for Zephaniah to pick up on it.

"Monument? What kind of monument? Why would they want *those* bricks, or even know about them? And you kept them? Joshua, what *aren't* you telling?"

Joshua's face flushed. He could hardly breathe. Zephaniah saw. And it was too late to go back. The only option was for him to press forward. Tears threatened the corners of his eyes but he choked them back.

"It was...murder!" Joshua blurted out finally, emphasizing each word.

"It was no accident!"

"They wanted those bricks for a monument...to the martyrs!"

He breathed a long slow sigh of relief.

Over the next half hour, the brothers made not one brick, as Joshua spilled the actual and complete story and Zephaniah listened, interrupting only a few times with questions for clarification.

Joshua told him how Abba and he had been making bricks like always. How he had gone up onto the roof to retrieve the trowel they had left there. Of the soldiers' arrival and their accusations. Of father's attempt at protest. And how they killed him in cold blood and then made it to look like an accident.

Joshua told how they had left and how he had gone to help and how one of the soldiers had returned and surprised him. How Cassius hadn't killed him on the spot but threatened to if he ever told anyone.

"You can't tell, Zephaniah, you can't! Please!" Joshua now insisted. "The soldiers will most certainly kill me just like they did Abba, maybe all of us, if we make any trouble!"

"Jacob said that they had taken care of it, but…I still don't know for sure that it is okay."

Zephaniah assured him that he wouldn't say anything, at least not right away.

"So, you haven't told Ima any of this either, have you?" Zephaniah now asked just to confirm his suspicions.

Joshua lowered his eyes and slowly shook his head.

"Really? Oh Joshua! You haven't told her? Oh little brother, we must! And soon! You…we can't keep *this* from her forever."

"Oh, my! And you have carried this burden all alone for all of these months? That's horrible!" Zephaniah said, smothering Joshua in a bear hug as he did so.

"Do not fear! Don't worry!"

"We will figure this out!"

Joshua knew that it had felt good to share with Simeon and Jacob the actual events surrounding his father's death, so freeing.

And although he later questioned the blunder he had made, now that the secret was out and known to Zephaniah, his own flesh and blood brother, it felt a million times better. He was a true brother. And it was an even bigger relief to finally have someone so close who now shared the burden.

Joshua *had* opened up to Zephaniah about Abba's death, had accidentally forced himself to, in the course of having told him about his encounter with the sons of Judas.

But so far, he had not mentioned the prospect of any future meeting or meetings with Jacob and Simeon.

Joshua had wondered since that first encounter with the brothers whether the Fourth Way might be part of *his* calling? He had so enjoyed the brief moments that he had shared with them and felt so connected to them.

But he was confused. Things were so much better at home now. Maybe he didn't have any reason, maybe he didn't want to leave anymore.

Family was good again.

Very good.

Besides, wasn't he needed at home?

The work would not get done without him.

Still, he knew that he looked forward to seeing them again. Talking with them.

He would simply meet with them to find out more, he told himself. Whenever that would be. *That* would most certainly be okay, he thought.

Maybe then, after he knew even more of their ways, he would talk with Zephaniah about it.

Who knew what the future would bring anyway?

He realized that he hadn't actually thought about the Qanaim for a few days.

He and Zephaniah had just been too busy enjoying each other's company.

Oh...and making bricks for the big order.

So far at least they had been able to stay on track.

Chapter 19

REUNION

As they continued to move forward with their Imperial order, the brothers soon began to feel that they were on top of things, somewhere beyond just trying to keep up.

Just recently, they were to the place where they had a second order ready and waiting even before the present installment of bricks was slated for delivery. And the garrison was starting to take definite shape.

At first, Joshua had wondered if and how they would be able to make it happen. So, to finally have a handle on things was wonderful.

One of the side benefits, and one of the results of having a larger workforce, was that they were now free to take on other small orders and fit them in around the Imperial contract. It had been several months since they had been able or willing to do that and they had needed to turn away a fair bit of business just so that they could fulfill the one large request. Some of their regular customers hadn't been too happy being neglected, even if they all said that they understood.

One of those smaller requests came from Joshua's boyhood friend, Caleb, whose family now resided in the city of Magdala, the largest urban center on the west coast of the Sea of Galilee, just slightly less than two miles away from Rakkath.

Caleb had appeared one day last week, much to Joshua's delight, and they had spent the better part of the day together catching up on all that had happened since Caleb's family had moved away about three years earlier. They didn't actually live that far from each other but even that small distance and the rigors and busyness of life and circumstance had somehow kept them apart.

Joshua had questioned spending so much time away from making bricks, but Zephaniah had assured him that it would be okay, that they would be okay, and actually encouraged him to take the time.

"Don't worry," he said. "We are ahead of schedule. And you haven't seen Caleb in years. The rest of us can look after everything else for a while. You owe each other some time."

"It's so good to see you! But, so sad to hear about your abba's passing," Caleb had begun. "I have prayed for your family and for you especially since the time that we heard. It must have been so hard for you. I can't even imagine what that must be like! We would have come but our family was in Jerusalem at the time Abba passed away and we only heard the news later after returning home. Then it was too late—to be here for the funeral at least. I have wanted to come and see you ever since but life is so busy…or, maybe just full of excuses!"

"I know what you mean. There always seems to be some urgent *reason* why you can't. Me too," Joshua said. "But thank you. Your prayers and the prayers of others are most assuredly what brought us through. It was definitely hard at first. I felt so overwhelmed and very alone. It did improve a lot when Zephaniah finally came home."

"At the same time, it would have been nice to talk to a friend…"

Joshua winced as soon as he said that.

He hadn't meant it to sound as condemning as it somehow came out.

"Sorry, I didn't mean..." he began to say.

"No! *I'm* sorry," Caleb said. "Sorry I wasn't here for you. I should have made a way."

"It's okay, Caleb. I understand. It just would have been nice, is all. Like now! I did talk to Jonathan some but it wasn't the same. He and I just aren't that close anymore. I guess that happens. People grow apart. Besides, you and I were always the closest of the three of us. And I still feel closer to you than to him even though we haven't been around each other much lately," Joshua said. "By the way, how is *your* family doing?"

"We are good. We have done well. Our fish salting and drying business is booming and our city is gaining quite a reputation. In fact, our city's name has even been changed! To *Magdala Nunayya*, or, 'tower of the fishes.' Which brings me to the reason that I am here."

"You came to sell me some fish?" Joshua jokingly asked, grinning.

Caleb laughed.

"I did bring some along to *give* to your family. But no, I came because we need to build some new pools for brining our fish and I was wondering if we could get some of your bricks. The regular clay ones we have been using deteriorate rather quickly. Nothing we do seems to help. I heard that your father added special ingredients to his bricks to make them much stronger and more durable. Would you fire them in the oven? Glaze them? I don't know. But I think that they would probably work very well for us. We have been talking about it at home for a while and I told father that we should just go ahead and give them a try. Besides, it was just a good excuse to come and see you!"

"Unfortunately, we have been rather consumed lately by a very large order for the new garrison the Romans are building just to the southwest of town. That one request has taken all of our time and energy," Joshua began, but then hesitated. "However, we have begun to see the light at the end of the tunnel. In fact, just this week, we have taken on one or two other small orders for some local residents. For you and your family we, most assuredly I, would be willing to work any extra that might be needed! I just need to check with Zephaniah. How many do you think you need?"

"Well, our pools are ten feet by six feet and two feet deep," Caleb said. "So, I don't know, however many bricks that would call for."

Joshua quickly worked out the amount of bricks needed and suggested a price. Caleb said he was not a brick maker but knew that was probably far less than they were worth. He insisted Joshua charge him the going rate, saying that they shouldn't give their bricks away even if he was a friend. Caleb said that Adonai had blessed them too and so they didn't mind paying fair price and blessing their friends.

Joshua quickly checked just to make sure they could fit this order in and Zephaniah said that it wouldn't be a problem. It wasn't that large of an order by comparison. In fact, he told Joshua he had just been informed that construction had slowed a bit due to something that had happened over the past few days and the next delivery to the garrison had been extended; it was now one week later than originally scheduled.

"Good news! We can do it!" Joshua said smiling at his boyhood friend.

He paused and moved on, or returned, to more important things.

"How great it has been seeing you!" Joshua said.

"I couldn't agree more!" Caleb replied, returning the smile.

"We must not let so much time go by ever again!" Joshua said.

Caleb nodded his agreement.

"No more excuses!"

"You should stay for the evening meal!" Joshua stated. "And you can spend the night. You can return home in the morning. I just can't get over how good this has been. A bit more time would be even better!"

"I didn't realize how much I, well...how much I missed you!"

Caleb grinned.

"What's for dinner?" he now asked, slowly licking his lips.

"I was thinking dried fish!" Joshua said wryly and with a big smirk.

They both burst out laughing.

"Just kidding," Joshua said.

"I don't actually care," Caleb replied. "Whatever your ima makes will be just fine by me. It is just so nice to be together with you and your family. I have missed all of you. And again, it's so sad that your abba is no longer with us. I miss him and you all must too."

Just then, Batiyah appeared.

"Thank you, Caleb. We do miss him for sure," she said. "You will stay for dinner, won't you, son?"

She didn't wait for the response.

"Joshua, you did invite him, didn't you?" she asked looking in the direction of her own son.

"Yes, Ima, of course, and I told him he should stay the night too."

"It's settled then?" she asked, or more truthfully stated, making her way to the fire pit without waiting for an answer.

"Yes, Ima, of course. And thank you," Caleb answered, even though Batiyah was already pretty much out of earshot.

Joshua spent the next hour or so showing Caleb around and explaining to him much of the process of brick making. He even shared with him some of the secrets that Abrahim had discovered to make the bricks stronger by adding limestone or local volcanic rock to the mix. Things that they would include in the bricks they would make for the brining pools. He showed him the kiln and explained how glazing and firing made the bricks that much more durable. Caleb had expressed his interest in the process and Joshua was only too willing to share with this lifelong friend the ins and outs of his trade.

He didn't realize how much he missed this kind of companionship.

It had been great when Zephaniah had come home and he had a brother again.

He recognized that Caleb was a brother of another sort and that he actually craved that kind of relationship as well.

When they sat down to eat, Zephaniah prayed the blessing and thanked Adonai for bringing Caleb to them, for the extra order that would bless their family, and for Caleb's family, that Elohim would continue to prosper them and *their* business.

Batiyah and Sarah then set steaming bowls of goat stew and fresh bread in front of each of them and they ate until they were full and maybe even a bit more after that, continuing to talk late into the night.

There was just so much to catch up on. Each story would provoke another. And on and on it went.

Finally, they all agreed that it was time to go to sleep. Morning was sure to arrive in no time at all. And they would all have much to do tomorrow.

At the same time, it was sad to say goodnight because that meant that their time together was ending.

They all made their way to bed, exhausted and energized at the same time. And within minutes, all that could be heard was the deep breathing of restful sleep.

Hezekiah crowed and morning came.

Sadly, it was time for Caleb to leave. Batiyah had packed him some food for the road even though Magdala was not that far away. They said their goodbyes and Caleb disappeared down the lane.

Joshua watched him leave and then walked back into the yard.

What a pleasant surprise this visit had been, he thought to himself.

And now, he could look forward to seeing his friend again in a week or so once the order was ready. He would deliver it to Magdala and have a chance to catch up with Caleb's family.

He so looked forward to that.

And he vowed to himself that he would make an effort to connect with Caleb much more often than had been the case in the last several years.

In some ways, he knew, a friend could be even closer than a brother.

Chapter 20

MAGDALA

Over the next week, Joshua took personal responsibility for Caleb's request, carefully weighing and mixing the ingredients and watching over the drying, finally glazing and firing each brick to make them even more impervious to the saltwater brine the fish needed to soak in. It meant that he worked quite a few extra hours, even late into the night, but it seemed to him no chore at all. This was one order he really cared about and a delivery he eagerly anticipated.

The wagon had been loaded with the bricks for Caleb's family the evening before. After a little bit of breakfast, Joshua hitched Samson to it, leaving for Magdala just as the sun came up over the Sea of Galilee, illuminating the western shore and the townsite.

Their delivery meant that Samson would be out of the picture for a day or so but that wouldn't be a problem, for their family had recently purchased a second donkey and cart. They had needed to, just to keep up with procuring materials and making deliveries for the Imperial building project. And Solomon had already proved himself a worthy addition, younger and able to pull heavier loads of clay, other materials, and bricks.

Joshua had thought it was funny that someone had named their first donkey Samson. Solomon? A wise and regal...donkey? That seemed like a contradiction.

Joshua loosened the cloak around his neck. There was still a bit of a chill in the air but he could already feel the warming effect of the sun and knew that it would be hot soon enough. Travelling was always better when it was cooler but mostly, he wanted to be in Magdala early in the day so that he could spend the better part of it with Caleb and his family.

Joshua and Samson travelled northwest for about a mile in the direction of the cliffs of Arbel. At the junction in the road, he then took a right turn, heading back in the direction of the Sea of Galilee and the city of Magdala. The whole trip was less than two miles, but with Samson and the load of bricks, it still took several hours to complete. Joshua didn't mind.

Samson had apparently decided that today was a good day to actually cooperate and the weather was lovely. It was warm and there was a gentle breeze blowing across the water and up into the hills. He drank in the beauty of the landscape, the green Galilean hills to his left and the deep blue-gray of the Sea of Galilee to his right. The air was rich with that *alive* smell that is present after the rain or heavy morning dew. Joshua was enjoying this break from the routine. It was nice to actually notice and enjoy the beauty that was around him every day. And he could hardly wait to spend more time with Caleb, the whole day in fact, scheduled to return early the next morning.

At least, that was the plan.

He arrived about mid-morning and they unloaded the bricks and gave Samson some hay and water. Caleb showed him around their fish-salting and fish-drying operation. He told him how they would go down to the seashore early each morning and load up their cart with fish that had been caught during the night. When they returned home with their day's acquisition, the real work would begin. Joshua was genuinely interested in the whole process of gutting the fish, then curing them in salt brine, and finally, putting them on racks out in the sun to dry. It was kind of similar to making bricks he thought, albeit much smellier, but the advantage was that you could eat the finished product. Fish just seemed to be more fun than bricks but he wondered if the novelty would wear off after a while. Maybe he had just had more than his fill of bricks.

It was good to see Caleb…again. They had shared so much together in days gone by. And it was wonderful to be together with Caleb's family too. Joshua had spent much time in their home during his growing up years. In fact, Zadok and Deborah were like second parents to him. In some ways, he felt even closer to them than to his own blood relatives. Just being in their house made him realize how much he missed them. It brought back so many good memories of a simpler time.

It was difficult though, being in this place that felt so much like home and yet still included a father. That seemed to aggravate a nerve that had not yet recovered from being rubbed raw. It was actually hard seeing Caleb and Zadok together, for Joshua found himself face-to-face with the very part that was missing in his own life. He was surprised at how potent and painful that was, how much he was reminded he still missed Abrahim every day.

He thought that it had gotten easier, only to now realize that in actuality, it was merely that with each passing day, he just thought about it less. He wondered if there would come a time when he would forget about his abba altogether. He hoped that would never happen, even if it did hurt.

"We were saddened to hear of Abrahim's death," Zadok said as they sat down to have some lunch. "And we would have come if we could have. It must have been so hard. Our prayers are even now with you and your family."

Once more, Joshua found himself on that painful and familiar road.

But he knew that he didn't need to run from it here. He was loved in this place. This was family. Joshua wiped his eyes. They all smiled at him through their own tears.

Zadok prayed a blessing on the food and on Joshua's family. And Deborah began to place food in front of them: fresh bread, steaming rice, vegetables, and dried dates and figs. They all helped themselves.

"Yes, it has indeed been difficult," Joshua began. "It was really hard at first, but then Zephaniah came home and that has helped a lot. We have much to be thankful for. Adonai has been gracious to us and blessed us so that we have been able to carry on and make a go of it. And, other than missing Abba, which we do, we are all well."

"It looks like He has been blessing you as well," Joshua continued. "Caleb tells me that the move to Magdala has been a good one."

"Yes indeed. The switch from being fishermen in Rakkath to the fish-processing end of things here in Magdala has turned out to be very good for us. Then too, the market here is much larger than in Rakkath," Zadok said.

"By the way, thank you for bringing the bricks we will need to build more brine curing pools for our fish. That will help us do even more. The bricks that you brought look like they will be perfect and do much better at standing up under exposure to the salty water."

"Speaking of that, would you like some fish, Joshua?" asked a young female voice.

Joshua turned around. And there, before his eyes was Caleb's younger sister Ariah, although she looked nothing like he remembered her. She had been a little girl, impish and somewhat bothersome before, but accosting his eyes in this moment was a stunning young woman!

He felt the immediate flush of his cheeks and knew by the glint in her dark eyes that she had caught it too. She may have been blushing as well, but it was mostly hidden behind the veil that hung loosely around her face. He realized too late that he was staring and rather abruptly turned away, trying to pretend like nothing had happened.

"Ahhhh, yes-s-s-s, p-p-p-please," he stuttered.

"Thank you, *Ariah!*" he then added, but with much too much enthusiasm to in any way redeem the situation.

Zadok smiled and Caleb began chuckling. They had not missed what had transpired. And Joshua could do nothing now but grin awkwardly, not knowing where to look, trying desperately not to make any more direct eye contact with anyone.

He coughed and cleared his throat, making sure he was looking in the general direction of Zadok.

"Well, if and when you need any additional bricks for more curing pools, just let us know, please," Joshua said, trying to reorient and bring the conversation back to a less awkward place. "I would be very happy to bring you more."

"I'm sure you would!" Caleb said, with a twinkle in his eye.

The awkwardness flatly refused to disappear.

Fortunately, it was interrupted by a visitor's arrival.

"Hello there, I was wondering if I could purchase some of your dried fish?" a young man asked in a rather loud voice as he opened the gate and began to make his way into the yard.

"Oh sorry," he immediately added, hesitating. "I did not realize that you were eating. I can return later."

The visitor turned to leave.

"Nonsense," Zadok responded. "We had only just begun. How much do you need?"

"Well, if it's not a bother, about five pounds then?" the man asked from where he was standing, somewhere directly behind Joshua.

"Can you go get that please, Caleb?" Zadok asked.

Caleb excused himself and rose from the table.

"Why don't you come and join us?" Zadok said to the stranger, gesturing to an open place.

Joshua was extremely grateful that the tension had been broken and that there was now something else, someone else, to divert the attention away from himself.

"I really can't stay," the man said. "But thank you just the same."

There was something vaguely familiar about this visitor and Joshua turned slightly to take in the man who had come calling. He almost choked and had to catch his breath, while at the same time trying desperately to appear as if it was nothing, as soon as he saw him.

For there, right behind him was Jacob, son of Judas the Galilean!

"Hello, Joshua," Jacob said. "How good it is that we meet again!"

"You two know each other?" Zadok asked, quite surprised.

"We do," Jacob said without hesitation. "Joshua and his amazing family have blessed us with some very special bricks, in the past."

Moments ago, Joshua had longed for something, anything to break the awkwardness of the situation, but this turn of events had taken things in a totally different and maybe even less comfortable direction. He didn't know where to look or what to do next and was rather terrified of what Jacob might possibly say.

He could barely breathe.

Thankfully Caleb returned quickly with the order of dried fish, packaged and ready to go.

Jacob took the parcel, thanked Caleb and Zadok and then turned to leave.

He hesitated.

"When are *you* returning home, Joshua?" he asked.

"Tomorrow morning, first thing," Joshua replied cautiously.

"I am going that way tomorrow as well," Jacob said. "Maybe you would welcome a companion and we could travel together?"

"We could…I would…welcome it," Joshua said, careful of his words to make sure that he didn't say more than he wanted to or give away his profound excitement at the prospect of spending more time with this most unexpected intruder.

"Okay if I meet you here at sunrise?" Jacob asked.

"That would be just fine. I'll see you then," Joshua replied, and then added, "I look forward to your company."

Jacob put the fish into his bag and made his way out of the yard.

Joshua was so very glad that everything had come to a pretty good place of resolution. And the meal concluded without further incident.

He spent the rest of the afternoon reminiscing with Caleb. He even helped Caleb with his work though it was obvious to all that he didn't really know what he was doing. It was just good to spend time together, continuing to catch each other up on everything. They enjoyed the evening meal together and again talked rather late into the night.

Caleb was much more than just a best friend.

At numerous points throughout the day too, Joshua couldn't help but steal glimpses of Ariah as she went about her daily tasks. Each time he saw her and even when he didn't, he knew that in some profound and mysterious way, something had happened to him. This was a brand-new feeling. But…it was quite pleasing.

Was this, could this be *the* woman for him, he wondered? Or was he getting way ahead of himself? He had always imagined that there was in fact someone for him, but to think specifically of *who* it might be was a place thus far unexplored.

At the same time, his thoughts often raced into tomorrow and his time together with Jacob.

He had wondered when and if and how they would meet, very much looking forward to that. And although the lead-up to it was anything but comfortable, it gave him great comfort to know that his much-anticipated meeting was now imminent.

Was this movement somehow part of his future, his destiny, his calling? Would more become clear tomorrow?

Then too...now...there was Ariah. Was *she* part of his future somehow?

And finally, what about things at home? Zephaniah was back now and Joshua actually once again enjoyed being *there*.

How did everything fit together?

Would it? Could it?

Joshua climbed into bed that night entirely confused but extremely hopeful. Nothing was resolved. In fact, if anything, things had gotten much more complicated.

But there was or so it seemed now, the possibility that all or even some questions might soon have answers? He didn't know, couldn't know, but he could hardly wait for the sun to rise on a new day and the rest of his future. Whatever that would be.

"Lead me into my destiny, Adonai Elohim, into *all* of it!" he breathed prayerfully as he drifted off into dreamland.

Chapter 21

Meeting

Joshua had no problem rising early. In fact, he had actually lain awake for what seemed to him a very long while just waiting for the rooster to crow. He kind of wondered whether he had slept enough or at all really; however, even if he had not, there was so much energy and so many thoughts racing through his mind and body that he didn't feel tired at all.

Not at this point in the day anyway.

Caleb was up to see him off. Zadok too, busying himself with his usual morning chores of getting ready to go to the seashore and get the fish for the day. Deborah and Ariah were hard at work by the fire pit and the smells of a hearty breakfast of fish and eggs filled the yard. When they had finished eating, Deborah gave him some additional food and water for the road. They all hugged each other and said that they would see each other soon and not allow so much time to pass again.

Caleb and Joshua ended up turning their hug into a bit of a wrestling contest just so that everyone would know that they were men. Joshua was a little surprised at how difficult and emotional this parting was. He loved Caleb's family almost as much as his own.

Particularly unsettling, although in a very good way, had been the moment when he had hugged Ariah. She had literally wrapped her arms around him, holding him in her embrace a little tighter and a little longer than social convention should allow. Or was that just his imagination? His heart sped and his cheeks burned and his head was spinning. She smelled good. She felt good. There were no words or categories for what this was, at least not in his vocabulary so far.

And what was this that he was feeling? The desire to love and be loved by a girl, a woman?

This was all so new. It was intoxicating. Dizzying. And amazing all at the same time.

As promised, Jacob arrived before sunrise, just as they were all saying their goodbyes. Jacob greeted Joshua and Caleb's family briefly, not wanting to intrude on what was transpiring, and then went and stood by the gate waiting for him.

Joshua eventually made his way in that direction, picking up Samson and the cart on the way. He turned and waved and the little caravan made their way out of the yard and up the street in the direction of home.

For a while, Jacob just let Joshua remain lost in his thoughts.

"Nice family," he finally said.

"Yes, the salt of the earth," Joshua replied.

He had to chuckle at his unintentional joke. He had called them salt of the earth people and they were in the fish-salting business.

"They are wonderful indeed! I didn't even realize how much I missed them. How much I missed..."

Joshua stopped himself short.

"Do *you* miss your father?" he now asked his travelling companion.

"Every day," Jacob said.

"You too obviously," he added.

Joshua just nodded, not really too concerned if Jacob saw his response in the half dark of the morning or not. Jacob had seen, and they simply shared some quiet moments together, interrupted only by the creaking of the cart on the dirt road and Samson's heavy breathing.

As the sun began to rise, erasing the shadows of night, Jacob stopped and turned toward Joshua.

"I am not actually going to Rakkath, Joshua. Too many Romans there, especially with the construction of the new garrison south of town. I am most assuredly a known and wanted man. But I did want to talk with you. Can we take a detour off of the main road, find a secluded spot, spend some time together, and then I will make my way back to Gamala through the countryside while you can continue on down the road toward home? I'm sorry but that is about all that I can risk right now."

Joshua nodded and his heart raced. He had heard, with the envy of every young boy, the stories of David before he was made king, stories of how he and his band of mighty men remained covert as they evaded King Saul, but he had never personally known anyone who was on the run. It was vicariously exhilarating. He wondered what it would be like to be one of those men on a mission of danger and intrigue.

Suddenly, all of the questions that had been left hanging when his father had been murdered and then later when Jacob and Simeon had paid him a brief visit, came flooding back into his mind.

Joshua opened his mouth and let go the barrage:

"When did you first meet my abba? And, what is this movement? The one you called the Fourth Way? What exactly did happen to *your* father? And how is the monument to the martyrs coming? You said that, 'you had *dispatched* them.' Are those soldiers really dead and gone? Is Gamala where you have your headquarters? How many of you are there? And how did you know that I would be in Magdala? Are you and Simeon the leaders now?

Do we have any hope of defeating the Romans and taking back the land...?"

He would have continued with more but Jacob burst out laughing and now held up both his hands in Joshua's direction.

"Whoa! Hold on, little brother! One question at a time please, Joshua! Let's find that safe place to sit, off of the road and away from any spying eyes or ears."

"*Then* we can talk!"

Eventually, they turned aside to the right, leaving the road, and walked down into a nearby ravine where they discovered a small creek and some lush grass growing next to it.

"Samson will be okay here," Jacob said. "And we can go on a little farther off the road. If we hear braying, if he hears something, I will know that someone is coming and can make my escape."

Once Samson was content, Jacob and Joshua made their way up the other side of the ravine to a place where the rocks provided coverage but allowed them a view of the road in either direction. They could see Samson from there too.

Joshua sat down and Jacob went a bit further, planning out his escape route in the event that became necessary, or so Joshua supposed.

When Jacob returned, he measured Joshua up and down for a moment with his dark eyes, stroking his beard ever so gently.

"Where do I begin?" he asked, probably more of himself than of Joshua. He paused briefly and then launched into his answer.[7]

"I, well, we come from a family that is descended from Judas Maccabees and the Hasmoneans, a family that almost 200 years ago now rose up in revolt and took back the Land of Promise, re-establishing the Jewish nation until such time as it was stolen from us again by the Roman Empire. We stand in a long line of the Chosen who are zealous to see a return to Jewish self-government, to see ourselves out from under the control and taxation of anyone, to once again be the people of Elohim under the reign of His Messiah, His Anointed One. At the core of everything we believe, it is idolatry for the Chosen people of Adonai to come under any secular rule."

"As His Chosen people, we are unique among all peoples on the face of the earth and it leaves a most bitter taste in our mouths to be forcibly subjected to the rule of this idolatrous Empire, an empire which goes so far as to attribute divinity to its emperors! Roman and Jewish life are at complete odds with each other, on a spiritual level for sure and possibly on every other level as well, and as a result, we long for a messianic last days' revival of the glory of Israel and the downfall of this kingdom of arrogance."

"Our family has a long history in this revolt. In fact, our grandfather, Hezekiah, from the town of Gamala in upper Galilee, was a freedom fighter and the leader of a Zealot movement during the rule of Julius Caesar. And even though his activities centered mainly in the area along the eastern edge of Galilee bordering Syria, he made enough of an impact that shortly after he came to power, Herod the Great hunted him down and then had him executed. This execution did initially provoke an outcry against Herod in Judea. He was even summoned before the Sanhedrin. However, little came of it. Herod couldn't care less about Jewish sentiment."

"My own father, Judah, or Judas the Galilean as he became known, rose to prominence in the rebel movement somewhat later since he was very young when our grandfather was murdered. But it was in his blood. And when there was a messianic revolt in Judea shortly after the death of Herod, father was part of it."

"The uprising was ill-fated. Varus, at that time the governor of the territory of Syria just to the north of us, a man known for his harsh rule and high taxes, moved swiftly first of all to occupy Jerusalem and then to crucify some 2000 of these rebels."

"Our father somehow managed to escape crucifixion on that occasion and returned to Galilee to later lead another group of freedom fighters in armed revolt, attacking the royal palace in Sepphoris, the capital of Galilee, believing that Adonai would come and fight with and for them, especially for those who gave no thought to their own survival. It was a relatively small band of rebels against Varus's four legions of soldiers. They didn't fare well either but this is what gave birth to what is now known as the Fourth Philosophy."

"Theologically, I suppose, we have most things in common with the party of the Pharisees, however we place a much greater weight than they on our freedom to be the people of Elohim. In fact, we accept Adonai alone as our master and leader. And we are freely and readily prepared to accept the most horrible of deaths or see relations and friends tortured rather than accept human domination under an evil and ungodly regime. Our father believed and taught that it was cowardice to pay taxes to Rome or to tolerate the rule of man when Adonai is our only ruler."

"Well, our father was severely wounded in that uprising and we, and many others with us, thought that he was going to die. He didn't. Some thought it a miracle. Father simply said it was Elohim coming to the aid of someone who cared not for his own survival, as he had taught. Having been restored to life and health, over the next decade or so, he continued to develop his ideology and proclaimed it wherever he could and to whomever would listen, also going out on raids and participating in various uprisings from time to time. He was often in hiding and gone from home for long periods of time."

"Toward the end of this time, Quirinius once again instituted a census together with heavy taxation. Our father and those he had gathered around him rose up in revolt. Father believed that it was wrong under Ha Shem's laws for us to pay taxes to anything but the

Temple of the Most High, to say nothing of how unfair it was that we were being taxed severely while Gentiles were hardly at all. Add to this the legislated census, that we were being *counted* among a nation whose control they did not feel they should be under at all, and the ground was ripe for an uprising. They considered the census to be outright slavery. Censuses are forbidden in Jewish law! Many Jewish brothers around him had rallied in agreement. They felt that this must be opposed and stopped. In reality, the only thing that was stopped at the time was our father's life!"

"He himself had taken the lives of some Romans and Jewish sympathizers to be sure, but in the process, he was captured and executed for treason against the Empire. Many other followers of the Fourth Way were executed with him. We knew them all like family. That event more than anything has forever marked us, Joshua, much as your father's death has marked you. Simeon and I had come to know all that our father believed in—we had been discipled in it as it were—but now we felt called, duty-bound to rise up and champion the cause in his memory."

Joshua had said nothing, asked nothing, while Jacob had related all of this. He gasped as though inhaling for the first time in a very long while and realized that he had barely taken a breath as he had listened to all that Jacob was sharing. This history was anything but dry.

Samson suddenly brayed and Jacob paused, straining his ear to listen.

"Goodbye, Joshua. Until next time," he said abruptly.

And just as quickly, he disappeared from sight down the far side of the embankment.

Joshua now heard sounds coming toward them on the road. It was clearly a band of soldiers, swords periodically clattering against the greaves that they wore to protect their shins. A few moments later they came into view on the road. For a brief amount of time,

Joshua thought they might continue on but then, they did turn aside at this very same stream to which he and Jacob had come. Samson was still there, chewing on the grass next to the water.

"What have we here? Does this donkey look familiar to any of you?" one of the soldiers asked aloud when he saw Samson and the wagon.

Joshua cautiously moved in their direction.

"Well, hello, Jesus!" Maneus said, when he caught sight of Joshua. "What are *you* doing here?"

Joshua knew him from deliveries to the garrison.

His heart was racing but he didn't think that they had seen Jacob. And he now took a long slow breath, to calm himself but also to carefully compose his answer.

"I...ah...I had a small delivery in Magdala and am on my way back home. I stopped to water my donkey and to have a little something to eat myself. And now...I really need to get going."

Joshua quickly moved to where he and Jacob had been moments earlier, gathering everything up into the blanket they had been sitting on. He hoped none of the soldiers had seen that there had been two portions on the ground. He didn't really want to try and explain that.

Fortunately, they were busy drinking and filling their water skins.

"I'll see you tomorrow," Joshua said hastily. "I must carry on."

"You won't actually," Maneus said. "We are going to Magdala and possibly even beyond. We are on the hunt for someone, a most wanted criminal. We have a lead that he is here somewhere in the area. Hopefully we will return with our prize. His head!"

"You haven't seen anyone, have you?"

Joshua shook his head. He gulped and hastily made his way back to the road together with Samson and the cart, now empty of all but the wrapped-up blanket from the meal and also the fish he was bringing back from Caleb's family. He encouraged Samson to move a little or a lot quicker than normal.

He wanted to be home before it got dark. Mostly, he just wanted to be anywhere but where he was.

Maybe this cloak-and-dagger stuff was more than *he* could handle.

When he was down the road a bit, he finally allowed himself to breathe…and then, to think. He knew that he needed to process all of this. He had received a lot of answers, it was true, but still, most of his questions remained unaddressed.

He walked on, lost in all of his thoughts. There were so many more things he had wanted to ask, to learn. Did this new knowledge make things better or worse? He wasn't sure.

It definitely made him even more hungry than he had been before.

And this Fourth Way certainly seemed to resonate with everything inside of him. He wondered why it seemed so easy to adopt?

And then it hit him!

His own father had been in sympathy with this movement. And, the reason it made so much sense to him, the reason it was so very familiar, was because it was cut from the same cloth as the convictions that Abrahim had shared with him, with all of them.

This was *already* part of his own beliefs. Was it or would it now be part of his destiny as well?

Chapter 22

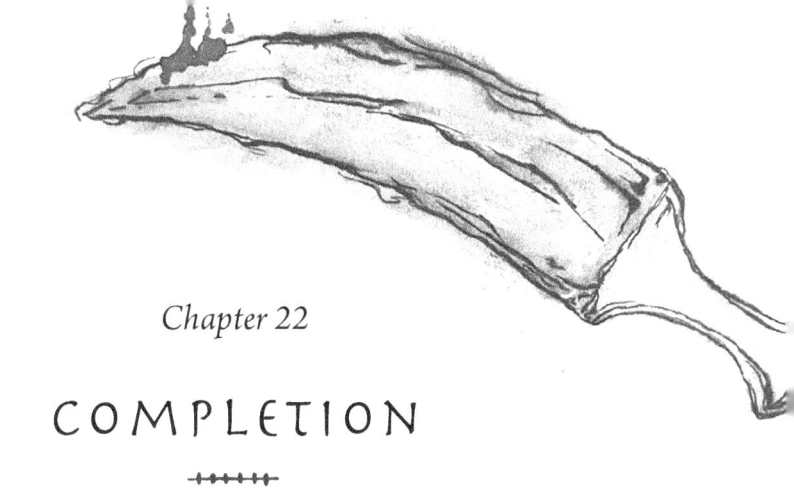

COMPLETION

Joshua was glad to be home.

But so much had changed in the last day or so.

His world had been opened up to all matter of new things beyond the bounds of Rakkath.

He was having trouble focusing on things at home.

He now wanted to spend more time with Caleb and his family and if possible, particularly with Ariah. Why had he not paid more attention to her in the past, not really noticed her before? Because she was just a little girl back then. She had certainly changed a whole lot from what he remembered.

Joshua recognized that he was changing, had changed, as well.

And then there was everything that Jacob had shared with him. It just seemed to fit. It all made so much sense.

His father Abrahim had been in sympathy with what they believed, these followers of the Fourth Way. With one notable exception: the fact that his abba had come to believe they should leave the vengeance to Adonai alone. This, in fact, had often been one of the topics of hot debate in their backyard: whether violence was the answer, or whether other alternatives were a better plan of attack.

Joshua himself had serious questions about that, especially now. Somehow, waiting for Elohim to act didn't seem to work. He himself had *stood by* once. Adonai clearly hadn't come through on that occasion. Maybe vengeance actually was, or should be, a *shared* responsibility of the people who called themselves by His name? Many Scriptures seemed to suggest that very thing. Had not King David been a man of war and yet was even so seen as a man after Elohim's own heart? Then too, Joshua thought it better to be an *active* part of something that at least tried to make a difference rather than letting everything just happen—to be part of a movement that was at least trying to change things. He had always thought that he might be a world changer. But, did he have it inside of himself to be that, to pull it off? He wondered what he would be like when push came to shove.

He remembered being on a roof, not that long ago really, and on that occasion, *he* had done nothing.

When he was too afraid to do anything.

He had changed, but how significantly since then? And in what way? That was a large unknown.

Everything and especially brick making, now seemed tedious. Maybe it was just that they were nearing the end of the order for the garrison. And that sometimes you want to quit just before you are about to finish? Had he simply seen one too many pieces of masonry?

It had been interesting to watch the progression of the garrison over the past weeks and months. It was awe-inspiring to see the gigantic structure approach completion and to know that they had played a large part in its construction. It really was quite a marvel to behold. There were only two more deliveries to be made, and then they would be completely finished.

They had actually made a half million bricks.

And all in just six months.

The impossible had been accomplished.

Adonai *must* be praised for that.

It had been good for them. But going forward, what about that Roman presence, he wondered. Having all of those Roman soldiers living so close, how would that be?

Joshua could hardly wait for it to end. It had been a long and difficult six months. It had been prosperous and good for their family, healing even. But they all needed a break. Just a bit of time to take a long, slow breath and regroup.

He needed it. Some time to think.

Several weeks had passed.

All of the bricks had now been delivered.

Joshua was busying himself cleaning up the yard. It had been severely neglected as of late, especially in those final days of completion. He wasn't sure how, but in this moment somehow, all of the others were somewhere else doing other things.

Joshua found himself alone in the back corner of the yard and the now somewhat tattered piece of canvas that covered the blood bricks once again caught his eye. He let his feet carry him in that direction and put his hand on the small pile of bricks that had such a large story.

"I miss you, Abba," he said out loud. "We can do most of what needs to be done around here, but I still need you, wish you *were* here."

Tears rolled down Joshua's cheeks and he didn't fight them.

How much feeling and emotion had he simply packed away like these stained bricks, to be dealt with another day? Joshua knew that his anger had at least lessened some recently, which was good. But there was still so much internal work to do. Today still didn't seem like quite the right time to try and deal with it.

Was his inner world very much like their yard, messy and unorganized because urgent things had demanded his attention? Maybe.

Maybe soon he could give his soul and spirit some attention. When he wasn't so tired.

He pulled back the cover and looked. The life was in the blood. And his father's life could be seen on, even in, those bricks.

That life was no more. And yet, that very same life was still... living. But now, living in him.

Very much *alive* within *him*.

They had been given a rich legacy even as Zephaniah had said a while ago. Joshua had received so much that was good.

Gratitude overwhelmed his sadness.

"Thank you, Abba," he said as he wiped his tears, treasuring them.

"Thank you for all that you have given me! Shared with me!"

He was talking to his earthly father, he supposed, but somehow, it seemed as if Adonai Himself was listening, participating, taking it all in, someplace alongside his own beloved abba. As a Heavenly Abba.

Joshua's mind wandered back to a poetic word of David, a message that was part of the very psalm that Batiyah had been praying on that wonderful night a while ago, that sacred place to which the two of them had regretfully somehow never returned:

YHWH is compassionate and gracious,
slow to anger, abounding in love...
As a father has compassion on his children,
so YHWH has compassion on those who fear Him...
from everlasting to everlasting
YHWH's love is with those who fear Him,
and His righteousness with their children's children.

Joshua wondered if Adonai could be similar to a loving earthly father, even though obviously far superior?

He laughed to himself.

Of course! Though he had it backward.

We are created in *His* image.

Abrahim had merely mirrored the character and the heart of Adonai.

"His love is with those who fear Him."

Not that difficult to grasp really, Joshua thought. He had certainly loved his father and had experienced his love in return, tenderness even. While at the same time having a healthy respect, one could even say, a fear of him. Love and fear together.

His thoughts were interrupted by a knock on the gate and the arrival of a messenger.

"Shalom, sir. Are you the brick maker, Jesus, son of Abrahim?" he asked. "I am Theocles, and I have a package from Zadok of Magdala."

"Yes I am. And thank you," Joshua said, reaching into his cloak to procure a half-denarius, at the same time extending his other hand to take the small package he assumed contained more dried fish.

Why they would go to so much trouble to send this, he wondered?

"I am told there is also a message…inside," Theocles said.

Joshua unwrapped the fish and tore off a piece for Theocles and one for himself. He thought it ingenious that the cloth was not only the wrapper for the fish but the medium on which to write a message.

He took a generous bite and just let it remain on his tongue, the taste of the fish and the salt somehow momentarily transporting him back to Magdala. When he opened his eyes, he now read their request:

"Please deliver two more lots of the same bricks you brought the last time. They work excellently! We couldn't be more pleased! Please bring them as soon as you can. We await your arrival.

Shalom, Zadok ben Jeremiah of Magdala."

A smile far too large to equal this relatively small order of bricks made its way on to his face.

He didn't bother to ask Zephaniah this time.

He tore off a piece of the fabric and quickly scribbled a reply to send back with Theocles:

"Yes. We will most certainly do that. I will deliver them personally within two weeks. I look forward to seeing all of you. Until then,

Blessings, Joshua ben Abrahim."

Joshua gave Theocles another healthy piece of the fish, a full denarius for the return trip, and now sent him on his way.

He stood there grinning.

This was almost too good to believe.

He would be returning to Magdala.

And so very soon.

Chapter 23

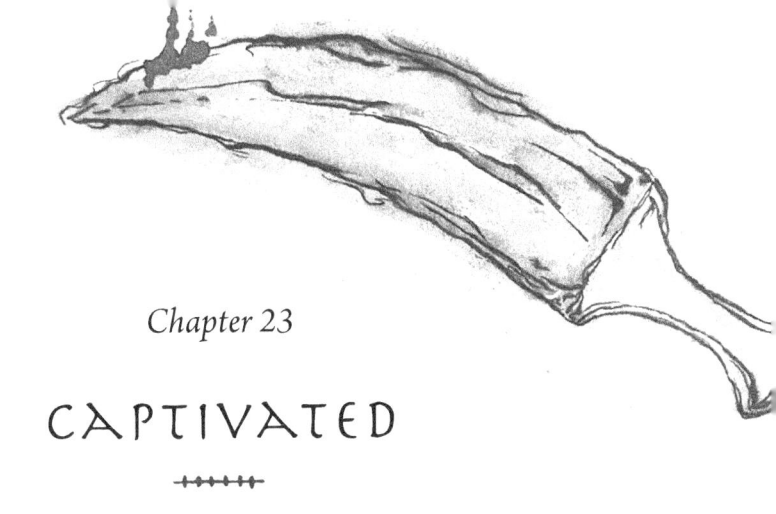

CAPTIVATED

Joshua's demeanor had definitely improved some after Zephaniah had returned home, and even more when the weight of the Imperial order was finally lifted.

But, because of everything else that was transpiring lately, Joshua found it much easier to work even more diligently than he ever had in his life before. Whereas previously, perhaps in the early days of the large order for the garrison, he worked hard only because there was no other option, his present enthusiasm was born out of choice. There were clearly forces at work in him that had never even existed before.

It was impossible not to notice. He was up very early every morning, and then worked almost non-stop throughout the day. He worked until late in the evening.

Maybe it was not even that so much. He had done as much on other days before. It was that he was joyful all the time. This was a Joshua that no one had experienced for quite some time.

There had been a few encouraging moments in the past several months, but they never seemed to last. But now, it appeared the angry, always tired, resentful young man they had come to know over the last year and a half, had gone to Magdala and someone else that looked very much like him but who was his very opposite, had returned.

Batiyah had certainly been the first to notice the change, and maybe she even knew what was going on. Mothers are often some of the most perceptive people on the face of the earth. Did she have a suspicion as to what or whom this newfound attitude was about? Probably, but if she did, she kept it to herself. Maybe she was just waiting for an appropriate time to open up the conversation.

Elijah however, didn't care a wit about such things as restraint or timing. Maybe he was too young to know about tact. Regardless, it seemed that if and when the opportunity presented itself, the chance to tease your older brother was just too good to pass up.

It happened at breakfast.

And on the Sabbath no less.

The whole family was seated together. The prayer of blessing had been prayed and they had all just begun eating the bread that Batiyah had baked the day before.

"Joshua likes a girl!" Elijah blurted out. "That's why he has been so pleasant and happy lately!"

Joshua immediately turned in Elijah's direction, glowering at his younger brother. Or maybe it was more a look of shock horror.

Everyone else turned to stare at Joshua.

"You don't know anything! You are talking nonsense!" Joshua said, though his angry face softened slightly as a blush made its way to his cheeks and ears.

"Oh, I know!" Elijah announced with emphasis.

After a slight pause, he boldly proclaimed, "I even know *who* it is!"

Now Joshua wasn't sure where or how to look. He secretly hoped that Elijah didn't actually know anything, but if he didn't, why would he have even brought this up?

"Ooooo, a girl. Who is it?" said Sarah who was always interested in other people's business.

"It's Ariah!" Elijah said without the slightest hesitation, "Ariah, the daughter of Zadok!"

Joshua gasped! And it felt as though his face would burst into flames. He knew that Caleb and his family probably suspected, but when would they, why would they, have had occasion to tell? And why of all people, his little brother Elijah? How he would have uncovered this secret was a complete mystery.

Joshua's face must have asked Elijah that very question, for he promptly looked at Joshua and gave the answer.

"Joshua, you talk in your sleep!" he revealed, proud of his most recent discovery. "At least you did last night. You just kept saying, 'Ariah, Ariah, Ariah!' over and over again. 'Oh, my sweet Ariah'!"

Joshua wasn't sure exactly what to do. He just knew that he needed *this* to stop. So, without warning, he lunged in his younger brother's direction, taking him off guard with the element of surprise and tackling him to the ground, now pummeling him with his fists. It took Elijah a second or two, but he quickly began returning volleys in Joshua's direction, blow for blow.

"That is enough!" Batiyah said firmly.

And they both knew that it would be unwise to persist.

Slowly, Joshua released his hold on Elijah and stood to his feet brushing the dirt from his clothes. Elijah quickly pulled himself up, giving his older brother another shot as the two separated. Joshua made a fist about to repay.

"I said enough!" Batiyah stated emphatically.

And that ended it.

Needless to say, the rest of the meal was rather silent.

Joshua inhaled his food, said thank you to Batiyah when he was done and excused himself. Later, it had been time to go to synagogue.

Joshua had trouble concentrating on what was being taught.

The next day, he was up quite early and decided just to hitch up Samson and go get clay on his own.

When he returned, Zephaniah was there, waiting for him, his eyes seeming to probe him with a thousand questions.

"Go away. Leave me alone!" Joshua said.

"I actually think it is quite excellent!" Zephaniah said.

"What?" Joshua asked, still angry, mostly at the fact that he had given himself away.

"Well, this, I mean *her,* as in, Ariah!" said Zephaniah grinning widely.

Joshua smiled.

Yes, it was excellent, Joshua thought. She was...

He realized he was totally at a loss for words.

"Do you know that I have my eye on someone too?" Zephaniah added after a slight hesitation.

"Ooooo, a girl. Who is it?" Joshua said in a high voice, imitating their little sister Sarah from the day before, and laughing.

Zephaniah laughed too.

"No, wait, don't tell me...it's Naomi, isn't it?" Joshua said.

"Do I talk in my sleep like you?" Zephaniah asked.

Now it was his turn to blush a little. He nodded.

"I knew it!" Joshua said, smiling. "Or at least, I thought it. Oh, Zephaniah, that's excellent!"

"She is...almost as wonderful as Ariah!"

They both laughed at that.

"By the way, I'm not going to ever go to sleep again until I'm sure that everyone else is asleep," Joshua added, laughing and knowing he did not really mean it, knowing that that was an impossible promise to keep.

"I don't want to give anything else away!"

The rest of the day, the brothers both worked hard at all of the new orders they had to fill, including the one for Caleb's family. Periodically they would glance in the direction of the other and smile. Once or twice, they caught each other's eye.

Zephaniah winked.

They were growing up.

After supper, Batiyah came and asked Joshua if he was all right.

"Yes, Ima, Elijah and I have made our peace. Everything is good."

"Fine then," she said.

"By the way, I don't know this grown up Ariah," Batiyah said. "But I always thought that she was a most wonderful little girl. If she is anything like her mother, Deborah, she would definitely make a great wife for someone, someday..."

Joshua feigned shock at the mention of marriage.

Batiyah's gaze probed Joshua with the question. He didn't counter her suggestion and Batiyah took that as her answer.

Joshua knew that she knew.

The next afternoon as Zephaniah and Joshua worked, albeit a little bit slower in the middle of the day because of the heat, he asked his older brother a question:

"Zephaniah, not that anything is being planned yet, but just kind of wondering, when ah...you, want to get married eventually maybe someday, how does that work since we have no abba to make the arrangements with, shall we say...Naomi's family?"

Zephaniah laughed.

"If Abba were still with us, he would most certainly be the one to make all of those things happen. But, in his absence, one of our uncles, probably Uncle Joseph, as the next oldest in the family, together with Ima would be the ones to negotiate on my...or, on *your* behalf."

"I know you weren't just wondering about me, were you?"

"Well, no," Joshua said, color appearing on his cheeks.

"Didn't think so," Zephaniah said. "Don't worry. It will all be fine. We don't have to remain single our whole lives!"

"All in time, little brother, all in time," he said.

Just like Abba.

Joshua smiled at that. But…

He still wished that Abrahim were around to take care of things.

Especially, important things like this.

Chapter 24

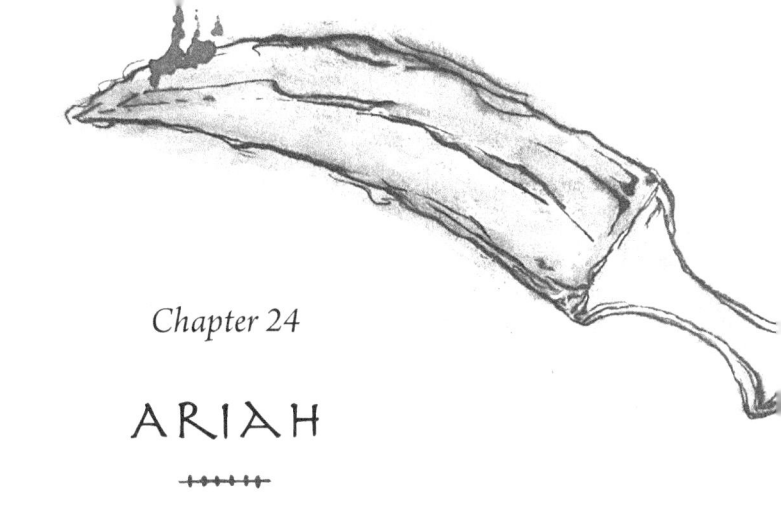

ARIAH

After several days, the first of the two additional orders of bricks was ready and it was decided that Joshua would deliver them to Magdala right away rather than wait for them all to be finished, especially since their wagon could hold one order comfortably but probably not both. Likely, even if they had a bigger wagon that could have held them all, neither Samson nor Solomon would be strong enough or favorably disposed to carry both installments that distance at the same time. Joshua would go and deliver what was now the second order and then return and almost immediately deliver the remainder. Zephaniah and the others would be able to have the rest of them finished by the time he got back.

Joshua thought this was a most splendid idea.

He would get to go to Magdala two more times in short order.

He had eagerly anticipated returning.

He thought that once would have been wonderful.

Twice was; well, twice as wonderful!

He could hardly wait.

They had loaded the wagon on Thursday afternoon. Joshua was scheduled to leave early Friday morning and arrive in lots of time to unload the bricks before the start of the Sabbath. He would then spend the Sabbath with Caleb's family and make his return on the first day of the next week. When he returned home, they could load up the wagon again, he could leave early Monday morning and they would have both new orders of bricks delivered even sooner than promised. Then he was going to spend Tuesday there and return home on Wednesday.

Such was the plan anyway.

Joshua hoped that he would have some time somehow, that he would be able to come up with some excuse to talk to Ariah, maybe even alone. They were kind of like family, so maybe he thought it might be allowed. Or possibly, it could just be overlooked. Caleb might even be willing to help create the circumstance so that could happen.

Friday morning was bright and sunny and so was Joshua. Samson was in a bad mood and fairly uncooperative. Joshua didn't even seem to notice or mind. He smiled and waved to his family as they drove away in the direction of Magdala. At the little stream where they stopped when they were about halfway, as Samson was busy drinking and chewing on some grass, Joshua's mind wandered back to the last time that they were here and his meeting with Jacob. He had learned much that day but still had so many questions unanswered. Their meeting had been cut short. Joshua wondered when and if they would meet again. He hoped that they would.

Of all the ways he knew, so far, the Fourth seemed most like *the* way.

Joshua took another drink from the stream himself and pulled Samson away from his grazing. It was time to finish the journey. Samson protested some but eventually gave in and the two of them were on their way again, arriving sometime in the late morning.

The gate to the yard was open so Joshua just walked in. He was about to call out a greeting, but immediately saw Ariah, busy at work, her back to him and not more than fifteen feet away. Her veil was loosely draped on her shoulders and her dark brown hair flowed down her back. She was singing softly to herself as she went about cutting up some vegetables for whatever it was that she was preparing.

Joshua stood frozen where he was, just inside the gate, looking directly at her.

She hadn't heard him.

A carrot slipped out of her hand and dropped to the ground. She spun around to pick it up and as she raised her head, she saw Joshua standing at the gate. Their eyes locked and she smiled in his direction—the most beautiful smile on the most beautiful face he had ever seen. He stared and grinned back, color immediately flooding his own face.

Ariah realized all of a sudden that she was not wearing her veil and spun around to fix it, dropping the carrot a second time. She retrieved the renegade vegetable and then, once her veil was somewhat in place, turned to face Joshua once more.

"Uh, ahem, shalom, Joshua, we did not know you were coming so soon!" Ariah said, coughing ever so slightly.

Her dark eyes were still smiling.

"Uh, I didn't know that I was coming so soon either," Joshua said, full on blushing, nothing to hide behind. He might have been able to pull his keffiyeh up to conceal his face, but...

"But, well...here I am!" he said red-faced.

"Yes, it would appear," Ariah said, giggling a little.

"Well, welcome," she said. "Don't just stand at the gate. Do come in. I, umm, we are glad you are here! I'll tell the rest of the family that you have arrived."

With that, she disappeared and within minutes Caleb and then Zadok appeared.

"Shalom, Joshua," Caleb said. "You have bricks for us already? That is excellent! I trust the journey was a good one?"

"Shalom. Yes. All is well," Joshua said, and proceeded to tell them how and why they had brought one load of bricks and of their plan to deliver the third and final installment.

"I trust that is agreeable?"

"Very good. Very good, indeed," Zadok said.

"It means that we can start even sooner than we thought, building yet one more of the new brining pools we need."

They went and got Samson and the wagon and brought him close to the place where they had staked out the second of the additional new brining pools and then the three of them unloaded the bricks into a pile. In almost no time at all, the wagon was devoid of its load other than a few bricks that had broken on the way.

"Come see the one your bricks already built," Caleb said and headed off in the direction of the recently completed pool.

Then turning to them, he said, "Well, the bricks didn't build the pool! We did…using the bricks!"

He laughed aloud at his own joke.

Joshua and Zadok joined in.

"So excellent!" said Zadok admiringly, once they reached the pool.

"Yes, that does look excellent," agreed Joshua nodding, though he had no clue what the difference would be between a good brining pool and a bad one.

He didn't have to wait long to find out though, as Zadok explained how the new pool using the bricks that they had made was superior to the old one in every detail.

It seemed as though the rest of Friday and even the next day which was the Sabbath, flew by before Joshua knew what had happened. Other than the brief moments they had shared when he had arrived, he had barely even seen Ariah. Oh well, he thought to himself, maybe when I return again in a few days.

"Men and women who are unmarried and unrelated don't get time together," Joshua said to himself as he drifted off to sleep. "What was I thinking? I wasn't thinking, is what. I was just wishing. Silly me!"

Early Sunday morning, Joshua tethered Samson to the wagon, gathered up his belongings as well as the lunch that Deborah had made him, and was about to set out.

"Joshua," Caleb said with a rather mischievous grin, "Ariah is on her way to the market to sell our fish there shortly. Maybe wait just a bit and the two of you could keep each other company on the way?"

Joshua could feel himself blushing.

Caleb grinned even more broadly.

"Sounds fine. I don't mind waiting a little while if needed," Joshua said as nonchalantly as he could.

Caleb gave him a wink.

Which made Joshua blush even more.

Ariah arrived almost immediately with her bags of dried fish.

"Ariah, Joshua is going to accompany you as far as the market," Caleb informed her.

"Caleb, I have been to the market by myself on my own many days before this one!" Ariah said in mock protest.

"But if this somehow makes *you* feel better, well then, I will comply with your wishes," she added.

Her eyes sparkled.

Joshua took the satchels of dried fish, marveling at how heavy they actually were, and loaded them onto the wagon.

"No sense you carrying them if you don't need to," Joshua said.

The first part of the journey, short as it was, was rather quiet, almost awkwardly so. Finally, Joshua could stand it no longer.

"Forgive me for being so forward, Ariah, but I like you. I like you a lot!" Joshua finally blurted out.

"I like you too, Joshua," Ariah said slowly and quietly, lowering her eyes ever so slightly.

Joshua felt dizzy, like he was going to fall over. He grabbed the wagon so he didn't and they walked in silence for a bit again.

And then they talked, the rest of the way. The easy conversation of longtime friends. About anything and everything.

The market arrived far too soon.

Joshua unloaded the fish and helped Ariah get ready for the day. He said his goodbyes and left. It was barely the second hour but it had been a good day.

He really had no desire to leave at all, ever, but the good thing was that he knew that he would be back very soon. And the door to whatever this was and whatever this could become had now been opened.

He and Samson hadn't made it very far down the road, however, when one of the wheels decided to fall off of the wagon. Joshua tried to repair it on the spot as he had so often done in the past, but the axle itself had given out and would need to be completely replaced. He would just have to return to Magdala and see if he could find someone to fix it. He wondered how long this would delay him?

The two of them made their way very slowly back to town. Fortunately, they had not gone far. But it was slow going since Joshua had to pretty much carry one side of the wagon while encouraging Samson to keep going. He was glad that the load was gone at least.

He inquired as soon as they reached the edges of Magdala, and someone pointed him to a shop nearby. The owner, a man named Bartholomew, said he could repair it, but because of his other commitments, it would not be until the afternoon, and even then, only if Joshua helped with some of the preparation. Joshua spent the better part of his day removing the broken part and getting the wagon ready. Finally, toward the end of the afternoon, Bartholomew was free and, in almost no time it seemed, they managed to put everything back together as good as new.

Joshua wasn't sure what to do now. Should he head for home even though it was late?

What would be the best plan?

Should he stay here in Magdala?

Go back to Caleb's for night?

His stomach growled and he realized that he hadn't eaten anything all day.

That gave him an idea. It at least answered what he would do right now.

He had the lunch Deborah had packed him but thought he would much rather return to the market. He would get something to eat that way, but mostly, catch just one more vision of this woman who was changing everything. He assured himself that he wouldn't be very long at all. Maybe he could figure out the rest of the plan on the way, or when he was there? Hopefully, she wouldn't already be gone for the day.

When he arrived, he paused at a little distance, just watching Ariah closing up her vendor's stall. How beautiful she looked.

All of a sudden, however, a Roman soldier who had been standing nearby rushed toward her small stand, grabbed her by the arm and pulled her down one of the long narrow alleys behind the shops. He was holding her from behind now and covered her mouth with his gloved hand.

Ariah was trying to scream.

Without hesitation, Joshua abandoned Samson and the wagon and pursued Ariah and her captor as they wound this way and that through the shadows of the city. Anger and justice rose up from deep inside of him. He knew that this wasn't right.

Knew that he must do something.

And he must act quickly.

For Ariah's sake.

"Aren't you a feisty little thing!" he heard the soldier mutter as Joshua watched them disappear into a nearby building. "This promises to be even more fun than I thought!"

"Oh no," Joshua thought. "This is not good at all!"

Joshua had followed as closely as he dared. He was trying not to be seen but knew that he could not stay hidden for long. Not if he intended to help. He moved to the doorway.

He could see now that the soldier had taken Ariah's veil and wrapped it around her head several times so that only muffled cries could escape her mouth. Her clothing was already torn and a bare shoulder could be seen in the half-light. The Roman threw her roughly to the ground and made a move to unbuckle his belt. Ariah tried to scramble into the corner, attempting to get away. There was nowhere for her to go.

Terror filled her eyes and her heart.

Secretly she hoped the beast would just kill her.

The soldier lurched forward in her direction but fell to the floor with a thud landing partly on top of her. Somehow, there was blood everywhere. Ariah had no idea what had just happened.

Was this the vengeance of El Shaddai she wondered? A miraculous deliverance? In those moments of terror, she had prayed, but she was surprised that He would answer so soon and so dramatically.

It was then that she saw Joshua, standing directly in front of her, standing over the fallen soldier, holding one of the broken bricks he had unwittingly picked up from the wagon before deserting it, and breathing so heavily he thought he was going to die. He immediately dropped the brick. It fell to the ground with a thud. Joshua glanced at Ariah, partially obscured by the soldier who had fallen on top of her. Bending quickly to one knee, Joshua rolled her attacker to one side and away from Ariah. He listened briefly for any breath and felt for a pulse, but there was nothing.

The soldier was dead!

Joshua's head was spinning.

He had no idea what to do next.

His gaze left the soldier to rest on the frightened child in the corner.

"Ariah, I'm so sorry. Are you okay?"

Ariah had somehow managed to unwrap the veil of her confinement, or maybe it had just fallen off, but now she was shaking and crying uncontrollably, her body heaving.

She said nothing.

Joshua slid down beside her and wrapped her tightly in his arms. She was small and weak at this moment, which made Joshua appear big and strong even though he felt anything but powerful.

He hoped that this was, that he was, some help.

He could feel his own heart beating wildly inside his chest. He tried desperately to appear calm, for Ariah's sake at least.

Ariah melted into Joshua's embrace.

And slowly, lost somewhere in this awful moment, the shaking at least subsided.

Joshua shushed her gently like a parent quieting a hurting child.

"Are you okay to move?" Joshua finally asked. "We have to get out of here. I have to get you out of here."

Ariah nodded, searching Joshua's eyes, agreeing. She smiled.

Joshua stood up and then helped Ariah to her feet. He tried to help her with her veil. But her knees buckled, and she would have fallen to the ground had Joshua not promptly grabbed hold of her again. He thought better of his original plan, forgot about the veil and now simply scooped her up in his arms and they made their way out of the building and down the street. Problem was, he didn't know where he was or how to get back to any place familiar, let alone Ariah's home. He had given little thought to directions in his hasty pursuit.

What he did recognize was that this was a strange, dark part of town, where unveiled women in scarlet stood on street corners brazenly talking to the men who visited there. Joshua saw one couple being much too friendly in public disappear into a building that looked like the one from which they had just come. He had heard about this place: the home of the adulterous woman. Something about it all made him shiver.

"Her house is a highway to Sheol," Solomon had said, "leading down to the chambers of death."

The realm of death indeed.

What would have, what could have happened to Ariah if he hadn't...?

"Do you know where we are, Ariah?" Joshua asked.

"No," Ariah said, shaking her head, "I've never been to this part of town. This is nowhere I would ever go nor is it where we want to be! If we just keep going though, I'm sure I will eventually see something familiar."

They walked first up one street and then down another, actually only Joshua walked, for Ariah was being carried, until they, by accident or by design, emerged at the river that made its way through Magdala. In reality it wasn't a river. The locals just called it that. It was actually just a man-made canal fed by the waters of the Galilean Sea that made its way from there to the base of the hills that overlooked the town.

Joshua gently set Ariah on the ground. He bent down and put the corner of his garment in the water. And with it he dabbed the blood spatters from Ariah's face and neck and wiped her hands. He unthinkingly began to wipe the blood off of her bare shoulder. When he suddenly realized what he was doing, noticing how soft her skin was to the touch, he pulled back as if he had too soon touched a brick just out of the kiln. He gasped and looked away, amazed at his own audacity.

Ariah hadn't noticed, or at least didn't mind.

She simply smiled up at him.

Joshua was about to pick her up again so that they could continue but she protested.

"I think I'm okay to walk on my own now, Joshua. Thank you."

The two of them made their way down the canal away from the hills and in the direction of the Sea, and at some point, Ariah said she now knew the way home. It was very late and would have been very dark were it not for the fact that the moon was fairly bright.

It didn't take them long to complete the journey.

When they arrived home, Ariah paused outside the gate.

She turned to Joshua and looked directly at him.

"Thank you for saving me, Joshua!" she said.

"I...love you!"

She stepped toward him, rising up on her toes, and kissed him gently on the cheek.

When she pulled back, Joshua saw tears in her lovely, dark eyes.

Moisture made its way to his eyes too.

The events of the evening apparently allowed social conventions to be completely and utterly overlooked. Not that anyone was there to enforce the rules anyway.

Joshua's heart was beating out of control.

He was having trouble breathing.

He was having trouble standing.

Ariah turned and knocked loudly on the gate that had been locked for the evening.

Joshua's head was spinning and he was sure he'd lose his balance.

They heard footsteps hastily crossing the yard.

"Who is there?" Deborah asked tentatively from the inside.

"It's me, Ima. Ariah. And Joshua is with me."

They could hear fumbling with the lock. But then the gate flew open and there was Deborah smiling at them. Almost immediately, the smile disappeared and the color drained from her face.

"Ariah, my dear, what has happened? You look dreadful! You've been crying? And there is blood on your clothes!"

"Joshua, my son, what on earth is going on?" she asked turning.

She didn't let him answer but tearfully embraced her daughter.

"Oh, Ariah, I'm so glad you are home. So glad that you are safe. When you didn't come home at the expected time, Zadok and Caleb went to see what was keeping you."

"We were all quite worried. Your father and your brother are still out looking for you. Where have you been so long and what *did* happen?"

Joshua was fighting to bring everything, in reality, himself mostly, under control.

Briefly, and avoiding most of the more lurid or gory details, he told Deborah the story of what had happened to her little girl. And Ariah added how Joshua had miraculously come to her rescue.

Deborah held her hand over her mouth, aghast.

"How was it that you were there, Joshua?" Ariah suddenly asked, giving voice to a question that had not previously crossed her mind. "Shouldn't you have been in Rakkath by this time?"

Joshua told her briefly about the mishap with the wagon and having to return to have it repaired. He avoided telling her why he had returned to the market specifically. Left her to assume that the place of repair must have been very nearby.

"It was gracious Adonai's providence is all I can say, that wheel falling off!" Deborah exclaimed.

"He made sure you were in the very place where you were most needed at the exact right time!"

She gave Joshua a big hug and then returned to Ariah's side.

"If you will excuse me, I should probably go back to the market and retrieve Caleb and Zadok," Joshua said. "That's likely where *they* will return when they come up empty. I will give them the good news that Ariah is found and we can all come home."

"That sounds good. But do be careful!" Deborah said. "And thank you so much, Joshua! Thank you for saving our little girl's life!"

With that, Joshua exited the gate the two of them had just recently entered.

Chapter 25

RETRIEVAL

THE MOON WAS NOW FULL, SO JOSHUA COULD EASILY see where he was going. Even so, he did struggle a bit to remember the way. On the way there and even on the return, he had been distracted by the conversation and mostly, by Ariah. And as a result, he did make a few wrong turns on this trip. Fortunately for him, his sense of the familiar let him know when he was somewhere he hadn't been before, and he could then backtrack and try another route that eventually proved to be right.

In time, he did find his way back to the market and to the place where Ariah had spent this day, and probably many others before, selling her family's fish. He recognized it in large part because he remembered the exact spot where he had been standing and watching Ariah, albeit unbeknownst to her.

All of what had been left there when she had been whisked away was gone. Everything. Joshua knew that anything that had been accidently left from the day's business became the booty of the gleaners, *street orphans,* that came to the market after dark and lived on whatever they could scavenge. But, was it possible that Zadok and Caleb had been there soon enough that they had been able to gather up whatever of their possessions remained?

Maybe. Hopefully.

At the moment, no one was there.

The market was deserted.

Joshua wondered where to go or what to do next.

And so, he prayed:

"Adonai Elohim, You see everything! You led me to Ariah's side today, and You know where Caleb and Zadok are now. Please, lead me to them. Or lead them to me. Come to my rescue and guide me now."

Joshua immediately felt a divine peace overtake him, a peace that he could only describe as the *Shalom Ha Shem*...peace that goes beyond understanding.

Things would be okay somehow.

He was convinced of it.

It was very good that such peace had come first, because hard on the heels of that wonderful feeling was the sudden grim realization that he, Joshua ben Abrahim, had truly murdered a man earlier that evening. Somehow, he had not actually entertained that stark reality until now. He had not killed in cold blood, mind you, but rather in self-defense, or at least, in Ariah's defense, someone who would have been powerless to help herself in this situation. Would that plea of self-defense hold up? Not likely. He was a Jew, and the man he killed was a Roman citizen and a soldier at that, a representative of the Empire itself.

He consoled himself in the fact that no one knew of his deed save Ariah and himself. Or did they? Had his action truly gone unnoticed? Unseen? Or was there a possibility that it could be traced back or linked to him in any way? Moses had imagined that he was in the clear when he murdered the Egyptian, only to find out later that others had seen.

He shuddered as he felt the onset of evening's chill.

Suddenly, Joshua felt a hand grip his shoulder from behind. He whirled around, nerves immediately exploding through his already tense body, raising his fists in the air, anticipating a fight, ready for anything.

Caleb held up his arms to defend himself.

"Joshua, it's me! Don't!"

Joshua sighed, dropped his hands to his sides and allowed at least some of the tension to drain from his body.

"Don't sneak up on someone like that," Joshua said. "You're liable to get yourself..."

"What are *you* doing here, Joshua? Shouldn't you be long in Rakkath by now?" Caleb asked. And then, turning quickly somber, he continued, "Joshua, Ariah is missing! We don't know where she could be. We have looked all over. Something awful must have happened!"

"All is well, Caleb! She is safe and at home. I took her there myself. The evil that threatened her was averted," Joshua said.

"That is most excellent news!" Zadok said.

"But wait...? She *was*...in danger?" he asked, now looking quite concerned.

"Yes," Joshua said, pausing, "she *was,* but..."

He proceeded to tell Caleb and Zadok the story of the wheel falling off of the cart, his coming back to Magdala to have it repaired, his return to the market and then seeing the soldier abduct Ariah. He told of how he had followed and eventually foiled the soldier's plans to take advantage of a young girl.

By the end of the story, Zadok was weeping, out of sadness for Ariah and the ordeal she had gone through, but also overjoyed at the fact that Joshua had so providentially shown up and come to her rescue, hopefully averting any permanent damage to his precious child.

"Adonai be praised!" Zadok said through his tears. "Thank you, oh thank you, Joshua, my son! You are rightly named! How can we ever repay you? We are most certainly forever in your debt."

Caleb smiled, tears filling his eyes too, at his wonderful friend. He was unable to speak.

"There is a friend who is closer than a brother," Solomon had said. Caleb knew he had just discovered exactly what he meant.

Zadok's face darkened as various thoughts suddenly assembled themselves in his mind.

"Joshua, you killed a Roman soldier! That makes you an enemy of the state, no matter whether it was justified or not! We are Jews, and you know that we do not have the rights of citizenry. Also, you may have thought that the soldier was alone, but soldiers are almost never alone. Is it possible that someone, anyone, saw you? And if someone saw you and can identify you, it is not safe for you to be here, most assuredly not here in the exact place, in the very market where Ariah was taken! We need to get out of here! We need to get *you* far away from here and fast!"

Zadok hurried the three of them off the street and into an alley where they would be less likely to be seen.

He paused.

"Caleb, do you know a way to get home from here, without going down any of the main streets in the market?"

"I think so," Caleb said. "Follow me." He turned to continue down the alley they had just recently entered.

"Wait," Joshua said. "As much as I would like to, I cannot possibly return to your home if I am now an enemy of the Empire. I don't want to bring any repercussions down on you or your family. Thank you for everything. You go. I must..."

Joshua hesitated.

His mind struggling to shape a positive scenario.

"...I don't know fully what I must do. But I can't have you or your family be any part of it. This is my cross to bear."

Both Zadok and Caleb knew that he was right. Knew that it was the wisest course of action given what had transpired.

"Ha Shem go with you, brother, until we meet again!" Caleb said prayerfully, tears welling up in his eyes. "I love you, Joshua!"

"And I, you!" Joshua replied, choking on the words.

He hugged them both.

They were about to turn and go.

"Joshua, if you go down that alley over there, it will eventually get to the river. It is not...well, that great an area...just keep your wits about you. But you should be able to make your getaway from there."

"Say goodbye to Ariah...to everyone, from me," Joshua said. "I hope I will see you again someday soon. My thoughts and prayers are with you all."

"And ours, with you."

And with that, they parted company, Zadok and Caleb to the right and Joshua to the left.

Joshua wondered momentarily if his escape route would take him past the scene of the crime.

He wasn't sure.

He couldn't remember where they had gone.

He continued now in the general direction he had started, careful to keep the moon steadily over his left shoulder. He did have to go left and right several times but at least he could always keep his bearings that way. He rounded a corner and sucked in his breath, almost colliding with the beast in front of him.

"Samson!" he exclaimed, laughing and definitely relieved.

He had completely forgotten about the fact that in the midst of all that had happened, he had simply left him and the wagon there in the market. Samson must have been aimlessly wandering around this whole time, as donkeys are prone to do.

Almost overcome, he gave Samson a big hug. His eyes rested on the empty wagon.

It was then that he saw them: the broken pieces of brick. And the stamp, two Hebrew letters: "Lamed Aleph." They were stamped on every single brick they had ever made. *"Lebhenah Abraham"* is what they stood for: "Bricks by Abraham."

In that instant, Joshua knew what he must now do. The Romans had seen at least half a million of these bricks in the last six months. They knew to whom they belonged. He had left one of those very bricks at the scene of the crime. It was a dead giveaway. At the very least, it would make things uncomfortable for him and for his family. The Romans would most certainly piece it all together.

Looking around, Joshua now realized that they were actually very close to the place where the soldier had attempted to take advantage of Ariah. His heart raced. He must retrieve that damning brick, evidence that would most surely condemn him.

The next thing he knew, he was standing inside the small dark room looking down at the personification of Roman lust and greed that yet lay still and unmoving on the cold, blood-soaked ground.

He quickly grabbed the broken piece of oven-fired and glazed clay that lay by the ogre's side. Sure enough, those letters could clearly be seen on the face of this instrument of death. Blood could be seen on its surface as well: Roman blood that Joshua had spilled.

Joshua surmised that someone eventually would find the body and discern that this soldier had been murdered. Had someone, anyone seen the soldier take Ariah, seen him go after the two of them? There had been a few people in the market even at the end of the day. Had they really just looked the other way? Maybe there was presently no way to connect him with this soldier. Hopefully.

There was no way to know for sure.

He had safely retrieved the brick but the thought now crossed his mind that if he disposed of the body, the soldier's murder could possibly remain a secret. They were headed in the direction of the river and it wasn't actually that far from here as he remembered.

Providence had reunited him with Samson and the wagon so hauling the body there would be a relatively simple task. He could simply drop the body in the river. Even if the corpse would resurface later, it would most likely be assumed that the soldier had spent the night carousing and then wandered off and accidently fell into the river in his inebriated state, bringing about his own demise. There would be no reason to suspect any foul play. Even the head wound could be written off as having been self-inflicted, something that had happened when he fell.

There was no time to waste. It would soon be morning. This was something that needed to happen under the cover of darkness.

Joshua rolled the soldier over onto his back, partially sitting him up, and then grabbed him by the leather straps of his breastplate and dragged him across the floor in the direction of the door and the wagon in the street. Once there, he clumsily rolled the body over again so that he could hoist it onto the wagon.

This was not easy. The expression "dead weight" came to mind. But he managed to shoulder the corpse and heft it onto the cart. He was thankful that brick making had made him so strong. Samson started to bray and Joshua shushed him. He took the canvas blanket and covered the soldier's remains, and they began the rather hasty funeral march to his final watery resting place.

As they approached the river, Joshua was grateful to have seen no one or heard anything. It was as if Samson and he were the only two creatures awake in Magdala.

"Thank you, Adonai!" he whispered.

They made their way along one street and turned the corner down the avenue that wound its way along the riverbank. The moon was making everything quite bright and Joshua didn't want to take any chances so he headed in the direction of a bend in the river where he could see that the surrounding buildings cast a long shadow across the road and onto the water. They were almost there.

A lone soldier suddenly appeared out of one of the side streets.

"Hello, Jesus," he heard the familiar though not altogether friendly or welcome voice say. "What are *you* doing...here...in Magdala? And so late in the night?"

Joshua froze.

Fear now pulsating through every fiber of his being.

He hesitated.

"Hello, L-L-L-Lysias," Joshua stuttered, his mind racing for some kind of explanation. "Umm, uh...just getting a load of clay... the kind we can't get in Rakkath. It has different qualities from the stuff at home."

Joshua knew his story sounded rather lame.

And why had he drawn attention to the cart and its contents?

That was stupid, he thought.

"And you can only get it in the middle of the night?" Lysias asked rather teasingly, though definitely intrigued and maybe a lot suspicious.

Lysias made his way close to and around the back of the wagon.

Joshua attempted to stay between the soldier and the cart.

"This clay also wears a Roman sandal!" Lysias said accusingly, his voice now rising to a crescendo. "Jesus son of Abraham, what have you done?"

Lysias reached for the covering, ready to pull it back and reveal all of what it concealed.

Joshua glanced at the wagon. He could see where the blanket had shifted to reveal the soldier's foot and give him away.

There was no time to waste.

He ran directly at Lysias and, surprising him, knocked him off balance, pushing him backward into the river.

Lysias plunged into the water with a huge splash.

Somehow Joshua managed to keep himself from going in together with his accuser.

He saw Lysias at the canal's edge, sputtering and straining to right himself and then claw his way out of the stream into which he had fallen. His armor and wet clothing were making his exit quite difficult.

Knowing that his slight, albeit fleeting advantage, would not last long, Joshua turned and fled, leaving everything behind.

There was no turning back now.

Chapter 26

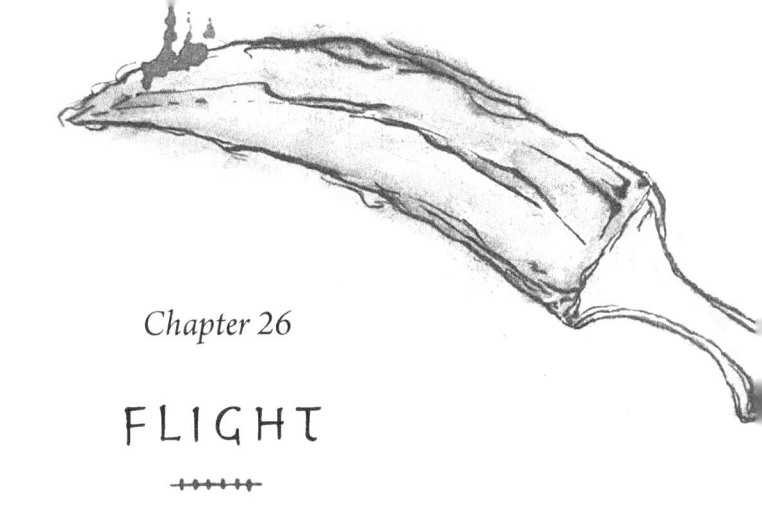

FLIGHT

As he ran in the direction of Rakkath, Joshua remembered his earlier prayer for Adonai's guidance and protection. He knew that he needed that now more than ever. But he wondered how, in any possible way, the chain of events that had been set in motion could come within the purview of His direction. Maybe it was rather mere circumstance, and evil circumstance at that, propelling him forward at this moment? Could there be a situation that was beyond Elohim's control? He knew what the theological answer was, but...? Well, what this was, he didn't know for certain right now. He only knew that he had to keep going, running toward somewhere...else.

Joshua was headed for Rakkath, even though he was keenly aware that there was no way he could remain there. His family would have enough trouble to deal with merely by their being related to him. Joshua had been found in possession of a dead soldier's body. And Rome could make up the story. He was now a *known* murderer. He had become an enemy of the Empire, a fugitive, who would most likely be on the run for the rest of his life, however long that would be, for as long as he could evade those who would pursue him.

He calculated that it would take Lysias only a little time to return to the military outpost in Magdala. And he knew that a search party would be dispatched almost immediately with orders for his arrest. They would anticipate his return to Rakkath, so he could not linger there more than a half hour or so. They would be hard on his heels.

Joshua's lungs were screaming but he willed himself to continue.

He could not stop.

Must not rest even for a second.

He had to get home.

Even if for only a few brief and precious minutes.

To explain as best he could.

To say his goodbyes.

And then to flee.

Forever…from this day forward.

He wondered if this was how Cain felt, when he was forced to flee after the murder of Abel was discovered.

Cursed.

Yes, Cain had killed out of jealousy and Joshua had killed out of justice, but wasn't the end result exactly the same?

Pursued by everyone.

Never completely safe.

Joshua arrived home just as the sun was making its entrance to the day from the east, extending its fingers across the Sea of Galilee and illuminating the waking town of Rakkath. He smelled breakfast as he entered the courtyard behind their home.

He would have to forego that.

Batiyah turned to see who was entering the gate. She smiled at the first sight of her son.

"Joshua! Welcome home…" she began.

But her demeanor instantly changed the moment she really saw him.

"Joshua! My boy. You look like...like you...I don't know what...! Did something awful happen to you?"

For a brief moment, she looked him up and down but then just held his panting and sweaty frame against her own, allowing her questions to remain unanswered for the time being, baptizing him in her own tears of joy at his safe return, whatever it was that had transpired.

Joshua struggled to catch his breath enough that he could speak. What followed came out amidst his gasps and pauses.

"Ima, something terrible *has* happened...while I was trying to prevent something far worse from happening!"

"I can't stay long."

"I surely must leave again almost immediately!"

"I fear it will not go well for all of you regardless, even if I go away. But I know that it would be absolutely horrible for all of us if I stayed!"

Zephaniah had joined the two of them, having come out of the house and into the yard.

"Joshua, *what* is going on? Why are you so long in getting home? And what's all this nonsense about having to go away?"

Joshua hesitated. He took a deep breath.

"Last night I killed a man and not just any man, I murdered a Roman soldier!" he blurted out.

Batiyah looked at her young son through eyes that held a thousand questions.

Horror filled those same eyes.

Zephaniah's jaw dropped open.

"What? Why? How?" Zephaniah asked. "Joshua, if this is some kind of joke, it is not funny at all!"

"I wish it were," Joshua said, shaking his head.

He proceeded to quickly tell them the whole story: of leaving Magdala, the wheel falling off of the cart and his having to go back.

He told of his return to the market and seeing the soldier abduct Ariah. How he had followed them and foiled his plans and then escaped with Ariah. About his return later. Realizing that the brick was there. Of his plan to get rid of the body. How Lysias had stumbled upon him at the river. And finally, how he had pushed him into the water and then fled.

"The very same Lysias that we know from the garrison here?" Zephaniah asked.

Joshua nodded and then continued.

"I know that I don't have much time. I do know that I need to go somewhere that is not here. But I couldn't just run away! I had to come home and at least let you all know what had happened, and to say goodbye. I didn't want to just disappear. I love you all so very much! I just couldn't do that to all of you!"

"Oh, and I'm very sorry about having just left Samson and the cart behind," Joshua added, mostly because he was at a loss as to what else to say.

Batiyah burst into tears. Joshua immediately hugged her but it didn't seem to help the loss that she already profoundly felt.

They all struggled to find words.

There just weren't any.

Zephaniah was still trying to figure out another way, even though he was pretty sure that there probably was none.

Joshua went and changed his clothes so he at least wouldn't match any description Lysias might include. He took a few of his other belongings and put them in a bag that he could carry over his shoulder.

Batiyah quickly found him some food to take on the road. Zephaniah gathered up a small amount of money putting it in a pouch and giving it to him, all that they had in the house at the moment.

Finally, they hastily woke the rest of the family so that they could all say their farewells.

"Joshua, where will you go?" Batiyah asked all of a sudden.

Where would he go? He hadn't really thought past *this* point. He had just been intent on getting home.

Where to indeed?

"I don't know," Joshua said flatly.

"I hadn't…"

Batiyah thought for a minute.

"You could, you should go to Gamala," she said. "It is far enough away. I have family there. At least I think I might. They may still be alive. You can ask after them when you get there."

Tears filled Batiyah's eyes as memories of a time not so long past came flooding back.

Joshua wondered about the manner in which Batiyah had just mentioned her family.

They *may* still be alive?

He remembered again that they had somehow never returned to his questions about her family on that night many months ago now.

He was feeling the loss of his own family already.

Joshua realized he was actually leaving home.

Right now…

…and maybe forever.

"His name is Jonas ben Haggai," Batiyah said. "He is my uncle and my adoptive father. I pray that you find him, Joshua. Please send word when you can, as soon as you can, if you can. And may Adonai Elohim, the El Shaddai, go with you!"

"And remain with all of you!" Joshua replied.

Everyone was a tearful mess. Elijah, Sarah, and Seth were beside themselves, having little or no idea what was happening. They just knew it was sad. Batiyah and Zephaniah could fill them in later.

"How do I get there?" Joshua asked.

"Just go north and then turn east after you clear the Sea," Zephaniah said. "And avoid the cities!"

Joshua hugged them all once more and disappeared into the night.

Alone, completely and utterly, alone.

As he ran, he tried to dry his tears and to calm his heaving body. He was certainly grieving the loss of his family, but he now realized and was almost overcome by the knowledge that life, his life, would never be the same again.

Destiny had taken over.

Or was it fate?

It certainly felt fatal.

Joshua cursed the Empire and all things Roman.

He watched Rakkath disappear behind him, grateful that the garrison was to the southwest of them and that he didn't have to pass it on his escape. His journey north, however, meant that he would have to go back past Magdala. That was equally unfortunate, but that being the reality, he made sure to choose a route that took him on a path far to the west of the city and away from the roadway.

He was thankful, in a way at least, that it was now daylight. It would make travelling easier though it also made it more precarious in that he could more easily be seen. He wondered how long it would take them to send out search parties. They would most certainly pay a visit to his former home shortly. And although he knew that his family wouldn't intentionally give anything away, he wondered what clues the soldiers would pick up on. They were trained in the art of interrogation. Even without clues, they could send search parties in all directions, some of them even mounted on horseback. Would they use dogs to sniff him out? Almost assuredly.

So, as he made his way north, after he had cleared the city of Magdala, his strategy was to keep fairly close to the shoreline and to stay on rocky ground as much as possible so he didn't make any visible tracks to follow. Then also from time to time, to plunge himself into the Sea and walk in the shallow water. The loss of his trail would at least slow his pursuers down. The water was refreshing, and he could scoop some into his mouth as he struggled against it. His lungs and his legs were screaming at him. Joshua simply commanded them to be quiet. Where the beach was sandy, he would head for the cover of the trees so that he wouldn't leave such noticeable footprints and couldn't be as easily spotted.

Thankfully, for whatever reason, his journey had been fairly free of other travelers. Not many people were on the road today. Not that he had been much on the road, in fact, he was purposely avoiding it, but he could often see it and at least hear when others passed by. He would hear them approaching and conceal himself at some vantage point until they were gone. It definitely slowed his progress but he knew that caution and speed needed to work together as best they could.

As he approached the town of Capernaum, about ten miles north of Rakkath, he decided to go further inland again, heading roughly in the direction of the town of Chorazin. There were far fewer people on this route and less likelihood that he would be spotted. He didn't want any southbound travelers notifying the soldiers of his whereabouts when they would eventually meet them on the road. He knew the soldiers would be asking everyone they met if they had seen anyone, asking everyone they met, if they had seen him.

Joshua carried on this way for the entire day and into the first night. He was grateful now for how hard they had had to work to fulfill the order for the garrison. It had actually built the stamina and strength in him that now allowed him to press on. Ironic indeed that the very garrison that had brought life to their struggling family was presently dead set on taking his life away.

Joshua knew that he had to keep going this way for at least a couple of days. After that, two things would happen. He would be farther away from his pursuers, at least from where they had started. The farther out he was, the more difficult he would be to find. And after two days he suspected, they would realize that continued searching would become more and more futile. It would be increasingly like looking for the proverbial needle in a haystack. They would then call off the search and simply put out a warrant, hoping that somewhere, somehow, they would stumble across him, or that he, Joshua, would himself do something careless and get caught. He hoped that would never happen. But…

…Even though the wheels of justice turn rather slowly, they always do turn.

And Roman eyes and ears, he knew only too well, were everywhere.

Chapter 27

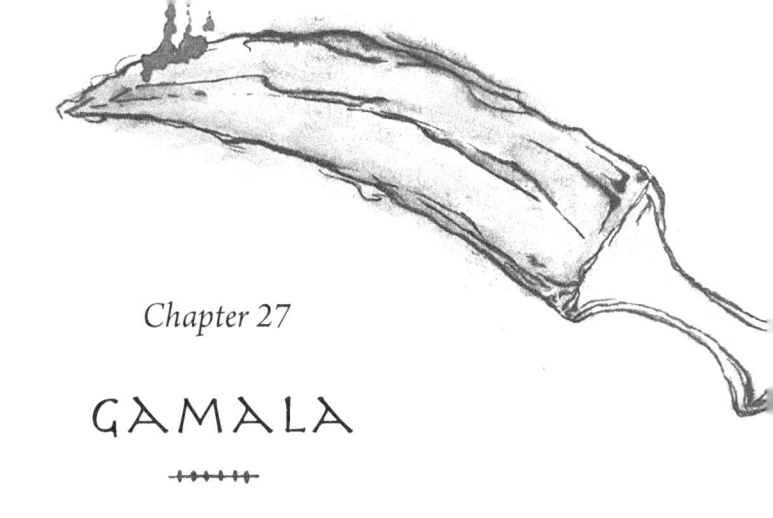

GAMALA

Joshua kept to the west of Chorazin continuing to make his way north. Progress was somewhat slowed since leaving the vicinity of the Sea of Galilee as the terrain turned more and more rugged the further north he went.

Once he had cleared the city of Chorazin, he finally felt it was safe to turn east and make his way toward the upper Jordan River. He now knew that he had to be extra cautious though, not just to remain unseen by the Romans, but also so as not stumble across bandits who liked to hide along these roads in the hills and valleys.

He felt less open to danger in a way though since he was not really using the roads, and jokingly contemplated that he was now an outlaw himself and so, need not fear other outlaws. If he was honest with himself, he had been permanently afraid this entire journey. He longed for Gamala and even a semblance of peace and safety.

He was still just a young boy, somewhat lost and definitely alone. Far too early in life to be on the run for murder. Where was life taking him? North, and then east after Galilee was all he knew.

Since passing to the west and then north of Chorazin, Joshua had been traversing the deserted hills of northern Galilee and had not seen or even heard a single other soul. He reached the Jordan just as it was getting dark on his second day. He continued north along the river until he came to a shallow part. It was wider here but he might be able to walk across. He did have to swim through some of it in the middle but managed to make his way safely to the other side. The water was refreshing and invigorating. He continued walking for a while as the moon now made its appearance over the horizon ahead of him.

He suddenly realized how tired he was. Two days of constant fear had been exhausting. Add to that the rigors of cross-country travel, and he was totally fatigued, inside and out. Was it safe to sleep now, even for a little while? He knew that he was far north of the road that went east to west around the northern side of the Sea of Galilee, and north even of the road that went east from Chorazin.

"Watch over me as I sleep, Adonai Elohim," he prayed and quickly succumbed to what he felt. It didn't matter that his clothing was still a bit damp. The evening was warm enough.

He drifted off to sleep.

Somewhere in the middle of the night, for it was still dark, Joshua awoke with a start.

He was being prodded rather roughly from behind.

He whirled around to face his attacker, drawing the knife that he had concealed in the belt of his cloak. He yelled and lunged forward, his voice annihilating the silence.

A small fox sprang back and immediately darted away. Joshua found his breath again...and then began to laugh.

There was nothing to fear.

At least not from this little fox.

Adrenaline now coursed through his veins and he was wide-awake. He knew there would be no more sleep this night. But he actually felt quite rested and realized that while it had only been for a short time, he had nevertheless slept like he had seldom if ever slept before. An answer to his prayer.

"Thank you, Adonai! For watching over me," he whispered, getting his bearings in the moonlight. "And for waking me to continue!"

Joshua now made his way south along the east bank of the Jordan River, finally turning east to head in the direction of Gamala when he came within sight of the Sea of Galilee. He tried as much as possible to stay off the road, but nevertheless followed it a little more closely since he knew only that Gamala was on the northern road running east of the Sea of Galilee.

He knew now that he didn't have far to go and could hardly wait to get there. Running for his very life, Joshua had not given much thought to his actual destination. But now, with the end of his journey almost in sight, he finally allowed himself this luxury.

Who was this Jonas ben Haggai, he wondered? He was his mother's uncle, but she had referred to him as her "adoptive father." What did that mean? Had they been close when she was growing up?

And what of his mother's own family? They were from here. Would he finally get to meet them? Why hadn't Batiyah said anything about them growing up? Even when Joshua had asked, granted not at the best of times, she had simply said that it was a long and involved story.

And then, in the early hours of the morning when he had fled, she had said that maybe they were alive? Did she mean her family, or Uncle Jonas?

What if...? What then?

Almost immediately, a parallel thought invaded.

Gamala. He was going to Gamala. That was where Simeon and Jacob were from! He could...find them? Spend more time with them?

Joshua broke into a run without even realizing it. And, within minutes it seemed, the town of Gamala spread out in front of him. He slowed and smiled, remembering the prayer he had prayed long ago:

"Lead me into my destiny, Adonai, into all of it."

Fueled by all of his unknowns, and by all of his imaginations, Joshua made his way into the small town, encouraged immediately by the fact that he noticed almost no Roman presence here.

No symbols of Roman power.

No soldiers.

Would he be safe here?

Could he live here without trouble?

Time would tell.

People had certainly noticed his presence but seemed to pay no special attention to him.

He was grateful.

As he made his way to the center of town, Joshua felt as though this place was somehow very familiar, maybe similar to the way that Rakkath had been, before…

When he saw a quorum of Jewish men sitting together in the town square, something that you were sure to find in any Israelite settlement, he respectfully approached them, waiting until there was an opportunity to make his request. It didn't take long.

They all turned to look at the newcomer.

Inviting him to speak.

"Shalom, fathers. I am Joshua ben Abrahim and I am looking for Jonas ben Haggai."

"Does he still live…here?"

"He does," said one of the older men. "Are you by chance a relative?"

"He is my ima's uncle," Joshua replied.

"Batiyah?" one of them asked rather tentatively, or so it seemed to Joshua.

"Yes," said Joshua.

A noticeable hush immediately descended on the gathered crowd.

They all just looked at him.

Were they sizing *him* up? This relative stranger?

"Jonas is a relation of mine as well," a younger man finally said, breaking the tension. "I would be pleased to take you there whenever you are ready."

Joshua did wonder what the mention of his mother's name had in fact engendered, what it was that hadn't been said, but passed it off as the stuff of future exploration.

He was anxious to complete his journey.

"That would be wonderful. Thank you," he replied.

"Can we go, now?" Joshua asked, impatiently.

The end was in sight.

"For sure," the young man said, rising from his seat.

"By the way, I am Eliazer ben Naphtali. Pleased to make your acquaintance, Joshua ben Abraham."

And with that, the two of them set off through the town, he assumed, in the direction of his great-uncle Jonas's house.

Conversation was relatively easy and it took only a few minutes for them to make their way, just long enough for Joshua to find out that Eliazer's father, Naphtali, was a son of his uncle Jonas's cousin, Solomon, making he and Eliazer fourth cousins, or something like that.

"At home we have a donkey named Solomon!" Joshua said.

The two of them laughed at that.

Though the mention of Solomon and home did tug at Joshua's heart just a little.

As they rounded a corner Eliazer announced, "Well Joshua, here we are!"

He knocked loudly on the gate and they entered the small courtyard.

A short elderly woman with a kind face greeted them, motioning them to enter.

"Shalom, Eliazer, always nice to see you. And who is the friend you have brought to our home?"

She called her husband's name, and he peeked around the corner of the house.

"Come over here, Jonas, we have visitors. Eliazer and uh...what did you say your friend's name was?"

"I didn't say yet!" Eliazer replied.

"Oh yes, silly me," she said, chuckling to herself.

Jonas slowly made his way over to the small group now gathered in his yard.

"Uncle Jonas and Aunt Anna," Eliazer announced, "this is Joshua, son of Abrahim and Batiyah."

The two of them almost simultaneously sucked in their breath, but immediately moved as quickly as their bodies would allow, to embrace Joshua, tears streaming down their faces.

Joshua was a little taken aback but allowed himself to be swallowed up in their warm, and emotionally charged greeting. What else could he do?

"So wonderful to meet you, Joshua. You are certainly welcome here for as long as you like. Our home is your home. You are family!"

Joshua thought it interesting indeed that they had *adopted* him too, having just barely met him. He *was* actually family, he thought to himself, but this must be what Batiyah had meant.

They were certainly inclusive and welcoming.

"You look like the journey has been a long and tedious one," Anna said. "How far have you come?"

"From Rakkath where we live...well, truthfully, from Magdala," Joshua said, correcting himself.

Anna looked shocked.

"That is only a two-day journey!" Jonas said, his own shock evident in his words. "My dear boy, did you run into bandits on the way?"

Given their reaction, Joshua wondered what he actually looked like!

He was about to start, not really sure of how much he should tell these people whom he had just met. Jonas waved him off.

"Later. You can tell us later, Joshua. All in time. Anna, can you please prepare us something to eat? I believe that we should kill the calf. Joshua, you must be starving. Do you have any clean clothes? I could maybe find you something if you don't."

"Stay there, I'll be right back," Jonas said.

"I do have a clean robe in my travel bag, thank you," Joshua called out as Jonas was walking away. He was convinced that the old man had not heard.

At this point, Eliazer excused himself saying that he still had things to do, adding that the day was not getting any longer.

"Shalom, cousin Joshua," he said as he turned. "It was really very wonderful to make your acquaintance. Hopefully we will meet again?"

"Shalom...cousin Eliazer. Yes, I trust we will meet again soon, and thank you, for all your help," Joshua replied.

Eliazer left. Anna went to start on food for later. Jonas was already gone to get clothes, Joshua supposed.

He was left alone in the yard for a brief moment.

Jonas returned shortly, not with any clothes, but rather with a bowl of warm water and a towel. Without a word, he bent down and began to unlace Joshua's sandals. Joshua opened his mouth to protest. But Jonas simply raised his hand motioning him to be silent.

Joshua did not know what to do. Washing feet was servant's work, reserved for the lowest person in the household, not the master of the house. At the very least, it was for young people to do for their elders, not the other way around.

Joshua tried to protest again. Jonas simply raised his wet hand and Joshua was forced to relent out of respect for his elder.

After a minute or so, the old man paused.

When he spoke, he did so with deliberate intent.

"Jehoshua, son of Batiyah…and Abraham, I am honored to have you in my house," he said with tears in his aged eyes. "Allow me to serve you in this way. It is the least that I could do for you…and for those from whom you have come. May Adonai Elohim bless you both now and always!"

Soft tears now found their way down Joshua's face as Jonas gently washed his tired and dirty feet, massaging them with his twisted hands. It was wonderful and humiliating and uncomfortable, stirring up all kinds of other feelings that he didn't even have a name for. This was so strange.

What was the meaning of all of this, he wondered?

Jonas took the towel and carefully dried Joshua's feet. As he finished, he looked up into the young man's questioning face. Joshua tried to get a read on what Jonas was saying without his saying anything at all.

It was like gazing into the deep.

Finally, Jonas spoke again.

"Why don't you go into the house and change your clothes. Rest for a while from your journey. You must be very tired. I will come and wake you when the evening meal is ready."

"We have *much* to talk about."

Chapter 28

CONNECTION

Joshua did as he was told but he definitely could not sleep. At least not right away.

His mind simply would not let him. Still, it did feel good to just lay back and close his eyes.

"We have much to talk about," his uncle had said.

If Jonas had not been smiling when he said this, Joshua would have been very worried.

Now he was just perplexed. And intrigued. And maybe a little bit anxious.

Would this be a place of more answers?

Then, there had been the way that the elders in the town square had reacted when they discovered that he was the son of Batiyah.

Why had they responded like that?

Jonas and Anna's initial reaction had shocked him as well: their tears and the honor that they bestowed on him. The embrace. Then, having his feet washed by his uncle Jonas and hearing the words of the blessing that was spoken over him.

He knew almost nothing of this part of his family. But here they were. And at first glance they seemed pretty amazing. Why had they never had any contact with them? Why had Batiyah never said anything about any of them?

And what about his ima's parents? Did she have any brothers and sisters? Were there cousins? Ones more closely related than Eliazer? Would he soon meet them too? What were they like, he wondered?

All of these questions raised even more in Joshua's mind.

Jonas had said there was much to tell.

Joshua could hardly wait for the evening meal.

How was he supposed to sleep?

At some point, which probably felt longer than it actually was, his fatigue did overwhelm his restless mind, and he drifted off to sleep.

A very deep sleep indeed.

Joshua woke with a start as Jonas shook him.

He sprang to his feet and the elder stumbled backward, cowering and raising his hands to defend himself.

Fortunately, Joshua realized just in time that he was standing there ready to unload a round of blows on a fragile old man.

He let his hands fall to his side, embarrassed.

"Sorry, Uncle. I..." Joshua began apologetically.

"Not to worry," Jonas said.

"I should have known better."

"The meal is ready!"

Jonas wouldn't have had to tell him. It was impossible to miss. Amazing smells permeated every part of the yard and house.

Joshua ran his fingers through his hair and straightened his robe and they moved themselves to sit at the table.

Immediately, Anna brought steaming hot veal seasoned with a mix of thyme, salt, sumac, and sesame seeds, as well as bowls of saffron rice, and a mix of leeks, onions, and fennel, seasoned with garlic and cilantro. There was fresh bread as well, wrapped in towels and still warm from the oven.

Joshua sat and just breathed it all in.

He felt like royalty.

But that just raised even more questions.

Why such special treatment?

Other than the blessing, they ate the first part of the meal in virtual silence. Joshua wanted to ask but didn't want to be impolite.

The phrase, "All in time," came tumbling into his mind and he smiled.

Jonas had said that very thing earlier and was most likely waiting until they were done eating. Besides, the meal was amazing. It would have been a shame not to at least give it all the attention that it deserved.

"Thank you so much for welcoming me into your home and for inviting me to such a splendid table," Joshua said as it became apparent that they had all had enough. "You honor me. And I give this house my blessing. That was delicious!"

"Thank you, Joshua. You are so very welcome," Anna said. "It is our privilege really!"

Jonas paused and took a long, slow breath, pushing himself back slightly from the meal spread in front of them.

"Let's see. Are you ready, Joshua? Hmmm, where do I start?"

He paused again.

"Actually, Joshua, why don't you first tell us how *you* came to Gamala? And to us? What course of events led you here? And please, what *did* happen on the way?"

The last thing that Joshua wanted to do at this moment was rehearse things with which *he* was already familiar. He rather wanted Jonas to share with him all of Batiyah's history, his own unknown history, which had forever been shrouded in mystery.

He supposed however that they were desperate to know more about him too. They were being polite, letting him go first. And really, what difference would a few more minutes make?

He would make the story as short as he could.

That way Jonas could get on with the *very much* he had to tell.

"Well, my father, Abraham, is...or rather, *was* a brick maker in Rakkath. He died about a year ago," Joshua began.

"That is so very sad. We loved your father!" Jonas said, tears welling up in his eyes.

"But Batiyah is well?"

"Yes, I believe so, although father's death has certainly taken a toll on her, on all of us."

The old man's tears brought tears to Joshua's eyes.

"Don't interrupt, Jonas," Anna said. "Just let him tell his story."

Joshua wiped his own eyes and continued.

"So, yes, a brick maker. He learned the trade in Bethlehem from a distant relative, Enoch, although they actually weren't there very long. They moved back to Rakkath shortly after my older brother, Zephaniah, was born. I was born three years later. I had an ordinary childhood I guess and we have a great family. And besides Zephaniah, I have a younger brother, Elijah, a sister, Sarah, and then the youngest is my brother, Seth."

Joshua realized that if he kept going this way, his story would take a very long time and they would never get to what *he* really wanted to hear. He determined to abbreviate the story as much as he could.

"My best friend growing up was Caleb ben Zadok. His family now lives in Magdala, and they have a fish salting and drying business. My father Abrahim over the years came up with all kinds of interesting 'recipes' and I was delivering a load of special bricks for use in their brining pools that would better stand up to the salt."

"On my way home from delivering a load of these bricks, the wheel fell off of the wagon, and I had to return to Magdala to get it fixed. Fortunately, I had not gone very far. It took the better part of the day, however, and I decided on my return to revisit the market where Caleb's sister, Ariah, was selling their family's fish."

"It was a providential thing I did too, I guess, for I returned just as a Roman soldier abducted her with obvious evil intent. And, as one thing leads to another, I accidentally…on purpose killed him."

Joshua scanned his audience for their reaction.

Both Jonas and Anna just sat there listening, wide-eyed, engaged, and waiting for more.

He marveled that it seemed so easy to tell these people whom he had just met something that was really quite horrific. Without a second thought, he had just trusted them. Then too, he hadn't hesitated telling them a story, within the details of which he openly confessed to being a murderer. He wondered if they now questioned their decision to open their home to him so quickly, but he sensed no apprehension on their part. That piece of the story did not seem to bother either of them in the least.

He must have hesitated, for they now encouraged him to continue.

"I took Ariah back to her family. Then went back to the market to look for Caleb and Zadok who had gone out to look for her. I found them but realized that I should not go back home with them. Zadok was sure that someone had probably seen me, and we all decided it was in my best interest to flee, at least for the time being."

"I also realized that the brick that I had used to kill the soldier had our family's imprint on it and returned to retrieve it. When I found myself back at the scene of the crime, I thought that maybe I could just dispose of the body and make this soldier's death look like an…"

Joshua stopped mid-sentence, slack-jawed in the shocking realization that he had tried to do the very same thing that four Roman soldiers had done to his father some time ago, make a murder look like an accident.

He shook his head and told himself that the two things were not at all the same, but it visibly rattled him.

He took a moment to catch his breath.

"Carry on," he told himself.

Jonas and Anna just waited patiently.

"...an accident. I had abandoned everything when I went to rescue Ariah initially, but when I returned, I providentially stumbled across our donkey, Samson, and the cart which had been repaired. I loaded the body onto the cart, carefully covered it with the blanket which we soak with water to keep the clay from drying out, and headed for the city canal to dispose of his remains."

"All would have gone according to plan except for the fact that Lysias, a soldier who I knew from delivering bricks to the garrison the Romans recently built southwest of Rakkath, appeared, doing night rounds I suppose. I don't really know why he was there. I thought I had been very careful to conceal the body, but he noticed a Roman sandal protruding from under the blanket. The body must have shifted in transit. I was sure he was about to arrest me. But I caught him by surprise, pushed him into the water and then fled the scene before he could recover."

"I made my way quickly back to Rakkath. To say goodbye to my family and also to decide where I would escape. Ima suggested here, unsure of whether you were even alive. But..."

Joshua hesitated.

"Knowing this, if you would rather I not stay, for your own safety, I will understand and move on. Not sure where exactly, but I would not want any harm to come to you. You have been more than welcoming and I appreciate everything that you have done...already!"

"Nonsense, Joshua, we are not afraid," Jonas said definitively.

"Do you think it is safe here, in Gamala?"

"Oh, and does my ima, Batiyah, have immediate family here? Her father and mother? Do you know where *they* are?" Joshua asked.

Jonas took a deep breath.

"Your last few days are quite a tale, young Joshua."

"It makes what I have to tell so much more..."

Jonas left the sentence incomplete.

Just let the words hang.

Anna had quietly disappeared and now returned with cups of tea for the three of them.

Jonas looked at her, and she returned his gaze.

"Yes, Jonas, you must...tell *all*," she said. "He really needs to know. Deserves to know. It will bring everything together."

"'All in time,' you always say?"

"Well, that time is now!"

All in time?

There was that phrase again. Joshua made a mental note to ask Jonas why *he* always said that. He wondered to himself why he had never asked his father why it was *his* favorite thing to say?

Chapter 29

HARBOR

Jonas began.

"Your story does not surprise us in the least, Joshua. It makes perfect sense. In fact, it fits hand in glove with what I am about to tell you. You have both a history and a destiny. Everyone is anchored somewhere and from there they lift anchor and sail. That place, *your harbor,* in a way I believe, is here!"

"Joshua, my son, have you ever, or always, wondered where you belonged, wondered what it was that Elohim had for you to do? Felt that there was something more...somewhere?"

Joshua nodded, his eyes widening. He felt as though his uncle Jonas was walking straight into some secret place inside of him, reading his thoughts and speaking directly to his heart. Like he somehow knew him like no one else other than Adonai Himself ever did.

"How much has Batiyah told you about her family? About growing up here in Gamala?" Jonas asked changing the focus slightly.

"Nothing," Joshua said. "Well, no, that's not true. I know nothing at all other than that she was from here. I guess I just grew up thinking that was normal. That a woman leaves her family behind to be part of her husband's?"

"I did ask her about it, I guess, not that long ago, but it was already very late in the evening and so she said that we would save that revelation for another day," Joshua said, remembering. "We never finished that conversation."

"So, you know pretty much nothing?" Jonas asked.

Joshua shook his head.

He had wanted to ask her again, but never did.

"Hmmm...interesting. But then again, not surprising," Jonas added, speaking more to himself than anyone in particular.

"She must have just blocked it all from her memory, or it was just too painful even to talk about," Anna said.

Joshua saw that her eyes were filled with tears.

Jonas turned his attention back to Joshua.

"Well, you asked about your mother's family..."

"They are no longer here..."

Joshua could not hide his disappointment.

Jonas took a slow deep breath.

He shook his head and forced his own emotions down. Some difficult place was obviously his destination.

"They are gone. Dead. My brother—your mother's father, who would be *your* grandfather, Gideon—was murdered by the Romans. The whole family in fact! Your grandma, Marion, and your ima's two brothers, Micah and Jeremiah, all of them were killed in the courtyard of their own home right here in Gamala!"

"We are pretty sure that the soldiers did horrible things to your mother too and then left her for dead! Batiyah couldn't remember or at least she couldn't tell us anything. That she survived was a miracle!"

"They obviously had assumed she was dead too, but she was not. Barely alive is still alive! And when she did regain consciousness, the first thing to greet her little eyes was the sight of her entire family, murdered and left to decay in the hot sun! Severely sunburnt and in immense pain from the ill treatment she had received, your mother was in severe shock. Somehow she made it to our place."

"For quite a while, we thought she might not make it. Her little body was physically ravaged, but even more so, she was emotionally scarred. She did have an amazing will to live, but we know for certain that it was only by the *hesed,* the grace and loving kindness of Ha Shem, that she actually did survive!"

"We were never able to have children of our own, but now, grateful to Elohim for this gift, we raised your mother just as if she were ours. It was as if Adonai had seen fit to lift our curse with this blessing. And miraculously, the evidence of His unceasing grace in her life, she grew to be a wonderful and sweet young lady, albeit with an extremely strong sense of right and justice. She had been aptly named, *Batiyah,* 'daughter of Ha Shem.'"

Jonas paused.

Joshua was holding his hand over his mouth, eyes wide.

"I'm sorry, son, if this is too much. I can..."

Tears were trickling down Joshua's face. But he was barely aware of their presence.

How was he so wonderfully blessed to have this woman as his ima? She was obviously even more amazing than he had ever thought. And he was proud to stand in her history, painful as it was.

This just confirmed what he had always known somewhere, that there was much more to her than met the eye, that Batiyah was a warrior.

Jonas shifted the conversation in another direction.

"What do you know of the movement they call the Fourth Way?" he now asked.

Joshua stopped short, snapping back to the present.

"A little bit. Some," he said slowly, wondering where this was going. "Why do you ask?"

"It is important to the next part of the story."

"Your father and mother met here in Gamala because your father, Abrahim, had come to find out more about the Qanaim. He was very sympathetic to the goals and ideals of the movement. Most likely he would have joined. That he did not in the end was because of Batiyah."

Joshua's mouth hung open, questions and thoughts now tumbling over each other and all over the place.

Jonas continued.

"I myself was, well, still am a member, though not very active anymore," he said flatly.

Joshua's face revealed his shock at this additional revelation, his mind struggling to put everything together.

"My brother, your mother's father, Gideon, had also been a prominent member, in fact, one of its leaders, and we are sure that it was because of this that their entire family was killed. Being part of a rebel movement clearly has a cost attached to it. It has certainly cost our family dearly. Your family!"

"When I shared her story with Abrahim, he made the decision *not* to join. He felt that as much as he was in sympathy with those who were zealous for Israel, he loved Batiyah far too much to put her anywhere close to all of that horror again. He chose to remove her from the fray of battle. He wanted to give her what she had never had growing up. For her to truly experience Shalom!"

"My father was here and was actually going to join the Fourth Way?" Joshua asked, even though Jonas had just told him just as much.

"Yes...he was! I can't deny the fact that we were disappointed in his choice not to. We would have loved to have him be part of what we believed Elohim wanted to do. But on the positive side, when Abrahim showed himself to be so caring and considerate of Batiyah, Anna and I had no hesitation blessing his decision. We simply knew that we could trust him to take care of her and always have her best interests at heart. She needed a special man to understand her, and we felt that your father was the man that Elohim had chosen to do just that. We knew that she would respond to his affection and care for him too."

"And so, betrothed to this man, she left Gamala and everything that she had ever known behind and went with Abraham to Rakkath where they were married."

Joshua just sat there shaking his head, trying to let the gravity of it all sink in. Everything made so much sense now. It was as if the windows of his understanding had opened wide.

Suddenly another thought presented itself.

"So, that's how my father Abrahim knew Simeon and Jacob? From before? From when he was here as a young man?" Joshua asked.

"Well, they would have been very young at that point, but yes," Jonas said.

With everything that had been happening lately, Joshua had not given the two brothers more than a passing thought.

"By the way, did you know that *they* are your relatives, Joshua?" Jonas said. "Simeon and Jacob. Their father Judah is, ah...was, my cousin."

One more revelation.

And something even more significant now impressed itself upon Joshua's young mind—that the Fourth Way was most assuredly tied to whatever sense of destiny he had felt.

Was he on the verge of walking into *it*?

He had told himself that being in Gamala might make it possible for him to truly discover what the Qanaim was about. He had thought he could reconnect with the brothers and discover more. Surely now that fate or providence had brought him here, that could be rather easily accomplished. And then too, now, there was his uncle Jonas, who was most assuredly a wealth of information about the movement.

This was all getting very exciting.

Batiyah's story just added fuel to the fire.

"How do you know Simeon and Jacob?" Jonas asked.

"Well, I met them initially some time shortly after father was murdered by the Romans. Then I later spent some time with Jacob alone once on my way from Magdala to Rakkath. And I was hoping I might see them again while I am here," Joshua said, feeling the freedom to hold nothing back and to make his intentions clearly known.

"Your father was murdered?" Jonas asked, focusing in on one part of what Joshua had just shared.

"Yes," Joshua replied rather quietly but without hesitation. "The Romans considered him a *Zealot*."

Jonas shook his head.

Anna was sobbing.

"There is clearly a cost. So much cost!" Jonas said. "This was exactly what he tried to spare her from. Oh, I feel so sorry for Batiyah. She has been through so much more than anyone should. Her entire family and now her husband, murdered."

"She doesn't know that it was murder," Joshua said, hesitating.

"No one knows. Except my brother Zephaniah and Simeon and Jacob...and now you," he added.

"She doesn't know?" Jonas asked in disbelief. "Oh dear! How is it that she doesn't know?"

"No one would know, if I hadn't seen them do it," Joshua said. "They made it look like an accident. And the soldiers threatened me and told me that they would kill me too if I told anyone."

"Oh, my poor boy! It would seem that you too have been through much more than someone your age should!" Anna exclaimed. She reached her hand to take Joshua's.

Joshua was convinced that she had experienced more than her fair share of pain.

"Actually, I wasn't the only one who had seen what the soldiers had done. I found out later that Simeon and Jacob also knew, that they too, or at least one of them had actually seen what happened. They told me so when they came back for the bricks," Joshua added, remembering.

"Bricks?" Jonas asked, intrigued. "What bricks?"

He waited for Joshua's response.

"The bricks that soaked up Abba's blood," Joshua said slowly. "For the monument to the martyrs."

"You know about the monument?" Jonas asked.

Joshua nodded.

Jonas smiled.

"We could go see it if you like," he said.

For maybe the thousandth time even just today it seemed Joshua couldn't believe what he was hearing.

Life had taken a turn but no longer was anything even remotely predictable or mundane.

Joshua had been attracted to the Qanaim.

That now made even more sense.

His father had been in sympathy with the movement.

Was even on the verge of joining.

His mother had grown up in it.

All of these people were his kin.

Zealous for Israel.

Related by blood.

Connected by the blood in their veins.

And the blood that had been spilled.

"Can we go now, or very soon?" Joshua asked, the anticipation already building.

"First thing tomorrow!" Jonas replied. "Now is probably the time for sleep. It has been a long, full day!"

For the second night in a row, Joshua didn't know if he would be able to sleep.

Long, full day was an understatement to be sure.

Anna showed him to his bed.

"Shalom, Joshua."

"Shalom, Aunt Anna. And thank you, for everything!"

Joshua tried to think it all through. He wanted to put it all together, to make sense of everything.

He tried...

...but within minutes, exhaustion took him prisoner.

Chapter 30

Martyrs Monument

Joshua awoke with a start, terror crashing over him like waves on the seashore in the midst of a storm.

But, quickly surveying his surroundings, he now realized with instant relief where he actually was.

Safe in Jonas and Anna's house.

No one was pursuing him. At the very least, they had not caught up with him yet.

He must have been dreaming something, dreaming that he was still fleeing, though he could not call to mind the content of the dream.

His breathing slowed.

He did not have to run today.

The sun was already well up in the sky.

How long had he slept?

He felt rested.

Refreshed.

Renewed.

Was this shalom? He wasn't sure yet. Maybe it was or maybe not. But so much seemed to make sense.

It was as if he made sense to himself, all of the things that he had thought and wondered and felt. Would this be the place of even more answers to all of his questions? Maybe.

Uncle Jonas had called it his "harbor."

And then, suddenly, Joshua remembered.

The monument!

Jonas had said that they could go today.

He would get to see what until now he had only imagined. He sprang out of bed, getting himself ready.

In the meantime, his thoughts raced back to all of the other revelations of yesterday.

About his mother's family. His grandfather. About Batiyah herself. And then, about his own father. And their marriage. All of these things he never knew before but that had now been brought to light.

His connection to the Qanaim. And that Simeon and Jacob were his relatives too. How was that for interesting?

Had Batiyah known that all of this would become clear when she suggested that he come here?

Possibly. Who knew?

Joshua wondered whether ultimately, this *would* be the place where he could walk into the destiny that the Almighty had for him?

All in time? Yes, but that time seemed to be now.

He needed to get going. There was not a minute to waste. How many had passed already?

He quickly dressed and made his way into the yard. Anna and Jonas were sitting and talking quietly to each other. Were they praying together? They smiled as they saw him approach. Anna passed him some bread and cheese, eggs and fruit, and a cup of water.

"Aren't you a sleepyhead?" Jonas said jokingly.

"Sorry," Joshua said, "I don't know what came over me. I hope you weren't waiting too long."

"Nonsense," Jonas said, "You were exhausted. Rest is a gift from Adonai, a gift you most desperately needed."

"And besides, we are old. What else do we have to do but wait?"

"Have a little nourishment," Anna said, "and then the two of you can make your way to the monument."

"Is it far?" Joshua asked.

"No, not too far," Jonas said with a grin. "This old man can still make it there without too much trouble!"

Joshua ate, more quickly than normal, thanked Elohim and Anna for the food, and then the two men set out on their journey.

"Shall we take anything for the road?" Joshua asked.

"No, I think we'll be just fine," Jonas replied, grinning.

And with that they walked out of the gate and across the lane, entering the yard directly behind them.

There in the center of the courtyard they entered was a semi-circular wall of bricks and stones of all sorts, somewhat haphazard in its arrangement, tapering inward from bottom to top, each one engraved with a name.

Joshua stood at a short distance for a moment, admiring it.

He was unaware that Jonas had busied himself searching for his father's bricks. He returned to Joshua's side, gently putting his hand on his back and then directing his attention to a section near the top of the wall, just to the right of where Joshua had been standing.

"Do you see them, Joshua? Right here." Jonas said.

Joshua moved in the direction of the bricks Jonas had pointed to, reached out and let his hand run over their familiar surface, now part of a much larger story. He could see the variations of light and dark, the color of the bricks and the stain where they had embraced the life of his abba. They had been varnished so that the weather wouldn't steal away the life that had been sown into them. All the bricks and stones had been similarly treated.

"Abrahim ben Jehudah," he read.

Tears made their way down his cheeks.

And he felt sad, at his own loss, but indeed sad for everyone whose lives had been stolen away and whose memory was treasured in this monument. The pain represented here was almost too much to absorb.

At the same time however, in a way that he could not have described if he had tried, Jehoshua ben Abraham felt emboldened, felt intense passion rising up in him. He just knew that *he* must make sure that the sacrifices of all of these people, his own family included, would not be in vain. All of these deaths needed to mean something, they demanded avenging. They demanded justice.

"How dare they insult the army, the people, of *Elohim Hayyim,* 'the Living God'!" he said aloud, growling now from somewhere deep inside.

He wandered around the wall, lost in his thoughts. And Jonas just left him to it.

"Joshua," Jonas finally interrupted after a time. "Do you know where you are?"

"No," Joshua replied. "What do you mean? I am standing in front of the monument to the martyrs."

"Do you find it strange that it was so close? That it is in this yard right next to mine?" Jonas said, just letting the questions hang.

Suddenly it all came clear to Joshua.

"This is...!"

Jonas nodded.

"This is the very yard where *they* were murdered? And the exact place where my own mother was mistreated and left for dead?" Joshua said very quietly, his own roots obviously now deeply planted in this sacred space.

His knees went weak and he slumped to the ground.

"There is something else I want you to see," Jonas said after another long while, directing Joshua's attention to several stones right near the base of the monument.

"Here, Joshua, are the stones from Batiyah's, from your very own family, stones lifted from this very yard."

Joshua saw the names, carefully engraved:

"Gideon ben Haggai."

"Marion, *ishah,* wife of, Gideon ben Haggai."

"Micah ben Gideon."

"Jeremiah ben Gideon."

He touched them. Let his hand linger and run over their rough surface and the letters engraved in them. These were his grandparents and his uncles, Batiyah's family. People he didn't know, who he didn't even know existed until yesterday.

They were his people.

If only he had known them.

Jonas put his hand on his shoulder for a moment and then quietly exited, leaving Joshua to himself.

Another stone with his mother's name might have been there too, were it not for the grace of Elohim.

But, had that happened...he, *Jehoshua ben Abraham,* would never have been.

Neither here now...nor anywhere.

He placed his hands on the dirt beneath him.

This was the very place.

He removed his sandals.

This was holy ground.

And there seemed even as Moses had experienced so long ago to be a fire here that simply would not, could not be extinguished.

Maybe Elohim would speak to him too from the midst of the burning.

Here in this sacred place.

Joshua remained, entirely consumed in the awe of it all. He knew beyond doubt that he was even now standing at some very crucial moment in his own history and destiny.

"Speak, Adonai," he prayed once more.

"Your servant is listening!"

Chapter 31

COMMITTED

"Joshua?"

"Ahhhh...Y-y-yes...Wh-what?" Joshua answered hesitatingly, his eyes searching the heavens.

"Joshua! It's me, Simeon," came a voice from directly behind him.

Joshua burst out laughing as he turned to face his actual visitor.

Simeon just looked at him sideways.

"I was praying, and I thought..." Joshua said.

"You thought that I was the Almighty...answering you? Oh my!"

Now it was Simeon's turn to laugh.

"Yes. And I must confess I was a little worried!" Joshua said.

And then, all of a sudden, Joshua realized who in fact *was* talking to him.

"Ahhhh...Simeon, it's actually you!"

"Yes, Joshua! That is what I said. And yes, it's actually me!" Simeon said, shaking his head.

"I mean...I know it's you," Joshua stated, and then asked, "But what I mean is, how come you are here now, in this very place?"

"The brothers in town told me that you had come, and when I went to Jonas's house, he told me that you were here," Simeon said. "He briefly shared with me the chain of events that brought you to Gamala as well."

"Joshua, I cannot believe that what has happened over the past few days was mere circumstance or was not in some way part of the Almighty's plan."

Simeon paused, took a long deep breath, and then boldly proclaimed:

"Jehoshua ben Abrahim, I believe that Adonai has raised you up and brought you here for such a time as this. I believe He is even now inviting you to embrace your calling and His destiny for you. I believe that it is here, in this place."

To Joshua, this declaration was like a prophetic pronouncement—a breath of the Spirit—even if it felt beyond his capacity to entertain as truth.

Wonder might best describe what he was feeling.

He longed for such lofty sentiments to be true.

"Jonas also told me that he shared with you for the first time the tragic history of your mother and her family. You should know that Gideon was a prominent member, a leader, of the Fourth Way, what we call the *Qanaim*—the Zealous Ones—or simply "Q" for short. Your great-uncle Jonas, too. They were compatriots and friends of my father Judah. Joshua, you have a powerful lineage and a most amazing family!"

Simeon was silent for a bit but then spoke again.

"That all being said, I ask you, Joshua: Where do you stand in all of this? Are you ready to take your place here, to walk into *your* destiny?"

Joshua didn't respond.

He had to think about all of this.

It was almost too much.

"Have you given any thought to where you will go or what you will do next?" Simeon asked after a little while, changing the subject slightly.

"No, not really," Joshua said, "except that I know that I cannot go back home. I believe that I have become a wanted man…"

His voice trailed off as he lost himself in that stark realization: He was a wanted man!

When he had first met Simeon and Jacob, he had thought it must be exciting to be a fugitive, on the run and in constant danger. Now he wasn't quite sure what to think about this state of being.

"You are safe here," Simeon said. "Well, safer than a lot of places. We are farther away from Roman power on this side of the river. And our home is your home. You are a brother. You are family."

He gestured toward the wall.

"*This* is your family, Joshua. All of these people."

Both of them were quiet for a while.

Finally, Simeon spoke.

"I will leave you now. Sorry for interrupting your prayers. Stay as long as you like. Wander around the yard. Even into the house. We can talk more later on if you like. Jonas knows how to find me."

And with that, Simeon turned and exited the yard, leaving Joshua alone with his thoughts.

Part of Joshua wanted to leave with him but he knew that he needed to remain here, at least for a while longer. He returned to the wall and to his earlier prayer.

"So, speak, Adonai. Your servant is listening. And do lead me, I pray, into my destiny…into Your destiny for me. *All* of it."

He spent the rest of the morning and the entire afternoon here at the wall, touching the bricks and stones. Those of his father and Batiyah's family but others as well, unknown to him, but known to Elohim.

After a time, he found the one that said, "Judah ben Hezekiah."

And he said a prayer for Jacob and for Simeon.

"Your brother's blood cries out to me from the ground," Elohim had told Cain long ago.

Joshua felt as though the blood of these martyrs was crying out to him. It was as if he could hear their voices. It was as if he was hearing them say:

"When will Adonai's deliverer come? When will He arise? Come quickly, Anointed One!"

"Adonai, have you truly, as Simeon said, raised me up and brought me here for a time such as this? Could it be *me*? Can I be that one? It seems to me now to be no accident that I did what I did on Ariah's behalf, knowing the heritage in which I stand. Is that why I so wanted to do something powerful the day that Abba was murdered too?"

Ariah. He hadn't really thought about her that much in the last few days. At the same time, he knew almost immediately that she had never actually been far from his thoughts.

He smiled.

His heart raced a little.

She loved him.

And he knew that he loved her too.

But at this, Joshua allowed himself to weep.

He knew that she could never be his. He was a fugitive, a man on the run with absolutely nothing to offer her. She would most certainly, should even, be given to another who could provide for her and look after her. That it was true, in no way lessened the pain he so deeply felt. For it was love. It was truly love.

Barely allowed to bloom before it had been rudely plucked away.

Joshua prayed for Ariah, thanked Adonai for her, and asked that He would care for her in all of the ways that Joshua wished he could be part of, but knew for certain he could not.

Sadly, he could not go back. Destiny was leading him forward. Or at least, circumstance was propelling him. But whatever it was, it would now most surely lead both of them in different and separate directions.

He thought of his mother Batiyah and of the rest of his family. He could not go back there either. At least he would not, probably should not, return for a very long time.

The events of the past few days had changed everything.

He was grateful at least that Zephaniah was home and that they would be able to survive, even prosper. Elijah was already helping out more; thankfully there was at least someone to take his place. And eventually, like with Abrahim being absent, they would learn to carry on. Without him.

He missed them all the more knowing that this part of his life was most likely gone forever.

"Adonai, make a way. For them. For me," Joshua whispered.

Then too, he was extremely grateful for the *family* that he had here in Gamala. Family he had just barely met. What would he be doing now if he could not have come here? Where would he be if not for them?

Was this place, as Jonas had suggested, now to be *his* harbor?

Jonas and Anna had so welcomed him into their home. They certainly made him feel welcome and safe. Was he truly safe here? Simeon had said that he was. Maybe as safe as could be expected given the circumstances. Few people even knew he was here. The Roman government certainly didn't. At least not yet. And that was a very good thing.

Maybe he could take on a new name. Change the way that he looked and dressed. Was there a way, a possibility, that the authorities would never find him? Could he just lie low here?

Joshua vowed that he would do whatever he needed to do to survive. And he hoped that somehow, someway, someday he would be able to go back…to the place that had been his first home.

For now, he was here. And this was now home. His only home.

And, what of the Fourth Way?

His grandfather, Gideon, and his uncle Jonas, and maybe others of his relatives he didn't yet know had been leaders of this initiative.

Would his father Abrahim have also joined were it not for the fact that he wanted to give a different life to Batiyah in the throes of all that she had gone through and endured? For certain!

His history was certainly here, even if he had never been here before.

It was all here, *in this place.*

And it was as if he knew who *he* was here.

"Have you ever, or always, wondered where you belonged, wondered what it was that Elohim would have you to do? Felt that there was something more somewhere?" Uncle Jonas had asked him yesterday.

That was what Joshua had always felt.

His heart had soared when he heard those words.

And then, earlier today, Simeon had said that he believed… that Adonai had raised him up and brought him here for such a time as this.

Suddenly, it all seemed to come clear.

It was no accident.

No coincidence.

"Ha Shem, it was You who raised up my hand to slay the 'Philistine' who was threatening Ariah! Who threatens every child of the Most High!"

"You have brought me to this place, and I now have a destiny to fulfill!" Joshua declared looking up to the heavens once more.

He stood and walked to the wall.

He knelt down and once more touched the stones that held the blood of Batiyah's martyred family.

He lingered there for a moment, then stood to his feet and moved to the bricks that had absorbed the outpouring of his abba's life.

"I know now that I have clearly and powerfully been moved by Your providence," he boldly began. "And so, here now in this place I give my life alongside those who are jealous for You. I Jehoshua, son of Abrahim and Batiyah, and grandson of Gideon ben Haggai, give myself to the overthrow of Roman power and the re-establishment of the messianic kingdom of David!"

"I will join these, my ancestors, who have gone before. I will pick up and complete what they have left undone. And if my blood be spilled in the process, so be it. Though it cost me all I have, there is little for me to lose and everything to gain! Truly, zeal for the house of Ha Shem and for His children consumes me!"

"My life is Yours, Adonai."

"Do with it what You will!"

"For Abba and for Batiyah!"

"For Gideon, Marion, Micah, and Jeremiah!"

"For all of them!"

"And most of all, for You!"

Chapter 32

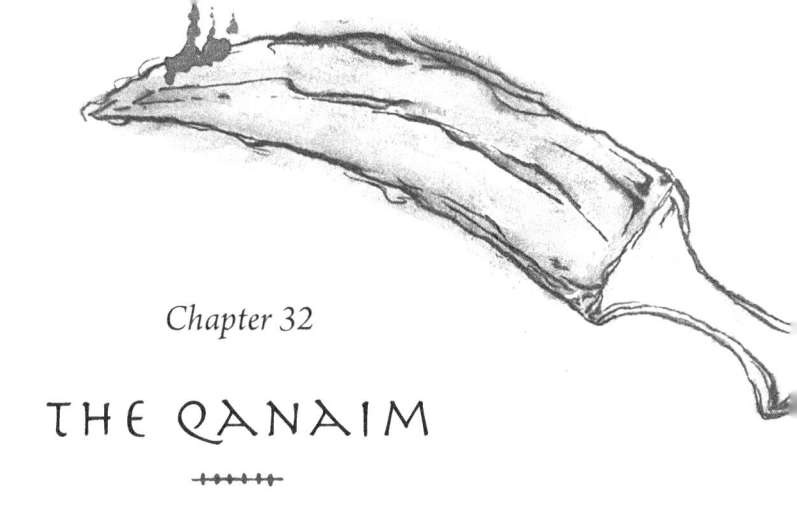

THE QANAIM

THE SKY WAS TURNING DARK. EVENING WAS COMING. Joshua realized that he had been here pretty much the whole day. He was tired, physically spent, not just from today but from all of the events of the last several days. At the same time, he felt energized. It was as if he had finally come to a place of peace on the inside, or in a different way than he had felt in years, maybe ever.

He now had purpose. He had a reason to live.

Turning from where he was standing, he made his way across the courtyard, pausing for one more look around. He put his hand on the latch.

"Thank you, Adonai," he said quietly. "For meeting me here."

He opened the gate and exited, closing it gently behind himself. Walking across the street, the smells of supper greeted his nostrils and Joshua realized just how hungry he was. He hadn't eaten anything all day. He had been focused on other things. Jonas and Anna were both there as if waiting for him to return.

"Shalom, sorry I am so late," Joshua said apologetically.

"Not to worry. We were in no rush," said Anna.

"Good day?" asked Jonas.

"A very good day!" Joshua replied.

"Very good indeed!"

Anna and Jonas were smiling at him.

He paused.

"I believe I have finally found my way. My 'harbor,' to use your words, Uncle Jonas, my destiny. And, knowing that I have much to learn, I believe that I am to commit my life to Q and to the Fourth Way. For Adonai and for His children. For Batiyah and for Abba," Joshua said.

And then reaching across the table to grab Jonas and Anna's hands, he added, "for my whole family!"

Now they were really smiling, and tears were filling their eyes. Joshua was having a little difficulty seeing as well.

And while it was joy for sure, it was not unblemished. This joy could make room for sorrow too; it needed to make room for it. As if the fullness of life could not but include both joy and sorrow.

It seemed as if Jonas was about to say something, but he must have changed his mind.

Rather, he stood up and made his way into the house, returning almost as quickly as he left, now holding something wrapped in a rather ornate piece of cloth. He set it down on the table and pushed it in front of Joshua.

"Here, Joshua," Jonas said. "This belonged to your grandfather, and I know that he would have wanted you to have it."

Joshua carefully unwrapped the gift. It was the most beautiful and ornate knife he had ever seen. The bone handle was inset with jade and amethyst and on the engraved silver sheath he read the words:

"EL NATHAN N'QAMAH."

"Elohim who gives me vengeance," he said quietly to himself, speaking the engraved words, taking the knife and letting his hands connect him not only to it but also with its former owner.

"Gideon, O mighty man of valor!" the angel had spoken over the hero of ancient Israel.

Joshua was convinced that his grandfather had probably walked in a similar anointing. And he felt as though that declaration now descended on him through this piece of holy history he held in his hands.

He trembled and took some deep breaths.

Anna eventually brought their meal of lamb and lentils, leeks, onions, and carrots to the table.

This was not his family, but it was.

He was *home*.

It sure felt like a safe harbor.

After supper, the three of them sat around the fire and Jonas told story upon story of what he called "the old days." He told of Gideon and himself teaching all who would listen the various tenets of the Fourth Way. He shared the major parts of what he believed with Joshua. He told stories of uprisings and victories. He told tales of hiding, being on the run, and of defeats too.

"By the grace of Adonai, I survived," Jonas said. And then added, with tears in his eyes, "there were many others who made the supreme sacrifice. Like my brother Gideon. Your grandfather. May Adonai grant him peace!"

"We all knew going in that death was a price we might have to pay someday. I was never afraid of dying. I think that I was more afraid that I may never really live, never do something that really mattered," Jonas said, now turning to his wife Anna.

"And you, dear woman, walked with me through all of it. I am so very grateful to Elohim for you!"

Anna returned the look of love. She laughed.

"What else could I do, you silly old man!"

"Indeed!" Jonas replied, joining her laughter.

Joshua marveled at the two of them.

He fell asleep thinking of them. And of Ariah. His family in Rakkath. His destiny now decided. And of Q.

Joshua tried to imagine his future. His hand rested on the precious gift that he had received, now strapped around his waist under his cloak.

Quite early the next day right after breakfast, Jonas looked at Joshua and simply said, "Follow me."

He mounted their old donkey and Joshua obediently walked alongside as they made their way up the main street and out of town. They continued up into the hills to the east and north of Gamala.

After a while, Joshua interrupted the silence.

"Uncle Jonas, the other night you used the phrase, 'All in time.' My abba used to always say that too. And I always meant to ask him why but never got the chance. But...I can ask you! Why do *you* always say that? At least, Auntie Anna says you always do!"

"Well, I think it's fair to say your abba and I probably say it for the very same reason!" Jonas replied.

"In a very passionate appeal that Simeon and Jacob's abba, Judah, made a long time ago, he used this phrase over and over. It comes from the book of Ecclesiastes. 'There is a time for everything, and a season for every activity under the heavens.' 'All in time, all in time,' Judah just kept on repeating on that occasion. And he talked about us discerning the times. 'What time was it?' he asked. He felt that it was the time to die, if need be. It was time to hate and to speak out. It was the time for war!"

"I guess 'All in time' just became something we all repeated from that day on! I guess it was our way of being thoughtful and purposeful about everything that we did."

"All in time," Joshua repeated to himself. "All in time. A time for everything."

Simeon had said that Adonai had indeed raised him up and brought him here for such a time as this. Maybe this really *was* His time!

Eventually, they left the road and made their way through some very dense undergrowth, haphazardly, or so it seemed to Joshua, turning left then right and then left again. Finally, they came to what appeared to be a cave. Jonas dismounted and walked into the opening, pulling the donkey behind him. Joshua followed. The cave, which was actually a tunnel, ended and they came into a clearing filled with tents and looking very much like a military outpost.

Joshua turned and looked at Jonas.

"Welcome to the home of Q, Joshua, and to the place we call 'Bereshith'!" he said with a smile, waving his hand over the camp. "This will be your base of operations now, though we trust you will come and visit with the old folks from time to time."

"Maqaba," Jonas called out as they neared the center of the camp, "there is someone I would like you to meet."

A battle-scarred man emerged from his tent. Joshua imagined Samson himself might have looked like this man.

"Shalom, brother Jonas," the man said bowing slightly. "Always good to see you. And how have you been?"

"Very well," Jonas replied.

The two men embraced each other.

Jonas set Joshua directly in front of himself.

"Maqaba, this is my relative, Joshua, son of Batiyah and grandson of Gideon. He has come to learn the ways of the brothers who are zealous for Adonai."

"Honored to meet you," Maqaba said to Joshua. "Simeon said that you had come. Wondered whether you might join us. Welcome, brother!"

Maqaba heartily embraced him and Joshua thought his ribs might crack. Thankfully, they did not.

"Daniel," Maqaba said to someone standing off to his side, a young man who was maybe a few years older than Joshua. "Could you please show Joshua around the camp? And then get him settled in. He can share your tent."

Daniel nodded.

"We will share the evening meal later, Joshua," Maqaba said.

Turning to Joshua, Daniel beckoned him to follow.

Joshua looked at Jonas.

"Go," Jonas said. "I'll be fine. So will you."

He turned and had to quickly catch up to Daniel who had simply assumed he was following, beginning their tour of the small cluster of tents, some for sleeping and other larger ones for supplies, meetings, and various other things.

"You are related to Jonas?" Daniel asked. "Did Jonas say you are Gideon's grandson?"

"Yes, I am," Joshua replied. "Yes, to both questions!"

"You should know that your grandfather is somewhat of a legend here," Daniel said. "I have heard many stories of his exploits. His and Jonas's both."

Joshua thought it strange that he didn't even know his grandfather existed until yesterday and that Daniel probably knew more about him than he did.

"So, Joshua, is that what brings you to Q?" Daniel asked, continuing without waiting for his answer. "I came here from Qumran. It was good, but I no longer believe hiding out in the desert and doing nothing to actually bring about the kingdom of Elohim is enough."

"My brother was in Qumran for a time," Joshua said casually, not totally sure how much to share in his first moments here, but as a way of making connection with his guide and now, also his tentmate.

"What's his name?" Daniel asked.

"Zephaniah ben Abraham," Joshua said.

Daniel thought for a minute or two.

"No. I can't say that I know him. Maybe we weren't there at the same time. I left there to join the Qanaim about two years ago now, I guess."

He paused.

"It was my own decision. But I was kind of forced to leave. You see, I had killed a Roman soldier and I knew it would make things very difficult for the community if I stayed," Daniel blurted out.

"I don't know why I just told you that," he said, hesitating. "I hope that I have not said too much too soon. Scared you away or something. You might want to sleep in a different tent now!"

He laughed a little nervously.

"But…to return to my earlier question: why did *you* come to Q?"

"You killed a Roman soldier?" Joshua asked slowly, avoiding his own question momentarily.

Daniel nodded.

"I had to. He was hurting someone I cared about."

Joshua's jaw dropped and he stared at Daniel wide-eyed, shaking his head in disbelief.

"We are truly brothers, Daniel! That very same circumstance has led me here!"

"What? Really? I can't wait to hear this," Daniel said.

They made their way to the tent that was Daniel's and would now also be Joshua's.

And Joshua told him about Caleb's family and the order of bricks. About the wagon wheel and returning to Magdala. He rehearsed how he had returned to the market and then saw the soldier intent on taking advantage of Ariah. Killing the perpetrator. The brick. About being caught trying to dispose of the body…and having to flee for his life.

Daniel told his own story of how they were in En Gedi getting supplies for the community. How Samuel, one of the community's young initiates, had tripped and accidently knocked over the table of an Imperial tax collector, sending money flying in all directions. A soldier standing guard obviously thought Samuel did it on purpose and began beating the young boy mercilessly.

"I don't know what came over me exactly," Daniel said. "Zeal for justice and Adonai's Chosen? Hatred of all things Roman? The next thing I knew, I was standing over this Roman brute holding a knife in my hand, while his blood ran dark red all over the ground."

"I heard shouting and saw other soldiers fast approaching. I grabbed Samuel and told him to return to the community. To tell them that I was leaving and why. To give them my good byes."

"How did you know to come here?" Joshua asked.

"A member of Q whom they called Zayin had been there watching the whole thing. He caught up to me as I fled the scene, told me that he was part of the Fourth Way and helped me to escape. I was so grateful for his assistance. He knew the countryside like the back of his hand. He brought me here."

"This is so amazing," Joshua said. "I have just barely met you and yet I feel like I have known you forever!"

"Same here," Daniel said. "Brothers! Blood brothers!"

"Now, let's get cleaned up and ready for supper."

They sat down to the evening meal across the makeshift table from Maqaba, whom Joshua had realized was somewhat of the leader here.

There were upwards of several hundred people in all, Joshua imagined, most of them young men his age or in their twenties, all seated at tables in the center of the compound.

The food was nothing fancy but it was tasty—simple meat and vegetables.

"So, Joshua," Maqaba said after they had eaten, "your uncle Jonas told me the story of how you came to Gamala and of your intention to join our movement."

Joshua nodded.

"Yes sir. If you'll have me?"

"Have you? Of course, we'll have you. In fact, you are highly esteemed here, simply because you are the grandson of Gideon ben Haggai. Add to that the fact that you have already disposed of one of the enemies of Israel! We consider you a *gibbar,* 'a mighty warrior,' a man who would make your grandfather proud!"

"You are most welcome here, Joshua," Maqaba said. And then, standing to his feet announced, "Recruits, meet your new *achi,* Jehoshua, the grandson of one of our most honored brothers, Gideon of Gamala!"

The whole company rose to their feet and applauded. Several *brothers* moved over and slapped Joshua on the back. Joshua blushed with pride. Had he ever felt so welcome, so special, in his entire life?

It was quite heady.

But it really felt like family at the same time.

Family lost and family found.

Memory momentarily pricked him.

But he quickly put that out of his mind.

He needed to focus on what was ahead.

"Get a good night's sleep now," Maqaba said. "Training starts tomorrow morning at daylight or...even a bit before!"

"Daniel, can you make sure Joshua is made to feel *welcome* here?" he added with a slight wink.

Daniel saluted and the two of them made their way to their tent.

Chapter 33

TRAINING

Joshua sat bolt upright.

Sputtering.

He was completely soaked and his hair was dripping.

"Whaaaattt?" he cried out.

Daniel, barely visible in the light of a dim lamp and doubled over, was holding an empty pail and laughing hysterically.

"Good morning, my little brother! And welcome to Q! A bucket of freezing cold water drawn especially for you! It's the way we greet all new recruits!" Daniel announced, still trying to compose himself.

Without any hesitation, Joshua lunged from his sleeping mat and tackled Daniel around mid-section, taking him to the ground, the two of them now wrestling in the dirt and attempting to best each other in this contest of strength and male bonding.

Somehow though, in a flash, Daniel spun around and broke free, immediately pinning Joshua to the ground face down.

"Say you give up!" he demanded playfully.

Joshua struggled momentarily but to no avail.

"I give," he finally said begrudgingly.

"You are certainly zealous, Joshua, and that is a very good thing, but zeal without wisdom only leads to ruin and defeat. Now, put

TRAINING

on some dry clothes, wash your face and comb your hair. What happened to you?" Daniel said. "You don't really want to be late on your first day, do you?"

Daniel took great pleasure in this part of his *assignment*.

What Joshua didn't know right off but gradually found out, was that this wasn't just the way new recruits were greeted on day one, it was ritual treatment for the entire first week.

He took it in stride but waited patiently for the last day when, rising very early, he took the opportunity to get one up on Daniel, sharing his own wet welcome with his new tentmate.

Now it was Daniel's turn to drip, and Joshua's turn to laugh.

"Well played!" Daniel said, drying himself off. "I had that coming!"

"I could not disappoint...a brother!" Joshua replied gleefully.

Training in the Fourth Way was many faceted, but two things were primary: imbibing their philosophy and then perfecting the art of close quarters combat and the efficient removal of targeted individuals.

"There are in Israel at present four approaches to living out the faith of the fathers," Maqaba taught them, beginning on day one.

"The Sadducees believe that everything is confined to the here and now. As a direct result, they do their best to accommodate to the world in which they find themselves while still maintaining a semblance of uprightness. Consequently, they do not shy away from involving themselves in all aspects of worldly things, though primarily and most often it would seem, for their own personal power and advantage."

"The Pharisees on the other hand, the party with whom we have the most affinity theologically, choose to focus on personal piety. They believe the good that they have done—how well they observe the Torah—will be weighed against whatever mistakes they have made, and that they will be judged accordingly. This is why they are so zealous about law-keeping and have added in excess of 600 'by-laws' to the ten commands that Elohim gave us to ensure that they do not even come close to sinning. They admit that they are present in the world but view themselves as set apart from it, even above all others."

"The sect of the Essenes sees the world for sure but even Judaism itself as corrupted and so they remove themselves in an effort to guard their corporate faith as Elohim's called out people. They consider it crucial to maintain separation from all of it. This is why they cloister themselves in their community at Qumran and shun contact with the pagan world, Jewish society, and the Temple, when at all possible."

"These approaches all have some value, but we believe that each one falls short, primarily on account of the fact that they do little to bring the kingdom of Elohim into fulfillment and turn us back to the way that Adonai's people were at the beginning."

"In a way different from all of the others, the Fourth Way believes that Elohim desires us, His people, to *be* the agents of reformation and revolt, throwing off the yoke of political oppression in the same way our ancestors threw off Egyptian slavery and then went on to overcome the Canaanites and take possession of the Land of Promise."

"We are His people. Subject to Him alone. It is for this reason that we abhor pagan taxes and refuse to pay them. It is the reason we refuse to register ourselves in any census. It is the reason we offer ourselves as instruments of Adonai's present end-time judgment on any and all, be they Gentile opponents or Jewish accommodators, who would bring us into servitude to an idolatrous Empire that believes its emperors to be divine and keeps us from being the Chosen race that Elohim promised."

"Ha Shem *alone* is our master. It is why we only refer to each other as brothers. No one here is over or under another. And, while some obviously do give leadership, we lead as servants. Gideon, one of the greatest judges our nation ever saw, told the people of his day, 'I will not rule over you, nor will my son rule over you. YHWH will rule over you.'"

"We recognize that we are in the midst of a pagan world and believe that Adonai wants us to be set apart from it, more than that, set over and against it! We are definitely not to be under it! We assert our high calling as Elohim's Chosen people! We believe and pray that Messiah will come soon and revive the glory of Israel and usher in the last days' community of the faithful and bring about the downfall of 'the kingdom of arrogance.' We stand against any and all integration into the Imperial system, and we will never submit to Roman rule! We believe in aggressive involvement within society to bring about this new order—violent men bringing about His kingdom by force! We fight and even die for our right to be Adonai's people here in the Promised Land! The most horrible death, even the torture of relatives and friends, is better than human domination. We fight for the freedom of Israel! *That* freedom is our highest value!"

Maqaba was a powerful and eloquent teacher.

And, although it was a lot to take in, Joshua had no issue with most of what he was learning these days, the majority of it being convictions he had been taught and had believed his whole life.

It all spoke to a familiar place inside of him. And, as he once again thought through all the possible ways of being faithful, he became ever more convinced that the Fourth Way was *the way* that made the most sense and the most perceivable difference.

Joshua loved the idea of taking a stand *for* something. And, of actually fighting, of really doing something to bring about a change.

One of the other things that Joshua appreciated was the fact that all of their beliefs were anchored in the Scriptures. They spent many hours studying them, poring over the Holy Writings. And, when open to the Zealot perspective, he was amazed at how many places in Elohim's revelation they found where this seemed to be the most logical reading of the text, indeed, where there seemed to be no other possible interpretation.

Had not the focus of most, if not all, of the prophets been the critique of Israel's accommodation to and with the surrounding nations?

Adonai was looking for a people set apart, separated unto Him, a Holy nation, righteous in their creation as His people, sanctified as He brought them out of slavery in Egypt, and furthering that identity even into the conquest of the Promised Land.

From the very first battle at Jericho in which everything and everyone, save Rahab and her household, was *cherem*, "devoted," to Ha Shem, they had been called to sacred war in which they destroyed every living thing that was against Him, men and women, young and old, cattle, sheep, and donkeys.

Adonai's overwhelming aim was a pure and holy people, set apart from the rest of the world. Evil removed. In a cleansed and Holy land.

He alone would be their king.

He would rule in righteousness and justice.

Both Moses and Joshua had stood on that *Holy ground*.

And even when Israel demanded a human king like the other nations, Saul had been told that, as Elohim's representative, he was to, "go, attack the enemies of Adonai and totally destroy all that belongs to them. Do not spare them." When he didn't do that as completely as Elohim had commanded, his kingship was taken from him.

David, who succeeded him, had often spoken against His enemies and all those who set themselves against the Chosen people. He had been a warrior who shed much blood and yet was one who Adonai described to Samuel as, "a man after His own heart!"

David had written those words down, and indeed, many of the *Tehillim* were prayers prayed for the destruction of these enemies of Israel, some of them extremely graphic in their requests.

The fifty-eighth had become one of Joshua's favorites:

> *Do you rulers indeed speak justly?*
> *Do you judge people with equity?*
> *No, in your heart you devise injustice,*
> *and your hands mete out violence on the earth...*
> *Break the teeth in their mouths, O Elohim;*
> *YHWH, tear out the fangs of those lions!*
> *Let them vanish like water that flows away;*
> *when they draw the bow, let their arrows fall short...*
> *The righteous will be glad when they are avenged,*
> *when they dip their feet in the blood of the wicked.*
> *Then people will say,*
> *"Surely the righteous still are rewarded;*
> *surely there is a God who judges the earth."*

The Qanaim were merely continuing what many others in Israel's history had been called to do.

They were working to bring to fruition what they were convinced was Adonai's blessed promise.

Often during this time, Joshua thought of his abba, Abrahim. His death to be placed squarely at the feet of the Roman Empire.

He thought of Batiyah, his ima, and the murder of her entire family.

And of Ariah, and what might have happened, had he not come to the rescue.

He thought of all of the others though more vaguely, myriads of people whom he didn't even know, but those whose lives had been taken from them by this demonic empire.

Joshua returned to the monument as often as he could, to remember and to pray and intercede for all of Elohim's people.

But especially for the martyrs.

Did not the Torah in fact demand atonement for all bloodshed?

Joshua thought it was time that Adonai once again bare His arm in vengeance.

The prophet Jeremiah had said in former days, "A curse on anyone who is lax in doing YHWH's work! A curse on anyone who keeps their sword from bloodshed!"

Joshua was ready to pick up his sword and do battle. To defeat the enemies of Adonai.

But as Daniel had told him, "Zeal without wisdom only leads to ruin and defeat."

He still had much to learn.

Jacob had told him much of the early history of Q when they met together that day by the side of the road, but with each passing day, Joshua learned more of how the Qanaim had come to be organized, to be what they were now, and how they came to exist here at *Bereshith*.

Hezekiah, Jacob and Simeon's grandfather, had discovered this place, an almost impenetrable natural fortress, during his early days as a leader of the freedom fighters in this area bordering on Syria. He had stumbled across it as he fled for safety and hid in what appeared to be a cave, about six miles north of Gamala. The next morning, he had discovered what Joshua found out when Jonas and he came: that the cave was actually open on both ends, a tunnel into this natural basin, surrounded on all sides by steep rock cliffs. Hezekiah had continued to be based in Gamala, but had used this fortress to gather and train his band of rebels for forays into northern Galilee and southern Syria.

When Judah took over the movement after Herod executed his father Hezekiah, he knew that the Fourth Way, as it eventually came to be known, had to be able to operate more covertly, to be more cautious about letting outsiders know its whereabouts. They became much more secretive about who was part of the Zealot movement and more careful about their public appearances.

This place: *Bereshith,* from the first word in the Torah, meaning "beginning" or "head," became the operations and training center. It seemed appropriate since this was the place where Judah had spent much of his time developing his philosophy in the ten years between the attack on the royal palace in Sepphoris when he was injured and the time when he was eventually killed.

Calling it Bereshith meant that they could talk about returning to "the beginning," and only those who were part of Q would know what that meant.

It was also very easy to guard. What Joshua had not known but later found out: when Jonas and he had made their approach, they had been watched by at least six sentries positioned in various places on the cliffs overlooking the entrance.

And there was a signal. Jonas had taken a drink from a stream on the way in. Three drinks in fact. But he had cupped his hands and brought the water to his mouth instead of drinking directly from the stream. It was the way that Adonai had chosen Gideon's 300. Qanaim everywhere identified themselves to each other this way: they would very discretely cup their hands and bring them to their mouth and the other would tap three fingers on his heart.

Only those who were members knew.

If there had been any danger, the sentries would have signaled those inside by means of ropes attached to small bells at which point the entrance to the compound at the inner end of the tunnel would have been blocked with a large stone rolled into its place. What had appeared to be a cave would seem to the intruder to be only that. He might stay for a night or so but would eventually leave. Even any footprints he would find would simply appear as though others had used this cave to hide out on prior occasions. The Qanaim had engineered a similar entrance/exit on the north side as well so that they could come and go even if the south entrance was blockaded.

The movement had grown monumentally in the years since Judah's death. Maqaba said that there were close to ten thousand members and adherents spread throughout the cities and towns of Israel and all over the Diaspora, those places in the Roman Empire where Jews were scattered. Even allowing for some exaggeration, the movement was so much bigger than just the 200 or so men that were here in training.

And many, if not most of the members of Q, were regular people carrying on regular lives with wives and children, houses, and jobs. They would band together when needed to carry out raids, rally to encourage others to embrace their philosophy, dispose of the enemies of freedom, or whatever was necessary at the moment.

He had discovered early on that every one of the men that he had approached that first day in the town square in Gamala were actually members of Q. His cousin Eliazer, who had brought him to Uncle Jonas and Aunt Anna's, was too.

Joshua was intrigued at the thought that many if not most of the Zealots lived almost normal lives. They lived in their own houses in towns throughout Israel. They had wives and children and jobs and carried on businesses.

He could not help but think once again of Ariah. And of what might have been.

He had erased the consideration that they could somehow be together from his imaginations in the early days as he fled, thought it would be impossible, but now he wondered: could there be a way that they could be together, maybe even be married and have a family?

He longed for even a bit of that kind of ordinary.

The Qanaim was a grass roots and covert movement of brothers, loosely organized but tight knit, powerful in part because its ideology rather easily appealed to the heart of every patriotic Jew.

His own father, while sympathetic to the Zealot cause, had chosen to forego full and complete affiliation in an attempt to save Batiyah from any more suffering, to separate her from all of the pain that her life growing up had dealt.

In the end, that hadn't turned out so well. She had lost Abrahim anyway, and now Joshua too had been taken out of her life. Joshua knew that Abrahim's sentiment could not be faulted even if he disagreed with his father's stand on non-violence.

Joshua himself had now chosen to fully align himself with the movement and, in a way similar to his abba, knew that he did not want to, could not put Ariah through any of this, even if he loved her.

Maybe, because he loved her.

She loved him in return, true enough, but this was maybe just too much to ask of her, maybe of anyone.

He thought that he would probably not be one of those brothers who got to live a somewhat *normal* life.

He decided to put all of those thoughts on a shelf somewhere, positive she could and would never be his.

All in time?

A time for everything?

Apparently not for that.

Training at Q's headquarters was also quite physical.

Joshua was pretty muscular from working long hours lifting bricks. Grateful for that preparation, he became even stronger with each passing day. Every morning, initiates would run several times around the perimeter of the compound in which they lived, the equivalent of three or four miles. As members of Q, they had to be prepared to flee if needed, running quickly and possibly sustained over a long period of time. It was imperative that they be swift of foot.

At other times, they would have to stay and fight. So, they sparred with each other as well, learning holds and throws and the best ways to overcome any opponent. Joshua had learned early on from Daniel that force and even surprise could be overcome if one fought wisely.

And then, most importantly in a way, they learned how to quickly and efficiently and permanently take out a target. They practiced on straw men and were taught exactly where to strike with the small curved blade of the *sicae,* the small dagger knife and weapon of choice, so that it did the most internal damage with the least amount of external blood loss.

It was all about attracting as little attention as possible, dressing just like everyone else and concealing the small blade until you were right next to the victim.

The knife must be extremely sharp and both the jab and withdrawal must be quick and precise, best just to the right of center and between the third and fourth ribs. In and out rapidly and then slowly disappear into the crowd, drawing no attention to oneself.

As the attacker, you could be at some distance by the time severe internal bleeding and a compromised heart took the victim out. The crowd would know soon enough that someone had been murdered, but they had not seen anyone do it nor witnessed anyone running away.

This had the added benefit of instilling fear.

Those in power especially never knew when or if they might be next.

Or, where their attack might come from.

From the front.

From behind them.

Everyone could be a suspect.

And, people in a crowd bumped into each other without noticing the other person all the time.

Chapter 34

ACTIVE STATUS

Not long afterwards, about four months after his arrival at Bereshith, Joshua was called upon to be a participant in an uprising that had been planned. On this occasion, he went along with Daniel and about thirty other Zealots intent on inciting the Jewish citizens in the city of Hazor in northern Galilee, many of whom were already active members of Q, to rise up in armed revolt against the harsh taxation policies of the local Roman proconsul. Joshua was there only as an observer, but was standing right next to Daniel when he took out the city treasurer, Terentius, in the midst of the crowd. The deed done, the two of them slowly retreated and when they were about thirty feet away, Joshua turned to see that the Roman leader had collapsed to the ground. Others there met the same fate that day, twenty-eight persons in all.

Of those members of Q who were involved, no one was arrested. Not one was caught. The immediate wave of fear that descended on the city was palpable. Politicians particularly, were afraid for their lives. The Qanaim celebrated long into the evening. And the harsh taxation relaxed. This kind of pressure seemed to achieve results.

Joshua's training continued.

About six weeks later, he and Daniel were in Jerusalem. It was Yom Kippur, the holiest of all days on the Jewish calendar.

Festivals were great times to carry out the aims of the Zealot movement. There were lots of people around with whom to share their ideals. Add to that the reality that they were *in* the city of Zion, Elohim's very place of habitation. Patriotism ran extra high at these times. It was easy to stir up a riot. And people, crowds of people, and commotion always made it much easier to conceal one's self and actions too.

Lost in a crowd as it were.

The one difficulty to be overcome was that on many festival days and on the Sabbath for certain, the Torah permitted absolutely no work or was severely limited. The Zealots however had simply come to the understanding that an exception could easily be made, given the fact that they were carrying out the work and the will of Elohim.

Joshua's target on this day, his first, was a particular Sadducee named Menachiam. Apparently, this Jewish leader had somehow got wind of the existence of a Zealot cell in the nearby town of Bethany, about one and a half miles to the east of Jerusalem. He had then hired several Jewish spies to pose as persons sympathetic to Q and attempt to uncover where they were meeting. When it was eventually discovered in the hills on the far side of town, Menachiam had shared the location with the Roman authorities, encouraging them to take action against the Zealots. This was obviously all aimed at securing Roman favor for himself and for the ruling party in Jerusalem, not to mention the fact that he also allegedly made some money in the transaction. He had *sold* them out.

The Romans and Herodian Jews had then monitored their comings and goings, waiting for just the right moment. Finally, on one particular evening, when about 120 of them were together, a large detachment had attacked and slaughtered them all. Some Romans and Herodians had been killed in the fracas but the Qanaim had been totally outnumbered.

One of the *spies,* a man named Zeboiim, had become truly sympathetic to the Zealot cause during the time he was supposed to infiltrate the movement. And, by some miracle, he had managed to escape death, even though present when all the others were murdered. They had indiscriminately killed all of the infiltrators along with the membership of Q. He realized afterward that the Jewish leaders' intent from the beginning was to sacrifice them as well, "for the good of the many." When he came to the next morning, wounded but alive, surrounded by all of the dead, Zeboiim decided to join the movement for real and, knowing Menachiam's plot, now proceeded to share all of its details with the rebel movement; most specifically, to reveal its author.

Joshua relished this assignment from the moment he was given it. He felt honored to be given such a high-profile victim. He viewed it as payback to those Jewish brethren who had in the past been so willing to sacrifice his father for their own political advantage and position. He felt that these men were traitors to the people of Adonai in the worst possible way. And they deserved what was coming to them.

He saw it as retributive justice. Personal vengeance. Payback.
For Abba.
A life for a life.
And, he carried out his assignment flawlessly and with precision. He was in and out quickly and quietly and Menachiam was now dead. Daniel congratulated him on a job well done.

When they were a fair distance away, now on their way back to Gamala, Joshua took out the *sicae* that his uncle Jonas had given him, the one that had belonged to Gideon, wiped the blood off of its blade, and breathed:

"For You, Adonai. Vengeance. May Your kingdom come!"

As he slid the knife back into its sheath, he once again rehearsed the words inscribed there:

"EL NATHAN N'QAMAH."

"Elohim who gives me vengeance," he repeated quietly to himself, now pressing the knife and its sheath to his chest.

He was making a difference. Making an impact.

The next day, however, this whole incident bothered him. Quite a lot actually. He thought that he would feel different. Better. Vindicated.

He did not.

Was Menachiam an evil man? Most certainly.

But did he deserve to die for what he had done?

The members of Q and those he had hired as spies were dead because of what Menachiam had orchestrated.

So probably.

But what had he ever done to Joshua, personally?

He didn't even know this Sadducee existed until a few days ago. He had never met him until yesterday. Joshua hadn't seen him until he was identified out of the crowd as his target three days prior.

It had made sense and had not really bothered him to kill the soldier that was threatening Ariah, he thought. No, he hadn't known him either. But he had known Ariah. Loved her even. And the soldier was hurting this innocent young girl. The threat was immediate.

He was simply defending her.

This seemed different somehow.

Joshua shared his struggle with Daniel the next day as they were trying to enjoy a few minutes of downtime.

"We were simply defending, or avenging, 120 or rather, 119 of our brothers who were killed at this man's hand," Daniel said.

That seemed to make sense at the time, but Joshua didn't sleep well at all that night either.

Daniel suggested that he talk with Jonas and maybe revisit the monument. Get some wisdom and perspective.

Ideals seemed to make more sense when left in the abstract realm, Joshua thought. There seemed to be no mess as long as they were only ideology. The problem, he imagined, came when what one believed was translated into biography, when you tried to live it out. That was when any flaws in your thinking would become evident.

Maybe it was just seeing a man die at his very own hand.

What if he were not cut out for the Zealot life?

Not enough of a man?

Or had his abba been right?

Maybe violence and bloodshed wasn't the way of Adonai. Or at least it should be left to Him to carry out.

The next day, Joshua did take his questions to the monument, and then to Jonas and Anna.

He spent several hours reconnecting with the bricks and stones, praying, and then went across the lane and into his relatives' yard.

He had been there to visit on several occasions over the past months and every time, he was welcomed with open arms. It felt good. Q had become a family for sure, but this was somehow more truly *family*.

"Hello, Joshua, so good to see you as always!" Anna said, almost running to embrace him.

"And you too, Auntie," Joshua replied.

"How have you been since we saw you last, my son?" she asked.

"Good. Really good," Joshua said, realizing that it wasn't true, even as the words left his lips.

He was sure she saw right through him.

"Jonas went into town for a bit, but he should return shortly," Anna shared. "Can I get you a little something to eat while we wait?"

She set herself to the task without waiting for Joshua to respond. Joshua just watched her work.

When she brought some food to the table, he boldly asked, "Auntie Anna, what was it like? Being married to a freedom fighter?"

She didn't answer the question posed.

"Why do you ask? Is there someone you might want to…?"

That caught him by surprise.

Joshua blushed a little and she had her answer.

"It is hard, Joshua. I'm not going to lie. She would need to be a very special girl. It was the life that Jonas had chosen even before we met and he invited me to be a part of it. I guess I went in with my eyes open. I had grown up around it so it wasn't a total shock. But…"

She paused, thinking.

"Maybe the hardest thing was when he would go out on a mission. And I would never know if he would return or not. I simply had to learn to entrust him to Elohim, our protector and defender. I would invoke the words of Psalm 91: 'A thousand may fall at your side, ten thousand at your right hand, but it will not come near you…' Fortunately, he always returned."

Tears filled her eyes.

Tears of gratitude he imagined.

"Did you, did he, ever talk about the…ah, actual killing?" Joshua asked.

"No, he told me that he wanted to spare me from that and I shouldn't have to give that part any thought," Anna shared. "But I sometimes knew that something, maybe *that* was bothering him when he returned. He would be lost somehow, far away in his thoughts. I would just leave him alone. And he always came…back."

And with that, Jonas returned.

"Hi Joshua, good to see you as always!" he said as he entered.

"Good to see you too, Uncle," Joshua replied.

Jonas sat down. Anna put some food in front of him and then made her way into the house.

"What's wrong, Joshua? Why the cloud?" he asked.

"Is it that obvious?" Joshua replied.

Jonas just waited.

"I murdered someone. My first *target*. An evil man really. But it still bothers me. I don't know what to think. I need your wisdom. Your experience, I guess. I'm hoping to find some answers. This calling all seemed to make sense until three days ago. Now, I just don't know if I can do it."

"I'm hoping that you can help me through this. I'm kind of questioning everything."

"Hmmm," Jonas said, stroking his beard. "The big questions!"

He thought for a minute or so, remaining silent.

"Joshua, we do not *murder* anyone. The ten words forbid it. '*Lo tirtzach*,' it says. Do we *kill*? Yes. But not indiscriminately or with malice. We simply target the enemies of Adonai. David *killed* Goliath. Israel was told to kill the ungodly nations who would detract them from being who He was calling them to be."

"I struggled whenever I made it personal, whenever I was acting on my own initiative. I fear you made it about avenging your father, or actually about avenging yourself for what they did to you. Am I right?"

Joshua nodded.

"We must never act on our own. We are Elohim's representatives. We are merely extensions of His arm. 'Vengeance is mine. I will repay,' says Ha Shem. Never forget that."

"We are part of His army in the world. We fight His enemies."

"That is not to say that killing is ever easy or that it doesn't or even shouldn't bother us from time to time. I just found that I had to give whatever I was struggling with to Adonai in prayer, and know that I was bringing about His kingdom on earth."

"Leave whatever personal avenging needs to happen to Him."

Jonas smiled a broad and loving smile.

He moved over and embraced his young relative.

And Joshua did feel better at that.

It was okay to struggle. He had been given permission.

"Oh, and some of us did give ourselves new names," Jonas added. "To change the focus a bit, as a reminder that we weren't fighting for ourselves. A name that identified us as servants set apart for and in the Holy War of Ha Kadosh, the Holy One."

"Doing that may be something to consider."

"I suggest you ask Maqaba about it when you return!"

Chapter 35

BARABBAS

As soon as Joshua arrived at Bereshith that evening, he sought out his leader. He found him resting in his tent.

"Uncle Jonas tells me your name isn't really Maqaba," Joshua said as he entered, not wasting any time with small talk.

"So, you're struggling with the killing part?" Maqaba asked, immediately grasping the issue at hand.

Joshua nodded.

"Jonas did help me some though," he added.

Maqaba was silent for a minute.

"My parents actually named me *Barenos!*" he finally said when he did speak.

Joshua stared at him in shock, holding his hand to his mouth. He was grinning widely and struggled not to burst out laughing.

"Yes, exactly!" Maqaba continued. "It translates as 'son of man,' but it actually means or usually ends up meaning, 'son of weakness' or, 'the weak one'!"

"I was scrawny as a child and needless to say, I was teased a fair bit. After I joined the movement, I thought it hardly a fitting name for a freedom fighter!"

"So, I became *Maqaba*: 'The Hammer!' I renamed myself a mallet in the fist of Elohim. Choosing to see myself as strong, not weak! I wanted to be a son of Adonai and a weapon of El Shaddai!"

Maqaba chuckled, with a somewhat sinister grin.

"Much better, don't you think?"

"*Joshua* on the other hand is a great name!" Maqaba said.

"But you too may choose another, if need be."

"May I suggest that you spend time with Adonai and ask *Him* to suggest a new name. He changed Abram's name to, 'Abraham,' and Jacob's name to, 'Israel.' I'm sure he could find one for you as well!"

"Thank you...*Barenos!*" Joshua said, pretending to cower.

Maqaba just scowled at him, pounding a fist into his other hand.

"Don't you dare tell!" he threatened.

Joshua knew he was joking.

Well, sort of.

But it set *him* on a quest.

For a new name.

Not that his wasn't good. It was a great name.

But...

Named Jehoshua ben Abrahim at his circumcision, he had been called Joshua his whole life, well, other than Yoshi, when he was a small boy growing up at home. In the Roman world, he was known as *Jesus*. His name meant, "YHWH who saves." It was a very good name as Maqaba had said.

But still, Joshua now asked Adonai for a new name—a new identity.

Maybe a more *zealous* name.

Eventually, he took to calling himself, *Barabbas*, a name that means, literally, "son of the Father." He had chosen this alias both to identify himself as part of Adonai's army as Jonas had suggested, but also for the protection of his family, so that he would not be easily identified as connected to them or vice versa, them to him, shielding them from the possibility of having to suffer any repercussions as a result of his chosen mission of violence and aggression against Rome, their sympathizers, and the Herodian dynasty specifically.

His family had suffered enough already, he imagined.

How had he come to choose the name *Barabbas*? He had thought long and hard before it came to him. Prayed much about it even.

In the end he chose it for three reasons: First of all, because his earthly father had often been called Abba, by his children for sure, but also by many others as a term of respect and a shortened form of his actual name, Abrahim, which meant "father of many," or "father of nations."

Calling himself Barabbas was Joshua's own personal way of honoring the one person who had meant so much to him and whose untimely death, his murder, at the hands of the Roman Empire, had been a large part of what propelled him into this mission and his affiliation with the Fourth Way in the first place.

But then, he also chose the name as a way of remembering his mother, Batiyah, especially now that he knew the full story of her family and his own heritage within and connection to the Zealot movement through her side of the family. She had suffered significantly and gone through so much. Joshua was doing this for her as well.

Finally, he did want to imagine himself as a, "son of the Father," as a son of Elohim. And although it was maybe even frowned upon in most devout Jewish circles, to view the Almighty as one's father, Joshua had discovered it on David's lips in several places in the Psalms and knew it was what *he* most wanted and most needed: A Father.

And so, he took to calling himself *Barabbas*: for it's obvious and primary meaning: "son of the Father," son of Elohim. He was committing himself to be about his Father's business. But he also chose it because he felt it a fitting combination of the Aramaic *Bar,* meaning "son of," *Ab,* to represent "Abrahim," and *Ba,* short for "Batiyah," his ima. Hence, *Bar-Ab-Ba* or when he put it together with his given name: "Jesus Barabbas!"

Jesus Barabbas: spiritual son of Father Elohim, and earthly son of Abba and Batiyah, true heroes of faith in his eyes.

Over the next twelve years, Jesus Barabbas made steady progress up through the ranks of the Qanaim even though they staunchly affirmed that there were no ranks, always referring to each other as brothers and holding that each member was equally important. On a practical level however, a functional level, there were obviously those who were giving direction and leadership to this movement.

Barabbas gradually evolved as one of those leading brothers, in all areas of their endeavors.

Early on, Barabbas had shown himself quite adept at thievery. This was part of how the Qanaim could afford to support themselves and carry on their mission. Yes, many of the members worked regular jobs and contributed money to the cause, but it never hurt to swell the coffers, particularly with Roman money, even better if it was money taken from affluent citizens. They would quietly break into the houses of these wealthy and prominent officials and not only kill them in their sleep but then also, help themselves to the coins and jewelry that were stored away, most often buried somewhere in the floor of the house and usually concealed by a mat or piece of furniture. Barabbas seemed to have a knack for knowing exactly where to look.

At other times, they plundered the treasuries of the Empire directly. This was always a great adventure and one they would celebrate when they reassembled. If they got wind of a stash of money, most often when it was being transported from one location to another, they would simply hold up the caravan at knifepoint, take the cache, and make off with it. If a few Romans died in the process, so much the better.

Truth be told, often these *outings* were even more about sticking it to the Romans than the money per se. Steal from the pagans and give to the pious. They wanted the Romans to fear the recompense of Ha Shem. Besides, hadn't King Solomon said that, "the wealth of sinners is stored up for the righteous?" It was simply taking back the fruit of a land that they believed was rightfully theirs as the Chosen people.

Each member of Q also needed to be able to teach at least the basic tenets of their philosophy to others one-on-one. And from time to time, they would hold larger meetings, albeit fairly secretive ones, in various towns and cities, encouraging their fellow Jews to throw off the shackles of Roman slavery and oppression, maybe even to join them in armed revolt.

Knowledgeable and eloquent, Barabbas emerged as one of Q's leading teachers and preachers of freedom from Roman oppression. He showed himself an extremely passionate proponent of the cause.

He was a Zealot of some mean reputation.

There was no one like him.

He was a model of everything that Q stood for.

And through his years, he had become somewhat of an iconic hero within the movement as a result of all of the targets he had successfully eliminated.

If you wanted to eliminate an enemy quickly and efficiently, Barabbas was the one to learn from.

The one to watch.

Not that killing was or should ever be easy, as Jonas said early on. It wasn't.

Joshua had changed his name to Barabbas to keep the actual killing part at some distance from his heart. And that had helped some.

But by far the biggest relief had come rather early on, at the suggestion of his relative Eliazer.

The key was to never look back in the direction of your target, not even when you were at a safe distance.

Barabbas found this simple suggestion to be a great help to him personally and it became his inalienable rule, something he shared freely with all that he trained. He found that he did not struggle at all to watch others take targets down or to see their victims fall to the ground, it was just in the case of the ones for whom he was personally responsible that he was particularly vulnerable.

And it seemed that as long as he remained detached in this way, he found, there was little or no struggle with this rather gruesome but necessary side of his destiny.

Recently however, several events had indeed shaken him to his core, forcing him to question every one of his beliefs and aspirations.

Chapter 36

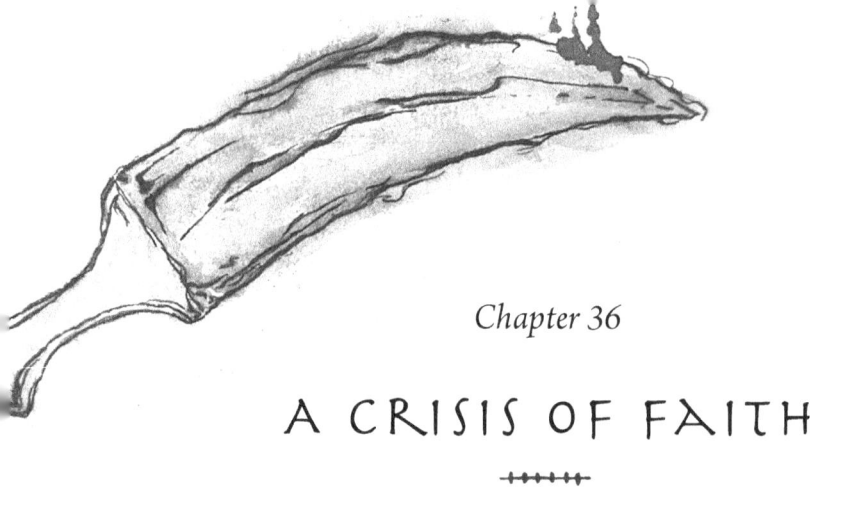

A CRISIS OF FAITH
++++++

THE FIRST HAD HAPPENED SEVERAL MONTHS AGO.

He and Daniel and a number of others had been sent out on a mission to the coastal town of Joppa, about thirty miles northwest of Jerusalem. They had met with many sympathetic Jews over the two weeks that they were there and had definitely stirred up the zeal of Ha Shem among them. It had been decided that they would rise up in revolt against the local Roman government on the upcoming Sabbath, fortuitously the Day of Atonement, the holiest day on their calendar of holy days.

Everything was made ready.

Blood would be spilled and atonement would be made.

Whenever and wherever a crowd of Jews gathered it seemed, Roman attention was aroused, bringing them out as well. This occasion was no different. A large number of Jews had congregated in the heart of the city. And Rome was on alert. Soldiers had come in force. Politicians watched nervously. Jewish leadership too, scribes, Pharisees, and Sadducees especially, were there, to guard their positions and their power.

All that Barabbas needed to do now was to induce a riot; that would lead to confusion and provide the necessary cover and distraction for the attack. He was prodding the people of Elohim with his words, purposefully inciting them.

The guards began moving. They obviously intended to arrest him. They would hold him. Maybe threaten him. Then be forced to release him. Or he would break free. He had been arrested numerous times in his career. However, being able to evade arrest was always to be preferred.

Much easier just to avoid the inconvenience.

It just made everything so much better.

And so, without a moment to lose, feeling he had sufficiently whipped the crowd into a frenzy, he shouted his final crescendo:

Awake, Awake, Arm of Adonai,
Clothe Yourself with Strength!
Awake, As in Days Gone By,
As in Generations of Old!

These words of the prophet Isaiah were the prearranged cue and the Qanaim who were scattered throughout the crowd quite literally "awoke their arms" and began to take down their targets.

Mayhem erupted as soldiers ran at Barabbas and he disappeared into the fray. Targeted individuals began falling to the ground all over the crowd. When this happened, many of the soldiers gave up chasing him, and now started scanning the crowd for the killers. Barabbas himself ran around the back of one of the shops and up onto the roof so he could survey the results without being seen.

But now, as he peered over the parapet of the half wall, the first thing Barabbas saw was his friend Daniel, grimacing in pain, a Roman sword protruding up and out through the front of his chest. He had been pierced from behind by one of the soldiers.

The two of them locked eyes for a sliver of time.

"Adonai, my vengeance!" Daniel mouthed.

Barabbas desperately wanted to return. To help. But he knew that he could not. There was nothing that could be done for his companion now. To try to save him would be pointless. And unwise. Daniel knew it too.

This was a cost that many had shared.

And now Daniel had just paid the ultimate price.

Anguish threatening to undo him, his legs struggling to hold him upright, Barabbas quickly made his way down from the roof and began his own flight, running east, away from the city and the sea and into the hills.

Until he was far away from everything.

He remained there throughout the night. Weeping. Grieving. Pouring out his soul to Adonai. Begging Elohim for answers.

Daniel had been his closest friend, his brother. They had shared the last decade and some together, been through so much. There was no one closer to him in the world. But now, he too was gone.

He had been called upon and had willingly made the final sacrifice. But...

Would Barabbas ever recover, he wondered?

He had lost so much over the last decade of his life. Had lost so many people that he had loved. So very many brothers in arms.

It seemed as though losing Daniel however, was the proverbial straw that broke the camel's back.

And in reality, what had he gained through all of this? What had *they* gained?

The uprising would probably be judged *successful,* but at what cost?

He wondered whether he was just losing his nerve.

Once more he had been on a roof looking down, and once more he had done nothing. He'd been unable to. The irony of that was almost too much.

They had shed much blood. All in the name of Ha Shem, calling it the vengeance of Adonai.

But, was it what *He* really wanted?

Was it what the Divine One had asked of His people?

Of him?

Barabbas knew that this was a much deeper and more profound struggle than the one he had when he joined the movement. More significant than any struggle he had experienced in the intervening years.

He was now questioning everything. And he realized that he had been for a while.

Maybe his abba *was* right.

Daniel's death just seemed to make it that much more urgent that he find an answer.

The answer.

None seemed to be forthcoming.

The Holy One seemed rather far away. Absent.

Eventually and just as the sun was breaking over the hills, Barabbas succumbed to his own exhaustion.

When he finally awoke, he began, albeit rather slowly, to make his way back to Gamala. Mostly because he did not know what else to do or where else to go. He had a considerable distance to cover and it might take him several days, maybe even the better part of a week.

He looked forward to the time alone.

He needed time.

To think, to process all of the things that he was feeling, everything he was struggling to bring sanity to.

On the way, he somewhat unconsciously detoured in the direction of Rakkath. He knew that he so wanted to see his family. To re-establish connection with them. Was that the *sense* that seemed to be missing in all of this *non-sense* at the moment?

He missed them.

Did they miss him too?

Had enough time passed that it might be safe?

Suddenly, or was it now too late for him, he knew that people themselves were far more important than one's ideals, more important than any cause.

He knew in some inexplicable way that love, a love deeper even than the brotherly affection they felt for each other within the ranks of Q, was possibly the missing ingredient in his life.

Maybe it was not to be found. Or not his to have?

Family.

He made his way south into the familiar town of Rakkath, but it was not familiar at all.

In fact, it seemed almost abandoned.

Where had everyone gone, he wondered?

He made his way down the street where he used to live, that is, after he was able to get his bearings and find it. He approached their old house.

It was obvious that no one lived there anymore.

His family was gone too.

He wandered into the yard.

Nothing was left.

This place was only vaguely recognizable.

He made his way across the street.

Nathanael and Elizabeth were gone too.

Everyone was…gone.

He was at a loss as to where to turn next.

Wandering rather aimlessly, he found an old man on one of the streets nearby.

He didn't recognize the man.

"What has happened here? Where is everybody?" Barabbas asked.

"What do you mean?" the old man returned.

"Does no one live here anymore? Where did they all go?" Barabbas asked.

"Well, a number of years ago, maybe four or five or even six now," the old man related, "Emperor Tiberius began building a new city surrounding the garrison that had been constructed. He named the city after himself and then made it the capital city of the region. Most people eventually abandoned the city of Rakkath to go and start over there. Rakkath was overcrowded anyway and the Emperor made it very attractive to move, subsidizing building materials, giving land to any who would make the move and promising no taxes to those who made their new home there. He has since gone back on his word, as I told people he would, but only when it was too late for everyone who had made the shift. In fact, the taxes are now much higher in Tiberius than they ever were in Rakkath, at least for the Jewish people who live there."

Barabbas had kind of avoided this piece of geography lately. Had he heard anything about this development? Not that he could recall.

As a young man, Barabbas had struggled with the Romanization of Rakkath. But now, the fact that the Chosen people had abandoned this Jewish refuge for a Roman capital city named after an unholy emperor was the worst thing he could imagine.

And it would appear that even his own family had joined in, been taken in.

Once again, Barabbas cursed the Empire and all things Roman.

"And what about you, sir? How is it that *you* remain almost alone here in Rakkath?" he asked.

"I, Jeconiah ben David, a patriot of the tribe of Judah, remain because I refuse to come under the rule of or pay taxes to Rome. I believe that is slavery."

Barabbas smiled. This was familiar rhetoric.

"I believe in the absolute freedom of the people of Elohim," the man continued. "I believe that we are to have no king but Adonai. I would rather die than accept the evil human domination of this unholy regime!"

Barabbas cupped his hands and brought them to his mouth. The old man, Jeconiah ben David of the tribe of Judah, put three fingers to his heart and then just stared at Barabbas, looking him up and down. The two embraced each other.

"I myself am an active participant, a leading brother I suppose, in the movement," Barabbas said. "I am Jesus Barabbas. Though originally, Joshua ben Abraham, from Rakkath."

"Abrahim, the brick maker?" Jeconiah asked.

"Yes. Do you know him? Did you? And my family? Do you know them?" Barabbas asked excitedly.

"Sorry," Jeconiah said, shaking his head and thinking. "I have only heard of him. I moved to Rakkath just shortly before it was abandoned."

"Well, it was good to have met you, *brother*," Barabbas said, emphasizing the last word, as he turned to leave.

"And you," Jeconiah said. "Shalom, brother...uh, did you say that you are *Barabbas?* You are *him? The* Barabbas?"

"Yes, brother, I am."

"Well then, I have most certainly heard of *you.*"

"*You* are...legendary!"

"I am just a brother among brothers," Barabbas said smiling. "And now I must be going."

"Well, I am thrilled to have met you, most esteemed brother!"

"Shalom, brother Jeconiah."

"Indeed. Shalom. May Adonai grant you success!"

The two parted company and Barabbas made his way back to what had been home growing up. He spent the night there feeling that it was quite safe. Rakkath had been abandoned after all.

And no one other than this Jeconiah person knew he was here. He slept well.

And in the morning, he began to make the trek south-southwest to Tiberius. He wasn't sure that he would go through with it but he started in that direction anyway. As he got close however, he was about to encounter a rather large detachment of soldiers on the same road heading north. He decided not only to abandon the road but his reunion as well and turned aside, now making his way north cross-country in the direction of Gamala.

He convinced himself that he had no family other than Q, and no home other than Bereshith.

It was a lie.

It seemed easier but pained him deeply.

Maybe another day.

Two days later, when he made his way past the sentries and into the camp, he was welcomed with open arms.

"So good to see you, brother Barabbas!" Maqaba said, giving him one of his famous bear hugs, although maybe not quite as strong as it had been in days gone by, age taking its toll.

"No one was quite sure where you had disappeared."

"I was forced to come home a roundabout way," Barabbas said. "And I just needed some time."

"Daniel didn't make it." Barabbas stated although he was pretty sure Maqaba knew. Maqaba shook his head.

"Some of the brothers told me," he shared.

"It's sad. I miss him dearly," Barabbas said.

"As do we all," Maqaba added. "He was a valiant warrior and a most beloved brother!"

They paused, silently remembering their fallen comrade for a minute or two.

Finally, Barabbas broke the stillness.

"Maqaba, can I tell you something?" Barabbas asked, speaking rather quietly and moving close to his elder brother, not really wanting to be overheard by the others.

"Daniel's death has hit me hard. I find myself struggling like never before. I don't know what to do."

"It's just the loss of a dear friend. I know. I have lost many. Get yourself cleaned up, Barabbas. Supper will be in a little while. Let some time go by and then we can talk more. Remember what brought you here in the first place. I know you will be fine in a few days."

"There is someone else here who is struggling too, though for different reasons. Maybe you could help each other. He might need someone like you to talk to."

It felt good to clean up and the food tasted particularly delicious at supper. His bed, his own bed though nothing fancy, felt far better than the hard ground that had grown somewhat familiar. He had been on the road for a long time. At the same time, it was hard, knowing that Daniel would never again sleep in the other bed.

Nevertheless, Barabbas awoke with renewed energy and zeal the next morning. Maqaba was right he surmised. Just give it a few days.

He steeled himself to do as he had learned to do in days gone by. Kind of ignore what he was feeling, pass it off as falling short of the ideal, pray, and move on. On to the next mission, and the next uprising, and the next target. This was just one of the hazards of his chosen calling.

"Above all else, guard your heart," Solomon had said.

Barabbas knew that his was under lock and key, under vigilant surveillance. And if anything, he secured it even a bit more.

Too much thinking.

It could drive anybody crazy.

A few days later, Maqaba introduced him to "the someone" he had mentioned he wanted Barabbas to meet with. To try to help. Barabbas recognized him and knew that he had seen him on a few occasions over the last several years but remarked to himself that he had somehow never actually talked to this young man or had gotten to know him. He simply chalked it up to his own intense involvement in the movement and also that he had been gone for much of the time lately.

"Barabbas, this is Simon." Maqaba said.

Barabbas looked at the young man in front of him. He appeared to be similar in age, very muscular, with dark features. Most would even describe him as handsome. He looked the picture of health.

Barabbas wondered what it was that could be troubling such a fine young man. But then he thought of his own struggles of the last while. Did they have similar questions? He wondered if he would be able to help.

"Hello, brother Simon. I am Barabbas."

"Yes, sir. I know who *you* are."

The two embraced each other as members of Q often did.

It was affectionate and manly at the same time.

They were comrades.

Blood brothers.

"Maqaba says you have some questions. He seems to think that I can help…and I will…if I can," Barabbas began, smiling.

Simon looked up at him and returned the smile.

Barabbas liked this young man, he thought to himself. There was definitely something winsome about him, shining through the dark cloud that shrouded his countenance at present. He thought it would be interesting to get to know him and knew that the best cure for one's own struggles always seemed to be helping someone else overcome theirs.

The two walked away together, and Barabbas simply waited for Simon to speak. For a while they talked about nothing in particular. After a while, Simon led Barabbas to a topic they often revisited in this place. Past uprisings. Past targets.

And then he came out with it.

"Brother, what I am struggling with is just that: Murdering people! Our cause. All of it, I guess. I just don't know if I can do it anymore...!"

Barabbas was just about to say that he understood, to share with him what his uncle had shared many years ago...and his strategy for never looking back in the direction of his victims.

Simon didn't give him the chance.

"Not since I met *him,* anyway," Simon continued.

"Him?" Barabbas asked. "Him, who?"

"The prophet from Nazareth," Simon said. "Last week I was home in Cana for my brother's wedding and a man miraculously turned water into wine when it ran out. A man named Jesus. Intrigued, we followed him around for the next couple of days and discovered that he was stirring up the people in his own way. He was preaching a kingdom of love for one another, even enemies. He spoke about grace and forgiveness and said that these things are not only far more powerful than hatred, they more than anything else reveal the heart of our Father Elohim."

"I know that I have never met anyone like him! He taught with such authority! Bested the scribes and Pharisees! And even performed miraculous healings and set men free from demons!"

"And then, this Jesus looked directly at me, called me out of the crowd, and said, 'Simon, son of Clopas, come follow me. I am zealous for my Father's house, and true zeal can empower you too!'"

"He was blessing my zeal but calling me to be zealous for something greater!"

"Or, rather, calling me to Someone greater!"

"And I don't know how exactly, but he knew my name!" Simon said in disbelief. "More than that, it felt as though he actually and totally knew *me*, his words somehow making their way into a deep place inside of me that I maybe didn't even know was there. But it wasn't condemning. It was freeing and forgiving. Like fresh wind blowing over me!"

Barabbas just stared at him.

Suddenly a gigantic smile made its way onto Simon's face, and he laughed out loud.

"Barabbas, brother, thank you! You have helped me beyond what you know! I must leave! I must follow this man! I should have never walked away!"

Simon got up and ran off.

"Thank you, brother!" he called out as he sped away.

Barabbas just stood there…dumbfounded.

What had just happened?

Simon's questions had seemingly been answered. Barabbas knew that he hadn't answered them.

And now *he* had even more questions than before.

Like, who was this man, this prophet Simon talked about, this Jesus of Nazareth?

A kingdom of love?

One that included, even welcomed its enemies?

Gentiles? Romans?

Seriously?

That was…

…ludicrous!

Could such a thing even be imagined?

When Barabbas eventually returned to camp, Simon was gone. Apparently, he had gotten clarity.

Barabbas came away more confused than before.

Chapter 37

LAYING LOW

"What happened," Maqaba asked when he saw Barabbas the next morning. "Where is Simon?"

"Gone," said Barabbas shaking his head and shrugging his shoulders.

"I'm sorry, Maqaba. I was no help at all! There seemed to be no reasoning with him. It was as though his mind had been made up… or more like, remade somehow!"

"Don't feel too bad," Maqaba said. "I tried talking to him and got nowhere either. I just thought, hoped that you might have greater success than I."

Barabbas was glad his wasn't the only failure.

He did wonder who this crazy sounding prophet from Galilee was, this man that had so turned Simon's world upside down, but maybe it was rather easy to dismiss. In reality, it was as if someone arose every other week claiming to be or being touted as *the* Messiah. This one too would most likely come and go, just another hopeful.

At the same time, when would Messiah come? *The One.* It seemed as though things just went from bad to worse with each passing day. Was it not time for an actual Messiah to appear, *The*

Messiah, Someone who could and would deliver them from this evil Roman domination?

"Maqaba," Barabbas began, "I really think that it would be wise for me to lie low for a while. I took far too public a role in Joppa and our opponents now most definitely know who I am. I have never been worried about being a wanted man but I believe I have probably been made one of Rome's prime targets. I am certain now that I should have taken a less visible and forward role in leading the uprising there. It would have been wise to be far more covert. I don't know what I was thinking!"

"It would appear the fervor of the brothers there just got the best of me!"

"Or maybe it was just the impatience of old age," Barabbas said, laughing at the thought.

He was all of twenty-eight years old.

"I was thinking the same thing," Maqaba said. "Not about you being old! But about you possibly backing off for a bit. You have been going hard at it for a long time. That is why I myself am mostly here at Bereshith now. It is not safe for me out there either! And I could really use the help. We have a large group of new recruits to train over the next few months. I would welcome your presence here, brother."

And so, it was decided. Barabbas would shy away from leadership in the public forum and concentrate on readying new recruits. Confine himself to Bereshith.

This was good and bad.

It did let the dust settle a little. Let the Romans give up on finding him when their search turned up futile. Maybe if he didn't resurface anywhere for a long while, they would lose interest, forget about him.

Maybe.

At the same time, it made things difficult for him, because at arm's length from active and public participation in the movement, the only thing he had known for the last decade or so...

Barabbas had time to sit back and look at things. At everything. Maybe too much time.

Time to examine his life. What he had done. What he had missed. What he wanted. Where he was headed. Thoughts that sometimes took him to crazy places.

Daniel's death continued to haunt him. He knew that he himself could just as easily be dead. And maybe he was amazed in a way that he was not.

Maybe he should be. It would be easier.

Then too, the desertion of young Simon kept coming back to his mind. Had this young man really discovered something better, a more significant way? He had left Q to pursue it, to pursue this man he talked about.

Barabbas wondered whether there was now a *Fifth* way—*a way of love?*

He wondered on many days whether *he* could ever do or be anything else.

If he laid low for long enough, maybe changed his identity, could he somehow sneak back into society and live a *normal* life? Would he be allowed that luxury?

But then, would he be able to live with himself, even if he could pull that off? Or was he just so full of idealism that he could never settle for normal? He just didn't know anymore. Not for sure, anyway.

And he thought more all the time it seemed, about family. Other people in Q allowed themselves those joys.

But here he was...alone.

He had his Zealot brothers, but...

He had been very close on his way from Joppa, had even slept on the roof of his former home in Rakkath. He had so longed to see them.

What was family life like in Tiberius he wondered, if that was in fact where they now were?

Batiyah, his ima? Would she still be as he pictured her? Was she well? And what of Zephaniah? He was probably married, likely even had several children by now. What was his wife like? Had he married Naomi after all? And his children? Boys? Girls? How old would they be? And then there were the others. Elijah would be…twenty-four or so. And Sarah, she would now be a young lady. She was likely married herself, or at the very least betrothed to someone. Barabbas wondered what her husband was like, what kind of man he was? And finally, Seth. He would be eighteen. All grown up in his own right.

All that he had missed.

He wondered about Caleb and his family too.

Was he married by now?

And then too, again, what about Ariah?

She had most likely been given and had given herself to some other man. They probably had children together. He was convinced of it.

Barabbas knew in some way that he should be that man. Should have been that man.

He loved her, then and still, he was certain, more than anyone else ever could have. Dangerous places to let one's mind wander indeed.

Over the next several years, Barabbas was only a casual participant in uprisings and completely shied away from actively engaging targets. He shared his talents in eliminating them with those in training at Bereshith. He concentrated on teaching recruits the ideals that Q valued and believed: all that he had learned through the years.

At times he wondered if he was actually a hypocrite: did he fully believe what he was teaching anymore?

Much of his time was spent poring over and sifting through each of the scrolls Q had in their possession, most of his pursuit now focused entirely on what the prophets had foretold regarding the coming Messiah.

What Simon had said on the day of his departure had set Barabbas on a quest.

Exactly what it was that he had said that had so arrested him, he couldn't remember.

Only that he simply knew that he must discover the truth. Must seek it out.

The whole and the complete truth.

About the long anticipated One that Adonai had promised He would send.

Chapter 38

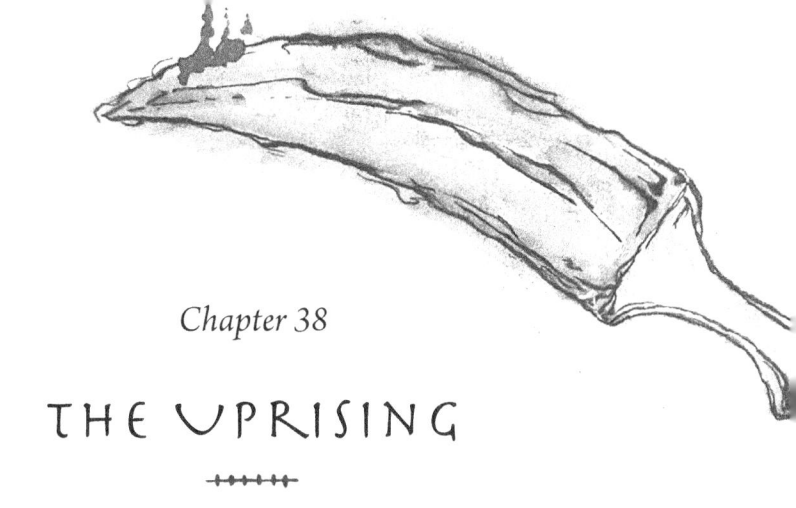

THE UPRISING

Festivals, the high and holy days on the Jewish calendar, were always the best times for the Qanaim to incite riots, hold uprisings, and further the aim of the movement: the overthrow of Roman power so as to bring about the freedom of the Chosen people.

The festival that they loved the most, however, was definitely the Feast of Purim, celebrated exactly one month prior to Passover.

It was not a scripturally mandated feast but had evolved from the time when the Jews of Queen Esther's day were delivered out of the hands of evil Haman and saved from his sinister plot to destroy them.

On the thirteenth day of the twelfth month, the month of Adar, it seemed certain that their enemies would triumph but then somehow, things miraculously turned around and the Jewish people began to prevail over their oppressors. By the fourteenth of Adar, they had clearly won the day and, as a result, that day came down in history as a day of feasting and gladness, a day of sending delicacies to each other and of giving gifts to the poor.

Of all of the Jewish holidays, this one lent itself to the most consumption of strong drink. That in itself made it much easier to take down Jewish targets at least. Many of them were quite inebriated and could barely stand.

They would hardly know that they had been attacked. And when they did fall down, death would not be anyone's first thought.

Then too, the fact that this feast celebrated the nation of Israel ridding itself of its enemies and throwing off their domination?

It was a perfect fit.

This festival seemed tailor-made for the Zealot cause.

Barabbas had lain low for almost three years now. Not only he, but Q as a whole, had been rather quiet for the last several years.

It had been much talked about lately and was ultimately decided that, as a movement, they should plan possibly the largest uprising known to date, to take place in Jerusalem at the time of the upcoming celebration.

Plans were made. Members were notified. Targets were chosen. In all, almost one thousand people had been slated for elimination.

The Qanaim were planning to show their strength like never before. And that meant that all members who were able needed to participate.

Barabbas was the one chosen to lead the offensive. He was definitely the most experienced and skilled in combat and had probably eliminated more targets than anyone else still living. He was certainly a symbol of passion for the Zealot cause. Then too, he was an eloquent spokesperson, an excellent organizer, and his charisma always seemed to encourage others to achieve beyond what they thought was possible.

Everyone thought him the man for the job. They told him he had lain low long enough.

In secret, Barabbas questioned whether he was up to it. But he hoped and prayed that this might be exactly what he needed. He could put his own questions or concerns or apprehensions aside for later or for good, and pour himself into the task at hand.

What he was good at.
The only life he had known.
It was his calling.
Enforcing the justice of Ha Shem.
He became a man on a mission.
Consumed by zeal once again.
He was very excited; more and more as the day drew near.
Purim finally came.

Members of Q had come from far and wide to be in Jerusalem to participate in this uprising. Over the course of the several weeks leading up to the fourteenth of Adar, they had held many secret meetings and even recruited quite a few new members.

Barabbas himself had chosen a young man named Abiathar to shadow him. He was one of the promising new recruits he had come to know over the past few months at Bereshith. Their particular target was a Roman consul known as Decimus, a man responsible for some of the harshest taxation policies to date, in Jerusalem specifically but indeed, impacting the entire province of Judea.

Coincidentally, the Romans had a rather large festival of their own occurring at the same time as the Jewish Feast of Purim, though truth be told, they seemed to celebrate one of their many gods almost every other day. This was big though, the beginning of their New Year, which happened just slightly before the Jewish New Year. It was the time when they celebrated the birthday of the god Mars after whom the month was named. On this day, the sacred fire of Rome would be renewed. And, at the height of the celebration, they held a parade in which young men called *Salii* danced their way through the streets decked out in military garb celebrating Rome's armed forces and military might.

For them to do this in Rome would be one thing. But this blatant affront to the worship of the one true God and to the Jewish state was more than the Qanaim could stand within their borders, especially within Judea. They had largely been able to resist Roman tyrrany until about thirty years ago. But now it seemed each year brought greater Roman influence and control, especially right here in Zion.

The sun rose bright and clear on the fourteenth of Adar. Both Roman and Jewish targets had been chosen and assigned. Q had spent the day before celebrating their victory, though careful to avoid the consumption of alcoholic beverages that usually went with the Feast of Purim. They wanted to make sure that they had their wits about them and were stone cold sober, completely up to the task at hand.

Everyone was in their place.

The Imperial parade was making its way down the street, the young dancers in their military costumes leading the procession. Roman dignitaries followed. The crowd cheered. The parade invaded streets that were already filled with Jewish revelers celebrating their own strength and victory in the Feast of Purim celebrations.

The parade destination was the large paved area outside of the Roman garrison that had been constructed adjacent to the Temple. This was after all a celebration with military overtones.

It was a clash of two cultures.

A holy temple and a demonic empire.

The collision of sacred and secular.

A battleground.

Barabbas saw Decimus, and motioned to Abiathar. They moved toward him as the procession slowed and began to gather, merging with the Jewish crowd. Decimus's face showed his pleasure at all of this. His smile seemed to Barabbas the epitome of the politician. A man who loved the accolades of the crowd. Barabbas edged his way, ever closer to this symbol of Roman power and sovereignty.

His hand was inside his cloak gripping the handle of his dagger as he came alongside.

Barabbas didn't know this man at all, but hated him all the same. Allowed himself to hate him for all that Rome had done to him and to those that he loved and cared about. Hated him for what he represented. Hated him for all that he had lost, for all that he'd had to go through as a result. Hated him even for the fact that he had not really been able to choose the direction for his life.

Barabbas moved around to face him. And for a moment they stared each other down. This Roman and this Zealot. Barabbas sneered at him. And he saw the change of expression on Decimus's face, unsure as he was of this Jew who had invaded his space. Abiathar watched.

"For Adonai And For...Barabbas!" Barabbas shouted in words reminiscent of Gideon's attack on Midian. Right in Decimus's face.

Loudly enough that everyone could hear.

Mayhem broke out throughout the crowd as the members of Q sprang into action.

On this day, Barabbas had decided to be even more openly aggressive than ever before. Was he tempting fate? He pulled the knife from its hiding place and drove it home, deep into Decimus's chest, holding him for a moment's time. He withdrew the knife and went to move away. But he had remained just a little too long. Decimus grabbed Barabbas to steady himself. At the same time, someone crashed into the two of them from behind and they now fell to the ground together, Barabbas still caught in this Roman's death grip. He struggled to free himself. Decimus hung on with every bit of life that remained.

Abiathar grabbed at Decimus's hands in an attempt to free his mentor. The whole scene around them had erupted into riotous confusion. Finally, Barabbas managed to break free and quickly scrambled to his feet. He grabbed Abiathar by the hand and motioned which direction he thought the best option to guarantee their escape.

As he did so, however, he made one more bold mistake, he turned again to look in the direction of his target, something that he had trained every member of Q to avoid. For the first time ever or, at least since that very first time, Barabbas broke his own rule. Why he did it, he did not know.

But, as he did so, he could not but notice that there was now a young man all decked out in full parade garb, maybe about fifteen years of age he guessed, bending over Decimus's limp form. His eyes were filled with tears and a groan escaped his lips. He looked up toward the sky, his young mind most likely awash with questions. Barabbas had not noticed this young man in their vicinity, this boy he could now only assume was Decimus's son. Did not know that the one who danced right next to him was in all probability the Roman legislator's very own flesh and blood.

Barabbas froze…

…at the very moment when he should have been making his exit.

Memories of another young man whom he knew only too well, a boy of about the same age kneeling next to his murdered father, ambushed by a million questions, came flooding back, clouding absolutely everything.

Barabbas stared at the young man. He could not have averted his eyes even if he'd wanted to.

So deeply he felt his pain.

Pain that *he* had been the one to cause.

Pain that *he* knew first hand would never go away.

The young man looked up. And as he did so, their eyes locked. Barabbas was powerless to do anything but stand there and return his gaze.

What Barabbas beheld was a young man searching this stranger's—Barabbas's very own—eyes for some answer.

"Why? Why did *you* do this?"

"What did my father ever do to *you?*"

He held out an arm in Barabbas's direction, pointing.

Barabbas could barely breathe, felt himself choking. Thought he might vomit.

Immediately, soldiers surrounded them taking a firm hold. Barabbas was almost unaware of what was going on.

They were being arrested.

He had been apprehended.

He didn't even resist.

The soldiers grabbed their arms, pulling them roughly around behind them. As they did so, Barabbas lost his grip and the still bloody dagger clattered to the ground.

In that very instant, Barabbas knew that he had already been judged and found guilty. This would be different from all the other arrests.

A despised Jew had evidently murdered a prominent Roman citizen.

He had been caught as they say, "red-handed!"

Holding Barabbas and Abiathar from behind, the soldiers took them to the ground, crushing the two of them into the pavement with their full weight.

"You will pay for this, dagger man," one of the soldiers snarled. "You will most certainly pay for this with your life!"

Maybe this was the end.

In a way, Barabbas didn't even care.

Relief might be the thing he was actually feeling.

Strange musings, he thought.

The reality was...

His destiny had just taken a rather abrupt turn.

And life, as long or as short as it might now be, would most assuredly never be as it was before.

Chapter 39

ARREST

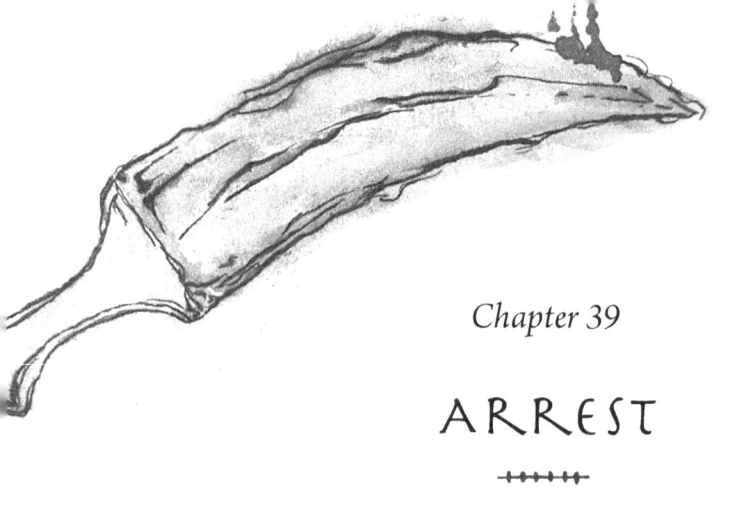

Many freedom fighters were apprehended that day. Upon arrest, they were stripped naked, ensuring they had no other concealed weapons, but this was also a great way for the Empire to publicly humiliate and shame them, something Rome loved to do to its enemies at any opportunity.

And now, shackled hands and feet, their particular group was paraded through the streets and then brought right back to the Antonia Fortress—a military post that had been built adjacent to the northwest corner of the Temple in Jerusalem almost seventy years ago, during the early building program of Herod the Great—publicly paraded and then returned to the very place they had been captured.

Upon arrival, they had been led down a significant number of steps, through a locked iron door that opened itself upon a small holding cell. In the center of that room was a hole, a shaft actually, maybe about four feet in diameter, and the iron grate covering it was secured with several large locks. Barabbas had noticed a ladder leaning against the wall to their right, but the soldiers, once they had roughly removed his shackles, simply opened the hatchway and then quite literally cast him, or rather, simply dropped him, down the short *tunnel* and onto the dungeon's floor some twelve or so feet below.

He had landed in a heap on the dirt. Though injured, he had been able to shuffle himself to one side to get out of the way just as Abiathar crashed to the ground in the same way Barabbas had just seconds earlier.

"Abi, quick, get out of the way!" Barabbas called out.

But his trainee, Abiathar, had not been as quick on the draw and a rather large man named Josiah, the next member of their group to be thrown into this prison, had landed in a heap on top of him.

Abiathar cried out in pain.

"Are you okay?" Josiah asked, scrambling to move the two of them out of harm's way, knowing that others would soon follow.

One by one they crashed to the ground behind them.

Barabbas and Josiah both knew without being told that Abiathar had definitely fared the worst in all of this. They had heard maybe his collarbone or a rib loudly complain as Josiah had landed on him.

Josiah felt around and finally put his hand on Abiather's shoulders. The slight pressure made Abiathar scream out in pain. It was warm and sticky on his left side and bone, broken bone, protruded through the torn flesh. Josiah kept his hand on the wound in an effort to stop the bleeding but it seemed futile.

The attempt to help just increased the pain.

Other than the bit of light coming down the shaft through which they had entered, there was no other source of illumination. Barabbas waited for his eyes to grow accustomed to the dark, surveying his surroundings as they did. He heard other people moving around in the room beyond the small circle of light but was not sure exactly where the others were or how many of them were there.

He slowly moved away from the illuminated spot the three of them and then the others had entered, straining his eyes and holding his hands out in front of him. As soon as he was away from the opening however, the smell of urine and excrement and sweat and death immediately overwhelmed his nostrils and he involuntarily vomited up the little bit of food that he had eaten earlier that day.

What he saw was that the underground room in which they now found themselves, stone walls and a dirt floor, was about thirty feet long, about twenty feet wide and maybe about six and a half feet high. Water, or possibly sewage, from the city above ran down the one wall and onto the floor below. And, he counted some twenty or so other prisoners who were there in that cavern, all awaiting trial or more likely like him, like the rest of them, simply death.

As he moved around, Barabbas saw a pile of clothing to one side and tore off a piece to help stop the bleeding from Abiathar's wound. As he did so, however, he realized that a dead and decomposing body was concealed in the garment. If he hadn't already vomited the contents of his stomach, he was sure he may have again.

He took the piece of cloth to where Josiah was holding Abiathar, already unconscious as a result of the pain. Josiah took the makeshift bandage extended to him and placed it over the injury. Barabbas didn't tell him where he had procured it.

"This is an awful place!" Josiah said. "More horrid than Gehenna! And, for better or worse, I fear that our little brother... will not be long here."

Barabbas nodded in agreement, though in the darkness, he was pretty sure Josiah had not seen the gesture. The group was now all huddled together against one wall by themselves.

Barabbas thought it was very unfair that Abiathar, someone who had only been there as an observer, had been arrested and cast into this prison just as if he was a full-fledged member of the movement and a murderer like the rest of them. He would die here.

Almost immediately, his thoughts rushed back to another young man whose world he knew he had just turned upside down.

Decimus's son.

That tortured face haunted him.

Yes, he was a Roman.

The enemy.

But he was human.

And in reality, just an innocent child.

Barabbas had always known that others, family members, were impacted by the death of whomever was his appointed target. At times they had killed entire families.

But at a distance, as long as it remained only a conceptual reality, he could remain largely unaffected by it.

Here was a boy, still living, who needed a father. And now, it did not matter whether he had been a good, bad or mediocre one, his abba would not be part of this young man's life anymore.

He would grow up without…him.

Barabbas groaned.

His own pain rubbed raw again.

"What have I done?" he cried out, his thoughts now tormenting him.

He knew the boy would be asking, why? Wondering if it was a nightmare from which he could awake? Supposing it was some kind of mistake? Wondering why this stranger had done this to him?

Barabbas knew because they had been *his* questions.

He wondered what *this* young man would do with all of his anger and confusion?

Would this victim become a fighter, fueled by rage, as Barabbas himself had done? Had he unknowingly created yet another enemy of the Chosen people, even one with some justification for his hatred?

Barabbas must have eventually drifted off to sleep, if that is what is what it could be called. More like passing out from absolute mental and physical exhaustion.

The mission, as far as he was concerned, had failed miserably.

It was an absolute disaster. His taking the lead had not been a good idea at all.

He had been too bold. Too aggressive. Too vested.

Zeal...without wisdom.

Chapter 40

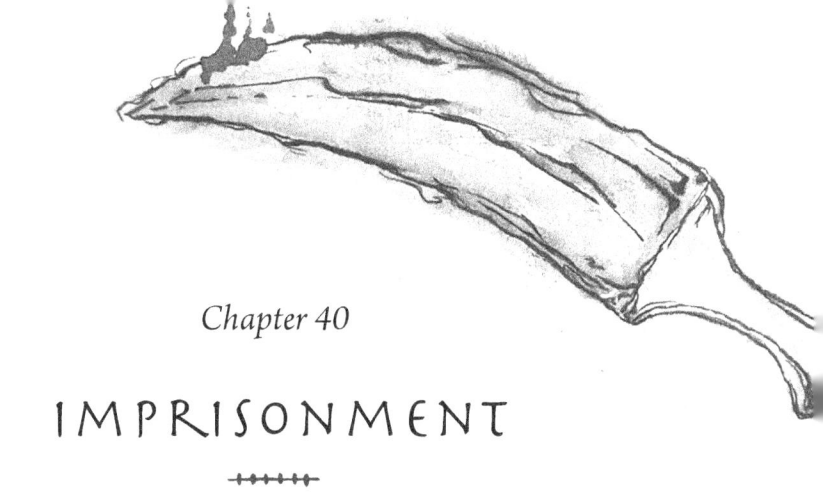

IMPRISONMENT

Barabbas had been in prison.

Quite a few times in fact.

But this place was unlike anywhere he had ever been detained before.

If he had been wealthy, he wondered, might he have simply been placed, like most who were people of means, under house arrest? That is, as long as he behaved, until he could stand trial. He didn't have money, he would have had to steal it, but even if he had, that probably wouldn't have happened.

Could they, would they, have trusted him to cooperate? Not likely.

He was a murderer all but convicted of treason against the Empire. A Jewish Zealot caught in the act of killing a Roman citizen.

In actuality, he had killed *many* others, probably somewhere in the hundreds, but so skillful was he that he had never been caught in the act.

Until now.

He was very good at what he did. Or had been…

Still, as one of the leading figures in the movement, he would most certainly have broken free, waiting for an opportunity to overcome, even kill his Roman keepers, and run away. One of his compatriots could have and would have surely been willing and able to somehow smuggle him some type of weapon, for that very purpose. Or the Qanaim may have come *en masse,* killed the guards and broken him out. Those kinds of escapes had happened before.

He knew that he at least, was most certainly in the Antonia Fortress because it was far more secure, home to no less than 600 Roman soldiers at any given time and sometimes occupied by several thousand.

If he had been someone of little consequence or notice, if he had not made such a reputation for himself, maybe justice would have been swift and fatal, like he had witnessed years earlier... in Galilee.

He thought once more of Abba. And Batiyah. He had told himself he was doing this for them. But...was this what they would have wanted him to do?

Abrahim had most assuredly been opposed to violence, bloodshed, and vengeance. And his ima...?

Had he been wrong about everything?

He now questioned every decision he had made.

His thoughts were driving him mad.

But in prison, one can do little else but think.

How long had it been, here, in this dungeon; confined in this awful place? "And there was evening, and there was morning... *another* day." How many times had that happened?

At this very moment in the half-dark of early morning, Barabbas didn't know exactly. There was little sense of time here. It was like one very long night. He thought it must surely be close to a month or so now.

Was it Passover already?

He would most likely not be celebrating this year.

Why was it taking so long? Barabbas didn't know that either. Prisoners were given very little if any information. All he knew for certain right now was that he was starving and ill and that he was, physically, emotionally, and spiritually, the most miserable he had ever been.

Barabbas cursed the Empire and all things Roman.

The only good in all of this he supposed, was that he was still alive, even though he knew that it was a gross exaggeration to describe his present state of existence as *living*. His life had been far from easy or comfortable, especially for the last decade or so—a Zealot, almost always on the run for his very life it seemed—but being imprisoned in this hellhole, he wondered whether full-on death might be the preferable option.

Despair made constant assaults.

He longed for it all to just end.

Of the eight brothers who had been arrested and brought here after the most recent uprising, he was the only one still alive or at least so he assumed. Given his condition, he might soon join them, he thought.

Abiathar had died almost right away from the injuries he'd sustained when they were cast into this abyss. Josiah and all of the others had been removed about a week later. Most likely, they had been crucified.

Why he of all people had been spared the cross and left to die a secluded and secret death here in this nether world made no sense.

Surely, even in his worst nightmares, had Barabbas ever imagined that this would be where his life would end?

Part of him had always known and more so after joining the rebel cause, that he would probably not live to a ripe old age.

But here, like this…

Were the Romans saving his death for some special occasion?

Barabbas knew that he had come to be part of the Jewish Zealot movement by choice in a way, but maybe more so through circumstances that had been beyond his control. He had simply been in the wrong place at the wrong time, or maybe the right place at the wrong time, or the wrong place at the right time…he wasn't sure what wording best described what had actually happened.

He *was* grateful that he had been there. If for nothing or for no one else, then for *her* sake. But, could things have turned out differently?

If only.

The Qanaim had taken him in and given him a semblance of family when he had lost everything. Had he believed what they taught only because of what he received in return? No, it had made sense to him even before he joined. It still made sense to him. The ideals anyway.

But…and this was the thing troubling him the most: what about the means they used to achieve those ideals? He had wondered about that often over the past few days and weeks, and truth be told, even before he had been imprisoned.

Did all of the bloodshed, all of the violence, really accomplish their goals? More than that, was this really the way that Elohim intended to bring about His kingdom, His reign on the earth?

Barabbas's biggest question, the one that loomed large: Did all he had done please Adonai?

Was this a crisis of faith he was experiencing?

Everything he had come to believe now seemed to be called into question.

Or was it that he just did not have the stomach for this way of life anymore?

His thoughts seemed to be taking him all over the map and in every direction at the same time.

But here, in this place, Barabbas was forced to ask himself what each of us must ask ourselves at some point:

Has my life, my unique contribution within history, in any way made a positive difference in the world?

And on a more personal note:

Have I *myself* mattered to *anyone?*

That latter question felt like a dagger thrust deep into his own heart.

He knew that people were far more important than any ideology. They matter. Family was important. Relationships were paramount.

He thought of all of the people that he had killed.

They were not without significance.

And then, once more, he thought about the boy, Decimus's son.

Barabbas had begun calling him, "Marcus."

He was almost positive that probably wasn't his name, but he knew that the boy did have one.

Barabbas was pretty sure that *naming* him was a mistake. Add it to all of the mistakes he had made on that day, and on many others.

But he knew that the boy was a *someone,* someone who mattered.

How many other sons and daughters and wives had he hurt?

Was there any hope for him?

Or was it too late for redemption?

Barabbas buried his head in his hands and wept.

Profound sadness and pain surfaced, bubbling up from the center of everything that was churning inside.

And yet, there was some kind of striking clarity.

In the past, Barabbas had always forced those hurts and life-size questions way down deep inside and invited anger and hatred to take their place. Those emotions seemed easier to control. To channel.

Less vulnerable. More powerful.

But maybe he didn't need or want to respond that way any longer.

Where had anger and hate taken him?

Nowhere good it seemed.

Too little, too late?

Impossible?

He didn't know.

Tears were streaming down Barabbas's face. He made no effort to stop them. In fact, he welcomed them.

And then, a thought, a revelation, appeared from some forgotten, or maybe from some brand-new place within him.

Hope wrestling to be born.

"Adonai," Barabbas began, and then somewhat tentatively declared, "David said that even if I make my bed in *Sheol*, You are there, and that even the darkness will not be dark to you. That your light will shine!"

Surveying his surroundings momentarily, his hands reached out for something, or maybe...

...for Some One.

"Are You really…are *You* actually…*here?*"

"If You are, then I beg You, shine Your light and find me please, Abba!"

Barabbas gasped at that last word. It had escaped his lips before he had thought about or could stop it.

But it was the one thing he knew he craved.

And he was now keenly aware that he was a man who had nothing to lose.

Or maybe, more correctly, that he was at the core of his being, simply and once more…a desperate and lonely child.

Chapter 41

BROUGHT OUT

Barabbas blinked.

He was not dreaming. Sure enough, he found himself standing once more on the Stone Pavement in front of the Antonia Fortress.

Outside.

No shackles.

No smell.

For the first time in…

How long had it been?

He was free.

They had taken off the chains of his imprisonment and he had heard the words, "You're free to go, dagger-man."

What in the world had just happened?

The last several hours had been a whirlwind on every front.

It had not even been light when he had been rather rudely awakened, not that he ever really slept in that awful place.

"Jesus Barabbas! Get up! You've got an appointment with the governor. Now!" his keeper had called out.

"Whaaat? Now?" he had groggily replied.

But then, he was suddenly and completely and totally awake; terror filled his heart.

"I am being crucified today!" he whispered to himself.

His mind raced. No light penetrated the prison opening. What was the rush to have him executed so suddenly in the middle of the night?

His jailer had lowered a rickety ladder down into the cell. With some difficulty, because he was rather weak and because he was still barely awake, he climbed up and out of the netherworld that had been all he had known for the past twenty-nine days and nights. It was indeed still dark outside, but he blinked a little because even the darkness of night seemed bright after having not seen it for so long. Fresh night air assaulted his nostrils and lungs. It was glorious. And almost overwhelming.

He was led out of the small room above the dungeon, down a short alley and into another larger room where the jailer was now joined by several others. They proceeded to tear off the rags that used to be his clothes, by now so rotten that they gave way easily. He stood there, chained and manacled, and once more, completely naked.

They began to cut off his long and matted hair and beard, trimming it close to his skin. Why would they go to all this trouble just to kill him, he wondered?

And now, the guards took soap and water and began to scrub him down. Rather roughly, but it felt wonderful. Water! It was freezing cold, but it was amazing! He opened his parched lips and let some of it enter his mouth. He could have done without the soap, but to a thirsty soul, it still tasted wonderful.

They stood him to his feet and quickly if not completely dried him off. They put a clean robe on him, undoing each of his fetters just long enough to pull his arms through.

He felt vaguely human for the first time in a long time. Having tasted fresh air, he now longed for more. For freedom. But alas, that was only a dream. He was still a prisoner, not free at all. A captive of this idolatrous empire. They could do whatever they wanted to him.

And that, it appeared, was exactly what he was shortly to experience in a most final way.

Chapter 42

PONTIUS PILATE

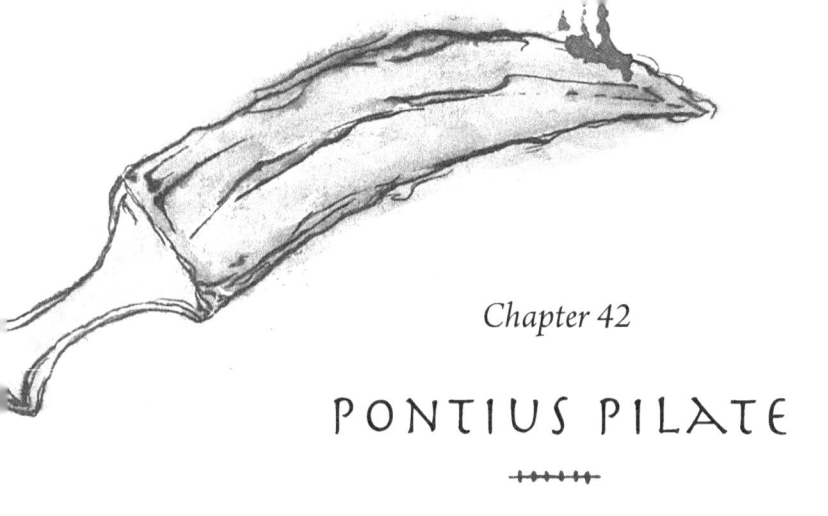

BARABBAS WAS LED BETWEEN TWO GUARDS UP A wide staircase into a rather large room within the palace. This was the upper section of the Roman fortress of Antonia, a place that Barabbas had never seen; so very different from the familiar part of the fortress.

On the far side of this room, a man was standing and staring out through one of the arched openings.

It was none other than the governor himself.

Pontius Pilate.

Barabbas was led in his direction and as they approached, Pilate turned to face them.

Barabbas was not even ten feet away from the Roman governor. If only he had some kind of weapon. Yes, two guards stood at his sides to restrain him. But, even with his chains, even in the midst of his keepers, he imagined that he could force himself in Pilate's direction and bury a knife deep into his flesh.

Certainly, he would be apprehended and killed, most likely on the spot, but he was going to die anyway. How wonderful to be able to take out one very influential and important Roman dog on this, his final day. He was pretty sure he wouldn't have any qualms about killing *this* man.

Pilate spoke directly to Barabbas.

"It has been my custom on occasion to release a prisoner at your Jewish Passover festival. Today, some of your rulers, persons of some influence, have come to me and petitioned for *your* release."

The last word slammed itself into Barabbas's consciousness.

"Release!"

What?

My Release!

He thought for sure that he was being crucified.

Today. Now.

He was certain it was all over.

But, could it be? How could it be…that he might go free?

Had the Empire gone mad?

He almost smiled at the thought.

And then, why him?

He? Barabbas?

And who were these persons of influence who had talked to Pilate on his behalf?

Pilate turned to look out onto the Stone Pavement once more. A commotion could be heard outside.

Just then, a guard entered from that direction and motioned for Pilate to come.

Barabbas wondered what was going on out there. He could hear only muffled sounds. Whispering back and forth. Questions. Answers.

Whatever it was, something big was going down.

Finally, he heard Pilate out on the front steps of the palace address the crowd: "What charges are you bringing against this man?"

One voice from the crowd, Barabbas thought he recognized it as belonging to the high priest, Annas, spoke up, "If he were not a criminal, we would not have handed him over to you."

"Take him yourselves and judge him by your own law," Pilate said.

"But we have no right to execute anyone," they objected.

This certainly is big, Barabbas thought. If it was indeed the Passover as Pilate had said, and Barabbas had thought that the celebration must be near but had kind of lost track of time during his incarceration, the fact that the Jewish leaders wanted to have someone executed seemed strange indeed.

Why the rush?

Who was this that they hated so much that they would risk killing him and having some see him as a sacrificial lamb? Killing someone during the Passover could very easily start a riot, especially if the victim was popular with the people.

With that, Pilate came back into the room. And, at a short distance behind him another man entered, a Jew, bound at the wrists, and escorted by several guards.

The man looked completely exhausted, as if he had been through much abuse already that morning or even all night long.

Barabbas wondered what he himself must look like?

Barabbas simply stared at the man, now quietly standing directly across the room from him. He wondered what horrible thing he had done that the Jewish leaders so wanted him dead. He didn't think this man looked like a criminal at all.

And why the strange combination of his release and this other individual being put to death for his crimes?

Pilate stood in front of Barabbas and the other man.

"Jesus..." Pilate began.

Barabbas jerked his head to the right and in the governor's direction, jolted out of his reverie, thinking he was being addressed.

He was about to answer.

Pilate was looking at the other man.

Chapter 43

THE MAN

Pilate paused. He drew a deep breath, as if he was pondering what to say next or what to do.

"Are you the king of the Jews?" he asked the man.

Barabbas's mind raced.

King of the Jews? Someone claiming to be the Messiah? No wonder the Jewish leaders had taken a dislike to the man. At the same time, people claimed to be the Messiah almost every other day.

Messiah? Pilate had called the man Jesus.

Was this, could this be that Jesus, the Jesus of Nazareth that Simon had talked about? The one who changed everything?

Barabbas was trying to get a sense of the man.

"Is that your own idea," the man replied, "Or did others talk to you about me?"

Wow, Barabbas thought, he might not look like much but there is definitely more to this man than meets the eye! That was some response. He seems to have absolutely no fear of the Roman authorities.

Barabbas now looked forward to what else this man might say.

Pilate laughed a little, albeit somewhat nervously.

"Am I a Jew? Your own people and chief priests handed you over to me. What is it you have done?"

Yes, what had this man done, Barabbas wondered?

And, at the same time, he had another more sobering thought. What would all of this uproar mean for his imminent release?

Pilate, or so Barabbas thought, had been ready to pronounce him free and release him.

And now, this other Jesus, claimant to the throne of David, was diverting all the attention.

Might his own release be forgotten in all of this?

His thoughts were interrupted by the other man's speech.

"My kingdom," Jesus said, "is not of this world." And with that, he turned and looked directly at Barabbas, his eyes seeming to search the very depths of Barabbas's soul. "If it were of this world, my servants would fight to prevent my arrest by the Jewish leaders. But now my kingdom is from another place."

Barabbas's mind reeled. Who is this? And even the mighty Pontius Pilate seemed a little taken aback by the man's answer.

The governor hesitated.

"You *are* a king, then?" asked Pilate.

Or, was it more of a statement: "You *are* a king then!"

Barabbas wasn't entirely sure.

"You say that I am a king," Jesus answered.

Clearly, he picked up on the fact that, know it or not, Pilate was making it more of a statement than he was asking a question.

"You say that I am a king. In fact, the reason I was born and came into the world is to testify to the truth. Everyone on the side of truth listens to me."

Barabbas was riveted. He could not take his eyes off this man. Had he ever heard anyone speak this way? He now knew for himself what Simon had talked about, what was so appealing, drawing.

This Galilean Messiah had to be that same man.

He was clearly baffling Roman power.

Barabbas smiled at that thought.

"What is truth?" Pilate said, in a way to himself and under his breath. It was obvious he was troubled with all of this, and he left the room to go out to the crowd once again.

"I find no basis for a charge against him," Pilate said to the crowd who immediately clamored in uproar.

"He stirs up the people all over Judea by his teaching. He started in Galilee and has come all the way here," someone shouted.

Pilate returned and asked the man if he was indeed a Galilean. The man nodded.

"He is a Galilean and Galilee is Herod Antipas's jurisdiction," Pilate said to the soldiers. "Herod is in Jerusalem right now. Send him there."

And with that, Jesus was escorted out and away.

Pilate left the room and Barabbas and the guards watching him remained where they were...waiting.

Jesus of Nazareth returned after about an hour and a half, though now dressed in a purple robe.

Barabbas knew that it was meant mockingly, but found it interesting that in their *humiliation,* they had in fact dressed him as if he were king.

"Herod says that the man wouldn't talk to him, but that he too finds nothing against him," the captain of the guard relayed.

Pilate was clearly thinking all of this through.

He went back out to the crowd.

"You brought me this man as one who was inciting the people to rebellion. I have examined him in your presence and have found no basis for your charges against him. Neither has Herod, for he has sent him back to us. As you can see, he has done nothing to deserve death. Therefore, I will punish him and then release him."

The crowd went absolutely wild, erupting into shouts and screams. They wanted none of that. Not today. The incited mob was hungry for blood.

Pilate quieted them with his upraised hand. He stroked his chin gently as an idea assembled itself in his mind.

"It is customary at the time of the Passover for me, Pontius Pilate, to release a prisoner to you."

> "Whom do you want me to release to you:
> Jesus, who is called Barabbas, or
> Jesus, who is called the Christ?"

Barabbas couldn't help but hear the irony

He was Jesus Barabbas, son of Abba-Father.

Jesus Christos, *Yeshua Ha-Mashiach,* Jesus the Messiah, the Anointed One, was the way he referred to the other man.

But wait! Was he hearing right? Could this other Jesus be released? What then? Was there a possibility this other man might be released and that then he, Barabbas, would not? Was that the possibility that had just been placed in the hands of the crowd and the Jewish leadership? Barabbas's mind raced.

Within seconds, however, he heard the chant of the crowd gathered outside:

"Barabbas, Barabbas, give us Barabbas!"

His heart leapt inside his chest.

He would be released.

But that also meant that the other man, the other Jesus, would not.

His heart sank at the same time.

Jesus Barabbas would go free only because they hated this other Jesus even more than he.

He glanced in the direction of the king of this other-worldly kingdom. Their eyes locked. What was it that he now saw for himself in those eyes? It seemed like they were filled with an eternity of love and compassion, like it was entirely okay that Barabbas's freedom came at the price of his own misfortune.

It was too much. Barabbas ripped his gaze away. He could not look at the man any longer.

He knew that he actually deserved to die even if he didn't want to.

He *was* a criminal.

But this other man?

What had he done?

Pilate had asked that question and had never received a satisfactory answer.

But, Jesus of Nazareth?

He had done nothing worthy of death.

Chapter 44

CONDEMNED

Taking their cue from a subtle wave of Pilate's hand, the soldiers removed the man's garments.

They promptly and with seeming relish grabbed the whip, the cat-o'-nine-tails, and began the flogging. Thirty-nine times, they brought the whip down on his bare back, ripping into the flesh. But this was more than just an ordinary flogging. They also twisted together a crown of thorns from a nearby bush and forced it down on his head. Blood trickled down his forehead.

Once finished, they clothed his bloodied body once more in the purple robe.

"Hail, King of the Jews!" they said over and over, bowing before him in feigned worship.

Barabbas found himself turning away in horror and disgust. Again, that deep and familiar anger rose within him as he watched these Romans treat one of his kinsmen with such hatred and disrespect.

"'Vengeance is mine. I will repay,' says YHWH." How badly, Barabbas wanted to be the instrument of that Divine vengeance on the enemies of Ha Shem once more; now in defense of this man.

Once more, Pilate left the room and went out to the swollen crowd of Jewish leaders and common people gathered outside, those gathered *outside* so as to avoid ceremonial uncleanliness and still be able to eat the Passover later that day, since entering the Gentile palace would have made them unfit.

Barabbas wondered to himself how they could do something so filthy, so vile, and still be considered clean in Adonai's eyes?

Was being unclean only about outward actions?

Was it not more about the condition of the heart?

"Look, I am bringing him out to you to let you know that I find no basis for a charge against him," Pilate stated.

It appeared that Pilate really wanted to release Jesus of Nazareth.

What that would mean to Barabbas for Pilate to succeed, he did not know. In a way, he no longer cared.

The soldiers led Jesus of Nazareth, now bloody and beaten and wearing the crown of thorns and the purple robe, out onto the balcony where Pilate had gone.

"Ecce homo!" Pilate pronounced.

"Here Is the Man!"

But, as soon as they saw him, the chief priests and the leaders began shouting, chanting,

"Crucify, Crucify, Crucify!"

The crowd was clearly incited, maddened with rage.

Pilate held up his hand and as soon as they quieted somewhat, he answered, "You take him and crucify him."

In a very forceful and yet calm voice he said again, "I find no basis for a charge against him!"

For the third time Pilate had repeated his findings:

"I find no basis for a charge against this Jesus!"

But the crowd, spurred on by the religious leadership, didn't care for Pilate's ruling.

"We have a law," one of the Jewish leaders replied, "and according to that law he must die, because he claimed to be the Son of our God!"

At that, Pilate took Jesus's arm and led him back into the palace. Barabbas thought that he saw fear written all over Pilate's face.

"Where do you come from...and I don't mean Galilee?" Pilate asked the man.

"Who are you?"

Jesus remained silent.

Pilate waited.

Jesus said nothing.

"Do you refuse to answer me?" Pilate asked. "Don't you realize I have power either to free you or crucify you?"

The man had been quiet, but now he spoke, evenly and with amazing conviction.

"You would have no power over me if it were not given to you from above," Jesus said. "Therefore, the one who handed me over to you is guilty of a greater sin."

Pilate was visibly shaken. He wanted desperately to set this man free. He tried several more times to reason with the riotous crowd. But as much as Pilate wanted to free this Jesus, immeasurably more, it seemed, the Jewish leaders pushed for his death.

Finally, one of the Jewish leaders yelled from the crowd, "If you let this man go, you are no friend of Caesar! Anyone who claims to be a king opposes Caesar!"

That was Pilate's undoing.

He was, like all the other Romans, it seemed to Barabbas, a political opportunist. And, whatever he may have thought or felt about this Jesus, he was going to protect himself and his rising position.

Yes, that was what Barabbas hated most about Rome. And he saw ever more clearly, though not for the first time, that the Jewish leadership had been afflicted with the same evil self-preservation and self-interest at any cost, human or otherwise. He had seen it here this day, right before his eyes.

Pilate had Jesus brought out once again onto the *Pavimentum Saxum*, the Stone Pavement. He sat down on the judge's seat.

Judgment was about to be pronounced.

From where he was standing, Barabbas could not see the man, Jesus. He could only see Pilate seated on the judge's seat. Suddenly a woman, looking somewhat disheveled and distraught, came in from the back of the room and went right to the opening, blocking even Barabbas's view of Pilate. Barabbas wondered for a second who this was that had such access to the governor, such audacity, but quickly realized that it must be Pilate's wife, Claudia Procula. She called to the governor and he looked in her direction.

"Have nothing to do with this man," she said, in a whisper loud enough for Barabbas to hear. And then, pointing in the direction of where Barabbas could only assume Jesus was now standing, she continued, "this man is innocent. And I have suffered greatly today in a dream because of him. Please, have nothing to do with him!"

As she turned to leave, Barabbas saw tears and terror. And he saw that Pilate was maybe even a little more rattled.

"Which of the two do you want me to release to you?" Pilate asked once more.

Barabbas was pretty sure that he himself favored the other man. Again, the crowd called for Barabbas.

When Pilate saw that he was getting nowhere, and that a riot was a very clear possibility, he called for a bowl of water to be brought to him. And, ceremoniously dipping his hands in the water and wringing them together, he looked in the direction of the crowd.

"I am innocent of this man's blood," he said. "It is your responsibility!"

Someone from the crowd called out in a loud voice, "His blood be upon us and upon our children!"

The crowd took up the chant.

Pilate lowered his gaze and shook his head. Then he raised his hand to once more silence the crowd.

"Here Is Your King!" Pilate announced in a very loud voice.

Barabbas marveled.

Did anyone else realize?

Pilate had just *judged* Jesus of Nazareth to be the King of the Jews. Had proclaimed him as such.

But they shouted, even more vehemently now, "Take Him Away! Take Him Away! Crucify Him!"

Pilate went at them again.

"Shall I Crucify Your King?"

After a pregnant pause, the chief priest spoke.

"We have no king but Caesar!"

Barabbas could not believe what he was hearing. The divinely ordained leaders of his nation were not only abandoning Adonai as King but were pledging their allegiance to a pagan demi-god, a man who was not the One and Only True God?

Their only king was the Roman Caesar, Tiberius? What had happened here? This was demonic and ugly in so many ways. What had happened to the faith?

With that, Pilate motioned to the guards.

"Crucify him," he said ever so quietly and without looking up, refusing to look in Jesus's direction.

The soldiers knew what to do. They had done this before to many others.

Jesus of Nazareth was not the first, nor would he be the last. Was it simply their job, Barnabas wondered, a rather gruesome employment, or was there some ugly place in each of them that rather enjoyed torturing their victims?

He thought he was going to be sick.

Chapter 45

FREEDOM

Before he even knew what had happened, one of the guards at his side removed the shackles from Barabbas's wrists and ankles.

"You're free to go, dagger-man! The crowd chose you!" he said with a sneer in his voice.

He was led out of the palace and onto the Stone Pavement in front of the Antonia Fortress. The soldier gave him a shove, just for good measure and because he could do nothing else.

Barabbas stood there for a moment, hardly knowing what to do.

He was a free man.

He blinked, waiting for his eyes to become accustomed to the bright sunshine of the outside world.

"Hey, brother!" he heard someone call out from behind him.

He turned to see Tobias and Levi, two of his fellow freedom fighters smiling broadly in his direction.

They came over and embraced him heartily.

"Let's get you out of here," Levi said, "before they all of a sudden change their mind!"

"It's so good to see you, brother. I really can't believe Pilate actually granted your release, although it seemed in question for a bit," Tobias said. "We weren't sure which Jesus they would choose."

"It has been a crazy day!" Levi added. "Can you believe it? The Sanhedrin petitioning Pilate for *your* release? Crazy!"

Barabbas just shook his head.

Crazy didn't even begin to describe it. Could it be more insane?

Barabbas wondered how it was that *he* had been freed. And the thought that the Jewish leadership had somehow orchestrated it just made the whole thing that much more complex.

"Who cares," Tobias interrupted, "Our leader is free!"

And with that, after a quick glance around to make sure no one was watching them, he passed Barabbas a *sicae*, complete with its sheath and belt.

"Here," Tobias said. "You will need this. It is the Passover and we still have work to do here."

Barabbas received it and quickly concealed it underneath his robe, reaching between the folds to experience again the touch of the smooth bone handle.

It was not Gideon's knife. Sadly, that one was gone forever, but it felt almost the same. Familiar. Comforting in a way. Things could now go back to the way that they were before.

Or...could they? Should they?

Did he even want his old life back?

Barabbas looked over at Tobias and Levi. They were busy now, conversing with James and Joachim, two others from the Fourth Way who had just joined this reunion of rebels. Barabbas imagined they were talking about what Q had planned here in Jerusalem over the next few days.

He had been, still was, a leader in the movement. He would be brought up to speed eventually.

Barabbas hesitated.

Maybe later.

Right now, he felt compelled, knew what he had to do, what he must do.

There was not a moment to lose.
He had his own mission to fulfill.
There was someone he must find.
Immediately.
Before they were gone.

He darted into an alley to his right and then turned left at the street on which it opened. He ran down the street and returned in the general direction he had remembered the crowd slowly moving.

He was pretty certain that he could catch them.

He must.

The moment, his opportunity, dare not be lost.

Chapter 46

THE CROWD

As Barabbas rounded the next corner, he thought he saw him.

But he must get closer.

He wanted to be close. Very close.

And there was already quite a throng.

It hadn't taken long for the crowd that had been on the Stone Pavement at the Antonia Fortress and was now making its way to the place of crucifixion to swell as others joined the ranks.

Jewish leaders, both Pharisees and Sadducees, members of the Sanhedrin who had brought the man to Pilate, were there in full force. Common people. Many were present simply because there was going to be a crucifixion.

And then, there he was.

The one Barabbas was after.

None other than the man he had just met.

Not weak by any means, Jesus of Nazareth looked exhausted. He had been mocked, spit on, slapped and scourged, whipped, and beaten.

He was in the middle of the moving multitude, carrying the heavy wooden crossbeam which usually weighed somewhere between 75 and 125 pounds, securely tied to his arms.

He would eventually be nailed to it.

The Romans had invented several types of *crucifixes* but, with the exception of an actual dead tree used only on rare occasions, the one they seemed to choose most often consisted of an upright in the ground on which a wooden beam, the *patibulum,* was then hoisted up.

It was this crosspiece that the condemned were most often compelled to carry to the place of crucifixion.

This accomplished several things. It was heavy and uncomfortable on the back of the neck, especially with one's arms wrapped around it. It definitely contributed to the parade of scorn, as criminals were forced to walk through the crowded city streets on their way out of town and on to the crucifixion site. Everyone would know who the condemned person was.

And they were closer to death by the time they got there. In more ways than one. If they tripped and fell, they would smash their face and body into the ground, since they could not use their arms to break the fall. In fact, the weight of the crosspiece would only add to the brute force of the impact with the road.

It was the *Via Dolorosa:* "the way of suffering."

At the same time, all of this torture was intended to invoke fear and intimidation in the hearts of a conquered people and also to convey the clear and present message: "Don't you dare mess with the Roman Empire!"

Barabbas could not but follow; not because he enjoyed this kind of thing. He detested it.

But because he had met the man.

"*Ecce Homo*—Behold the man!" Pilate had said.

And Jesus of Nazareth was like no other man he had ever encountered. They hadn't even talked...not really. But this man was so different from anyone Barabbas had ever known before.

Like Simon, his ex-Zealot brother, had told him.

Jesus had looked at him. Looked into him. And that look, the depth in those eyes, had somehow penetrated his guarded heart.

It drew him to this man.

And it absolutely amazed Barabbas that hatred or anger seemed entirely absent from those eyes.

Even now.

It was not very far from the Antonia Fortress to Golgotha, "The Place of The Skull," located just outside of the city of Jerusalem where all crucifixions took place, hardly a quarter of a mile. But Jesus barely made it as far as the Fish Gate, the portal where they made their way outside of the city walls. It was there that he stumbled and fell headlong onto the street further bloodying his already bloodstained face. And it was there that the soldiers conscripted some bystander named Simon, from Cyrene, to carry the cross the rest of the way.

Why had the soldiers chosen this one particularly?

Probably because just as Jesus had faltered and fell, the Cyrenean had reached out to catch him, somehow right beside him at the precise moment Jesus had stumbled.

He had shown compassion to a criminal and would now be punished along with him.

And, then again, Barabbas thought, anyone would probably do. Why would the Romans not abuse one more Jew in the midst of torturing another? Was it all just sport to them, treating any non-Roman like little more than an animal?

As he followed along and watched Jesus make his way to the place of his execution, the words of the prophet Isaiah screamed in his ears:

"He was despised and rejected by mankind, a man of suffering, and familiar with pain. Like one from whom people hide their faces he was despised, and we esteemed him not."

Did this man not resemble Elohim's suffering servant?

Indeed, it seemed to Barabbas as if this Jesus was carrying the weight of the world on his own shoulders, even though they had now laid the crosspiece on Simon. Yet, even in the midst of all this, Jesus of Nazareth still looked at the people he passed by with that same look that had pierced Barabbas's own soul.

Was it…how could it possibly be?

Loving!

The crowd following Jesus, Simon, the soldiers, and two other criminals that the Romans had decided to crucify along with Jesus, continued to grow in numbers.

Some of the women who were following were mourning and wailing for him. He rebuked them. Or, did he rather use this as an opportunity to prophesy?

"Daughters of Jerusalem," he turned and said to them, "do not weep for me. No, rather weep for yourselves and for your children. For the time will come when you will say, 'Blessed are the childless women, the wombs that have never bore and the breasts that have never nursed!' Then they will say to the mountains, 'Fall on us!' and to the hills, 'Cover us!' For if people do these things when the tree is green, what will happen when it is dry?"

Indeed, Barabbas thought, what other evil could this Roman machine invent, to assault and mock the people of Elohim? What *was* yet to come as Rome continued ever more to assert itself as ultimate sovereign on the world's stage?

Chapter 47

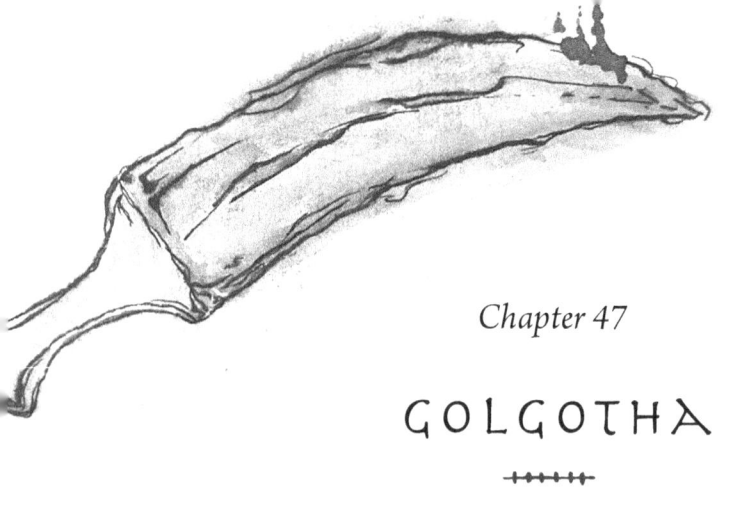

GOLGOTHA

The mob reached Golgotha, "The Place of the Skull" it was called because of how it looked, at the third hour, at around nine in the morning.

And first thing, the soldiers offered Jesus the customary wine mixed with gall, a rather strong painkiller.

Jesus refused it.

Barabbas thought that that was…strange.

He knew that *he* would not have wanted to face crucifixion stone cold sober.

They relieved the man from Cyrene of the crosspiece he had been forced to carry and proceeded to nail Jesus to it. One long nail was driven through each wrist, making sure to miss the major blood vessels.

They didn't want their victims to bleed to death and die quickly.

This was torture after all.

Then, using a rope, the crosspiece with Jesus now hanging from it was raised up the stake that was already in the ground and firmly tied in place. Lifting his feet slightly and laying one over the other, they then nailed them to the upright.

By pushing against the lower nail with one's feet, the crucified one could raise his body slightly, albeit with excruciating pain, and gasp for a bit of breath while the pressure constricting the lungs was lessened for a few brief moments.

Those crucified die of slow suffocation, a most horrific way to die.

Barabbas had witnessed crucifixions in the past. Many members of Q had been executed like this.

But this was different.

This man was so different.

Barabbas somehow knew that *this man* shouldn't be here.

In keeping with Roman custom, as soon as Jesus was lifted into place and his feet had been nailed, one of the soldiers raised a ladder against the cross and climbed up, nailing a plaque at the top of the vertical stake just above the man's head.

It detailed Jesus of Nazareth's *crime*:

"This is Jesus. The King of the Jews," was what was printed there.

Barabbas was amazed at the fact that Pilate boldly proclaimed *this* as Jesus's crime. He had heard him say it several times at the trial and guessed that, in a way, it *was* treason if it were true, especially since Herod, "Herod the Great," some had taken to calling him lately, had bought for himself that very title: "King of the Jews."

Not surprisingly either, as soon as it was nailed there, Barabbas heard many of the Jewish leaders complaining about what was written and saying they must go to Pilate and get him to change it.

Once Jesus had been secured, the soldiers proceeded to carry out the same thing with the other two criminals who had been led out together with him, one on his right side and the other on his left. They too had plaques nailed above them. "This is Dismas, murderer of Flavius Paulus," one read. "This is Gestas, robber of the treasury of Rome in Jerusalem," read the other.

Barabbas knew the two of them somewhat. Like him, they were Jewish freedom fighters who had been arrested in the uprising.

He wondered where *they* had been imprisoned?

Barabbas knew that the cross in the middle should have been, but for some miraculous accident—*his* cross.

An innocent man now hung there in his place.

His plaque would have said, "This is Jesus Barabbas, leader of the insurrection and murderer of Decimus," or something like that. He was a criminal. How many crimes against Rome he had actually committed, he probably couldn't count. This was just the most recent one for which he had been apprehended. He had not been careful enough.

He had turned back to look.

Broken his iron-clad rule.

He had locked eyes with the boy.

And that...had been his undoing.

He paused.

Barabbas knew what he himself had done.

But what had this Jesus done? He had said that his kingdom was not of this world, a kingdom without fighting.

What could that possibly mean?

Could that work? Accomplish anything?

It seemed to have failed miserably too.

Barabbas knew that he knew almost nothing about this Jesus but he was sure that he must find out more.

After all, he was free because of *him*.

Simon had left Q because of this Jesus.

Barabbas wondered whether he was seeing something similar to what Simon must have seen in this man?

Barabbas now watched as Jesus surveyed the crowd around him, much smaller than a while ago. Some of the women who had followed him were huddled together, weeping. The soldiers were off to the side, throwing dice for his clothing. The contingent of Jewish leaders of various stripes: scribes, zealous Pharisees, teachers of the law, and Sadducees of the ruling elite, compliant with Rome so as to solidify their political power were still present, giving their approval to everything.

He watched as Jesus lifted his gaze toward the sky.

"Abba," he prayed aloud, "forgive them, for they do not know what they are doing."

Barabbas sucked in his breath.

Had he just heard what he thought he heard? Forgive them? Forgive them...because they don't know what they are doing?

Who? The Jewish leaders? The Romans? Of course, they know what they are doing, he thought.

They are evil—all of them.

Who ever said anything like that as they were being crucified? Barabbas knew that he wouldn't have.

He most assuredly would have cursed them all.

And then, there was that opening word of the prayer.

This man had addressed the Almighty as his "Abba!"

David had talked about Elohim this way. Barabbas himself had accidently spoken it just within the last day.

But who *was* this Jesus?

This man seemed to truly know and relate to the Name as Father.

Barabbas hardly knew what to think.

Heretic or not, Barabbas couldn't tear himself away.

Here was this man lifted up on a cross, cursed, and yet it felt as though something or more like *someone,* was drawing him in.

Many others were shaking their heads, insulting this man.

"You said that you would destroy the Temple and rebuild it in three days," one in the garb of a Sadducee said. "If you could do that, why don't you save yourself?"

"Go ahead, come down from that cross you, 'son of Elohim'!" he said with venom in his voice.

Those of the Jewish leadership all reviled him.

Chief priests.

Elders.

The teachers of the Torah.

"King of the Jews. Ha!"

"He saved others but he can't save himself! He's the King of Israel? Let him come down from that cross right now, and we will most surely put our faith in him!"

"He trusts in Elohim. Let Adonai rescue him now if He wants to for he claims to be His son!"

Even the two who were crucified with him joined in the insults.

"Aren't you the Messiah?" said Gestas, "Save yourself, and us!"

At that, Dismas, the one on the left, who had been participating in the insults before, suddenly fell silent. After watching Jesus for a while, he now turned to Gestas and reprimanded him.

"Don't you fear Adonai," Dismas asked, "since you are under the same sentence? We are punished justly, for we are getting what our deeds deserve. But this man has done nothing wrong."

Dismas's words, like the nails in Jesus's body, pierced Barabbas's heart. He knew that the crucifix on which he hung was rightfully his. And that was what his own deeds were, they were evil, that the cross was what he deserved. But this man, *this Man*, what had he done to warrant this shameful treatment at the hands of everyone?

"Jesus," Dimas requested turning to the One in the middle, "could You please remember *me* when You come into Your kingdom."

"Truly I tell you," Jesus said as he now looked at the man hanging next to him, "truly I tell you, today you will be with Me in paradise."

A single tear made its way down Barabbas's cheek.

He knew he had just witnessed the rescue of one man by another unlike any man he had ever met. In the midst of suffering. And he wondered whether in some strange way he was being rescued too. It was all too much. It was so undeserved. But it was the very thing for which he had prayed.

Barabbas backed up and slumped to the ground. He turned away. He buried his head in his hands and pinched his eyes closed. It was beyond anything that he had ever seen or experienced.

Grace. *Hesed.* Loving kindness.

In the few moments that Barabbas's eyes were closed, he sensed that it had all of sudden become very dark.

What on earth was happening? It was only noon, or so he thought by where the sun had been.

Now he was terrified.

When he dared to open his eyes, it *was* indeed dark, so very dark. He simply sat there, lost in his own thoughts.

Again, it seemed like only a few moments had passed but it must have been longer, maybe even hours. Had he slept? He was physically and emotionally exhausted from the events of the day.

He was jolted out of his sleep or his daydream or whatever it was.

"Eli, Eli, Lema Sabachthani!—My Elohim, oh my Elohim, why have you forsaken me?" Jesus said from the cross in a very loud voice.

Barabbas echoed the prayer taken from the twenty-second of the *Tehillim.*

"Adonai Elohim, where are you?"

Someone of the few who were still there said they thought that he was calling for Elijah.

Elijah indeed. Where was the Adonai of Elijah?

Another offered Jesus a sponge soaked with wine vinegar.

"Leave him alone," one of the scribes said, "let's see if Elijah comes to save him."

Once more Jesus cried out.

"Abba, into Thy hands I commit my spirit."

Again, that audacity.

But with that, Barabbas saw Jesus's head bow and his body go limp.

The man was dead.

Now tears streamed down Barabbas's face. Hot, salty tears.

He found himself weeping profusely, overcome by something he had maybe never even felt before. Daniel's death had certainly impacted him. And there had been other occasions when he had cried.

But like this?

It was probably almost fifteen years, he thought. Fifteen long and lonely years since his own abba had forsaken him that he had felt anything remotely like this.

He suddenly felt silly.

In reality, he didn't even know this man.

They had not exchanged a single word.

He was a nobody.

Maybe Jesus of Nazareth was a lunatic.

Anyway, what good was a dead messiah?

Was he letting the craziness of this day get the better of him?

Or…was he seeing things more clearly than he had in years?

Before he could fully explore all of the thoughts racing through his head, assaulting his mind, he felt the ground beneath him tremble and then begin to heave back and forth.

An earthquake?

Could this day get any weirder, he wondered?

He held tightly to a nearby tree even though it was moving too.

After a minute or two it subsided. And although there were one or two more aftershocks, their movement was minor in comparison.

"This *is* crazy!" Barabbas thought to himself, "*I* am going crazy! This is not at all like me!"

"Abba, into thy hands I commit my spirit," Barabbas said, replaying the last words of the man on the cross.

Did he speak it as a question? Was he simply amazed that one could say such a thing? Or was it something more...personal?

Barabbas shook his head.

He closed his eyes trying to focus, as he sat leaning against a rock.

He was trying to make sense of everything he had experienced. Everything that he had felt.

He wasn't allowed the time to figure it all out.

He discovered that he had no energy left.

And almost immediately, the full weight of the day's events, the craziness and his own exhaustion could no longer be kept at bay and somehow overwhelmed him.

Slumber once more snatched him from this world and took him prisoner.

Chapter 48

NEXT STEPS

A FEW HOURS LATER, SOMETHING STIRRED BARABBAS.

The darkness of evening was approaching.

He knew that he had slept, but how long, he did not know.

"I must have been totally exhausted," he said to himself. "Have I slept at all in the last month?"

The pungent smell of lilies assaulted his nostrils.

In an instant, he realized again that he was no longer in the prison but outside in clean, fresh air. He sat up rather quickly, trying to remember everything, now completely awake and on full alert.

No. This was not a dream.

He glanced around in an attempt to recover his bearings.

It all came back in a flash.

There were the three crosses but now the middle one was empty except for the plaque still affixed to the top of the stake.

Jesus's body was gone.

It had been removed while he slept.

The other two still hung there. Barabbas could see that their legs had been broken to hasten their death. The soldiers were standing around waiting to remove them, waiting for them to die.

The Jews wouldn't want the bodies there on the Sabbath, at least not on this one, the Sabbath of the Passover.

Barabbas was at a loss as to what to do next.

He felt very alone.

He wondered what had all happened while he slept this second time.

On a practical level, he was hungry.

Maybe he should go back into the city and find something to eat. Then he could decide what he should do next. So, he made his way back into Jerusalem the same way that he had come out. Only difference was, where before there had been a large crowd leaving little room to move, now, he pretty much had the street to himself.

It was eerily quiet. It was almost dark now. Night was falling. The Sabbath was almost here. However, he did manage to find one street vendor who was still in the final stages of closing up shop. At the same time, Barabbas realized that he had no money. He smiled as he approached.

"Hello, sir, my name is Joshua, and I have fallen on hard times. I wonder if you might have a little leftover that you would be willing to share with a brother?"

The man eyed Barabbas up and down. Barabbas saw him smile a little. That was a good sign.

"I have a little fish and bread here," the man said. "It was my own lunch but you're welcome to it. I wasn't very hungry today."

He passed Barabbas a small package wrapped up in a rather worn piece of cloth.

"Thank you, sir. May Adonai richly bless you!" Barabbas said.

"And Shalom to you, brother Joshua," the vendor replied. "May Adonai bless you and keep you and make His face shine upon you."

Barabbas watched as the man finished cleaning up. He watched him load everything onto the small cart that was tethered to his donkey. And then he watched him disappear.

He unwrapped the small package that had been given to him and ate the few small fish and the little loaf of bread that it contained.

Barabbas shook his head.

He had called himself, *Joshua*. Without really thinking about it.

He wondered who he was. Really.

He had been Barabbas, the violent rebel Zealot, for as long as he could remember.

Could he be anything, anyone else?

He was free for the first time in a month.

Maybe for the first time in his life.

Or at least since being a young boy in Galilee.

Could he, now, be someone else?

Or was he fated to return to the life that he knew. The only one that he knew. What was at least familiar.

Joshua.

He had called himself, *Joshua*.

Could he be that person again?

He wasn't sure. Who was that man?

He had taken on the persona of *Barabbas*.

Maybe that was who he now was. Maybe there was no one else left.

And then, suddenly, it hit him.

He was free! Free to *be* anyone.

Free to go anywhere, without fear.

He could go back home. To Galilee. To family.

He could go back. And see. And then decide.

Maybe even decide who he really wanted to be.

He could be *Joshua* again.

Barabbas wandered around the streets lost in his thoughts. He had slept so soundly during the afternoon that he was not at all tired now. Yes, these streets could be dangerous after dark. He himself had at times been the danger lurking in the shadows.

But there was no danger, he told himself. He was not in danger. The world was now a glorious realm of possibilities.

He could change.

He was not a leopard, unable to change his spots.

Adonai Elohim could change him. Yes, even him.

"Gotcha!" Barabbas heard someone whisper loudly in his ear just as he was grabbed tightly from behind.

The hair stood up on his neck and he was about to try and break free and run, or maybe turn and fight, his hand instinctively reaching into his cloak for his dagger, but the voice sounded vaguely familiar.

His assailant's grip relaxed, and he turned to see Tobias now laughing hysterically.

"You shouldn't laugh, you silly fool," Barabbas said. "I was just about to run you through!"

"You and which army?" Tobias asked. "I had you, Barabbas, so had you, dead and gone."

"You're crazy!" Barabbas said.

"I learned well, from the best," Tobias replied. "You trained me!"

"Barabbas, where have you been all day? You were there with us one minute. We were talking to each other and when we turned around, you were gone. We looked for you but couldn't find you anywhere. Where did you go and what was with giving us the slip?"

"There was just something I needed to do," Barabbas replied. "Sorry I bailed on all of you. I'm here now."

"C'mon. Let's get out of here," Tobias said. "I'll show you where we are hiding out."

"That is, unless you prefer the place where you were formerly residing?" he added teasingly.

"Oh, right, for sure, can I please go back there?" Barabbas said jokingly.

The two of them made their way off together as the moon began to show itself over the ancient city.

"What were *you* doing here in the city in the middle of the night?" Barabbas asked, his own question suddenly coming to mind.

"Why, looking for you of course!" Tobias replied.

Chapter 49

BEGINNING AGAIN

Tobias led him to a makeshift camp that had been set up to the east of Jerusalem near the Wadi Jimel, in the hills but with a good supply of water. It was definitely further than any religious Jew should walk on the Sabbath, but they didn't have a whole lot of options. And anyway, Barabbas knew that he had actually broken so many of the commandments or at least the bylaws, this one would just add to the mountain that was already there.

How did being zealous for a cause lead you to believe you were allowed to break the law in certain situations? Barabbas realized they were no better than the Jewish leaders they condemned. They just considered their own reasons more valid.

There were about fifty or so tents scattered haphazardly in a hundred or so foot radius. A campfire burned in the middle and several members of Q were sitting around it having breakfast. They greeted Tobias and Barabbas warmly, standing to embrace them as they joined the circle. Food was immediately brought to them and Barabbas was encouraged to share all of the details of his imprisonment and then his miraculous release.

"I still can't get over the fact that the Sanhedrin petitioned for my release," Barabbas said. "Does anyone here know anything about that?"

"We have only heard rumors," Levi said. "But they must have really wanted this Jesus of Nazareth dead, is all I can say! To have fought for *your* release over his? They hate you!"

"By the way, Barabbas, did you see him? Meet him? This Jesus of Nazareth they crucified? I've heard stories about him, and some of our own have even gone to see him. Apparently, he teaches that we should love our enemies, heals people, and...supposedly has even raised the dead," Joachim said. "Was he for real or just another crazy lunatic claiming to be the Messiah?"

"Not sure," Barabbas said. "Truth is, I barely met him. We didn't exchange a single word."

Barabbas knew that he didn't want to share any of what he was feeling and thinking regarding this man with the brothers.

Did he himself even know all that he was contemplating?

"Pilate sure didn't know what to do with him! And, this Jesus of Nazareth certainly had no fear of Rome or of any power other than Adonai, it seemed. It was fun to watch!"

"I don't suppose any of it matters now. He is dead."

"He did seem...I don't know...sort of genuine?"

Barabbas found himself lost again, captured in that gaze, that look, those eyes that had penetrated his own heart, in judgment yes, but in judgment that was somehow overcome by mercy.

"Truth, what is truth?" Pilate had asked.

Jesus had said that he was a witness, a martyr, to the truth.

Barabbas actually longed to know this man.

To know what was, well...really true. His quest.

Sadly now, that would never happen.

Jesus was dead—a dead messiah.

If he had been messiah at all.

"Enough of that," Barabbas said, interrupting himself, not sure where the road of all those thoughts would lead him. Or whether he was willing to travel there to find out. Not here and not now at least.

"What is planned for the rest of the Passover week? Which houses will the angel of death visit this year?" Barabbas asked.

They proceeded to tell him some of the events that had been planned for the days that remained.

"Are you up for a target?" James asked when they finished.

"Only one way to know," Barabbas said, acting braver than he felt.

"Then," Tobias said, looking over the list. "Let's see. How about a young man named…Marcus Andronicus? He is the…"

Barabbas gasped, reaching out to grab hold of something, trying to get a grip on anything. His face went white. He could feel the ground moving beneath him.

The next thing he knew, he was lying on his back, his face and hair was soaking wet, and there was a crowd of his Zealot brothers standing over and around him, looking very concerned.

"What just happened?" he asked, shaking his head and sitting up.

"That's what we were wondering," Joachim said.

"You just passed out. It took a bit of effort to bring you back around. Appears you're not at all ready to take on a target! You can barely stand on your own two feet!"

"Maybe not," Barabbas replied.

"It seems I should just return to Bereshith."

They all agreed that he needed to go back and spend some time recuperating at Q's headquarters. They imagined that prison had been harder on him than he thought.

Barabbas knew that he needed to get back.

Though not to the place they all knew as "Bereshith," but to the true *beginning*.

His own real beginnings.

Would it be possible?

To begin again? To start afresh?

He desperately hoped he could.

Chapter 50

GOING HOME

Barabbas remained in the camp at Wadi Jimel for several days. Mostly because he couldn't or wouldn't do anything else. He confined himself to his tent. He avoided conversation with others. He felt he couldn't stomach interaction. He hardly even ate although he knew that he must if he wanted to regain his strength. Perhaps, as they had suggested, imprisonment really had taken more out of him than he had thought. Maybe he was in no condition to do anything.

Most of all, he suspected that his heart was just not zealous anymore, at least not in the way it had been. How had that happened? He had wondered about that even before his arrest. It now seemed full blown.

And Marcus...? Marcus...!

Was it just coincidence that the target they had chosen for him shared that very same name?

Barabbas had made it up, he thought, but had Adonai been the One influencing his imagination? Even in that? What was He up to?

One image haunted him more now than ever.

The vision of that young man, arms raised, beseeching the heavens, grieving for his fallen father.

A father forever lost to him.

A young man now destined to grow up without the one he needed most in this world. How was that young man doing, Barabbas wondered?

He himself could have been killed by the Roman soldiers on the day that his abba was killed, but he was forced to live on.

Had had to struggle to try and make it.

Had he done so?

He had struggled for sure.

But...had he in any way *made* it?

He was pretty certain he had failed miserably.

He seemed sure of very few things any more.

Some...or more likely, everything had to change.

Barabbas quietly made his way out of his tent early the next morning before it was light. It was a day prior to the one when they were all slated to break camp and everyone would leave. He had taken a little bit of food for the road. He now set off in the direction of Galilee.

He told no one, none of his Zealot "brothers."

He was going home.

Back to his real home.

Home was calling him.

Back to the beginning.

His real beginning.

He would begin again. Somehow. If he could...

The journey was difficult. And slow.

But at least he could stick to the road.

He wasn't running for his life anymore.

Well...maybe he was.

Though, not as in days before.

He somehow knew that, in a tangible way, his very life was hanging in the balance.

Barabbas felt old. He was barely thirty years of age, but life, his chosen life, had taken a huge toll on him. How many years had even just the most recent thirty days in prison stolen from him? He no longer soared on wings like an eagle. He knew that there was no way he could run and not get weary, at least not now. He prayed that he would be able to simply walk and not faint again.

"I will wait on You, Ha Shem," he said to himself. "Renew my strength and bring me home again, Ha Kadosh Baruch Hu."

The journey took a total of six days to complete. And every sunset and sunrise, whether because he was getting closer to his destination, or because Adonai was actually renewing his strength, he didn't know, but each day he made more ground. By the end of the journey, as the city of Tiberias came into sight, he actually felt almost like himself again. He had been careful to eat well and to drink water often and to rest when the sun was its hottest. He contemplated breaking into a mild run but thought that might be pushing things.

He wondered how difficult it would be to find his family once he arrived. If they had still been in Rakkath, it would have been relatively easy, he thought. He would have just gone home, to the house he knew and to the place where they once lived.

That thought sparked something.

Barabbas knew in a heartbeat what he would do. He could simply start by returning to that place. To their family home in Rakkath. He had stayed there once before not so long ago it seemed. And he would spend the night there again. It was late in the day anyway.

He could pray and prepare himself for...

He really didn't know what to prepare for.

Or how to ready himself, really.

...For whatever was to come.

It was dusk as he made his way down the deserted street, entered the yard, and then went into the familiar building. The few windows had been boarded up, and he secured the door behind himself. He pulled out his mat and blanket and lay down.

"Adonai, grant me Your favor in my quest," he prayed. "May I find an open door before me?"

And with that, sleep wrapped Barabbas in its tender arms.

Chapter 51

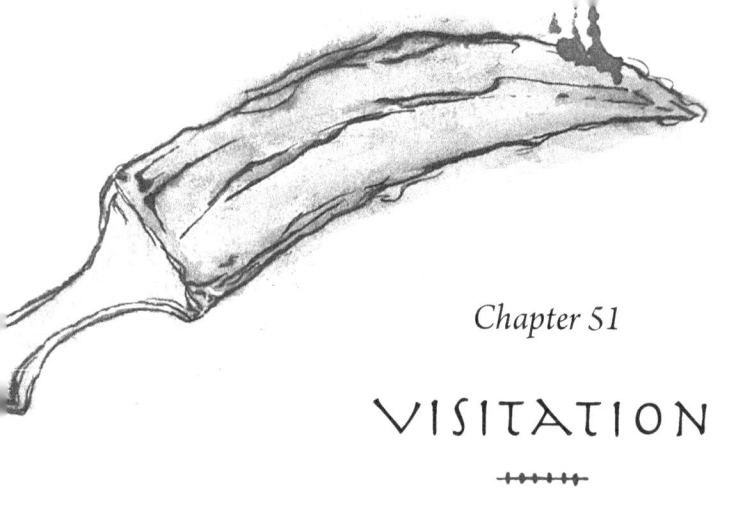

VISITATION

Barabbas awoke on high alert.

He knew he didn't dare move a muscle even though every fiber of his being was quivering. He had definitely heard something. He was positive that there was someone in the room with him.

Unable to see anything in the darkness in front of him, he was wary about rolling over and giving away his advantage of surprise.

How someone could be there in the house he didn't know, since he had made sure all was secure before he lay down to sleep. Very quietly, with measured and deliberate movement, he slowly reached for the small dagger in his cloak. He would be ready for whoever this intruder was. Someone who might want to do him harm.

"Joshua," he heard a vaguely familiar voice softly say. "Release your grip on the knife. I come in peace."

With that, light from somewhere suddenly appeared in the room. Not totally convinced it was yet safe to do so, Barabbas nevertheless rolled over, his hand still gripping the hilt of the knife.

He wasn't sure he should believe the intruder had come in peace.

He blinked.

And then blinked again.

He was staring into the eyes of *the* man.

That other Jesus!

The one he had seen crucified.

Now he was really afraid.

Barabbas sat bolt upright.

His mouth dropped open.

"Whaaaat? You're dead!" somehow escaped his lips.

Jesus just smiled at him.

And Barabbas allowed himself to relax a little even if his heart seemed to be pounding ever more vigorously within his chest.

"Am I dreaming?" he asked.

"You're dead!" Barabbas asserted for the second time.

He continued.

"Am *I* dead?" he now asked, trying to make some sense of this.

"No Joshua, *you* are not dead!" Jesus said, rather emphatically but then, laughing to himself, added, "And *I'm* not either..."

"Even though I most certainly was!"

Barabbas stared, his eyes honed in on this man illumined by some otherworldly light.

This was no dream. He was completely awake and fully alert.

It was as if Jesus knew it and he now spoke.

Deliberately. Prophetically.

"Do not fear, Jehoshua ben Abraham! I am Jesus of Nazareth. I am Elohim's Anointed One. His Son. I came to earth to show people the Father's heart and the way back to Him. I was crucified for the sins of the world and for yours. And I have been vindicated by My Father and have been raised to life even as the prophets of old foretold. I am the Messiah who was to come. And I am calling you to come follow Me. You have a destiny, a calling. You have known it, sensed it, for most of your life. But it is not to kill or to bring about the kingdom of heaven through violence, at least not the kind that you are used to. It is to bring life and healing and restoration to all people. It is time to lay down the ideas of man and embrace the

ways of My Father, Yahweh. Our enemies are not flesh and blood, but rather principalities and powers. Do not be afraid! I have overcome them and you will too. I am calling you to be My witness in the power of My Holy Spirit. Most of all I want you to learn to love once more. I have loved you since the day you were born and even before that and I was right there beside you sitting in the clay on the day that your abba was murdered and your world changed forever. My Father, your Heavenly Father, cried with you then and has every day since. And He is now calling you to Himself. He wants you to be His beloved son."

Barabbas just sat, transfixed.

Eyes wide. Mouth open.

Sweet tears were running down his cheeks.

His heart felt strangely warm.

"Joshua, I know that you need to be here now, need to reconnect with your family. It's important. And I bless you in this good thing. I *will* grant you favor even as you prayed. Go and meet your brother Zephaniah down at the seashore when he comes to get clay for the day's bricks. He will be in a new spot a half mile south. He will take you home. And enjoy this time with your family…brother!"

"Just be sure that you are back in Jerusalem for Shavuot, the Festival of Weeks, fifty days from Passover. It is very important that you be there at that time. I promise to meet you there. It is an appointed time. And all will become clear, well…clearer," he said.

And then with a chuckle he added, "There is always the need for faith, however small, to be part of the process!"

"Oh, and one more thing. Leave the knife here. You don't need it anymore. You are not that man. You were zealous and did not know what to do with your zeal. You thought that you had to choose that life. Thought that was what our Abba was like. I understand. But you are no longer 'Barabbas.' You are a true son of the

Father. And free to be Joshua again, though now renewed, one who brings salvation and deliverance to people, to all people."

Jesus smiled broadly again, pulled Joshua to his feet, gave him a big bear hug and then promptly disappeared.

Not that he walked out of the room. He just vanished somehow.

And Barabbas, *Joshua,* was left alone.

Shaking, sweating, and barely breathing.

He still wondered if it had been some vivid dream.

But no! He was clearly awake right now and actually knew he had been the entire time. In fact, had he ever been *more* awake?

He had most certainly felt Jesus's hug.

This was not his imagination.

And his heart was burning inside of him.

Dream or not, this Man had...

...taken him back to his very beginning.

To his creation. His calling. His destiny.

"What is truth?" Pilate had asked just days ago.

Barabbas felt as though he had just heard the truest words ever spoken—words that somehow penetrated the very marrow of his bones.

More than that, it was as if the One who had spoken to him was the embodiment of truth.

As though he *was* Truth.

He realized in that moment that he was shaking, vibrating on the inside.

Barabbas was positive that he would assuredly never be the same. That he could not now or ever go back to the way things had been.

It was as if he had been given life all over again.

Or rather, a brand-new life.

Except for the fact that *the Man* had left.

And he now, or still, had questions that positively demanded answers.

"Jesus, if you're real, and alive as you say, then I want to know more...to truly know *You!*" Barabbas whispered to no one.

And...to Someone.

He smiled.

"I *am* going crazy!" he said aloud.

"But I kind of like it!"

And then he laughed out loud.

He shook his head.

However, what he felt inside was undeniable.

Shavuot? The Festival of Weeks. In Jerusalem? It would all become clear? Maybe, more clear? He would meet him, or *Him*, again? So much mystery.

Barabbas felt hope surge inside of himself.

He laughed again and realized that he couldn't get rid of the grin that now felt glued to his face.

"Wow! I really *am* going crazy!"

After removing, and not without significant effort, the bar that held the door closed, he made his way out into the yard.

He glanced back at the windows. They were still secure.

How had Jesus entered?

And when He left, how had He just vanished?

Barabbas had *seen* it.

He shook his head again.

In the early morning moonlight, he made his way to the very spot where he imagined Abrahim had been murdered. He took the knife out of his belt and used it to dig a small hole in the hardened ground.

"Swords becoming plowshares," he thought.

He placed the knife in its tomb and covered it with loose soil.

And then, kneeling at the place where his life had been so radically changed years earlier, Barabbas, rather now, Joshua, raised his hands and looked up toward the heavens once more.

"I lay down not only this knife but all that it represents. You said I no longer need it. I want to be a Joshua. One who brings life to people."

And then, once again borrowing the words he had heard the other Jesus say, not that long ago when He laid down His own life, he made them his own declaration:

"Abba, into Thy hands I commit my spirit."

Chapter 52

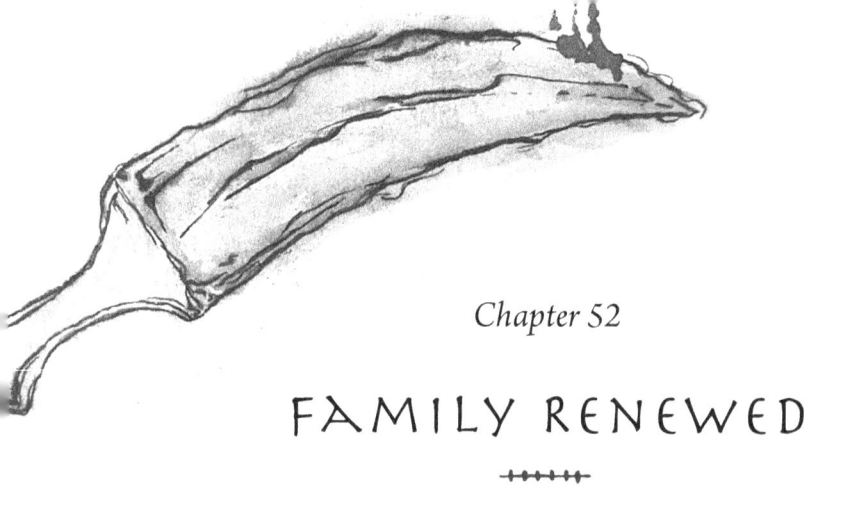

FAMILY RENEWED

JOSHUA WAS DOWN AT THE WATER'S EDGE FOR QUITE some time before the sun showed its face that morning. In the place where he had been told to wait and at peace because of what Jesus had promised, he was a bit anxious nevertheless.

Just waiting.

It was clearly a somewhat more mature Zephaniah and a rather old, graying donkey that appeared after a time. It made Solomon look wiser. And Joshua laughed, as he considered he might suggest they change the beast's name to Methuselah.

Zephaniah immediately noticed the other person present, as he approached the newly discovered deposit of clay. He was puzzled why some stranger would be here at this hour. Joshua thought he could see the questioning look on his brother's face from twenty feet away.

"Shalom, big brother! And how are you this fine day?" Joshua called out, breaking the silence that hung between them.

Joshua heard a gasp.

"Joshua? My brother? Is it really you?" Zephaniah rhetorically asked, now running, half-tripping, across the sand that separated them.

"It's definitely me!" Joshua said, laughing aloud and narrowing the gap between them from his side.

The two brothers crashed together in a manly embrace.

Emotion flowed like the sea that they stood beside.

And while neither one apparently ever wanted to let go of the other, Zephaniah finally broke himself free.

"Joshua, oh my beloved brother, you are…alive!"

"And…here! May El Shaddai be praised!"

"And I'm free!" Joshua said emphatically, the words like music to his own heart. "I was declared a free man by the Empire just days ago. No longer on the run for my life; I have come home!"

Joshua paused, backing away slightly.

"I take it I am welcome here?" he asked with a smirk.

"Are you kidding? Welcome? We will kill the fatted calf!" Zephaniah screamed, with a chopping motion of his arms as if he was butchering it right then and there.

"Well, can I at the very least help you get your load of clay for the day?" Joshua asked. "I haven't forgotten everything!"

"Clay?" Zephaniah said. "That's the last thing on my mind! There will be no brick making today! Maybe not tomorrow either. Forget clay! My little brother who we all thought was dead has come home! This is a day to celebrate!"

"Joshua, how did you know where the new clay pit we are using was?" Zephaniah suddenly asked.

"He told me," Joshua said matter-of-factly, not sharing too many details.

Zephaniah gave him a puzzled look.

"I will tell you later," Joshua said.

Not sure he really wanted to wait, with that, arm in arm, they turned Solomon around and headed for home, their wagon completely empty but their hearts loaded full to overflowing.

Zephaniah couldn't get Solomon to move fast enough. Joshua, on the other hand, was no longer in a hurry for anything. He just wanted to savor every moment.

The trip home was filled with easy conversation.

Brothers reunited.

Zephaniah told Joshua about his wife Naomi and their family. His oldest son, Abram, now ten years old; his daughter, Ruth, age eight; another son, Simeon, age six; and their youngest, Hannah, who was three.

Joshua choked up a little when he heard that Zephaniah had named his oldest son after their father. *How wonderful,* he thought!

Zephaniah told him that their brother Elijah was just recently pledged to be married to Eliyah, the youngest sister of Joshua's boyhood friend Jonathan.

And Sarah was already married to a young man named Josiah whose family had moved from the town of Capernaum.

They talked some about business and how things were going at home. Zephaniah told him that Batiyah was alive and doing well.

Joshua talked a little about *his* life since leaving home all those years ago, careful to omit most mention of all of the bloodshed and violence. There may be time for that later. Or maybe, Joshua thought, that particular part of his history would just never be revisited. Maybe it could just disappear into the mists of the past.

Forgiven.

Forgotten.

"By the way," Zephaniah added shortly after the two of them entered the city of Tiberias, "We continue to deliver those special bricks to Caleb's family. You should see. They have quite a massive operation there now."

Zephaniah paused.

"I have even visited with Ariah once or twice in my travels there!"

"Is she well?" Joshua asked, not at all concerned now if his interest clearly showed.

"She is, I believe. But…we will have to finish that conversation another day," Zephaniah said. "Because we are…home!"

Yes indeed, that would have to wait.

Zephaniah burst through the gate.

"Hey, everyone, would you look at who finally wandered home!" he shouted out in a loud voice.

Family almost immediately appeared from every corner; some, no, many of whom, Joshua had never even met.

"Ya tuv! Joshua!" Batiyah cried out, running toward her son.

Tears streamed down her face.

"Hallelujah! Adonai be praised! Oh, my long-lost Joshua!"

She had obviously aged, but Joshua thought she looked absolutely radiant as she came toward him and then embraced him. Maybe even better than she had appeared when he left.

Joshua couldn't find any words.

Then again, were they even necessary?

He could do nothing at this present moment but weep for joy.

Hugged on every side by everyone.

It felt amazing! It *was* amazing!

They would all stop for a minute and just look at each other and laugh and cry and then embrace some more. Celebrating.

"Time for breakfast," Naomi finally announced, wiping away her own tears. "Ruth, would you please help me find some food to set in front of your uncle Joshua? We don't want him dying of hunger when he has just recently been restored to us!"

Joshua laughed to himself that women could be so practical in times like this. He knew that was a good thing. Somebody had to be the one to make sure the human race survived.

The two of them busied themselves with meal preparations and in no time at all, the table was spread. Not quite the fatted calf, but lovely nonetheless. The entire family sat down together. Everyone. Even Josiah and Sarah had been summoned to come and join them. They lived not very far away Joshua found out, just down the street in fact. Eliyah too had been called and appeared after a bit.

After all of the introductions had been made, Zephaniah prayed the blessing and they began eating.

"Oh, Ima, I have missed you," Joshua said, and then, looking around, he added, "I have missed you all. I have missed so much!"

"And how *have* you been, Ima?" Joshua asked. "Zephaniah says you are doing good."

"I have not been well," she said without hesitation. "Not well at all. And yes, you have missed much!"

Joshua frowned, somewhat perplexed, but there did not seem to be any concern in Batiyah's statement even though directly contrary to what Zephaniah had told him.

He shook his head. She didn't look unwell.

Batiyah pressed on with a huge smile that seemed somewhat out of place given what she had just shared.

"Not well at all, Joshua…at least that is, until a couple of years ago. Until that day when I met someone like no one I ever met before."

Joshua slowly withdrew the bit of bread he was about to put in his mouth. He was about to interrupt but waved the small fragment in her direction, encouraging her to continue.

"You weren't aware of it, Joshua, but when Abba was murdered, I was pregnant with our sixth child."

At Batiyah's outright mention of murder, Joshua rather quickly shot a glance at Zephaniah.

"She knows. I told her," Zephaniah said. "Or rather, she actually figured it out and told me that she suspected that Abba had been murdered. She asked me point blank if I knew anything. At that point I felt that it was okay to tell her what you had told me."

"But how did you…?" Joshua's look asked.

"I was a little suspicious right from the beginning," Batiyah said. "Simply because I knew that Abraham had maintained some interaction with the Qanaim over the years and these things do happen from time to time, but I dismissed it as just my overactive imagination."

Joshua's jaw dropped.

"So, you knew about father's ongoing sympathy with the Zealot movement?" he asked.

She nodded.

"But we can talk about *that* another time."

"As to how I actually knew," she said and then continued, "On the morning that you left, one of the things Zephaniah did was to give you a pouch containing what little money we had in the house. That triggered something. I wondered to myself where the money belt that Abrahim would have most certainly been wearing on the day he died had disappeared? I realized I hadn't seen it and asked those who had readied his body for burial about it. I knew that neither you nor anyone else here would have taken it. So, where had it gone? Somehow it just kind of all came together in my mind, and I confronted Zephaniah with the possibility that Abba's death was not accidental but made to look that way. And that the money had been stolen."

"Joshua, I don't blame you at all for withholding. I understand. I am just so very sad that you had to carry that burden all by yourself for that whole time, even if I know why you thought you must."

Joshua stared at her in amazement, shaking his head. Batiyah gave him a squeeze and a smile and then continued.

"But, back to my story. We can talk about all those other things another time. Where was I? Oh yes, when Abba was snatched from this life into the next, I was pregnant, but the child to be born miscarried several months later. Probably had something to do with all that had happened, I imagine. I guess I should have told you about it, but you were so busy and so tired, I didn't want to worry you with any of my problems. You had enough of your own things to think about. And it is also just not something that we women usually talk about with our children…our male children anyway. There is so much that we just keep to ourselves. Or did. Part of the curse? Then too, I wondered if it was actually a blessing. Like we needed yet another mouth to feed!"

"My body bled quite a bit after the miscarriage. I knew that was normal so I just ignored it for a while. However, the bleeding would not go away. It just continued day after day. It refused to stop. I knew *that* wasn't right!"

Joshua interrupted.

"Ima, are you sure you should you be telling me this? Now? In front of all of the younger children?"

Batiyah just smiled.

"I tried to keep it quiet," she said. "But *he* wouldn't let me! Told me that part of my healing was to testify!"

"And so, I have told it many times already," she said, now absolutely beaming. "They all know. It would be nonsense to keep it quiet. It is a most wonderful story!"

"And who is this *he?*" Joshua asked.

Batiyah just held up her hand and carried on.

"I went to see doctors about it and no one was quite sure what to do or how to help me. They suggested all kinds of different medicines and treatments, and I spent a lot, it felt like all, of our hard-earned money trying to remedy the situation. All to no avail."

"We were getting poorer by the day. And I was growing weaker. I was losing hope. Thinking that I might very soon join Abba in the life to come. Thinking at times that was the better option by far even though I didn't want to leave my family."

"And then, at the very moment when my hope was almost gone, I heard tell of a man from Nazareth. A prophet. I heard stories of him having healed people. Deaf ears opened. Blind eyes seeing again. He cast out demons. Cleansed lepers. He even raised people from the dead."

"And I thought, that if he could do that for all of the others, then maybe, if I could just get close to him, touch him, could I be...?"

"No, I thought, I should probably not touch him since I didn't want to make him unclean. Maybe just quickly touch the hem of his garment, I thought. That might be okay. No one would even need to know. Might I then be healed like all those others had been?"

Joshua was grinning now but he didn't dare interrupt. He had a very good idea how this story ended. And of who the *he* was in her story! He was sure he now knew how such a horrible affliction could in fact be transformed into something you couldn't help but tell.

Batiyah didn't notice.

She was passionately wrapped up in the re-telling of her story.

"Well, I heard that he was passing through Tiberias and I went to see him. He was on his way from Gadara on the east side of the Sea of Galilee where it was reported he had just healed an extremely demon-possessed man. And he was on his way to the house of a man named Jairus in Capernaum. This man's little daughter had died, and he had asked Jesus to *heal* her! Heal her of death? I thought that was a very funny way of looking at things! You can't really be *healed* from death, can you?"

"It was difficult even to see him. There was such a huge crowd. A slow-moving throng actually. Which made it so very difficult to get near him, everyone jostling each other just to be close to him. I wondered whether I should even go through with it. I knew that I was unclean and that each person that I touched would be unclean. But I didn't care. Couldn't care. Not anymore. I was convinced that if I even just touched his cloak, I would be healed. And I guess I imagined that if I was healed, I would no longer be unclean and then none of them would be unclean anymore either! Adonai Himself would have to figure that one out!"

"Well, I pushed through the crowd, feeling faith growing in me as I came closer. I reached out my hand. And...touched. And immediately I felt the bleeding stop. I hadn't felt that way, that good, for twelve long years."

Batiyah was glowing.

"It was...absolutely amazing!" she proclaimed.

"I was about to slip back out of the crowd having received what I came for. Unnoticed."

"But then, this man stopped. 'Who touched me?' he asked. His disciples told him he was being silly. 'Who touched him?' Everyone was touching him! But he said that he knew someone had touched him for he had felt power go out from himself. I had certainly felt the power he was talking about! Power I had received! But now I was terrified! Was I going to be rebuked for my impertinence? I had the audacity to touch a Rabbi, a woman, and unclean at that! But no, he didn't seem angry at all. And so, I made myself known. I came, trembling, and fell at his feet."

"'Rabbi,' I told him, 'I have suffered greatly with bleeding in my body for twelve years. I have spent all I have on doctors and no one has been able to help me. But I heard of you and the wonderful things that Adonai has done through you, and I thought that if I even just touched the hem of your garment, I would be healed. And so, I came, and I touched, and I was instantly healed.'"

"And then," Batiyah related, choking up even as she did so, "He looked at me, with a gaze that somehow seemed to contain all of eternity in it, and said, '*Bati,* my daughter, *Bati-yah,* daughter of Adonai, your faith has healed you. Go from here in the Shalom of the Father.'"

"He called me by name, Joshua! He knew my name! Knew me! And in that instant, I knew that I was healed, not only of the bleeding, but indeed, healed and forgiven inside and out, of everything that had ever happened to me, and everything I had ever done!"

"I continued to follow him to the synagogue leader Jairus's house, where I witnessed him raise another daughter of Elohim to life, a little girl who had been sick for the twelve years of her life and had succumbed to her illness. He said the time for mourning was over!"

"It seems as though he is in the business of raising up sons and daughters for the kingdom!"

Batiyah stopped and shook her head reminiscing.

"He called me by name, Joshua! This Jesus of Nazareth spoke to my very soul. It was the way he said my name: *Batiyah*. Like he was reaching back to some place prior to my creation, prior to the creation of the entire world."

"I wondered if he was our long-awaited Messiah. And I committed myself to be his follower from that day forward. But then, I heard just a few days ago that he was crucified in Jerusalem. Now I don't know what to think!"

Joshua was on the edge of his seat. He could hardly contain himself. This was an amazing story. It had happened to his own mother.

A miracle of healing.

And then, there was her fervor. Her courage.

She had always been bold but there was something here now way beyond what he had seen growing up. Had it had been there all along and Jesus had just called it out. She was clearly a changed woman. A radical.

He suspected that something similar had just recently happened to him as well. Even if he really hadn't had time to process it all yet.

Beauty for ashes.

Joshua stood to his feet applauding.

"That *is* a most wonderful story, Ima!"

"And I...know the more of this story!"

"You see, I too have met this Man! Twice now, in fact! Once on the day that He was crucified. In the natural. He is the reason that I am free! And I watched Him die...on that Roman cross. And then, a short while later, I met Him in the...I don't know exactly... in the super-natural? I saw Him again! He *was* crucified, dead, and buried. But He has risen! He is no longer dead! And I believe He is now both Adonai and Messiah!"

Joshua hesitated, wondering what in the world he was doing. He felt foolish in a way, and then, not at all.

Everyone cheered!

"Do tell," said Batiyah, her dark eyes shining. "Do tell! Oh, dear Joshua, this is most wonderful news indeed!"

Chapter 53

JOSHUA'S STORY

"Who would like some tea?" Naomi interjected during the momentary break in conversation, and she and Ruth disappeared to make some for everyone who wanted it.

As soon as they were all settled again, Zephaniah, who had already been fortunate enough to hear some of Joshua's journey, encouraged him to share his whole story with all of them.

The others nodded in agreement. They all wanted to hear it and, besides, it was clear they weren't doing anything else today.

"Where do I even begin?" Joshua asked aloud, mostly of himself.

"Probably at the beginning," Elijah said, jokingly. "But it's your story. I suppose wherever you start...will be the beginning!"

Joshua took no notice of his younger brother's sarcasm.

"At the beginning..." Joshua said, venturing deep into his own thoughts, absentmindedly stroking his beard. "Bereshith indeed!"

He smiled at the thought.

He was back at the beginning.

Starting over.

Starting afresh.

It had been his hope, his dream.

It was Adonai's plan for sure.

And now, here he was.

Ready, anxious…to begin again.

"I think that I should probably start from Abba's death, his murder! I'm just so glad that you all know the truth about that now!"

He freely allowed himself to return there.

"That day I felt like such a coward. Like I had done nothing to prevent his death or to stop them. I had hidden on the roof like a frightened little boy and let them do their worst to our abba."

Joshua was quietly amazed that he had found it relatively easy to share this painful detail, one he'd always before kept so carefully guarded.

He wondered how things had changed.

How much he had changed?

"When the soldier returned and threatened to kill me, then I really did clam up! Told no one all of what actually happened."

"And, Ima, I'm sorry that I kept that from you especially. I just didn't know what else to do!" Joshua said.

"Oh, dear boy, like I said before," Batiyah replied. "I'm just so sad that you had to carry that by yourself. And on top of everything else!"

She moved over to sit directly next to her recently returned son.

Joshua continued.

"It all made me so mad. At the soldiers. At Rome. But mostly at myself. Because I had done so little. I came away from that experience wanting to do something. Needing to do something. To make things right somehow. Even if they would never be right. To get vengeance for Abba's death. I vowed that I would never again do…nothing!"

"I didn't realize it at the time, but that promise together with all that was going on inside of my head and my heart, made me ripe for my involvement with the Qanaim. Anger was forcing open that door."

"By the way, Ima, you knew all along that Abba still had some dealings with Q? That he met with some of them from time to time?"

Batiyah nodded.

Joshua just shook his head.

"I do want to talk more about that later. About all of it. But..."

He pressed on.

"What transpired with Ariah was different but in many ways the same. What was new on this occasion was that I actually did something! Right or wrong, I did something! I could not stand idly by and do nothing. I had done that once before. And I vowed that I would never be inactive again."

"Though I did not know it at the time, that one decision set in motion the whole course of events that followed: my having to flee for my life, my going to Gamala at your suggestion. Meeting Uncle Jonas and Auntie Anna. And my involvement in..."

He stopped for a moment remembering.

"They are such beautiful people, Ima. Why hadn't you ever told us about them? Why had we never gone to visit? They are...could have been our grandparents!"

"Not easily done, Abba thought it best that we leave all of that in the past. We were trying to escape...it," Batiyah said, "and I agreed with him. Unfortunately, that meant leaving the good behind too."

"Uncle Jonas told me about your family," Joshua said. "About your father Gideon and your mother, Marion. And your two brothers, Micah and Jeremiah. Murdered by the Romans! And you, Ima, so mistreated by the soldiers and on the brink of death. Yours is quite a story!"

"Why had you never shared any of that with us?" Joshua asked.

"Like I said, we made a decision to leave that in the past," Batiyah replied. "And I think, or rather I know now that I had kind of erased it from my memory. It was just too painful to think about. Then too, my new life here with Abraham was just so good. Our wonderful little family. We finally felt safe and at peace. There just seemed to be no reason to ever revisit such a horrific past. Adonai had delivered me from all of that!"

She paused, remembering a former time.

"Jonas and Anna were good to me though," Batiyah continued. "It is so good to hear that they are still alive and well. I think that I would love to go and visit them now. We all could. Should. I know that I would love to share the conclusion or at least the *more* of my story with them. The immeasurably more that Jesus has done for me. And, especially now that I know that He is alive, I would love to share that good news with them too. But, continue with *your* story, Joshua. Sorry, I interrupted."

Joshua obeyed.

"In Gamala, in your own yard, the very place where your parents and family were killed and you were left for dead, Q has built a monument to the martyrs. Remember the two men that came late that one night shortly before I left? Simeon and Jacob, sons of Judah of Galilee. They did come for bricks, not to place an order, but rather to get some of the ones that I had hidden away in the back of the yard, bricks that had soaked up Abba's blood when he was murdered."

"Abba's bricks are there in the monument. And the stones from the ground where your parents and brothers were killed. They are there too."

"And many others. Hundreds. Thousands."

Joshua let himself wander back there for a moment.

"I felt the call of Ha Kadosh there, in that place. It was a call to action. To take up the sword of Adonai. I believed it was my destiny. I knew that I could not come back home. I had to move forward. And I felt like life and death had somehow prepared me to be a Zealot, to bring about the kingdom of Elohim on earth. It seemed so logical, especially given what had led me there and our family's long history in it."

"I shared with Uncle Jonas and Aunt Anna what I was feeling and Uncle Jonas took me to their headquarters. The Qanaim took me in and welcomed me and gave me a semblance of family. Something that I did not even realize how much I was missing, grieving the loss of. I was so very thankful for the brothers there."

"And that has been my life ever since. A Zealous one. Constantly on the run. Teaching the patriotic the philosophy of the Fourth Way. Killing any and all those who opposed Adonai and the re-establishment of the Jewish nation here in the Promised Land."

"I'm sorry," he said, hesitating. "I can stop if this is too much."

He looked around.

No one seemed bothered.

They were anxious for him to continue.

"It all made sense at the beginning but over time, I came to question it, particularly the violence and bloodshed. I wondered whether I had really made, was in fact really making, a positive difference in history. Whether what I was doing was something worthwhile? And I guess in a way, I wondered whether *I* really mattered? And ultimately, was Adonai pleased?"

"Finally, at the Feast of Purim just passed, I was in Jerusalem. The Qanaim were there in numbers unlike anything in the recent past. A massive uprising had been planned. But things went wrong, and I was arrested. I had been arrested and imprisoned numerous times before, but this was different. This was the very first time that I was caught red-handed. With blood on my hands. Blood still on my knife. The very lifeblood of a man who now lay dead at my feet."

Joshua had to pause as all of what he was feeling now threatened to overwhelm him. He knew that he had callously taken someone's life from him, even if he was a Roman. And he really wasn't sure what to make of this...new feeling which seemed to refuse avoidance, and would not be glossed over as in the past. He bit his lip and waited for a minute or two.

Compassion for Romans?

He would have to revisit that later.

Finally, he took a deep breath and continued.

"I knew that I was as good as dead. Knew that I would most surely be yet one more Jewish nationalist forced to submit to the Empire in a most complete and final way: on a Roman crucifix!"

"Some of us who were arrested were taken and imprisoned in the Antonia Fortress in Jerusalem. But by the end of the first week, one brother had died there, and each of the others had been removed, most likely to hang on a cross. I remained incarcerated there for an entire month. I wondered why it was taking so long. Had I been forgotten?"

"And then very early one morning, I was summoned before Pilate, so early it was not yet light outside. As was his custom, Pilate was going to release a Jewish prisoner at the Passover. And this year it was going to be me! I hardly knew what to think! It seemed too good to be true!"

"It was there that I met Jesus of Nazareth for the first time. In the middle of *my* release. The Jewish leaders had brought him to Pilate demanding *his* death. Pilate questioned him and then wanted desperately to release him, knowing that he had done nothing worthy of death. Numerous times he tried and each time they refused. They adamantly wanted Jesus of Nazareth dead, and they would not be dissuaded."

"I must admit, I wondered what that would mean for me. For my release. All of that now seemed to hang in the balance. Maybe it wouldn't happen after all!"

"It was then that Pilate placed a blatant choice before the crowd: Me or Him?

'Whom shall I release to you,' he asked.

'Jesus, who is called Barabbas, or
Jesus who is called the Christ'?"

"They chose me!" Joshua related with a hint of sadness.

"'Give Us Barabbas! Give Us Barabbas!' they chanted, clearly incited by the Jerusalem religious leadership."

"'And what shall I do with this other man?' Pilate had asked."

"'Crucify Him! Crucify Him!' the crowd had screamed in reply."

"I was released. A free man. And this other Jesus was flogged and then led away to Golgotha to be crucified. On my cross. His cross should have been mine! He paid the price for my crimes!"

Joshua paused, the monumental weight of what he had just said once more sinking in.

What a profound thought—a revelation. His misdeeds had in fact been paid for by this other Jesus.

He had been redeemed.

Life for life.

Emotion of a different sort now threatened to overwhelm him.

He looked around at his family. Most of them were teary-eyed. But smiling.

This too was a wonderful story.

But only because of how it ended.

Even though it was far from over.

"I followed the crowd to Golgotha. Watched the whole horrible thing. Saw Jesus die. Witnessed the heavens go dark."

"I was exhausted and must have fallen asleep. When I awoke, he was gone. And maybe my hope with him. The Jewish leaders had taunted him to come down from the cross. To save himself. They said that if he did, they would believe in him. I just wanted him to show them. To come down from the cross in power and establish the kingdom he had talked about. Maybe I wanted to believe in him too."

"Well, as much as he may have impacted me, he was dead and so I went back to my Zealot brothers. Didn't know what else to do. I guess I was just going to carry on as if nothing happened even if I wasn't sure I could do that. But it was the only life I had known for so long."

"I soon realized however, that through all of this, something had changed. Actually, that *I* had changed. Had in fact *been changed* somehow, even in my brief encounter with this Man!"

"I had so many questions. My old life really did not make sense anymore. I realized that I desperately wanted to come home. I knew that I could now because I had been granted my freedom. All was paid for! All was forgiven! I had been given a second chance at life! I thought that coming here might help me to find some of the answers I was looking for. And so, I broke camp in the early hours of the morning about a week or so ago now. To finally come home for the first time in forever!"

"I spent last night in our old house in Rakkath. I had done that once before actually. But last night was completely different from the time before. For Jesus came and met me there! In a vision? I don't think so. No! It was so much more than a vision! He met me! He was really there! He hugged me, and I most definitely felt His embrace. I wondered whether I was going crazy. And yet knew that I was not. I know now that He is alive! He is risen from the dead! Adonai has raised Him to life!"

"And He spoke these words to me, over me: *'Do not fear, Jehoshua ben Abraham! I am Jesus of Nazareth. I am Elohim's Anointed One. His Son. I came to earth to show people the Father's heart and the way back to Him. I was crucified for the sins of the world and for yours. And I have been vindicated by My Father and have been raised to life even as the prophets of old prophesied. I am the Messiah who was to come. And I am calling you to come follow Me. You have a destiny, a calling. You have known it, sensed it, for most of your life.*

But it is not to kill or to bring about the kingdom of heaven through violence, at least not the kind that you are used to. It is to bring life and healing and restoration to all people. Our enemies are not flesh and blood, but rather principalities and powers. Do not be afraid! I have overcome them and you will too. I am calling you to be My witness in the power of My Holy Spirit. I want you to learn to love once more. I have loved you since the day you were born and even before that and I was there beside you sitting in the clay on the day that your abba was murdered and your world changed forever. My Father, your Heavenly Father, cried with you then and has every day since. And He is now calling you to Himself. He wants you to be His beloved son'."

"It was amazing! He told me to go and enjoy the time with family. He told me, Zephaniah, to go and meet you down at the seashore this morning. Even told me about the new spot! He said that family was a good thing. That I would find favor with all of you even as I had prayed."

"And then He told me to lay down my *sicae*. That I didn't need it anymore. That my name was no longer Barabbas but Joshua once more and that, true to my name, I would bring salvation and deliverance to many. To all people!"

"I'm still not sure what to think of all of this. But He said that I needed to make sure that I am back in Jerusalem for Shavuot, fifty days from Passover. That was very important! He said He would meet me there and that all would become clear, or at least…a little bit more clear."

Joshua realized that he was smiling from ear to ear. He was happy. No, he was ecstatic.

When was the last time he had felt anything that even approached the joy that he was feeling right now?

He had been changed. Knew he would be changed even more in the days and weeks and months to come.

And now, led by Batiyah, his family—his real flesh and blood family—stood to their feet and clapped and cheered.

"Joshua, I have prayed for you every day since the day that you left. Prayed that Adonai would watch over you and keep you safe and bring you back home to us. And especially, after I met Jesus—after I experienced what He could do—I prayed even more then that if you were still alive, and I guess I just knew that somehow somewhere you were, I prayed that He would find you and raise you up and bring you back to the place where you belong—that Adonai would lead you into your true destiny!"

"Yours too is an amazing story; a *redemption* story!" Batiyah said.

"And it is clear that Adonai has answered and is even now more than answering all of my prayers!"

Chapter 54

HOME AND AWAY

BEING BACK AT HOME WAS VERY DIFFERENT FROM all that had been his *normal* life for the last fifteen years, but it was just so good. And Joshua thought he settled rather easily back into the daily routines. He went with Zephaniah to gather the necessary clay the next morning. The morning after that, he accompanied Elijah. It was wonderful now to also work alongside his younger brother and to get to know him as a young man in his own right.

In many ways, Joshua felt like a new hire. The fact that Seth was present and doing things that Joshua had never learned was a bit of a shock. He had been so small when Joshua had left. He didn't really know this brother at all. But it was excellent getting to know him now too.

Joshua had to pinch himself. He was truly a free man. Free to do what he wanted. When he wanted. Free to be wherever he wanted.

Galilee

Home!

Part of his very own family once again.

What a treasure it was not only to get reacquainted but to get to know *all* of these people who he had only imagined existed until just a few days ago.

Zephaniah's wife, Naomi—he had known her a little before; knew who she was but not really much more than that. Joshua found her to be truly wonderful, even more exceptional than he had imagined. All of Zephaniah's children: Abram, who had been named after his grandfather, and then, Ruth, Simeon, and Hannah. Zephaniah had a lovely family. And he seemed to be very happy. He should be extremely happy, Joshua thought.

Then there was Elijah's betrothed, Eliyah. What a sweet young woman. Joshua did think it a little funny that they shared variations of the exact same name, but he wondered whether that was part of why Elijah and Eliyah complemented each other so well? They were truly made for each other. He imagined that they too would one day have a wonderful home filled with adorable children.

"All in time," he said quietly.

And he chuckled to himself.

Indeed, all in time.

Too bad Abba wasn't here to see, to enjoy all of this, Joshua thought. But then again, in a way at least, he was here. He wasn't sure if his abba could see or not. But, all of this was here because of him. It was his heritage. It flowed out from him. Represented him. These people all bore his image, his character. Joshua saw hints of him in each of them, from the oldest to the youngest.

Sarah's husband, Josiah, was a carpenter and a young man as solid as the things that he built. He was loving and caring as well. And, how excellent it was that they could now get their brick molds and other things made right within their own family.

Finally, Batiyah, his ima, seemed younger, much younger even than when he had been forced to leave home. Joshua now knew why. She had actually been quite ill when he had seen her last and now, she was well! Completely healed and entirely renewed!

Family as a whole had almost fully been restored.

Recreated. And it was good...very good!

Shavuot, or Pentecost as it was called, was fifty days from Passover. Joshua kept that date firmly in the back of his mind. Ten days had passed already.

Jesus of Nazareth had said that it was *very* important that Joshua be in Jerusalem for that. That *he* would meet him there. That all would be made clear. Joshua knew that this was one *appointment* he for sure did not want to miss.

He looked forward to *seeing Him* again.

A few days after Joshua had come home and reconnected with his own family however, Zephaniah said he had a special request.

"For sure, name it," Joshua said.

"We have another load of bricks to go to Magdala," Zephaniah related. "And I feel you should be the one to deliver them!"

"I think that you really should reconnect with Caleb and...well... with *all* of their family!" he said with a wink, strongly emphasizing the "all."

Joshua could not miss the mischief in Zephaniah's eyes. He knew that his older brother was up to something and prodded him.

"Don't ask so many questions, little brother," Zephaniah said smiling, "I just think that it is 'really important' that you visit them. Just go. It will 'all become clear, well...more clear,' when you are there!"

It was obvious Zephaniah was holding back, not telling him everything...or, something. He wondered if he was right about what that was.

He agreed that it would be great to see Caleb and now most likely also, his wife and family. Good to see Zadok and Deborah. But what about Ariah and her husband and their family? That might be hard.

Were they living in Magdala too?

Even if he didn't get to see her, he could for sure ask about her. Just to know that she was okay. To hear how her life had been.

"All right," Joshua said, trying to be nonchalant. "I suppose I could do that."

"How about the day after tomorrow then?" Zephaniah said. "Your homecoming definitely put us behind a bit, but we should be able to have the order ready by then."

Joshua was a bit concerned about going away so soon, but at the same time, he did look forward to this trip. It was not far and not for long he told himself.

He had slept little the last few days. So many things were vying for his attention. One more thing didn't help that at all.

And last night was maybe the worst. Did he sleep at all, he wondered?

Morning did eventually come. And their new rooster, who didn't yet have a name, crowed. Apparently, and sadly, Hezekiah had just recently given his last wakeup call.

Joshua climbed out of bed and got dressed.

Zephaniah was already up and had Solomon hitched to the wagon, complete with its load of bricks.

They had a little bit of breakfast together. Said prayers. And Joshua and Solomon were off.

In the direction of Magdala.

In the direction of…

Joshua wondered what he would find there.

He was nervous and anxious and excited and a whole lot of other things wrapped together, or maybe more likely, unwrapped.

He had tried on several occasions to get more information out of Zephaniah but his brother had remained tight-lipped.

"All in time," was all he said.

Joshua pushed Solomon fairly hard, his own excitement spurring him on. And Solomon seemed to respond. Which was good. The last thing that Joshua wanted was to have to fight an unruly donkey all the way there.

The day was glorious. The sun was warm and the familiar and exquisite smell of the sea was carried in on the light breeze that was blowing from the southeast. As they approached the city, it was hard for Joshua to resist breaking into a run. But Solomon and the load of bricks would definitely not have gone for that. Joshua exercised his patience.

He suddenly realized that he hadn't even asked but had just assumed that Caleb and his family had not moved. He thought Zephaniah would have most certainly said something if they had.

Joshua made his way down the somewhat familiar streets even though he hadn't been there in many years. He finally came to their property, larger than it had been, but still in the same location. They must have bought out some of their neighbors. He knocked on the gate and ventured into the yard, Solomon and the load of bricks in tow. Somehow, he half expected to see Ariah there. And he laughed to himself at the thought.

The memory.

He was greeted by a young man about twelve or thirteen years old.

"Hello, there! I recognize Solomon and the wagon," the boy said. "But who are you?"

Joshua chuckled. He knew the boy hadn't meant to be rude.

"My name is Joshua! Joshua ben Abrahim. And I am here with a load of bricks for..."

"That's funny! My name is Joshua too...although everybody calls me Khiya. I'll be right back," the boy said, running off before Joshua could complete his sentence.

"...for your father?" Joshua said, now finishing what it was he was going to say, his voice trailing off as he watched the boy disappear.

Caleb had a son, his eldest maybe, whom he had named Joshua?

Joshua was flattered that his friend had named the boy after him.

He smiled to himself.

He was intrigued by the nickname though: *Khiya.*

"He lives," would be the literal meaning.

Caleb and the young man reappeared within moments, running across the yard in Joshua's direction.

He too had aged, but it was definitely Caleb.

The two lifelong friends embraced.

"Unbelievable!" Caleb said speaking first. "Khiya said that there was another Joshua here, a Joshua ben Abrahim. I couldn't believe my ears, thought he must surely be mistaken. But here you are, alive, and I presume, well?"

"I had asked your family, well, Zephaniah and Elijah actually, when they would make deliveries, if they had heard anything from or about you. No one knew where you were or even if you were alive."

"Oh Joshua, it's just so good to see you in the land of the living, brother! What has all happened to you since we saw each other last?"

"And when did you make your way home?"

Joshua gave Caleb a very brief history of his life's journey starting from the last time they had seen each other, from the night he left Magdala after Ariah's rescue up until he returned home just a few days ago. And Caleb listened intently, shaking his head in disbelief on more than one occasion.

"Yours is quite the story, Joshua! And I'm sure that there is most likely even more to it than you have told me," Caleb said. "Mine certainly pales by comparison."

"Let's see. I got married. We have had three children. I just recently inherited the fish drying business from my father, Elohim rest his soul. And well, that's it!"

"Zadok is gone?" Joshua asked. "Zephaniah didn't tell me that. I'm so sorry! And your mother?"

"Yes, sadly, father has passed on, I guess about six months ago now. And thank you for your sympathy, Joshua," Caleb said. "Mother is well. Aged some, but well. She still lives with us here."

"And your wife?" Joshua asked.

"Her name is Mariyah," Caleb said. "You will meet her. Very soon, I think. She and the children should return from the market shortly."

"I do think that *your* life is wonderful, Caleb!" Joshua said. "I would have traded mine for one like yours in a heartbeat!"

"Oh, and I am most honored that you named your son after me," Joshua continued, looking in the direction of the young boy. "He seems like a most wonderful young man. Just like his father!"

"Young Khiya here, you mean?" Caleb asked pulling the boy directly in front of him.

"He's not mine," Caleb said, shaking his head. "He is Ariah's. Her only child. *She* named *her* son after you!"

Joshua's breath caught in his throat, and he paused briefly to take in the young man's features once more. How had he not seen it before? Ariah was written all over him.

Now, he had a whole host of questions.

"There is much to catch up on, friend!" Caleb said smiling; a knowing smile.

"Ariah too will be back soon. She went to the market with Mariyah and the other children, my children, our children, Rehoboth, Susanna, and Zadok."

"She has quite the story as well, Joshua…and I'm sure she would love to share it with you, of all people. That is, after she gets over the shock of your being here. Alive."

"She has never forgotten you. None of us have. We have been, still are, indebted to you, for what you did!"

Joshua felt passions never dead rise up inside.

Caleb smiled again at his long-lost friend.

Now found. Restored.

Joshua could not but wonder about Ariah's *story*. He now knew that she had a son, which meant that she was married. But what had all happened to her since that night so long ago?

That remained yet to be discovered.

And the truth now. Not just his wild speculations.

He looked at the boy. He did seem full of life, the picture of health and vitality.

Joshua shook his head. Ariah had a son, and *his* name was Joshua.

"Shall we get this load of bricks unloaded?" Caleb said bringing it all back to the present. "And you can tell me more about the last fifteen years. I can share more about what has happened with me too."

When Joshua had been here last, there was only one brining pool with plans for two more. Now there must be almost thirty of them.

"This is quite a spread you have, Caleb. Very impressive," Joshua said.

"Yes, the business has most definitely grown. We currently employ six other people beyond our family just so that we can keep up," Caleb replied.

They pulled back the blanket and began unloading the bricks.

They hadn't gotten far when the gate flew open and in bounded three little ones playfully laughing. Their mother was right behind them.

"Hi Caleb, we are home," Mariyah called out, relieving herself of the baskets of groceries she had brought back from the market.

She stopped herself now looking directly at Joshua.

"We have a visitor?" she asked, smiling and looking from Joshua to Caleb and then back again.

"Yes, Mariyah, come here. I'd like you to meet my long-lost boyhood friend, Joshua! And Joshua, this is my beautiful wife, Mariyah."

"Joshua? *The* Joshua?" she asked looking at her husband.

Caleb nodded, smiling broadly.

Mariyah unhesitatingly greeted their visitor with a warm embrace.

"Well, welcome, friend!" she said as she stepped back. "I have heard so much about you, at least from days long past. So good to see you—to meet you finally! Alive and well! Adonai be praised!"

She smiled at their guest. And Joshua thought to himself that Adonai had indeed given his friend Caleb a most lovely woman as his wife.

"Where's Ariah?" Caleb asked.

"Wasn't she with you?"

"Yes," Mariyah said. "But she stopped to look at one more thing just as we were about to leave. She said she would be home shortly."

And with that, Ariah entered the yard.

Just barely through the gate, she stopped abruptly sucking in her breath.

"Joshua?" she said in a voice barely above a whisper.

Joshua nodded.

It really was her!

It really was him!

She remained static for only a second or two. Then dropped the baskets she was holding, ran across the yard and threw herself into Joshua's arms, tears already streaming down her face.

She held him tightly, refusing to let go.

Joshua welcomed her in his embrace.

He felt his head spinning.

It was as if no time had passed at all.

He wondered if he was dreaming.

But then, suddenly horrified that he had acted so brazenly and inappropriately with another man's wife, Joshua rather clumsily pushed Ariah away.

He was amazed that he could have been so unthinking.

By the way, he thought, where was her husband?

It was then that he saw what had escaped his notice in the initial fury of their reunion, that Ariah was dressed in the black garb of a widow.

Chapter 55

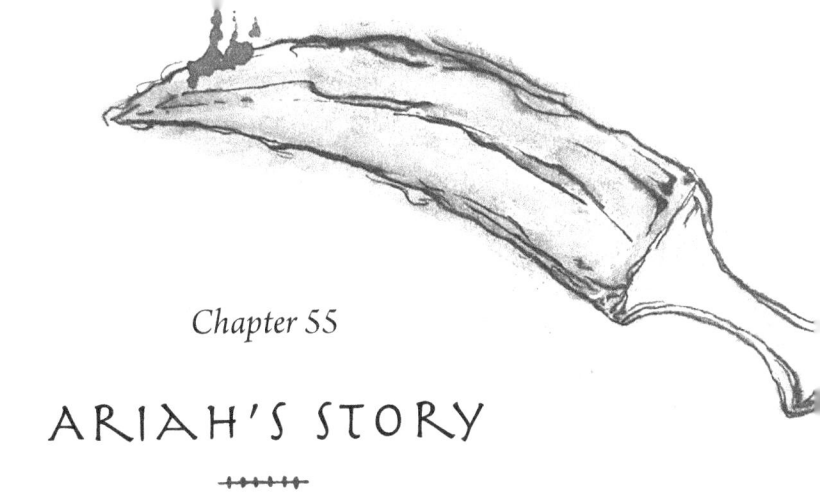

ARIAH'S STORY

Ariah was hurt. Wondering why Joshua had so rudely pushed her away.

It was obvious in her expression.

And Joshua tried desperately to explain himself.

"Sorry, Ariah, I didn't mean to hurt you, I just suddenly thought that it was so improper of me to be embracing you…ah…another man's wife like that. I didn't see, didn't notice…at first. But then, why would you have hugged me as you did if you were married? You are a widow? Oh, Ariah, you are a widow! I'm so sorry. I…I…didn't…know."

Joshua looked around; he was completely and utterly bewildered. He paused.

"And now I don't know what to say! I've been blubbering on like a crazy man."

He was trying to catch his breath.

Trying to compose himself.

But he was having a lot of trouble.

"Oh, I am sorry, Ariah! Caleb said you had…well, a story. Apparently! There is obviously much that I don't know. That I have missed. But I really would love to hear it if you don't mind," Joshua finally said.

Ariah was now grinning, shaking her head, and giggling almost uncontrollably.

"Still the same old Joshua! You haven't changed a bit!" she said.

Joshua knew that she was mostly laughing *at* him. He didn't mind so much.

This was Ariah after all.

And he did know he had most certainly carried on like a lunatic.

"It is a wonderful story, Joshua! And I would love to tell it!" Ariah said.

Joshua wasn't sure how this, her story, could be anything but tragic given what he had surmised of it so far, but he had also recently discovered that things were not always predictable.

Not anymore, at least.

At the same moment, Deborah, who had been visiting a friend down the street and had not been there when Joshua had arrived, returned home.

"That can happen soon enough, but first of all, allow an old woman to give her greetings," she said, interrupting as she joined the circle.

The elderly woman made her way to Joshua and embraced him.

She was crying but radiant through the tears.

"And welcome home, Joshua! It is so good to see you again after so many years. We have thanked Elohim for you every day and lifted you up in our prayers, praying for your protection, even while not knowing if you were dead or alive. But Hallelujah! Adonai has clearly answered! He has brought you back to us! Most blessed be the Name!"

"It is so very good to be home again, Ima," he said respectfully, welcoming her embrace. "I do love you all very much!"

"I was saddened to hear of Abba Zadok's passing though. I'm sure he is dearly missed by all. I know that I miss him," Joshua added.

The two just held each other now, quietly grieving but celebrating too.

When Joshua looked up, everyone was smiling and looking at the two of them.

"Thank you, son," Deborah said. "How wonderful of you to return. We have missed *you!*"

Joshua thought it was like no time had passed at all, as if nothing had happened.

This had always felt like family.

Even more so today.

Elohim was truly renewing all things.

And rather quickly it seemed.

"Why don't you boys unload the bricks and you can show Joshua around?" Mariyah said to Caleb. "There is lots that he hasn't seen since he was here last. We will have some food on the table shortly and we can all sit and talk then."

With that, Mariyah, Ariah, and the women busied themselves with meal preparations and Caleb and Joshua with young Khiya in tow went to inspect the spreading operation.

They were beckoned to the table after a short while.

They ate in relative silence. Everyone must have been hungry. As they were finishing, Caleb invited his sister to share her story.

"I would love to, Caleb. Thank you."

"Let me begin by saying how good it is to see you Joshua! I am so glad that not only are you alive but that you can be here with all of us!" Ariah began, a huge smile now gracing her lovely and unveiled face.

"Yahweh, be praised!"

Joshua almost choked on the little bit of food in his mouth at her boldness, at the fact that she simply spoke the Name, His Name, without hesitation. She had always been rather forthright, but this...? He looked around. No one seemed to be bothered by her audacity.

"First of all, I want to thank you so much for rescuing me that day, Joshua! I'm not sure I ever really got to thank you," Ariah began.

"Oh, you most certainly did!" Joshua said hastily, remembering the kiss but then immediately blushing. He instantly regretted his verbal outburst but it was too late to recall the words. They had been spoken.

And the color that instantly appeared in his cheeks and ears would not allow him to retreat unnoticed or easily.

Ariah apparently also recalled the kiss in that moment for she too blushed. How could she have forgotten that she wondered? She smiled as she paused briefly to revisit that moment.

She sighed. And then took the conversation in a very bold direction.

"I did love you, Joshua, in a young girl sort of way. I had thought that we might even marry someday. But then you were forced to flee. You didn't even return to say goodbye. I understood why, but it made me very sad. We could not even explore or discover what might have been!"

Her words made Joshua feel strangely at ease and wonderfully uncomfortable at the same time. He felt his cheeks burning even more than before and hoped it wasn't quite as noticeable as it felt.

"It's true," Caleb interjected. "She was a mess!"

Joshua smiled at that, looking in Ariah's direction, anxious for her to continue. Her eyes shone.

Once again, it seemed somewhat odd having the entire family around to hear all of this, and yet, somehow, not strange at all.

"I waited for a while. Hoping you would return. Waiting for you to return. Wondering if, wishing that we could maybe start a life together. In fact, I waited several years for you, Joshua. But you never came!"

Joshua's heart ached at those words. He knew his own anguish at being forced to spend life apart.

Ariah continued.

"Finally, father said that someone else had asked for me and had actually been after him about me for quite some time. He was a relative from the town of Nain about thirty miles southwest of Magdala. His name was Simon ben Naphtali, and Abba said that he was considering giving me to him. He asked me how I felt about that. I wasn't sure at first. I told him that I wanted to be *your* wife. I waited some more. But you were nowhere to be found. So eventually, I met this other man, and found him to be extremely sweet and loving. And since no one had heard anything of your whereabouts or even if you were alive, and I wasn't getting any younger...I finally said, yes."

"We were married and moved to the village of Nain, tucked up against the mountain on northwest edge of the great plain of Megiddo. And we were happy there. Simon was a shepherd, and the area where we lived was surrounded with green pastures. We began our own 'flock' there too, shortly after our marriage. In due time, Joshua was born. I asked Simon to name him Joshua in anticipation of the Messiah, and he thought that was a wonderful idea. But, if truth be told, I was thinking more of you than of Elohim's Messiah. It was my way of remembering all that you had done for and meant to me."

Again, Joshua blushed.

Ariah just smiled and continued.

"Things went along very well. We were quite happy. We were a wonderful little family. And Simon's sheep herd was growing with each passing season. He was often gone for long periods of time grazing his sheep. But one day, just shortly after Khiya's *bar mitzvah*, Simon didn't return home when I knew he should have. I waited another day and another and finally sent a relative to look for him. Jared returned several days later with the grave news that they had found Simon's body up in the hills, mauled to death, they supposed by a lion. The sheep had scattered and only a few of them could be found. Most of them must have perished and become food for the wild animals."

Tears now filled Ariah's eyes. However, she pressed on with her story, undeterred by her own emotions.

"Everything came crashing down, Joshua. I was now a widow with a young son in a place that somehow never quite felt like home, and I had little way to provide for myself. We tried to look after the few sheep we had left as best we could. We sold a few of them and ate some as well, but it was only a matter of time before I knew we would be completely destitute. And then, just when I thought it couldn't get any worse, my little Joshua got sick and then he too died!"

Ariah almost completely broke at this point, but continued. Joshua looked at Khiya and then turned back to Ariah.

"I don't know why I am so emotional today," she said. "I have told this story many times already!"

She shook her head.

"When Simon had been taken from me, I still had my son to focus on and to keep me company. But now, my whole world had collapsed. I traded the few remaining sheep to take care of the funeral costs."

"And now, I actually had nothing and no one!"

"For the second time in a very short while, I found myself on the way to Simon's family's tomb. This time to bury my only son! All that I had left!"

"I wanted to bury myself with them. My grief was overwhelming. The pain was unbearable. I could not stop weeping, and at the same time I was terrified, trying to imagine how I would continue. I knew that I must somehow. But I really didn't know if I could find it in myself to carry on. And really, did I even want to?"

Joshua found himself agonizing, hurting even as Ariah told her story, and feeling her anguish as if it was his very own. Why did this one precious woman need to experience so much pain in her life? If only he had been around to save her from all of that, he thought. To give her a different life from the one that she had experienced.

Ariah had tears in her eyes but she was still smiling, the fruit of joy that is born in one's heart and can't help but show itself.

Suddenly, Joshua began to piece it all together.

Khiya *had* died, but was obviously not dead now.

Hence the nickname: *Khiya*—"he lives!"

Ariah continued.

"In the middle of my grief, in fact, in the middle of our funeral march, a man made his presence known in the crowd..."

"...*a Man* unlike anyone I had ever met...!"

"It felt as though his very heart...reached out and embraced me in the midst of my sorrow!"

"'Don't cry,' the man calmly said."

"And then, without another word, he went over and put his hand on the funeral bier, forcing Simon's cousins to stand still and the funeral procession to come to a halt. I wondered who this crazy Rabbi was, a holy man who had no qualms about making himself unclean! I had absolutely no idea what he was doing!"

With each sentence, Joshua watched Ariah's joy increasing, if such a thing was even possible. He couldn't help but smile himself.

At Ariah. At Khiya.

It was contagious.

"The man spoke...to Joshua! He spoke to my dead son! I thought he was crazy! But he said, simply, 'Young man, I say to you, get up'!"

"And with that, my deceased Joshua sat up and began to talk!"

"I wanted to know what was going on!" young Khiya blurted out. "And why I was all wrapped up!"

"It was so uncomfortable!"

Everyone laughed.

"Of course you did!" Ariah said. "It is not everyday someone wakes up in the middle of their own funeral!"

"Jesus, the prophet from Nazareth, gave me my son, my only son back to me, Joshua! Back from the dead! My boy, the one we now call Khiya! We were all filled with awe and could not but praise Elohim! Adonai had come to help his people! He had come to help *me*! Who was I that He should come to my rescue?"

Passion radiated from Ariah.

"My life, none of our lives, have been the same since that day! Joshua's for sure. Khiya's. There is life where there was only death before! He was dead and he now lives! Yahweh be praised!"

"I was convinced that this Jesus of Nazareth was Messiah, come to deliver us from sin and death and disease and everything else! The kingdom of Elohim had appeared among us!"

"And then I heard maybe two weeks ago that this same Jesus was crucified in Jerusalem and my heart sank! I had so much hope! He had raised my son from the dead! Who but the Messiah can do such things? I didn't know what to think. I was so sad to have been so wrong!"

"But then, just days ago, a woman named Mary, a woman who had been possessed by many demons in the past, returned to Magdala, completely free...but even more than that, declaring that Jesus was in fact not dead! That He had appeared to her! Raised to life!"

"She was convinced He was alive!"

"And she was...convincing!

"Days later, other disciples returned to Galilee testifying to this very same thing! And I now feel certain that this same Jesus, the very man who raised my little Joshua back to life, has indeed been vindicated by Adonai and raised to life again Himself!"

Joshua rose to his feet applauding. For the second time in only a few days Joshua had heard someone very close to him tell of how Jesus of Nazareth had invaded circumstance and changed their world.

All was silent for a moment.

"He wants you to be his disciple too, Joshua!" Ariah said with urgency in her voice.

Things went quiet again.

"I know," Joshua said slowly, now breaking out into a large grin. "That's why He, the very same man, came and found me. Alive after I had seen Him die. Met me in my despair. Called me by name. My true name. Called me unto Himself. Called me to take up His mission."

Now Ariah was staring at him, wide eyes probing.

"I absolutely loved your story, Ariah! And *your* story too, Khiya!" he said.

Joshua paused. Then spoke.

"Would you like to hear *my* Jesus encounter?"

"Would I?" Ariah said moving toward him, so very eager to know everything about this man.

A man she had thought was forever lost to her, but who had just returned *from the dead* in a way.

And especially since it now appeared that Jesus of Nazareth had shown up and radically changed everything in his world too.

Chapter 56

CLARITY

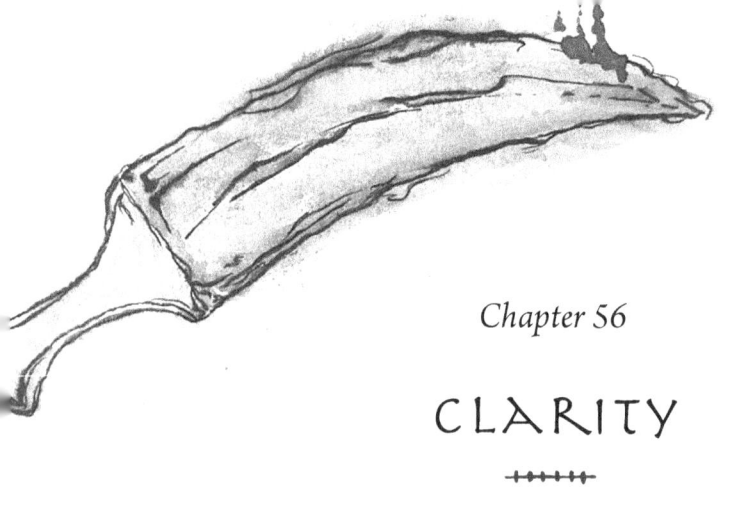

"Please, Joshua, do tell," Ariah urged. And then added, "It would appear that Jesus has given both of my Joshua's back to me alive!"

Joshua was just about to launch into the rehearsal of his life in more detail for the second time in only a few days. Deborah interrupted.

"Can it wait until we put some more food in front of us?" she said, and then with a twinkle in her eye, she added, "We don't want anyone to expire in the middle of a story, necessitating yet another resurrection!"

Everyone laughed at that.

The women busied themselves again with meal preparations.

Joshua, Caleb, and Khiya finally got around to unloading the delivery of bricks that had been abandoned earlier in the day, carrying them to the site of the next brining pool that was scheduled to be built.

Joshua had trouble not staring at Khiya.

The boy had been dead.

And now he was clearly not.

"You really are someone...amazing!" Joshua finally said aloud.

"I am!" replied Khiya without hesitation. "But our Adonai is so much more! I am amazing because of *Him!*"

The boy's eyes shone in a way identical to his mother's.

"Right you are!" agreed the elder Joshua, nodding.

"Out of the mouths of babes truly does come wisdom!" he thought.

The younger Joshua now turned to look full in the face of the one after whom he had been named.

Speaking unguardedly.

"I know why my mother loved...or rather, *loves* you!" he blatantly stated.

And without warning, the elder Joshua now found himself swallowed up in the younger Joshua's embrace. He couldn't help but choke up.

This was emotional beyond any words he could use to express it. Overwhelming even!

And he laughed that this was the second time in only a few days that he had been hugged by someone who had been dead and was now alive.

Joshua knew that he was loved.

He meant something to someone. To a good number of someones, actually.

And, ultimately, to Someone.

He had known that as theology, in his imagination.

But here it was. Tangible.

He could physically feel it.

"Taste and see that Adonai is good!" Isaiah said.

He knew without doubt that was true, and that he was more alive than he had ever been before.

"And I love you too, even if I have just met you!" Khiya interjected, interrupting Joshua's thoughts and compounding what he already felt.

Joshua had wondered not that long ago if all of this, if everything like this, had been lost to him.

But here it was. Better than ever before.

It had been recreated.

He had been recreated.

Reborn.

Made new.

"Thank you, Jesus!" he whispered.

Joshua knew that this time he would not leave.

He did not need too.

Indeed, everything was compelling him to stay.

His heart had found, was finding…home.

Family.

With that they were called for…what exactly? Was this supper or just the continuation of lunch?

Joshua wasn't sure.

They had spent the majority of the day around the table talking.

They certainly hadn't accomplished much. At least not much that was measurable.

At the same time, none of it felt like time wasted.

They had left the table only to almost immediately return to it.

But this was family.

Breaking bread together.

Celebrating.

Renewed.

And he and Khiya returned now, walking hand-in-hand, making their way toward an absolutely beaming Ariah.

She embraced them both.

Joshua was amazed at how good, how natural this actually felt.

When they were all seated, Caleb asked Joshua to pray the blessing on the food and on all of them. He did so.

And when they had eaten, Joshua launched into his story.

They all listened with rapt attention, especially Ariah.

As he finished sharing the details of Jesus's visitation, Joshua paused, realizing more deeply than ever, that his answer to his Savior, his Deliverer, his Yeshua, was indeed:

"Yes."

A resounding, "YES!"

He would be His witness!

There was nothing else he would rather do.

At the same time, another parallel thought somehow presented itself.

And with that, he stopped rather abruptly.

Almost in mid-sentence…

Chapter 57

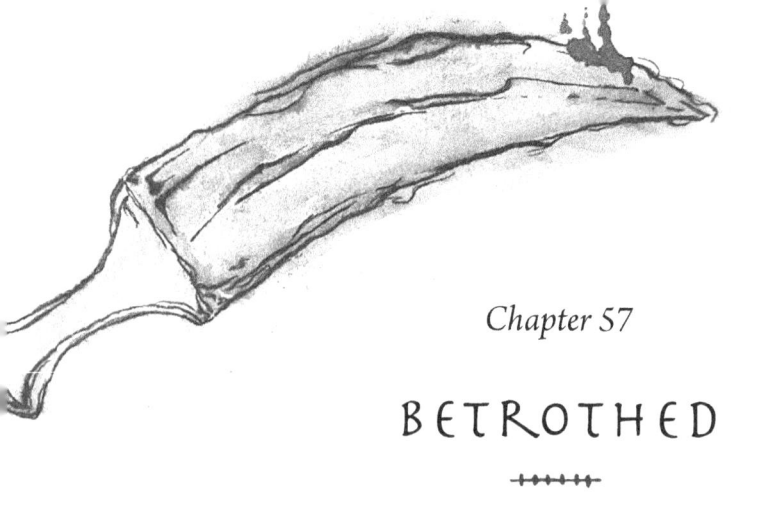

BETROTHED

"Caleb, Khiya, Deborah...I don't know who all actually. Most of all you, Ariah, I guess..." he said rather hurriedly, looking at each one in turn but finally resting his gaze directly on her.

They all stared back, somewhat unsure of what was coming.

Joshua pressed on, not wanting anything to weaken his resolve.

"I now know for certain that I truly want to be Jesus's disciple and His witness. But I don't want to, nor do I believe that I am supposed to, do it *alone*. I have spent the majority of my life so far 'going it alone.'"

"And Elohim Himself said in the garden long ago that, 'it was not good for the man to be alone...'"

Joshua was feeling extremely bold.

And a virtual volcano of words now erupted from his lips.

"Ariah, I love you! I always have. I have never stopped loving you. And I think...no, I know that you love me too! I have no idea how this will all work out and I don't know at all what the future holds, but can we, will you, walk together with me into whatever Adonai Jesus has for me...and for...us?"

With that, Joshua reached into his small moneybag, hunting for a specific coin.

A single denarius.

As was the custom, he extended it to Ariah.

His heart was in his throat.

But without any hesitation whatsoever, she reached out her hand to receive what was offered.

Joshua now spoke the weighted and necessary, ancient, words.

Slowly and deliberately he spoke.

"Ariah, be thou consecrated to me according to the law of Moses and of Israel," he said, or rather, asked.

Tears were streaming down Joshua's face, as he spoke. Ariah's too, even though she was beaming.

She shot glances at Caleb and then Deborah and finally Khiya. They too were crying and smiling.

Each one nodded, giving their approval.

Ariah swiftly moved in the direction of her about-to-be-betrothed.

"Yes, Joshua! Yes! Yes! Yes! I offer myself to you as your wife."

Joshua scooped her up in a soggy embrace.

After only a few moments, Khiya joined them.

"Finally!" Caleb said.

"Adonai truly works in mysterious ways, His wonders to perform!"

Chapter 58

WEDDING

THIS SET IN MOTION A VERITABLE FLURRY OF activity.

Caleb, Deborah, Ariah, and Joshua sat down and wrote out the wedding contract, the *Ketubah*, as custom dictated. The coin that Joshua had given Ariah was symbolic of the *bride price* that now had to be negotiated. Not that the bride was actually being purchased, it was more like a promise to take care of and provide for the woman who was to be entrusted to the man.

"So, one hundred denarii, then?" Caleb suggested.

That was after all the going *price* for a widow. If Ariah had been a young virgin, it would have been two hundred.

"Make it three hundred!" declared Joshua.

They all stared at him in shock.

"Ariah is worth more than all other women combined!" Joshua said loudly, a huge smile on his face.

He looked adoringly in her direction.

Ariah blushed and lowered her eyes.

Caleb and Deborah smiled and nodded their agreement.

"Three hundred it is!" Caleb said, knowing that most often no actual money was ever exchanged, especially when the parties involved were from the poor or working class. Only the very rich ever actually handed over any money. All of the other *terms* of the *Ketubah* were discussed and written down. It was a way of the bridegroom being held to all that he agreed to do for his bride.

The next day, a Friday, Joshua and Ariah made their way to Tiberius to share with Joshua's family the good news of their betrothal. Joshua had so much energy, he felt as though he could have run home. Ariah and Khiya alternated between walking and riding in the empty wagon that Solomon now pulled back to Tiberius. The weather was pleasant and travel was fairly smooth.

They talked the whole way home and Joshua got to know Khiya in particular, a whole lot better. He was a most likeable young man. That didn't surprise Joshua at all since Khiya was understandably very much like Ariah. Joshua wondered what Ariah's husband, Simon, must have been like. Some of who Khiya was had most certainly been passed down from his biological father, and given all that he saw, Joshua imagined that he too must have been a most wonderful person. What Ariah shared with him about Simon as they traveled just confirmed that his suspicions were true. He was very glad that someone had been there for Ariah in a time when he could not be and that he had been a man worthy of her.

At one point, Joshua absentmindedly got a way ahead of the small caravan. He stopped, turned and waited for them to catch up. He couldn't help but smile as he watched the two of them come toward him. Ariah would be, indeed she already was in a way, *his*. Khiya too. This would be, was, his very own little family.

He loved it!

Let that thought linger in his imagination:

His family!

He had a family!

He would soon be both a husband and a father. And, as he considered this, he thought of Abrahim. And he prayed again that he could be even half of what his own father had been. He was so grateful for the heritage he had been given and was now eager to pass it on.

In no time at all it seemed, they were home.

In Tiberius.

They quietly entered the yard.

Joshua saw Zephaniah, Elijah, and Seth busy making bricks. Batiyah and Mariyah were over by the oven cooking. The children were playing happily nearby. One of them looked up.

No one else had really noticed them enter.

"Hello. We have company!" Joshua called out.

Everyone stopped what they had been doing and moved in the direction of the trio.

"Well, not company exactly," Joshua said as they approached. "Say more like...family!"

Batiyah looked at Ariah and then at Joshua and back to Ariah.

She held up the coin that Joshua had given her and grinned.

Batiyah looked back at Joshua.

He smiled broadly and then nodded.

"Ya tuv!" Batiyah shrieked. "Joshua and Ariah are betrothed!"

The small family was now swarmed and surrounded by their larger extended family. All of them.

When the initial wave of commotion subsided, Joshua spoke.

"Hello, everyone, I would like you to meet my bride-to-be, Ariah, daughter of Zadok and Deborah. And this fine young man is her son, soon to be my son. His name is Joshua, though he most often goes by 'Khiya.' He'll have to tell you why later. And, Ariah and Khiya, this is, these people are my, and now your...family."

There was laughing and smiling.

And no shortage of joyful tears.

"Welcome to the family," Mariyah said after a few moments. "I have found them all to be welcoming and crazy and wonderful, and I trust that you will too. Some of them obviously know you,

Ariah, from birth. But I for one look forward to getting to know you. How would you like to help us finish getting the noon meal ready? We women can talk! I want...we all want, to hear all about it! This is quite sudden, no?"

"I just sent you to deliver the bricks and thought that it would be nice for you to *see* Ariah! I didn't know that you would bring her back as your wife!" Zephaniah said, shaking his head.

"Well, truth be told, I had no idea either!" Joshua confessed. "But it just seemed to be the right thing to do. Like Elohim Himself had ordained it. The words seemed to leave my mouth almost before I knew what had happened!"

"It's about time! You have been dreaming about this for years!" Elijah declared, and then added, "Ariah, Ariah, my sweet Ariah!"

Everyone laughed, remembering.

The rest of the day was a celebration of family. Enlarged as these new people were adopted in, rather easily it seemed.

The next day was the Sabbath, and they all observed it together. As family.

After two days, Joshua and Ariah and Khiya returned to Magdala with another installment of bricks for the brining pools, although truth be told, construction of any new pools was put on hold for a bit.

Joshua remained in Magdala for another couple of days and then headed back to Tiberius to await the time when he would come as bridegroom to fetch his bride and bring her home to be his wife.

He had asked Caleb to be his "friend of the bridegroom," his best man. To supervise and watch over the preparation of his bride.

"No question," Caleb responded. "I would love to do that for you, my friend and brother, and for Ariah!"

Whereas a normal *kiddushin*—a word that actually meant "sanctification" or a setting-apart, used to show the significance of a betrothal—in situations when the bride-to-be was a young girl and a virgin, would last six months to a year, in the case of an adult or a widow, both of which Ariah was, the wedding could happen within one month of the initial proposal.

Joshua hadn't really thought about all of that when he asked Ariah to join him on his life's journey. He hadn't thought about it at all. On the other hand, he had thought about marrying Ariah for most of his life, just none of the actual details. But the fact that they didn't need a lengthy engagement actually ended up working very well with his need to be in Jerusalem as Jesus had said he should be, for Shavuot.

He imagined that if all would be made clear or at least clearer for him, he wanted Ariah to be a part of that. Khiya too. They were going to be a part of whatever his future was now to be, after all.

Almost four weeks later, at midnight, Joshua got all dressed up in his festive garments and went, together with a small entourage, to Magdala, to get his bride. They met her attendants on the road as they approached the house. They in turn ran back to the house to let everyone know.

When they all arrived, Caleb joyously went out to meet Joshua and now called out in a loud voice:

"Behold, the bridegroom cometh!"

"Go you out to meet him!"

And of course, Ariah, bathed, purified, perfumed, richly clothed, and adorned with jewels, was ready and waiting for him.

The rest of the family and friends were notified and hastily assembled. Even though they too knew this day was coming, they just didn't know exactly when it would be.

When everyone was gathered, Caleb and Deborah spoke their blessings. Ariah was given a crown. And now they all made their way back to Tiberius in joyful procession in the wee hours of the morning. When they got to Tiberius, all of Joshua's friends and family were called upon to join them. Indeed, many had seen him go and had been waiting for him to return.

When everyone was present, Joshua took his own garment, spread it over Ariah and the two of them made their retreat into the house. And now, exactly twenty-eight days after their betrothal, on a Thursday, the day of the week on which widows were typically married, Joshua and Ariah became husband and wife, consummating their marriage.

Since Ariah was a widow and obviously not a virgin, there was no blood-stained sheet to display to everyone in the window, but Joshua nevertheless threw the bed sheet out of the window just for fun and everyone cheered.

That was the cue for the celebration to begin.

Since this was a second-time marriage, for Ariah, there was no call for a weeklong celebration as was usual with weddings. They didn't actually have time for that anyway. But they celebrated nonetheless for the rest of Thursday and all day Friday, and then spent the Sabbath together with everyone in Rakkath.

The plan was to be on the road to Jerusalem early the next day. If all went well, they would arrive there with two days to spare.

Just enough time to catch their breath…

Before…what exactly?

Who knew, other than Jesus, what it was that they were in for?

Chapter 59

JERUSALEM

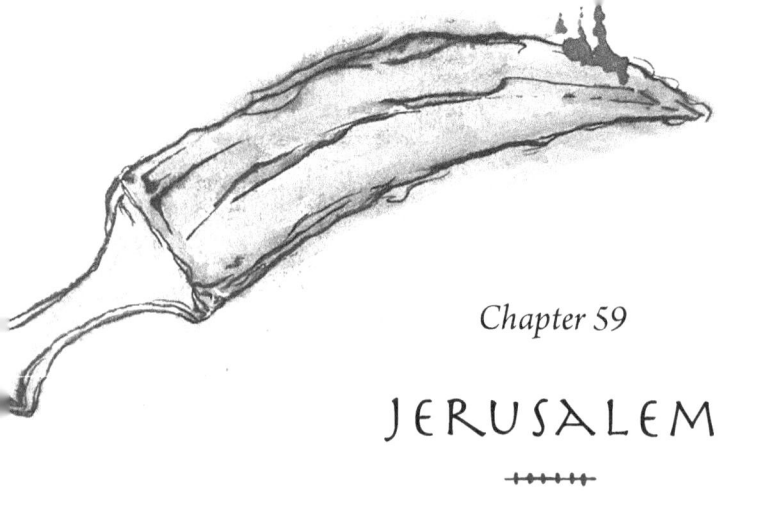

Joshua, Ariah and Khiya arrived in Jerusalem with only a day to spare. There were, as they had suspected, no accommodations available. They had made their plans much too last minute for that to be a possibility. And with Jews flocking to the city for the one-day festival, everything had already been spoken for. Fortunately for them, Ariah had a distant uncle and aunt, Zedekiah and Miriam, who lived very close, in the town of Bethany, less than two miles from Jerusalem. The threesome had just shown up at their door, explained their plight, and had been welcomed in.

Joshua took that as the blessing of Elohim on their journey.

It felt good to imagine that He was smiling on them.

The journey had been a good one.

He found out that Khiya really liked to talk—and ask questions. He sure had asked Joshua a lot of questions. Not that Joshua minded. He imagined that Khiya just wanted to get to know his father-to-be.

He had taken to calling him Abba almost immediately. That made Joshua feel strangely wonderful.

He loved getting to know Khiya as they talked about whatever came to his young mind as they walked.

Ariah just smiled at the two of them engaged in conversation, building a relationship.

She too had a family again.

She had her Joshua back.

Both of them now.

And Khiya seemed to her, if it was possible, even more alive than ever before. He too had been enlivened by this other Joshua, whom Ariah had thought was gone forever, but who had now been brought back into her life.

This was far better than she could have ever imagined, she thought.

They settled in at their relative's place and had a really good sleep for the first night in several. The journey had been good, but camping out on the side of the road over the last few days had not been entirely restful. That evening, Miriam fed them a wonderful meal and it felt amazing to go to sleep safely in a house and on a full stomach.

The next day, Joshua took them on *his* journey, a journey that started at the Antonia Fortress on the Stone Pavement, the site of his release, down the streets of Jerusalem where Jesus of Nazareth had been forced to carry His cross. Joshua related to them each detail of the journey.

From the sham trial and Pilate's pleading with the crowd, to Jesus being flogged and mocked by the soldiers. Pilate pronouncing His judgment. Washing his hands. Surrendering Him to be crucified. And then, the grim parade. Leaving the city. Jesus stumbling and falling. Simon of Cyrene being conscripted to carry the crossbeam. The women of Jerusalem weeping for Him.

Finally, the Place of the Skull...Golgotha.

Three uprights still remained in the ground on the hill. And Joshua, Ariah, and Khiya, proceeded until they were directly underneath the place where Jesus of Nazareth had suffered and died. The blood, of Jesus and others, was clearly visible on the wood and the ground. And they all just stood in silence for a while, each one awash in their own thoughts.

"This should have been my cross," Joshua said at long last, interrupting. "It *was* my cross, but Jesus took it for me. Jesus who is called the Christ, the Anointed One, the Messiah, for me: Jesus who was called Barabbas!"

He held his head in his hands, overwhelmed again and afresh by the weight of that thought.

Ariah and Khiya surrounded him in a tight embrace.

"His was all of our cross," Khiya said. "Jesus of Nazareth was the spotless lamb of Elohim, prepared in eternity and slain for the world. But, praise Yahweh! Death does not ever have the final word! Not anymore at least!"

"Yes. Out of the mouths of children…!" Joshua marveled.

"Indeed," Ariah agreed, praying. "Thank you, Adonai, for all you have done for us. For all of us!"

The three of them remained there for some time, then made their way back to the city and back to Bethany for the night.

Tomorrow would be *Shavuot*.

Pentecost.

Fifty days from Passover.

Joshua was in Jerusalem as Jesus had told him to be. But suddenly, he wondered: where *exactly* was he supposed to be? Where would he meet Him? Jerusalem was quite a large city.

And the city had swollen even more over the course of the day that they had been there, as pilgrims flooded in from all over the surrounding area, anticipating the festival that celebrated the harvest with a wave offering of fresh bread from the wheat harvest and coincided with a celebration of the giving of the Torah to Moses on Mount Sinai.

The three of them returned to Bethany and to the house of Zedekiah and Miriam, and again enjoyed the evening meal together.

"Did you have a good day?" Zedekiah asked politely.

"A most wonderful day!" Joshua said.

He had a thought.

"Zedekiah, I'm going out on a bit of a limb, but would you happen to know perchance where I might be able to find the disciples of a man who was crucified here in Jerusalem at Passover, Jesus of Nazareth?"

Zedekiah remained silent for a bit.

Joshua wondered whether he had asked something he shouldn't have, had stirred up what he should have left undisturbed.

Zedekiah didn't answer the question exactly.

"I don't know what to think about all of this. I did see him once or twice. And I have heard rumors, some saying that he rose from the dead. But our leaders are saying that is a lie and that his disciples in fact stole the body. I don't know. People don't rise from the dead, do they?"

Khiya spoke before Ariah or Joshua could stop him.

"People *do* rise from the dead, Uncle Zedekiah," Khiya now boldly declared. "I did! I was dead, and Jesus of Nazareth raised me up!"

Zedekiah's jaw dropped open. Miriam's too.

They just stared at the young boy.

"It's true! I was dead. And then Jesus spoke. And I am clearly not dead now, see!" Khiya said, reaching out his arms for them to touch him.

They reached out and touched him.

What else could they do?

And with that, they turned to look at Ariah.

"It is true even as he says," Ariah responded. "He was indeed dead. We were on the way to the family tomb when Jesus of

Nazareth stopped the funeral procession. He told me not to cry and then spoke to my dead son telling him to get up. With that, Joshua sat up and began to talk."

"I wanted to know what was going on and why I was all wrapped up!" Khiya said, clearly enjoying telling this part of the story.

"That is some story!" Zedekiah said, shaking his head. "Now I really don't know what to think about all of this! I do want to hear more though."

He paused collecting his thoughts, bringing himself back to the initial question.

"Joshua, you asked about this man's disciples. We used to see them all the time in the Temple. But I have not seen them since the Passover. I'm not sure anyone has. Our leaders have made it clear that they are wanted for questioning and…for who knows what else? Look what they did to their leader! The leadership have let it be known that anyone who sees them should turn them in. I did hear it rumored, and rightly so, that they are hiding out somewhere, but whether here in the city or not no one seems to know."

"Okay. Thank you anyway. I just thought…I don't know exactly. Now, I don't know *where* in Jerusalem I need to be for Jesus to meet me," Joshua said absentmindedly.

"This Jesus fellow *said* that *he* would meet you?" Zedekiah asked.

"*When* did he tell you that?"

"Well…that too is quite a story," Joshua said. "I would be happy to share it with you if you would like. If you have the time."

"We are old. We have nothing but time!" Zedekiah said chuckling.

"Although maybe not as much of it as we used to!" he added.

"Share it, Joshua. Please. And young Khiya, we for sure want to hear your story as well!"

They sat with rapt attention for the next hour or so as Joshua rehearsed his whole story and particularly the part about his visitation on that night in Rakkath. Following that, Khiya and Ariah told their stories too.

"That is quite a story! *Those* are quite the stories!" Zedekiah said when they all were finished.

"You have made me quite curious. We were going to go into Jerusalem tomorrow for the festival, but I am wondering, would it be okay, for us to come with you?"

He turned to face his wife.

"We would love to know more, I think. Miriam my dear, are you up for a little adventure?"

She nodded.

"When do we need to leave?" she asked.

"Early," Joshua said. "Very early I think."

"Well then, we better get to sleep. It's already quite late," Ariah said. "Enough talking!"

And with that, everyone retreated to their beds.

"Where in the city are we going to meet Him, Joshua?" Ariah asked as they settled in for the night.

"I don't know exactly. At least not yet," Joshua said. "But I can't believe that the Spirit of Elohim has led us this far, to not lead us now."

"I will ask Him for direction as I am falling asleep, and whether He tells me specifically or just leads us in a mysterious way tomorrow is of little matter. I trust Him to accomplish what He has promised. He said that He would meet me. I believe Adonai is faithful."

"He did tell me that some faith is required on our part!" Joshua added laughing quietly.

Ariah just nodded to herself in the dark and thanked Elohim for giving her such a wise...and godly man.

"Adonai Jesus, please lead me to Yourself," Joshua prayed as he allowed sleep to embrace him. "Show me where I, where we, need to be. Where it is that You will meet us. And...thank You for everything!"

Chapter 60

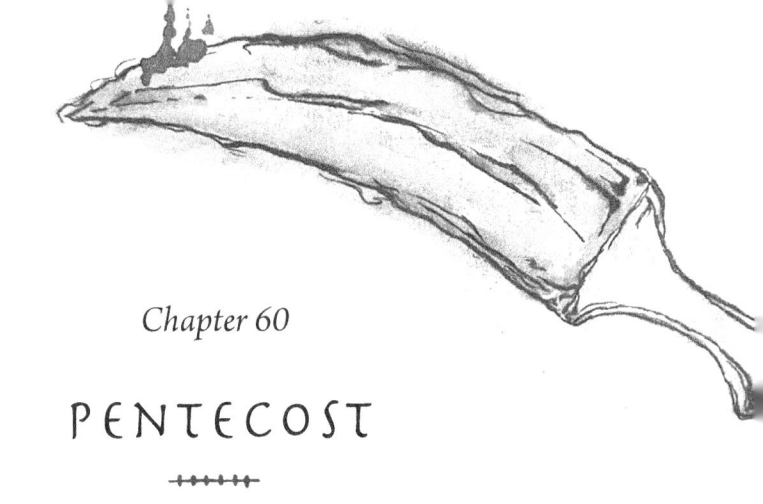

PENTECOST

The next morning, they were up early. In fact, Joshua had been awake for at least an hour before he heard the rooster crow. Praying. Patiently waiting for an answer as to where they were to be.

Suddenly it came to him.

Zedekiah said that he had often seen the disciples in the Temple. He needed to be in the Temple.

Where else would Jesus meet him?

Joshua wondered if Jesus's disciples would risk being there today.

Seeing as there would be many people there for the festival, maybe it would be okay today. Maybe the Jewish leaders would avoid causing a commotion on this day.

He knew all about being hidden in a crowd.

However, Joshua suddenly questioned why he thought he needed to seek out the disciples? Jesus had simply said that *He* would meet him. He laughed to himself and thought, He can walk through walls and locked doors, He can certainly find me wherever I am. But Joshua couldn't shake the nagging suspicion that the disciples were somehow meant to be there, to be part of this.

"So where are we going?" Khiya asked as they set out on their journey in the semi-dark of the early morning.

"I believe we should head toward the Temple," Joshua said, but then added, "though I know that Jesus can meet us anywhere!"

"To the Temple it is, then," Khiya said, boldly taking the lead.

He grabbed Zedekiah and Miriam's hands and placed himself squarely between them.

Joshua took Ariah's hand and the two of them fell in behind.

"I don't know how to get there!" Khiya whispered to Zedekiah.

"Don't worry," Zedekiah assured him. "I most certainly do!"

Their journey took a little bit longer than usual, since Zedekiah and Miriam were older and needed to go a bit slower, but they arrived within a couple of hours, at around eight in the morning.

Jerusalem was very crowded and people thronged the streets, more so as they neared the holy district. They pushed their way through the crowds and eventually, the Temple was in sight. But then...

Everyone suddenly stopped dead in their tracks.

It sounded as though a violent hurricane had descended upon them, yet nothing was blowing around.

All was still.

Fear was clearly written on many faces.

No one breathed.

They all just stared at one another.

Questions hung in the air.

And then, just as quickly as it had come, the wind, or at least the sound of it, stopped.

In the midst of the silence, a commotion was heard coming from a nearby house as a crowd of people rapidly descended the stairs from its upper room.

They were all speaking at once and moving to various locations within the court of the Gentiles.

Joshua didn't really understand any of the languages being spoken but there were clearly people, both Jews and converts to Judaism, who had come for the festival who did.

He thought that he recognized one of the local dialects of Judea.

"How is it that a Galilean is speaking fluent Parthian?" he heard someone else remark.

"And Cappadocian!" another one said.

It was then that Joshua saw Simon. He was smiling from ear to ear, and...almost...glowing.

Joshua simply stared at him. Simon too was speaking, preaching, though in some foreign language.

A crowd of pilgrims who clearly understood what he was saying was rapidly gathering around him. They looked like Egyptians.

Joshua wanted to go and ask Simon what was going on, but he also didn't want to interrupt whatever this was.

"What is going on here?" Zedekiah asked giving voice to everyone's question.

"I don't know," Joshua said, glancing at Ariah. "But it feels right. I think. As though I am where I need to be."

"These men have simply had too much wine!" Joshua overheard one dressed as a Sadducee say rather loudly.

"They are drunk," agreed another of the religious leaders.

Joshua wasn't entirely sure what caused all of this, but he didn't think that it could be attributed to strong drink.

After thirty minutes or so, one of those who were preaching stood up and silenced the crowd. Simon and the others gathered around him. Joshua counted twelve of them.

In a loud voice, though now in Aramaic, he said,

"Fellow Jews and all of you who live in Jerusalem, let me explain this to you—listen carefully to what I say."

Everyone grew silent.

The man continued.

"These men are not drunk, as you suppose. It's only nine in the morning! No, this is what was spoken of by the prophet Joel:

> *'In the last days, Elohim says,*
> *I will pour out My Spirit on all people.*
> *Your sons and daughters will prophesy,*
> *your young men will see visions,*
> *your old men will dream dreams.*
> *Even on My servants, both men and women,*
> *I will pour out My Spirit in those days,*
> *and they will prophesy.*
> *I will show wonders in the heavens above*
> *and signs on the earth below,*
> *blood and fire and billows of smoke.*
> *The sun will be turned to darkness*
> *and the moon to blood before the coming of*
> *the great and glorious day of Adonai.*
> *And everyone who calls on the name of Adonai*
> *will be saved'.*"

He continued, even stronger now.

"Fellow Israelites, listen to this: Jesus of Nazareth was a man whom Elohim accredited to you by miracles, wonders, and signs, which He did among you through Him, as you yourselves know. This man was handed over to you according to Elohim's deliberate plan and foreknowledge; and you, with the help of wicked men, put Him to death by nailing Him to the cross."

Joshua was almost positive such bold statements would provoke an outcry, maybe even a riot.

Would this preacher be arrested?

He had just laid the blame directly at the feet of the Jewish nation and particularly, the religious leadership.

Joshua knew first hand that it was a fair and right accusation.

The preacher paused now, surveying the crowd.

A broad smile broke across his face.

"But Elohim…" he said, raising his hand in the air, his voice reaching a crescendo, "…but Elohim, raised Him from the dead, freed Him from the agony of death, because it was impossible for death to keep its hold on Him!"

Had Joshua ever heard anyone preach with this kind of passion?

The preacher pressed on.

"In fact, David said about Him in the sixteenth of the *Tehillim*:

> *'I saw Adonai always before Me.*
> *Because He is at My right hand,*
> *I will not be shaken.*
> *Therefore My heart is glad*
> *and My tongue rejoices;*
> *My body also will rest in hope,*
> *because You will not abandon Me*
> *to the realm of the dead,*
> *You will not let your Holy One see decay.*
> *You have made known to Me the paths of life;*
> *you will fill Me with joy in Your presence'.*"

"Fellow Israelites, I can tell you confidently that the patriarch David died and was buried, and his tomb is here to this day. But he was a prophet and knew that Elohim had promised him on oath that he would place one of his descendants on his throne. Seeing what was to come, he spoke of the resurrection of Messiah, that He was not abandoned to the realm of the dead, nor did His body see decay."

"Elohim has raised this Jesus to life, and we are all witnesses of it. Exalted to the right hand of Adonai, He has received from

Abba the promised Holy Spirit and has poured out what you now see and hear!"

"David did not ascend to heaven, and yet he said,

> *'Adonai said to my Adonai:*
> *Sit at my right hand*
> *until I make Your enemies*
> *a footstool for Your feet'.*"

Joshua had never heard anyone speak like this man spoke. Except for the Man, Jesus. Such power and conviction—it was as if this disciple had absorbed the spirit of Jesus of Nazareth.

He stared and listened in wonder and amazement.

As he glanced around their small group, he noticed that Ariah, Khiya, and even Zedekiah and Miriam had similar responses.

Some in the crowd though, were murmuring.

The preacher was undeterred.

"Therefore," the man called out more loudly even than before, "let all Israel be assured of this..."

He now spoke with even greater conviction.

"Elohim has made this Jesus, whom you crucified, both Adonai and Messiah!"

A roar erupted from the crowd.

Some were jeering, but clearly many were cheering.

"What shall we do?" someone shouted from down near the front.

"Repent and be baptized, every one of you, in the name of Jesus Messiah for the forgiveness of your sins. And you will receive the gift of the Holy Spirit. The promise is for you and your children and for all who are far off, for all whom Adonai Elohim will call," the preacher replied.

"I want that, Abba!" Khiya said excitedly, turning in his abba's direction. "I want to be baptized and to receive the Holy Spirit of Adonai!"

"You took the words right out of my mouth, son," Joshua said.

"Jesus, thank You for meeting me here today! For meeting *us*," he silently prayed.

Tears were streaming down Ariah's face.

"Me too!" she said.

"I want that for every one!"

They looked over at Zedekiah and Miriam.

Zedekiah looked somewhat troubled.

Miriam was searching the eyes of her husband of forty-three years, waiting for his direction. It seemed as though he was struggling.

Finally, he spoke.

"As for me and my house," he said, "we will serve Adonai..."

He hesitated and then grinned.

"...And His Messiah, Jesus of Nazareth!"

The little group stood and hugged each other, smiling and crying and laughing.

Each one knew that what they were feeling was like nothing they or anyone else had experienced ever before.

Very soon, most of the crowd was making their way east toward the Kidron Valley and the pool that was there, created by the Gihon spring. When they arrived, a steady stream of people were making their way in and out of the water, being baptized by the preacher and the eleven other men with him.

Joshua and his small group had to wait their turn, but eventually, they all made their way down into the water. He stood praying now, eyes closed, waiting for someone to come to him, waiting for his turn.

"Barabbas!" he heard someone say from directly in front of him as he felt an arm smack his back.

He bristled and almost reacted violently.

But he had immediately recognized the voice.

"Simon," he said, turning to embrace him. "So good to see you. I actually go by Joshua now. My Barabbas days are behind me."

"Oh, and this is my wife, Ariah, and my son, Khiya."

Simon looked at him rather strangely, questioningly.

"Joshua, then..." he said hesitating slightly, and then turning, "and, Ariah and Khiya, good to meet you too."

His gaze remained fixed on Khiya and Ariah.

"Do I know you? I feel like we have met somewhere," he said.

"We have," said Ariah smiling.

Simon thought for a moment longer and then locked in on Khiya.

"You are the boy, that boy that Jesus raised from the dead in Nain!" he said.

"Good memory," Khiya replied. "And yes, I am!"

"Wow! So good to see you again! Alive!" Simon said.

He looked over in Joshua's direction once more. As though he was going to ask something but decided not to.

"We'll have to talk more another day. But for now, do you believe that Jesus is Adonai's Messiah and the atoning sacrifice for your sins?"

Simon looked at each of them individually, waiting for their affirmative response.

"I then baptize you in water, and pray that He will now baptize you with the Holy Spirit and with fire."

He proceeded to immerse each one of them in turn under the cold spring water, raising them to stand on their feet once more.

"Oh, and one more thing, brother: *'You are His chosen instrument, a carrier of His good news, and you will be mightily used by*

Adonai to turn the hearts of many people to Him! Actually, all three of you will'!"

Joshua just stared at him.

"Barabbas...sorry, Joshua, come and find me, after all of this craziness is done. Or I can come and find you. Where are you living?"

"In Tiberius...well, sort of...though, in Bethany right now," Joshua answered, composing himself.

"Could I come to *you*...here somewhere?" he said.

"I have a lot of questions. And I don't want to have to wait a long time for answers."

"Well, I don't really have a place of my own here in Jerusalem. But we often gather at the oil press on the Mount of Olives, or we used to, anyway," Simon said. "We meet in the evening to pray. That is probably the best place to find me. Us. I'm sure we will return there soon. Again."

And with that, he moved on to the next people. It seemed that there were probably several thousand who had come to be baptized.

Joshua, Ariah, and Khiya made their way out of the water and onto shore.

The noonday sun was warm, and they were already drying.

Joshua was sure that he had never felt this clean. As if the old was gone and something new had come.

"Baptize me in the Holy Spirit and in fire!" he said quietly to himself, repeating Simon's words to them just minutes ago.

They found Zedekiah and Miriam, eventually got something to eat, and then made their way back to Bethany.

Most of the way home was rather silent.

Everyone seemed deeply immersed in his or her own thoughts.

"Quite a day!" Zedekiah said to no one in particular at one point in their journey.

Quite a day indeed, thought Joshua.

But once they were back in Bethany, back at the home of Zedekiah and Miriam, and had sat down for the evening meal, it was difficult to get a word in edgewise. Everyone wanted to share what they had experienced and felt, what it had all meant to them. Now that they had all had some time to process all of it.

"I feel like I have been reborn," Zedekiah said. "It is like I have a new, divine life inside of me! It would seem that Elohim Himself has done what keeping the Torah could never have done."

"Little did we know a few days ago, that not only would relatives we didn't even know make their way to us, but that Adonai Himself would come and visit us! It is almost too wonderful to describe!"

Chapter 61

BETHANY

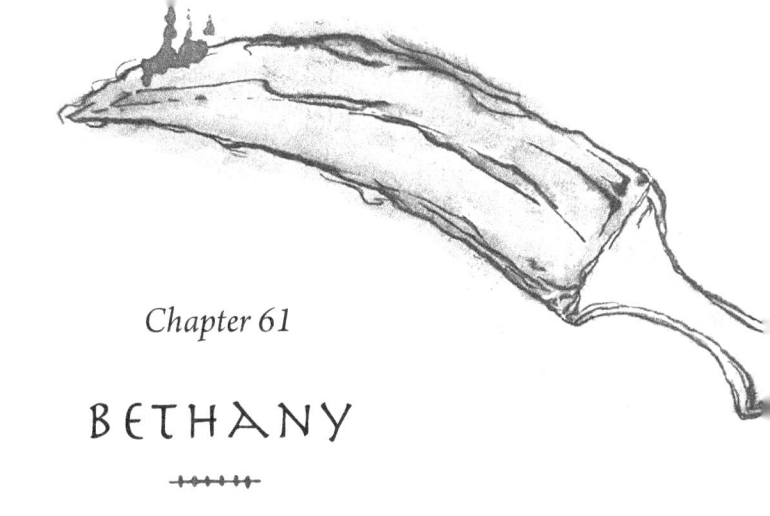

THE TRIO REMAINED WITH ZEDEKIAH AND MIRIAM for the next several days. It really was wonderful to have met these blood relatives of Ariah's and now also to share a bond in the blood of the Messiah. It seemed that many of their interactions were filled with "aha" moments as very familiar Scriptures somehow took on new meaning. It was as if Elohim's Spirit was revealing a new depth to the Holy Writings that had in fact been there all along, just waiting to be discovered. So much that had been mystery before now just seemed so clear. Each conversation just led to more. Revelation upon revelation.

But as wonderful as this was, Joshua was now anxious to make their way back to Jerusalem. To reconnect with Simon. Maybe to hear stories from some of the other disciples as well.

What hunger had been before was now intensified.

He was zealous to know even more about this other Jesus. The immeasurably more that seemed was waiting to be discovered. After four days, it was almost unbearable.

"You want to move on, don't you?" Ariah asked when they were alone.

"Is it that obvious?" Joshua replied.

"It is to me," Ariah said.

"I can read you like the weather, my love!"

"And I am not really that good of a reader!" she added with a giggle.

"How do we tell your uncle and aunt that we want to go just a stone's throw away without hurting their feelings?" Joshua asked. "They have been so good to us; I don't want to offend..."

"Don't worry about it," Ariah said, "I already told Miriam yesterday that we would probably be going back to Jerusalem shortly. They will totally understand. They are expecting it even!"

"Can we go then, and meet the disciples at *Gad Smane,* the garden of the oil press, maybe even this evening?" Joshua asked, not the least bit concerned that his impatience was showing.

"Yes, dear," Ariah said, "we can leave as soon as we have packed up our few belongings and said our goodbyes."

"Oh, and after eating something. I am sure that Miriam will insist on feeding us just one more time before we leave!"

Joshua and Ariah made their way down off the roof to find Khiya. They hesitated at the bottom of the stairs.

Across the small yard, Khiya was sitting with Zedekiah and Miriam, telling them once more of Jesus raising him from the dead.

Joshua marveled at the spirit and the passion that permeated his adopted son as he animatedly shared this life-giving story. It was Ariah's spirit. But he knew that even more, it was indeed the Spirit of the Almighty One that now filled this young man, full to overflowing.

Tears filled his eyes. He turned to look at Ariah. She didn't notice, for her gaze was firmly fixed on her son.

"Blessed beyond imagination!" he thought to himself.

Joshua momentarily turned his face toward the heavens and breathed an almost silent "Thank You," for all that he had received as of late.

The two of them decided to join the others without interrupting and let Khiya finish his story. It was a story that Joshua had now heard several times himself. It was something he knew he would never tire of hearing over and over and over.

When Khiya finished, Miriam spoke.

"Oh, my dear boy, that is a story I could hear again and again," Miriam said. "But it is time for you to go now."

She gasped.

"Oh, I'm sorry! I didn't mean for my words to come across the way they must have sounded!" she exclaimed.

Everyone laughed.

"I just meant..."

"Yes, yes, Auntie, we know what you meant," Ariah said, patting the old woman's hand ever so gently.

"We understand that you want to get going," Zedekiah said. "Adonai has much more in store for you. For all of us, I suppose. But can we please break bread together one more time before you go?"

"That would be wonderful," Joshua said. "Thank you so much for everything that you have given us over these past few days. For sharing yourselves with us! They have been some of the most wonderful days of my life!"

Within no time at all, they all sat down to eat.

And once they had finished, and then collected their belongings, it was time to leave.

They all embraced each other.

"May Adonai bless you and keep you," Zedekiah said. "May Adonai make His face shine upon you and be gracious to you. May Adonai turn His face toward you and give you peace."

The *Dukhanen*—the ancient Aaronic blessing.

How wonderful Joshua thought, a smile gracing his own face, to walk in the presence of Adonai, literally to walk in the light of His Face.

And Jesus of Nazareth, the man Adonai accredited to the world by miracles, wonders, and signs, had in fact come to earth for that very purpose: to put a face on the Holy One and to show us the Father.

"And to you as well," Joshua said to Zedekiah and Miriam.

"Shalom. And Adonai's blessing to you both. And to this house."

With that, the three of them made their way out of the yard and began their trek in the direction of Jerusalem.

Chapter 62

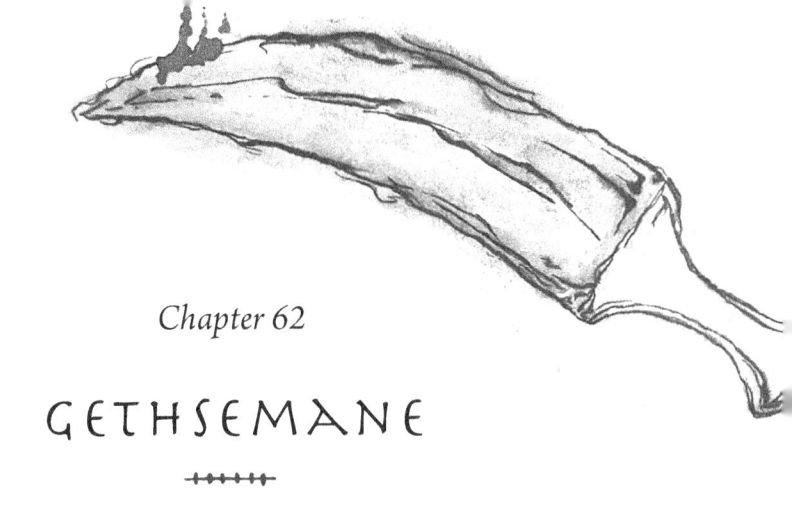

GETHSEMANE

As soon as they arrived in Jerusalem, their first task was that of procuring lodging, a job made much easier now by the fact that the majority of people who had come for the festival days had returned to their own homes. They rather quickly managed to find a good inn, at a reasonable price, not very far from the Temple and settled in. Ariah thought she might lie down for a bit. Joshua and Khiya allowed her some quiet and went to the market to get a few things they might want over the next several days. They certainly didn't *need* anything. Miriam had sent them on their way amply provided with everything that they would need.

While they were wandering around in the market, some treats called *ashishot* caught Khiya's eye.

It was a sweet cake made of toasted lentils that were ground up, mixed with honey and then fried. Sometimes people also added raisins, but these particular ones were devoid of that addition.

"Ima loves these!" Khiya said. "Can we bring some home, or… to the place where we are staying? To our home away from home?"

"Why not," Joshua replied. "These are days of celebration, I think! *Shavuot* is a celebration of harvest. And we have reaped abundantly this last week…and in all the days leading up to it!"

Khiya beamed, knowing how much Ariah would love them and how much he would enjoy surprising her with their extravagance.

The merchant handed Khiya the precious package and Joshua gave the man the money they had negotiated as the price.

They also stopped to buy some laundry soap at another stall before the two of them began their short journey back to the inn.

"Abba, can I ask you something?" Khiya said almost immediately.

Joshua enjoyed being called, "Abba."

"Sure, anything, *son*," he answered.

He loved the fact that he had a son.

"When we were baptized, Simon prayed that we would be baptized not just with water but with the Holy Spirit and with fire," Khiya began. "I knew that I wanted that! Even if I didn't know exactly what it was!"

"Okay..." Joshua said, leading him to continue.

"Well, when I came up out of the water, I heard myself speaking or maybe praying in another language just like the disciples had, though I didn't do it out loud. I stopped myself because it scared me a little, but at the same time, it was kind of...*warm,* I guess. I have found that I can start and stop myself anytime now. And when I pray like this, I just know that I feel so connected to Jesus and to Adonai Himself! It's strange though."

"It did feel...sort of like I was on fire!" Khiya said with a hint of a question. "Do you think I should have spoken it out loud? Maybe someone would have understood me? Do you think that was part of the other *baptism* that Simon was talking about?"

"I don't know, Khiya," Joshua replied. "This is all new to me too. But I had a similar experience, and so did your ima. We'll have to ask Simon about it when we meet with him. Maybe we can ask him tonight?"

Back at the inn, they made their way up to the room. And peeking in, they saw that Ariah was stirring, so Khiya made their return known.

"Look what we got!" he exclaimed, passing her the package, slightly askew seeing as how some of the treats had *escaped* on the way home.

Ariah rubbed her eyes and allowed them to focus.

A big smile broke across her face.

"*Ashishot!* Thank you, boys!" she said smiling broadly. "You are both so good to me. I am most blessed of women!"

She took a big bite.

"Mmmmmm," she said, savoring the confection. "Delicious!"

"By the way, how soon do we need to be ready to go?" she asked.

"Maybe in an hour or so?" Joshua replied. "If that's okay?"

"No problem," Ariah said. "Enough time for me to freshen up and for us to have a little something else to eat before we go. Khiya, I hope you're not filled up on treats with no room left for healthy food!"

Khiya shook his head and licked the honey from his lips.

After partaking of some of the bounty that Miriam had sent with them, they made their way out onto the street in the direction of the Temple. Once on the street, they headed north, then out of the city through the Lion's Gate, down through the Kidron valley and then back up the other side to the Mount of Olives and the particular grove known in Aramaic as *Gad Smane*, or in Greek as *Gethsemane*, meaning, "the oil press."

They arrived at around the eleventh hour, just as the light of the day was fading. No one was there. The garden was completely deserted. Joshua's heart sank. Maybe the disciples weren't meeting here anymore. Maybe Simon's supposition was only that. What if they had started meeting somewhere else, to avoid being seen by the authorities? But Joshua thought they had certainly been anything but cowardly or covert on the day of Pentecost so why the change, what would make them start caring about that now?

He soon saw a few people carrying torches on the road that led up the mount and into the garden of olive trees, some of which had probably been here when Abraham first laid his eyes on this land.

One of the first people to arrive held a torch in Joshua's direction.

"I know you!" he blurted out. "You are Barabbas! The one the crowd chose instead of our Adonai!"

"You are correct, brother," Joshua began. "I was that very one. But having met *Him,* I am a changed man, inside and out it would seem. My given name is Joshua. Jehoshua ben Abrahim of Rakkath."

"Simon, the one formerly also a Zealot, said I might find *him* here."

The man looked him up and down.

Was he being cautious?

"Well, Joshua ben Abrahim, you're right about that. My brother Simon will be here shortly. I am Thaddeus, Judas Thaddeus, though I have taken to calling myself Jude, as of late, so as not to be confused with another. I too was formerly somewhat of a Zealot!"

"Pleased to meet you, Barabbas...or sorry, Joshua!" he said.

Just then, Khiya walked up and joined them.

"I don't see him yet, Abba," he said.

"No, he hasn't arrived," Joshua said.

"Khiya, this is Judas Thaddeus, or just Jude for short. He too is one of the disciples of Jesus."

"I recognize him," Khiya said. "I remember seeing him after Jesus opened my eyes."

"The Master healed your blind eyes?" Jude asked, surprised.

"No," Khiya said. "He opened my *dead* eyes!"

"In the town of Nain!" Jude immediately exclaimed. "Now I recognize you! You are *that* boy! Restored to his grieving mother!"

"Yes, I am!" Khiya announced with pleasure.

"And your name is *Khiya?*" Thaddeus asked, somewhat perplexed.

"It's really Joshua," Khiya said. "But everyone calls me Khiya *now!*"

"*Alive!*" this disciple said.

"That is a great name you wear!"

Khiya just grinned. Joshua too.

And with that, Simon appeared.

"I see that you two have made yourselves known here," he said and then turning to his fellow apostle, added, "Thank you for making my guests feel welcome, brother Jude."

"No problem! Simon, this is that boy! The one our Master raised from the dead in Nain. And he goes by the name *Khiya* now!"

"I know! Talk about a great nickname!" Simon said. "'*He lives!*' I love it!"

"And where's your wife?" Simon asked turning toward Joshua. "Did she not come this evening? You do know that women are welcome in all of our gatherings?"

"Oh no, she is here somewhere," Joshua replied.

They noticed Ariah not far away, animatedly talking to another woman who was part of the growing band of disciples.

"Oh, there she is, talking to Josephine, Simon Peter's wife," Simon said and then added with a laugh, "They will have a fair bit in common, considering the kind of men to whom they are married!"

"By the way, Joshua, I wanted to ask you about that at Pentecost. It shocked me! I didn't know that you were married! And had a family? Nobody at Q ever said anything. You were married the whole time you were on the run and out on uprisings? Were you ever home?"

"No," Joshua said laughing. "That only happened within the last two months. And truth be told, it was quite a shock to me as well. A pleasant surprise albeit but one obviously orchestrated by Adonai!"

Ariah joined them and Joshua put his arm around her back.

"I can tell you more about this precious gift some other time!" Joshua said.

The rest of the evening was taken up praying, singing psalms, and sharing stories of what had been happening in various places ever since the Spirit of Adonai had been poured out.

Somewhere in the vicinity of three thousand people had confessed faith and been baptized even just on that first day. And every day since, more had joined the growing movement.

Joshua knew that the Qanaim had never seen that kind of response. But then again, they had never experienced anything that came close to this either.

They had been zealous, he thought, but this was a zeal unlike anything he had ever known. Adonai Himself had paid them a visit. And had come to stay.

As the evening drew to a close, Joshua realized he had not even broached the subject that had been his initial purpose. He found Simon once more and asked him when they might be able to spend more time together. Maybe without such a large group of people. So that he could find out more about this man, Jesus of Nazareth.

"For you, brother, most certainly, and soon," Simon said. "Seeing as how you *helped* me so much when we were at Bereshith!"

Joshua laughed at that.

He knew that *he* hadn't helped at all.

"How about we meet tomorrow morning, say around the third hour, at the gate called Beautiful?" Simon suggested.

"Sounds perfect," Joshua said. "Okay if we all come?"

"The more, the merrier!" Simon said. "You're all welcome!"

Chapter 63

SIMON

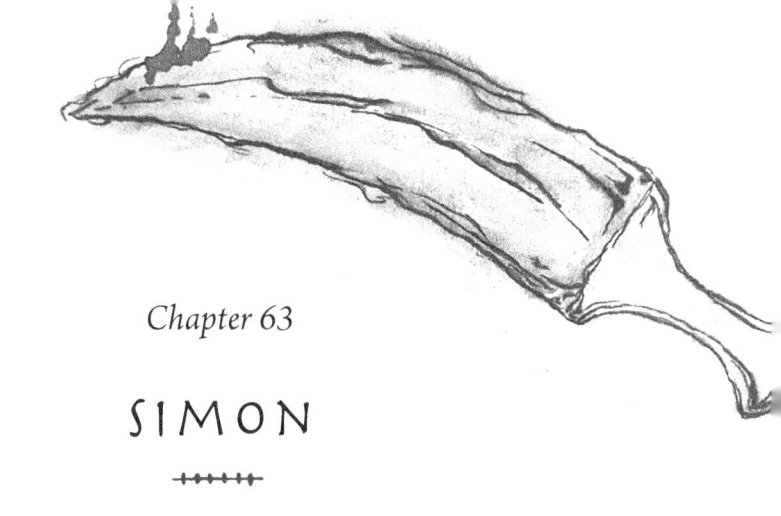

They had eaten breakfast, but hungry for more important things, they were at the Beautiful Gate very early the next morning.

Waiting. Eagerly anticipating.

Simon showed up pretty much at the third hour on the dot.

They exchanged greetings accompanied by hugs and then sat down in a shady spot just outside the wall of the city.

"So, what is it that you want to know?" Simon began casually.

"Everything about Jesus of Nazareth...from beginning to end," Joshua said excitedly. "Everything and anything you can think of. Well other than the few details I know...from the end."

Simon was shaking his head, contemplating how he could possibly accomplish what was being asked of him.

"So, everything...from beginning to end?" Simon said slowly. "I'll give it my best attempt off of the sleeve."

He paused.

Then spoke.

"I think that were I to actually share with you *everything* He ever said and did...a library of books could not contain it all! And besides, trying to compress into maybe three hours this morning all of what I experienced of Him over the last three years. Every day.

All day. And sometimes even through the night! Nearly impossible! I trust that I can at least send you away with more than you came!"

"Well, hopefully this will not be our only time together," Joshua said, playfully adding, "Unless you're going to run out on me again!"

"Not this time brother!" Simon said, fully enjoying the humor.

Simon bowed his head.

"Abba, Father…give us this day our daily bread," he prayed. "Holy Spirit, show me what Joshua and his family most need to hear!"

He took a deep breath.

"Where do I start?" he asked himself. "Jesus said so many things! But about Himself? Hmmm?"

"He said that He was the Good Shepherd. The fulfillment of the twenty-third of the Tehillim, I think—the kind of shepherd who deeply cares for and even lays down His life for the sheep. No matter what, He had compassion on the crowds of people who would come and often remarked that they were like sheep without a shepherd. He healed them and taught them, knowing that His sheep would recognize His voice and would follow Him. He said that He was also the gate of the sheepfold: the way in and out. How different the thief, our enemy, who comes in another way, intent only on stealing, and killing, and destroying. Death, disease, and demonization are the things Satan gives to the sheep. Jesus came in order that we might have life, Adonai's kind of life, and have it to the full."

"Life was in Him. The eternal life He shared with Elohim at the very beginning. Everything was in fact created through Him. His life was the light that dawned at creation. The light of all mankind."

"He is the living water, the only one who really satisfies. When we drink from a well, we will be thirsty again. But when we drink from Jesus, we will never thirst again and out of us will flow rivers of living water for others! A spring of water welling up to eternal life!"

"He said that He was the vine—the true vine. And we are the branches; if we abide, if we remain in Him. Along comes the Father and prunes us so that we may bear much fruit. Apart from Him, we can do nothing, any more than Jesus could do anything without the Father."

"He said that He only did what He saw the Father doing. That in fact, He did nothing apart from Him. He modeled the way for us."

"Right at the end, He had been telling us that He was going away and that where He was going, we couldn't come, but we would later. It was pretty confusing. That didn't sound like good news. But He told us not to be troubled about that. That He would go and prepare a place for us and then come back and get us. Thomas said that we didn't even know *where* He was going, so how could we know the way there."

"Jesus said that, '*He* was the way, *He* was the truth, *He* was the life.' And that if we wanted to discover the Father...to find our way to the Father, we would find it, get to know Adonai, through Him."

"Still confused, Phillip asked Him to 'show us the Father.' He asked Phillip how it was possible that he had been so long with Him and yet did not know Him. He said that if we had seen Him, really seen Him and knew who He was, we had seen the Father! He said that He was in fact in the Father and the Father was in Him, and that the words that He spoke and the work that He did was only the result of the Father, living in Him, doing these things through Him."

"When He first called all of us, He called us to follow Him. And I know that those are words that every rabbi uses to invite disciples to join him, but with Jesus, it was different, more real, more significant! It wasn't just to physically follow Him around and learn the lessons He taught, it was to follow *Him,* His very essence, the *Who* that He was, so as to become like and then do the very things that He did."

"Not that we were going to copy Him exactly though, He went on to say that 'Even greater things than these will *you* do because I go to the Father!' Even greater things, because He would send, would pour out, His Holy Spirit on us! That Adonai would fill us with His very self!"

"Jesus came to earth to show us what Adonai was like. Who He Is. And Jesus was and is, one with Adonai. He fully demonstrated who the Father was before our eyes, and He put His Spirit in us so that we could do the same!"

Simon came to a full stop.

Trying to rein it all in.

"Oh my," he said. "We'll never get anywhere, or maybe we will end up everywhere…if I keep on this way! Because each thing I remember Him saying somehow seems to provoke another and I end up chasing all of these little rabbit trails all over the place! I'm sorry."

"Don't apologize," Joshua interjected. "This is amazing!"

"I wasn't like this before," Simon continued, "but ever since we received the Holy Spirit in His fullness, it's like I am constantly reminded about everything that Jesus said and did. It is like the Holy Spirit has come alongside and become not only my Comforter, but also my Teacher, leading me back, as Jesus had said He would, into all the truth that He had shared with us. It's like I can suddenly recall all the things that He taught us where before I was, I guess we all were, so forgetful. We just didn't understand, just didn't get it, but now, in some miraculous way, we really do!"

"If only He could help my thoughts be more organized!"

Simon immediately laughed at that.

"Like He couldn't do that!" he said aloud. "Nothing is impossible for Elohim, the El Shaddai!"

He was about to start in again, but paused as something of paramount importance came to mind.

"Before we go any further, and maybe you've already grasped this one very important thing, Jesus's emphasis was never to know *about* Him. It was about actually getting to know *Him*. Who He was and is! His heart! And even more than that, to know Adonai as Father, His heart, His thoughts, His way of seeing! Jesus came to reveal *Him!*"

"This is wonderful and I'm glad that you are getting something out of it, but I suppose I should try and take us, all of you, on a more orderly journey through His life. I have to try anyway! At the same time, I know that the Spirit is like the wind and blows wherever He wants! We don't, can't, shouldn't even try to control what He is doing!"

"Take a breath, Simon," he told himself. "Start from the beginning."

Joshua, Ariah, and Khiya were just sitting there with their mouths hanging open, waiting for the next morsel. Orderly or not, this was just so good. It truly was the bread of life. And living water. It felt as if Jesus was right there, teaching them all things.

"Are you all doing all right?" Simon asked. "I haven't lost any of you?"

They all nodded.

Replying without any words.

Simon took a deep breath and started in again.

"I guess I'll start from where I last talked to you, Joshua. From the time I left the Qanaim. Well, actually maybe a bit before that. I should start with the event that led to my decision to leave."

"As I told you, Joshua, the first time I met Him was at my brother's wedding in Cana in Galilee. Somehow, pretty early on in the celebrations, they had run out of wine. The friend of the bridegroom told me later that several of the jars had somehow cracked and that all of the wine that they had prepared had leaked out. That would have been really bad for our family."

"Apparently, Jesus had told the servants to fill new jars with water and then serve that. They were more than a little afraid! Serving plain water would be in very bad taste. But they did as they were told and as they poured it, they immediately realized that it had miraculously been turned into wine! And the very best wine of the celebration at that!"

"Shall we just say that my interest was piqued?"

"I followed Him around for several days. As did a whole lot of other people. I listened to all of the things that He said. About a kingdom of love, even for enemies. How life was not just about keeping the Torah, but about finding out and following the heart of the Lawgiver. Jesus said over and over in His message that, while you have heard it said, 'you shall not commit murder' or one of the other commands, that was not enough. He would add, 'but I say unto you…do such and such.' And in each instance, what He was doing was actually intensifying the command! Not satisfied with the letter of the law, He was calling all of us to the spirit of it. So different from Pharisaic additions. Motivated by love rather than fear. I had never heard anyone preach like Him!"

"And then too, He healed. The demonized. The sick. Every kind of illness. He touched and cleansed lepers. The deaf heard. The blind saw. Lame people walked and ran and danced. People were set free from all manner of things that bound them!"

"And that was just what He accomplished in those first few days!"

"The most profound thing for me, however, was His personal call. I can remember that word for word: *'Simon, son of Clopas, come follow Me,'* He said. *'I am zealous for My Father's house, and true zeal can empower you as well if you let it.'* He called *me*—Simon the Zealot—to follow Him!"

"I returned to Bereshith. I didn't leave all and follow Him immediately as I know some others did. It was as though I knew the truth but I was still kind of confused. Not quite ready? Maybe.

That's when I talked to you, Barabbas...or...sorry, Joshua. And you actually did help me see what my *heart* really wanted!"

"I didn't feel like I helped at all," Joshua said. "And when you left, you actually left *me* more confused than I had been before! You see, I was struggling at that point too. Maqaba thought my talking to you might help me. It didn't at all! Or...maybe it actually did, now that I think of it. Whether you knew it or not, I guess you planted a seed in me, a desire to find out the truth. It put me on an almost three-year long journey to find out everything that had been prophesied regarding Messiah. I spent a lot of time after that day searching out the Scriptures."

"I'm glad for that, brother! But more than that, I'm glad that He found you and brought you here!" Simon said.

"So, I left the Qanaim and returned to Cana. And as soon as I found out where Jesus was, I went there. To Capernaum. A fairly sizeable group of people was following Him wherever He went. Taking in the things that He was teaching. Seeing the miracles. It was an amazing time!"

"At one point, very early on in the journey, we were all up on a mountainside. Jesus had disappeared the evening before, for the entire night. I think He had gone to be alone with our Father. To pray and just be with Him. He did that often, I later found out. When He returned in the morning, He called all of us who were following Him to gather around. And He chose twelve. To be with Him in a closer, more intimate way. To be His apostles—His 'sent out' ones. To preach and to heal. And, *I* was one of the ones that He chose! I felt so honored and blessed! And surprised! Me! Simon the Zealot! Chosen by a man preaching a kingdom of love for all! How's that for crazy?"

"Crazy for sure, but oh so wonderful!"

"I remember Him saying that if we only love those who love us, what good is that? Everyone does that! But, if we love those who hate us and even persecute us, by doing so we actually prove that we are true sons and daughters of Elohim, because He loves all men!"

"That was why Adonai had sent His Son to earth: to re-establish connection with us! He came to His own and many of them did not receive Him, they ended up crucifying Him, in fact, but as many as did welcome Him, they were included in the family, were made sons and daughters in His kingdom."

"Over the next three years, life was a whirlwind. All over Galilee and the rest of Israel. Preaching and teaching. Sometimes to large crowds of people."

"He constantly told stories, parables really. They were confusing but meant to make people think. To dig deeper. We didn't understand much of the time, but He would explain everything later when we were alone."

"And healing. He healed all who came. Of every disease. Never the same way twice it seemed. Each person was cared for. He touched them far beyond their physical ailments."

"And feeding people. Twice in fact! Five thousand men plus women and children the first time. And four thousand the next. And that with only a few loaves and a couple of fish!"

"Speaking of five thousand, I saw Him cast that many demons out of a man and into a herd of pigs in Gadara!"

"The man had been renamed 'Legion,' because of how many demons were in him! The locals had tried to chain him up at times, but he always broke the chains. He spent his nights and days running around naked, howling among the graves, and cutting himself."

"I saw the love of Jesus conquer even that and afterwards, there was that same man, sitting and talking with Jesus, clothed and in his right mind!"

"The pigs did not fare nearly so well!" Simon added with a laugh. "And in the end, the townspeople were so in awe, so afraid, they begged Jesus to leave. Which He did!"

"I'm not at all sure what they were so afraid of!"

"I was there when He raised you up, Khiya! When He gave you back whole and healthy to your grieving mother. And then, I remember a man named Lazarus from Bethany who had already been dead three days! Jesus raised him up and restored him to his sisters, Mary and Martha. There was a little girl who had died in Capernaum, maybe about your age, Khiya, the daughter of a man named Jairus."

"And there were others! Many others."

"My ima was there in Capernaum that day, when Jesus raised that little girl," Joshua said. "That was the very day *she* got *her* healing!"

"Your mother was *that* woman? The one who had been afflicted with bleeding for twelve years?" Simon asked.

Joshua nodded.

"Wow! That is so excellent! It would certainly seem that Adonai has taken a special interest in your family!" Simon said.

"And your mother, she is well?" he asked.

"She is better than ever!" Joshua replied.

"We saw so many miracles," Simon said, continuing. "But we found out that it wasn't just meant for Jesus to do these things, He eventually sent *us* out to do the same, in His authority. We were now to drive out unclean spirits, to heal all manner of sickness and disease, and to raise the dead. And, we did see all of these things happen at our hand! We were so excited!"

"We couldn't help but tell Jesus all about it when we returned. But I love what He did: He said that as good as all of those supernatural demonstrations were, the greatest miracle was that we could be rightly related to the Father, that this was the greatest healing, deliverance, or coming to life again—the way clear once more—people returning to how things were at the beginning, in the garden! Free from sin, free to just walk with Him in the cool of the evening. And He's right, by the way!"

"I saw Him questioned continually by the scribes and Pharisees. The Sadducees too. And every time, His answers confounded them and put them in their places. It was fun to watch, but it did nothing for their appreciation of Him. Their hatred only grew, probably starting from that very first day when He wove a cord and went into the Temple, overturned the tables of the money changers and drove out all of the animals. And for sure the fact that He often healed on *Shabbat* didn't help Him gain any favor with the religious elite either!"

"'My house shall be a house of prayer for all nations,' He said, as He cleared the Temple, 'but you have made it a den of robbers'!"

"He was probably the most zealous person I had ever met, more zealous for sure than any of the Qanaim! But it was zeal for His Father's house, for His Father's presence, for His Father's family, that consumed Him! Zeal that was motivated by and exercised in love!"

"Their hatred, which only grew throughout the years, eventually culminated in the events of Passover just gone by. Did they know that He was the Lamb of Elohim, sent to take away the sins of the world, as John the baptizer had proclaimed? If they had, I don't think that they would have crucified Him, the Adonai of glory!"

"He said that all of us who wanted to be His disciples must take up our own cross and deny ourselves and follow Him. That whoever tried to save their life would lose it, but whoever gave away—whoever lost—their life for His sake and the sake of the good news, would find it given back to them in abundance, even better than could be imagined."

"I think that Jesus knew all along that the cross was His destiny. That He would lose his life. In fact, He told us repeatedly toward the end that He was going to Jerusalem and that He would be delivered over to the religious leadership and be killed. When Peter protested, He told him that he was thinking earthly thoughts and did not have the ways of Elohim in mind."

"At the same time, He also told us that He would rise again on the third day, though none of us knew what He meant by that at the time!"

"I remember a time, just before that last week. We were in Bethany at the home of a man named Simon, a leper whom Jesus had healed, and a woman who had been a prostitute came in with an alabaster jar of very expensive perfume, made of pure nard. Weeping, she broke the jar and poured the perfume on His head and His feet and wiped them with her hair. Some of the disciples, especially Judas Iscariot, were offended that she had *wasted* the perfume. They said it could have been sold and the money given to the poor. Jesus told them to leave her alone. That she had done a beautiful thing. That she had in fact, anointed Him for his burial!"

"It all happened just as He said it would!"

"When we celebrated Passover together, He said that the bread was His body, broken for us. He said that the cup was the new covenant in His blood. None of us had a clue what He was talking about. And then, in the middle of supper, Jesus washed all of our feet and said that we should serve each other."

"I must admit, it was the strangest Passover meal I had ever been a part of! When Judas Iscariot, who was the self-appointed treasurer left after Jesus had shared the bread with us, we thought he was maybe going to purchase something we had forgotten. Jesus told him to do what he was about to do quickly? So strange. We ended up singing a hymn and then went to Gethsemane."

"Judas met us there later on, but brought with him a band of armed guards. He kissed Jesus. And they led Him away. And we all fled!"

"We have been told all of the events that followed by Peter, who followed at a distance, stayed for a while, and then left, and by John, who remained until the end. And by some of the women who were there through the whole ordeal. Of His trial. Of the mock justice of it all. Before the Sanhedrin. Pilate. Herod. Back to Pilate. The trek to Golgotha. And His crucifixion among thieves."

"I wish now that I had been there! That I had not been so afraid!"

Simon hung his head.

"I was...there," Joshua said quietly.

Simon's head jolted upright; his eyes wide.

"You were there?" he asked, staring at Joshua.

"Of course you were, Barabbas! You were the one who was released to the crowd when Jesus was led away to be crucified! Of course you were there."

Suddenly another thought presented itself.

"The Lamb of Elohim," Simon said aloud, although mostly to himself. "Who comes to take away sins..."

"He was our atoning sacrifice...our Passover lamb and our scapegoat...without spot or blemish."

"Joshua, my brother, do you realize that *you* were in a very real way, the very first person for whom Messiah Jesus died? The very first person for whom He gave Himself as a substitutionary atonement!"

Joshua exhaled slowly and then took a deep breath as the full weight of this realization descended upon him.

Again. But in even more fullness.

Tears made their way to his face.

Gratitude welled up inside.

Jesus had stepped in and taken his place.

In every way.

His punishment.

Both physically and spiritually.

He wondered how many times he would be overwhelmed by this blessed thought between now and eternity.

"I most assuredly did not know when I watched Him die on that cross the full significance of what He was doing for me. For everyone!"

Simon just stared at him.

"You were there? At the cross too?"

Joshua nodded.

"Well, then," Simon said. "I have heard the story from others, but I would love to hear *your* take on things. How His death impacted *you*."

"I will," Joshua said, thinking to himself. "But even more than the cross, even more than seeing Jesus there, when He appeared to me after His resurrection, that was far more powerful, and for me, life-altering!"

Simon sucked in his breath.

"He appeared to you, afterwards?"

"I mean, He appeared to us. And I know that others said that they had seen Him."

"But He appeared to *you,* in the flesh?"

Simon laughed.

"How wonderful! And how very much like Him!"

"I can't wait to hear all about it!" Simon said, eagerly looking at Joshua and trying to imagine what he would say.

"Okay, I will tell you. But, can we stop for a minute or two and eat some food before I begin?" Joshua asked. "I think maybe we have a few loaves and a couple of fish here…"

"Do you think that will be enough?"

Simon burst out laughing.

Chapter 64

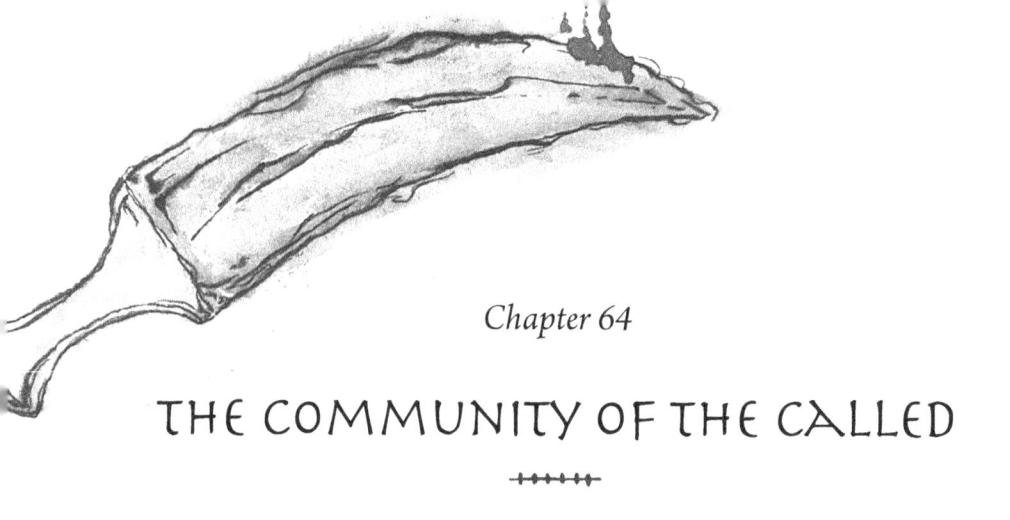

THE COMMUNITY OF THE CALLED

Joshua, Ariah, and Khiya remained in Jerusalem for several more weeks.

They met with Simon again so that Joshua could share additional details of that final day, and Simon also shared many more of his own memories of Jesus.

Ariah and Khiya both shared their stories with him as well.

And they met with the other disciples each day whether in the Temple or in homes, breaking bread together and being enriched through other testimonies of everything that Jesus had done, all of which the disciples here were privileged to witness.

It seemed that, even as Jesus had promised, now that His Holy Spirit had been poured out on all flesh, the even greater things He had talked about were most certainly beginning to happen.

It was a wonderful time, but they all felt that they could not remain here forever. Eventually they would have to return home.

To wherever that was.

After the wedding, they had spent the first few days in Tiberius with Joshua's family, the place that had been his home for the short time he had been back. After that, they had been travelling and staying in Bethany and then in Jerusalem.

Ariah and Khiya had lived in Nain for most of their lives and in Magdala for the last little while.

Where was *home?* As a new family, they had talked and even prayed about where that was. Where were they to take up residence as the little family unit that they now were together. They didn't really know, but they felt certain that Adonai would make a place for them wherever it was that He most wanted them to be.

Eventually, they felt led to settle in Tiberius.

Here and everywhere it seemed now, communities of faith, *ekklesia,* meaning, "the called-out ones," were springing up rather spontaneously, where followers of "the Way," as it came to be known, would gather.

On no particular day of the week.

On any given day.

To pray and be taught and to break bread together.

But always on the first day of the week.

On Sunday.

That was, after all, resurrection day.

Jesus had died and been buried on a Friday.

He rose on a Sunday.

And this was a community who saw themselves as children of the resurrection.

As Jews, they still observed the Sabbath.

But it seemed fitting that Sunday became in many ways right from the outset an even more important day.

There were already a number of gatherings of believers in various parts of Tiberius, but one had rather organically formed in their household almost right away, strongly encouraged by the testimonies and teaching of Batiyah, Joshua, Ariah, and even Khiya, who was now almost fourteen years of age. They were joined by the rest of their family and by others, some of whom had met Jesus but many who had not—people who were brought to faith simply through hearing what Jesus had done or through signs and wonders, miracles or healings, the things it was obvious He was still doing in their midst.

As had been the case with the original disciples, they felt sent out to preach the good news of Jesus, to heal the sick, to bring hearing to the deaf and sight to the blind, to see the lame walk, demons cast out, and the dead raised to life again.

And they did see all of these things happen at their hands throughout the next ten years or so, as they rose up in the power of the Holy Spirit to be Jesus's witnesses.

Elohim continued to prosper both them and their business and gave them a very fruitful ministry as well.

There was persecution for sure from both Jewish and Roman authorities. Believers were sometimes ostracized from their families and from society. And at times, even more than that, some were imprisoned, whipped, beaten, and even killed. Joshua thought that in this way, following Jesus was very much like being part of the Qanaim; the one very significant difference being that they were never the ones inflicting pain on others. They encouraged the persecuted, lifted up the broken, and walked together with those who were struggling.

They brought only health and healing and restoration and renewal just as Jesus had told Joshua they would when He appeared to him that night in Rakkath—even to their persecutors at times.

Early on, Joshua had been chosen as the lead elder of the *ekklesia* that was meeting in their home. He was still fully involved in the family business, in the making of bricks, but the others made sure to free up time that he could devote to his shepherding duties. He had been a powerful preacher of the ideals of the Fourth Way. He was now an even more passionate proponent and teacher of the Jesus Way. All of his upbringing, all of the Scripture that Abrahim had deposited in all of them, and all of that time spent at

Q's headquarters poring over what Elohim had said regarding His Anointed One came back to bless not only Joshua himself, but the entire community of believers.

Batiyah was quite a powerful proponent as well. On a Sunday not that long ago, she had shared again how she reached out and touched Jesus. In faith. How she had been instantly healed in that moment. And how it was still true that anyone with faith could reach out and *touch* Him and be healed.

They saw many receive their health that morning.

Batiyah had followed it up with a challenge.

Even as Jesus had challenged her.

"Who touched me?" she asked.

"'Who touched me?'" she said was a question that Jesus was still asking. "For I know that the power to heal has gone out today."

And then she had called all those who had been healed this day and on days before to "come out of hiding" and to proclaim in front of everyone, to their friends and neighbors, the wonderful things that Jesus had done for them and to call on those that they knew to follow Him too.

A most wonderful time of testimonies had followed.

Having met Jesus, his mother had become quite the evangelist, quite the preacher, Joshua had thought to himself on that occasion.

Apparently though, she didn't feel that was her only calling. Unbeknownst to Joshua and Ariah, she had spoken with Khiya several years ago and encouraged him to *seek out* the little girl in *her* story, Jairus's daughter.

She apparently felt that Khiya and the little girl having both been raised from the dead at the same age meant that they had some big thing in common, and she wondered what Elohim might be able to accomplish with the two of them *together*.

It's a very good thing she hadn't shared her thoughts with the two of them because Joshua and Ariah would have most certainly put a stop to it. Batiyah knew that. At some point, Khiya had innocently but boldly taken her up on the suggestion and had stopped in on the girl when he was out on a delivery together with Sarah's husband, Josiah, whose family was from Capernaum.

He had met with this young woman. They had shared their stories and, as Batiyah had predicted, they soon discovered that they did indeed have many things in common, but even beyond their resurrections at Jesus's hand—now shared an attraction to each other.

Eventually, the truth came out that Khiya had in fact made numerous clandestine trips in that direction and had feelings for the girl. And eventually, Joshua and Ariah had met her and then given their blessing to what had gone beyond friendship.

Tabitha, or *Koumi*, meaning "Arise," as she was now known, was a real sweetheart. And somewhere just over a year ago, Khiya had taken yet another trip, together with Joshua this time, to negotiate his request for Tabitha's hand in marriage.

And then finally, some two months ago now, Khiya had brought Koumi home to Tiberius as his bride.

It had been a lovely celebration.

Of life and love.

They were, as Batiyah had imagined or maybe prophesied, amazing together. They definitely shared a strong anointing. And as a couple, they had already brought one person back from the dead in Tiberius, a young mother named Melia who had succumbed to a very severe cough. The woman and her husband, Tobias, were neighbors of one of the families in the community of faith. They had asked Tobias if he was open to some people coming to pray. He thought that rather strange, but Khiya and Koumi and a few others had gone to the house where her body was being prepared for burial. They had prayed over her. And she was immediately restored whole and healthy to her overjoyed husband and her two young children. The entire family felt compelled to put their faith in Jesus and were baptized that same day.

Many times through their years of ministry here in Tiberius Ariah had shared her story. Shared the pain that she had gone through and then how Jesus had met her in her deepest, darkest hour and brought life where there was only death. She seemed to have a real gift for bringing emotional healing, particularly to women who found themselves in dire places: single women, and widows, and married women too.

"*Adonai is my shepherd. I lack nothing. He makes me lie down in green pastures, He leads me beside quiet waters. He refreshes my soul. He restores my life,*" David had written. "*He guides me along the right paths for His name's sake. Even though I walk through the darkest valley, through the vale of death, I will fear no evil, for You are with me.*"

Ariah had found that to be true. Joshua too.

They could all attest to the truth of David's words.

And they were witnesses to His love, His power, and His provision.

But still Joshua wondered if there was more.

He was feeling restless in a way.

"You will receive power when the Holy Spirit comes on you," Jesus had said to the apostles, "and you will be My witnesses in Jerusalem, and in all Judea and Samaria, and to the ends of the earth."

Joshua had seen it happen. He had been there when the Spirit was poured out. When cowards who were in hiding for fear of the authorities, had been turned into powerful witnesses.

The city of Jerusalem had been turned upside down. The community of the called out continued to grow. So did the persecution.

Maybe about six or seven years after Jesus's crucifixion, a deacon named Stephen, who had performed great wonders and miraculous signs among the people there, had been arrested in Jerusalem. He had spoken powerfully and passionately at his own defense, that Elohim did not dwell in a Temple made by the hands of men. The Sanhedrin were absolutely infuriated.

And on that day, Stephen had been stoned. He became a martyr, a *witness* in the full sense of the word.

A great persecution followed, breaking out against the ekklesia in Jerusalem and spreading from there. And while the apostles had remained for the most part in Jerusalem, disciples were scattered all over Judea and Samaria. They continued preaching the word wherever they went. After this, and maybe even because of this, to simply belong to the Way was enough to have one brought to Jerusalem and thrown into prison.

They had certainly felt the repercussions in Tiberius. Some in nearby communities had recently been arrested and had served time in jail just for being believers.

Joshua wondered when *he* might be brought up on charges and taken back to prison. It was certainly not a place to which he ever wanted to return. But, for Jesus's sake he thought, he would endure anything.

After all that He had done for him. He owed his very life to this Man.

And then recently, during the Feast of Unleavened Bread, Herod Agrippa had arrested a number of those who were followers of the Way and had the apostle James, the brother of John, put to death with the sword. When he saw how this met with the approval of the Jewish leaders, he had Peter thrown into prison as well.

The believers prayed.

And Peter was miraculously released.

Joshua wondered what was yet to come.

As Jesus had said, they had received power and boldness when the Holy Spirit had been poured out upon them. And they had been His *witnesses*.

Some of them, quite literally, His martyrs.

In Jerusalem, Judea, and Samaria.

But Joshua wondered, what about the ends of the earth? When would the Spirit send people there?

"Pray the Lord of the harvest, therefore," Jesus had said, "to send forth workers..."

It had already been ten years since Jesus had sacrificed his life.

Joshua knew now that it was for all mankind.

Jews and Gentiles too.

"Whom shall I send? And who will go for us?" Adonai seemed to be asking afresh.

A long time ago, and under totally different circumstances, Joshua had said, "Here am I. Send me."

Joshua shared what he was feeling with Ariah.

"The time here with the brothers and sisters and with our family has been so good," Joshua said, "but I can't help but feel as though Jesus is calling us out, away, to be his witnesses somewhere else. Exactly where, I don't exactly know right now, but some place beyond here."

Smiling, Ariah had simply echoed the words of Ruth, the Moabitess:

"Where you go, I will go...my love!"

Chapter 65

SENT OUT

A WEEK LATER, THERE WAS A KNOCK ON THEIR DOOR.

Joshua answered it.

And just stood there, speechless, for a few seconds, his shock evident.

Simon broke the silence.

"Well, Shalom, Joshua," he said. "And how are you and yours?"

Joshua shook his head, trying to collect himself.

"Simon! My brother! I'm not sure who I expected to be at my door, but it sure wasn't you!" he said excitedly. "Welcome here, my friend!"

The two men embraced, loudly slapping each other on the back.

"And what brings you to our little town, brother?"

"Well, to see you of course…and to meet with the brothers and sisters that gather in your house!" Simon answered.

"Where are my manners? C'mon in! Oh, this is a most pleasant surprise!" Joshua replied.

Joshua and Simon made their way through the house and out into the yard. The rest of the family was busy with various chores and of course, making bricks.

"Ariah," he called out, "we have a most wonderful visitor!"

She was up on the roof, stowing their bedding, tidying up and getting ready for a prayer meeting that was planned for later on that day.

She peered over the edge of the roof.

"Simon!" she squealed, and just as quickly disappeared.

They heard her rapidly making her way down the stairs.

"Simon!" she said again, giving him the biggest hug she could.

"How wonderful to have you visit us. What is the occasion?"

"Well, as I was telling your husband, to see you of course… and to spend some time with the community that meets here. To meet with your elders. I have something that I wish to request from them."

"A request?" Joshua queried.

"Yes, which I will share with you this evening." Simon said.

"Whatever it is, the answer is yes!" Ariah said.

"Are you sure?" Simon replied. "You haven't even heard what it is that Adonai might be asking of you!"

"We have learned, or have been learning anyway," Joshua said, "that it is best to choose obedience to Him first, even before we know what it is that He is asking of us. We want always, and in all things, to live in complete surrender to His will!"

"I like that!" said Simon. "I like that very much! So good! Obedience no matter what!"

"Can we sit for a while alone, and break bread?" Ariah asked.

"That would be lovely," Simon replied.

"Maybe you can give us a hint!" Joshua said with a wink.

"Maybe…" said Simon.

Ariah went to get things ready and Joshua took Simon around the yard, showing him their family's brick making business and introducing him to everyone.

After a few minutes, Ariah invited them up onto the roof where she had laid out a simple meal of bread and meat, some cheese, figs, and other fruits.

Simon prayed:

"Father, I thank you for this family. And for Your presence here with us. I pray that You would grant me success in my mission and bless us all as we spend time together now, and in the days to come. In Jesus's mighty name, Amen!"

They talked about rather mundane things for a bit.

Business. The weather. How Simon's trip had been. Some about family. Khiya's recent wedding and his new bride.

Simon asked about the fellowship and Ariah and Joshua shared many stories about what Elohim was doing even just in recent weeks. They shared the story of Melia being raised from the dead. And how another little boy named Samuel had heard his parents speak for the very first time. Another story about a Roman God-fearing family, neighbors of Sarah and Josiah who had come to meetings in their home and had just been baptized.

Simon just sat and smiled, soaking in all of their excitement.

"So, what have you been up to, brother? And how are the disciples in Jerusalem faring?" Joshua asked.

"Good, I think," Simon said. "I don't really know. I haven't been back there in quite some time."

"You haven't?" said Joshua. "Where on earth have you been?"

"In Egypt actually," Simon began. "For the last maybe eight months or so. Preaching. Teaching in the synagogue. Well, for as long as they let us. We appointed elders there before we left to carry on the work. There is a thriving community of disciples there now, in Alexandria, and it is already spreading to other cities as well."

"So, why are you in Tiberius? It's not even remotely on the way from Egypt to Jerusalem," Joshua said, laughing. And then a thought suddenly presented itself. "Wait...you have come here to convince us to join you in the work in Alexandria!"

Simon blushed.

Joshua looked at Ariah and back to Simon.

"I didn't think I was going to share this with you yet, but...not exactly," Simon said. "You see, I'm not going back to Alexandria. Nor are you. The community there will do fine without us. I feel Adonai's Holy Spirit leading me...to Persia. My brother Jude and his wife Mari are already on their way there. And I wonder whether He may not be setting the two of you apart for ministry there as well?"

Joshua looked at Ariah and then back to Simon.

He returned his gaze to Ariah.

She was nodding her head "Yes."

"Joshua, what did you just say to me maybe a week ago, that you somehow felt that Jesus was calling us out, away from here, good as this has been for all of us? You didn't know exactly where but you said that it was somewhere beyond here."

"And what did I tell you?"

"Where you go, I will go...!"

"Maybe this is...our *exactly where!* Adonai has revealed it!"

"So, what do you think?" Simon asked.

"Well, I do want to pray about it some," Joshua said. "And I would love to get the blessing of our family and of the elders here... But, yes, my answer too is a resounding yes, even if I have no idea what it is that we are walking into. I know that He will go with us!"

Many communities met in people's yards, but because their yard was almost entirely given over to brick making, the only other place that was available was the roof. So Josiah had built a framework, which they had overlaid with tarps to protect themselves from the sun and the rest of the elements. It seemed to work quite well.

They had jokingly said that they were, "closer to heaven" up there.

That was where they had eaten their meal together and Simon had shared what it was that he thought Elohim might be calling them to.

As the sun went down, brothers and sisters began arriving and taking up their places.

Within a half hour or so, quite a crowd had assembled. They had all brought food with them and soon everyone was busy eating and sharing life together.

As they were finishing, Joshua stood and invited everyone to take up a piece of broken bread. He asked Simon to lead them.

"On the night that Jesus was betrayed," Simon said, "Jesus took the bread and when He had given thanks, He broke it and gave it to us and said, 'This is My body which is broken for you.'"

"Jesus, our Adonai, I thank You for giving Yourself to us; Your body broken that we might partake of Your very life," he prayed.

Everyone ate.

"Then Jesus took a cup, and when He had given thanks, He gave it to us saying, 'This is My blood, the blood of a new and living covenant, which is poured out for many.'"

"Jesus, our Adonai, I thank You for the shedding of Your blood on our behalf. For being our sacrificial lamb and our atoning sacrifice. We live because the blood of our Passover lamb covers us."

They passed the cup around and everyone drank.

Celebrating.

Remembering.

And then they sang the ninety-sixth *Tehillim* together:

> *Sing to YHWH a new song;*
> *sing to YHWH, all the earth.*
> *Sing to YHWH, praise His name;*
> *proclaim His salvation day after day.*
> *Declare His glory among the nations,*

*His marvelous deeds
among all peoples.
For great is YHWH
and most worthy of praise.*

They had a brief time of silence.

Several people shared testimonies of some of those marvelous things that He had done among them even just in recent days.

Simon then taught the things that Jesus had shared with them when they asked Him to teach them how to pray. To speak to Elohim as Father but to fear Him and honor Him at the same time. For He is holy and loving, equally just and merciful. To ask for the things that we need, even though He knows all of our needs and bountifully provides at all times. To seek His forgiveness for the places where we fall short and the grace to forgive others for the times when they have done us wrong. That He would walk with us through every test or temptation and bring us out the other side victorious. That His will would be done on earth even as it is done in heaven. And that the kingdom and the power and glory is His both now and forevermore.

He shared the story that Jesus had told them of someone who went to a friend, maybe his neighbor, at midnight saying, "Friend, please lend me three loaves of bread; a friend of mine has just arrived on his journey and has come to me, and I have no food to offer him." His neighbor answered him, "Don't bother me. I have locked the door and my children are all asleep in bed. I can't get up to give you anything!"

"Well," Simon said, "that friend, your neighbor, may not want to get up and help you even if he is your friend because of the late hour, but if you keep knocking, I can guarantee he will arise and help you, in fact, he will give you more than just three loaves if you need!"

"Our Father is not like that friend, but prayer is as in the story. We need to be persistent. And it is never too late to ask!"

"And so, as Jesus told us, 'Ask and it will be given to you, seek and you will find, knock and the door will be opened to you. For everyone who asks receives; the one who seeks finds; and to the one who knocks, the door will be opened.'"

"Fathers," Simon continued, "If your son asks for a fish, what will you give him? You will most assuredly give him a fish! And if he asks you for an egg, would you give him a scorpion? Never! If you then, human fathers, far from perfect, know how to give good things to your children, how much more will your Father in heaven give good gifts, indeed, give of His own Holy Spirit to those who ask? Our Father wants to share with every man His bounty!"

"Elohim loved the world so much that He gave His one and only Son, and whoever puts their faith and trust in Him shall never die but enter into eternal life!"

"Jesus did not come to condemn us but to help and heal and save and deliver us!"

When Simon finished, you could have heard a needle drop.

"Does anyone here have a need, does anyone here want something more of what Jesus has to give?" Simon asked.

Pretty near every hand was raised.

They even heard someone call out from the street to say that he wanted to receive. It was a man named Timaeus. He had been standing nearby and listening to every word. He was a cripple so several of the men had to carry him up the stairs. They brought him in and began to pray for him and at the end of the night, he walked down the stairs, out the gate, and down the street to his home on his very own, whole and healthy, carrying his crutches under his arm.

People began praying for each other. Some were just silently praying by themselves. Others were confessing things to one another and receiving forgiveness.

One woman was healed from pain in her back that she had been experiencing over the past several weeks.

Beautiful and messy in a way, but orchestrated by the Holy Spirit.

Joshua watched on in amazement and wonder.

Adonai was indeed a loving Abba.

After a while, Joshua shared with the gathering that which Ariah and he had spent the rest of the day praying through, which they had already shared with each of the other leaders.

Adonai appeared to be calling them out of Tiberius.

And on toward the land of Persia.

Together with Simon and Jude.

The whole ekklesia gathered around them. The elders laid their hands on them and Zephaniah prayed:

"Father, we set apart Joshua and Ariah for the ministry to which You have called them. We have valued and appreciated the time, energy, and finances that they have invested in the faithful here in Tiberius. We will miss them dearly, but we know and trust that You will provide everything that they need and everything that we need too! May Your word go forth into all the nations of the world! For Your honor and glory! Eternal praise to You! Amen!"

Days later, Zephaniah was appointed the new lead shepherd of the community at Joshua's recommendation.

A week later, their whole community of faith, their entire family, and even some from other nearby fellowships in the city gathered to send them off.

Batiyah stood and prayed on behalf of everyone.

"Father, I thank You for my, for our, precious son, Joshua, and for his lovely wife, Ariah. Last time I sent him away, I know that I did so in fear. On this occasion, I send him, or rather, them, out in Your authority, knowing that You will go with them, provide for them and be their covering wherever they go and whatever they do. Empower them, Holy Spirit, for the ministry to which you have called them! Lead them and guide them always! In the mighty name of our Adonai and savior, Jesus Messiah!"

It was a long and tearful goodbye, knowing that they may never see one another again, this side of eternity. And more than a few tears were shed even in the moments, days, weeks, and months of their journey.

Three days after Pentecost, Joshua and Ariah began their two-hundred-mile journey north-eastward in the direction of Damascus and on to the port city of Nicephorium on the Euphrates River. The sky was overcast for most of the journey, which meant that it was not too hot while they were travelling. But the rain held off at least until they reached the river, and that was graciously received. The sky reflected their mood. It was sad to leave both family and the ekklesia in Tiberius. But Adonai had called them out and away, and they knew that they could not but obey.

It poured rain almost the moment they reached Nicephorium, long and hard. Fortunately, the two of them had been able to find shelter just shortly before the heavens opened. And when the rain did finally stop, the sun came out so bright and clear that it formed a beautiful double rainbow directly over the Euphrates. Joshua and Ariah took it as a promise and they thanked Elohim for gracing their travel so well.

Almost as soon as she had found out, Koumi had shared her new parents-in-law's plans to go to Persia with her father, Jairus. He had immediately felt led to underwrite their entire journey and even to provide them with enough money to find lodging and settle in once they had arrived at their new place of calling. Joshua and Ariah had been overwhelmed with his generous gift and had thanked both Adonai and Jairus profusely. How wonderful to feel so loved.

They had indeed been amply looked after.

The next day, Joshua booked them passage on a river vessel named the *Persephone,* which was loaded with grain, dried fruit, and vegetables mostly, and was bound for the Persian Gulf. He did think it a bit funny that they were travelling on a ship named after the goddess of the underworld, but Joshua knew that Jesus had overcome all principalities and powers and they needn't worry about any of that. Joshua knew they could have journeyed overland to Persia too, but it actually would have taken much longer and would have been much more tiring and trying, especially for Ariah.

After several days, all was ready and they boarded the ship and set sail down the river in the direction of the Persian Gulf. Not that they were going all the way there however, they were scheduled to turn and head back up the Tigris River when they met it, in the direction of the ancient capital city of Shushan or Susa, a total passage of almost six hundred miles.

Joshua and Ariah used the time together to talk and pray and ready themselves for whatever it was that Elohim had in store for them. It was wonderful to watch the sights go by and to simply *be* with no pressure to do anything. They had been pretty busy the last ten years or so. It was very special to now have the time just to reconnect as a couple and thank Adonai for all that He had led them through.

"I'm just so thankful for you!" Ariah said at one point in the trip.

"And I for you!" Joshua replied.

"I thought of you often in the days I wandered the countryside as a member of the Qanaim, but I never, other than in my wildest imaginations, thought that we could be together. I thought it would be too difficult, and I knew that I wanted to spare you from all of the danger, even as my father Abrahim had tried to protect Batiyah from it."

"I know," Ariah replied. "And I appreciate that you did that. But Joshua, please know that if you had asked me to join you back then, even to walk through all of that with you, I most surely would have!"

"And, well in no way to minimize how wonderful and loving my husband Simon was, when you returned and I was free to say yes to you, absolutely nothing was about to stand in my way! I could not and would not let you get away again!"

Tears sparkled in Ariah's dark eyes.

Joshua wondered how his own heart didn't explode.

He had almost no words.

"Thank You, Adonai," was all he could muster.

It was clear that He had made all of this a reality.

"Amen!" echoed Ariah quietly.

The two embraced each other, enjoying the view of the ancient city of Babylon as they passed to the south of it.

Several days after they reached the city of Shushan, they found a caravan headed north to Ecbatana, another of the capital cities of Persia, and then on to Rhages, the place that was to be their final destination.

It was a long journey. In all, almost two full months passed between leaving Tiberius and their arrival in the ancient city of Rhages. But they made it safe and sound, and soon found a wonderful little house, which they bought with money that Jairus, the members of the entire ekklesia and their immediate family had given them.

Chapter 66

TO RHAGES AND BEYOND

THEY BEGAN TO SETTLE IN.

To learn the language.

To befriend their neighbors.

Joshua hired himself out to a local brick maker.

And they also made connections almost immediately in the local Jewish community, attending a small synagogue in the city every week when *Shabbat* rolled around.

The ekklesia that began meeting almost right away in their new home in Rhages grew rapidly under the leadership of the five of them: Simon, Jude and his wife Mari, and Joshua and Ariah. They witnessed all of the things that had happened in Tiberius and other places happening here as well. Miracles, healings, even the dead being raised.

And it certainly seemed as though Adonai had set before them an open and fruitful door of ministry. It was as if Persia, the Parthian kingdom, had been divinely prepared for their arrival.

They began reaching out into neighboring communities and cities and saw other communities of faith being planted almost every other month or so it seemed. They went on missions north into Armenia. And everywhere they went, ekklesiae were established after almost no time at all it seemed.

It was a glorious season.

"I had a dream the other night," Simon shared with the group one morning when they were together for prayer after several years of ministry here.

"I saw a man from the Suani people, calling us to come. Or me at least. I invite you to pray about it with me, but I feel Holy Spirit leading me to go. I do not know what I will find when I get there for some feel the Suani to be an uncontrollable and invincible mountain people, but I just can't shake this feeling, this calling. Adonai willing, I have made plans to go a month from now."

The group did pray. Not just Simon, Jude, Mari, Joshua, and Ariah, but the whole of the ekklesia. And in the end, they all discerned that it seemed good to the Holy Spirit and to the community of faith to send Simon, Jude, and Joshua northeast to the city of Suanir.

Joshua was so excited. Each of the missions that they had been involved in had been good. But somehow, this felt even more like the fulfillment of Jesus's call to go to the uttermost parts of the earth. And *he* was privileged, called to be part of it.

He knew that he would miss Ariah, but she and Mari had become like sisters, so he was not too worried about her and supposed that the time would go by quickly.

They would be back before too long he imagined, Elohim willing.

Preparations were made for the journey up river to the Caspian Sea and then north-eastward across the water in the direction of the mountainous Suani region and particularly, the capital city of Suanir.

Five weeks to the day, the three of them knelt on the beach and thanked Adonai for bringing them there. They committed themselves to His service and prayed that He would grant them success in that to which He had called them. They made their way up into the mountains arriving at the gate of Suanir just as it was getting dark.

They approached the men seated there.

One of them rose and quickly made his way in their direction. He spoke to them in Farsi.

"Greetings! I am Abda. Are you the ones sent to tell us about the Man, the *God-man*, who came to earth to reveal to us the mysteries of the world and of the Divine One?"

Simon, Jude, and Joshua just stared at each other.

"He is the man that I saw in my vision!" Simon whispered.

Jude and Joshua looked at Simon in astonishment.

"You're kidding," Jude said, under his breath.

Simon just shook his head. He was anything but kidding. He was having trouble believing what he had just seen and heard.

Abda continued.

"Forgive me, but there is a legend among our people that one night, three men will appear at the city gate to tell us these precious things. I had a dream a short while ago that it would soon happen."

"You," he said, pointing at Simon, "I saw you in my dream and you said that, you were on your way!"

"I have been waiting for a month now for you to appear. Please tell me that I am not mistaken! Tell me that you are those men!"

"You are not wrong!" Joshua said boldly, taking the lead. "We know the One, the God-man of whom you speak. We are His disciples. Followers of the Way. His name is Jesus, *Isa*, of Nazareth. And we have most definitely been sent here to proclaim Him to you!"

"Elohim has made everything beautiful in its time," Solomon had written in the *Ketuvim*, in the book of *Qohelet*. "He has also set eternity in the human heart."

Indeed, Joshua thought, Adonai had put this legend in place in the heart of this people for just such a time as this. What a most amazing God He was. And how privileged did he feel to be part of this.

Plans were quickly made for a gathering to be held the next evening in the city square. Abda took them to his home to spend the night with him. The three of them were treated like royalty.

The next night when the three of them followed their host into the square, they all stared around in amazement. There must have been several thousand people gathered, just waiting to hear the message that Elohim had given to them to share.

There they stood, in the shadow of the temple to the Sun and the Moon, ready to convey the heart of Abba Adonai to all of these people so long immersed in animistic religion. It was almost overwhelming.

Abda began by rehearsing the legend that had circulated among their people for many generations. He told of his recent dream, and how the three men had appeared yesterday evening, just as he had seen in his vision. That the time of revelation was now. He told the crowd to give their complete attention, not that he had to say that, it had already been granted almost entirely. Everyone wanted to hear what Simon, Jude, and Joshua had to say, what Elohim wanted to share with His people.

He said that while the people were most comfortable conversing in their own Suani language, almost everyone understood Farsi, and that many, like their Persian neighbors, also understood some Aramaic.

Simon began by sharing, much as he had with Joshua, Ariah, and Khiya that day by the Jerusalem gate, the history, his own history, of spending three years travelling with and learning from Jesus, *Isa* in Persian or Farsi, up to the time that he was crucified by the Romans and then raised again to life by Adonai Himself. How this *God-man* came to earth to reveal the heart of Father Elohim.

Eventually, Jude stood up and whispered something in Simon's ear. What followed next was nothing short of amazing. Jude spoke for the next hour or so at least, in what Joshua could only assume was perfect Suani. He could see the expressions of delight on people's faces. The Spirit of Elohim was speaking and making Himself very clear to everyone there just as He had at Pentecost.

"What must we do?" one of the other elders standing next to Abda asked as Jude finished.

"Repent and be baptized in the name of Isa, the God-man, for the forgiveness of your sins, and you will receive His Holy Spirit!" Jude said.

Almost immediately, the man grabbed Jude's hand and began leading him in the direction of a river that ran down the mountain and into the Caspian Sea. There was a place not too far away where the river had formed a rather large lagoon.

Joshua, Simon, and Jude spent the rest of the night baptizing many of the Suani people who had come. Hearing them repent of their animistic ways, of worshipping something less than the Creator, and placing their faith in the one true God and His Messiah, Isa of Nazareth.

In all, some fifteen hundred of the Suani put their faith in Jesus on that very first evening. It was the most amazing thing that Joshua had ever seen, certainly the most wonderful outpouring that he had ever been a part of. Other than Pentecost.

And it was real. Very real.

Within a week, Abda and some of the other chiefs who had become believers began physically tearing down the temple to the Sun and Moon.

Many celebrated this with them.

But not all.

One particular individual was a priest in the temple, a man who called himself, Mainyu, "the Immortal One."

He was not happy at all. The fact that his one and only child, his daughter Vasni, had been present the first evening, had been delivered from the demons that tormented her, and had been baptized into the new faith, did not help.

He could not deny the fact that she was a new and very different person from the one that he had known before. But he and others with him were keenly aware that they were losing their power to this new way.

"I would like to hear more," he said to Simon one evening. "Would you be willing to share with me and a few others?"

Simon had asked Jude to come along with him.

And they had gone to Mainyu's house at the appointed time.

But it was an ambush.

Mainyu and the others had bound both Simon and Jude and taken them far out into the woods, to a local place of moon worship.

They had simply killed Jude once they arrived.

But Simon was sawn in two, and then Mainyu and the others had paraded themselves through the two halves of his body, over and over again in some kind of perverse demonic covenant ritual, a sacrifice to the spirits that held them in bondage.

They had celebrated their *victory* long into the night. Abda found out about this early the next morning.

"Joshua, it is no longer safe for you here," he said, waking him out of a deep sleep. "You must leave immediately. Run for your life!"

He shared with him the details that he knew. About Jude. And Simon. What he had been told by one of the other chiefs. What one of the priests who had been there had related to him. Someone who was now questioning what they had done.

"Don't worry about us," Abda said. "Elohim—our word for Him is *Khoda*—will look after what He has planted. We are not afraid!"

With a little food that Abda's wife had packed for him, Joshua fled. Heading south along the water's edge in the direction of

Rhages. Like in times long past, on the run as a member of Q, he made his way carefully out of Suanir and in the direction of home.

This felt very much like another time when he had fled Joppa after Daniel's death. And yet this was so very different. Somehow this time, even in the midst of something that was horrible and tragic and awful...he had hope.

Jude's murder.

Simon's torture and death.

He knew they were accomplishing something.

That their deaths meant something.

No, Joshua did not understand at all. Not in this moment anyway.

But he was convinced that Adonai had all things in His control. Their lives had been in His hands to do with as He saw fit. It had been no different for the One that they now followed.

"Into thy hands, I commit my spirit," Jesus had said.

Jude and Simon had done the same thing with their lives. Joshua knew that he had done it with his own.

Why he had been spared, he knew not.

Other than that Adonai still had a purpose for him.

It would be hard to tell Mari the news about her husband. He knew that. Hard for the whole community.

But the Holy Spirit was a Comforter.

And there was also a certain glory, a glory in being declared worthy to be a witness in the true sense of the word, a *martyr*.

Elohim had most certainly done, and would bring to completion the work that He had begun among the Suani.

In His own wonderful way, He would do it.

Several weeks later, Joshua walked his exhausted body through the city gate of Rhages.

It was not at all easy, even as he suspected, to share the sad reality with Mari. But Ariah had stood beside him. And the three of them together had shared the news, the good and the bad, with the entire ekklesia the next day. It was sad but a celebration nonetheless.

Adonai was in control, even as promised.

They heard later that, as he was wooing a king cobra in a ritual cursing of Joshua, Mainyu had been bitten by the snake he was attempting to charm. He had died almost immediately of his injuries.

Vasni had become a deaconess in the ekklesia in Suani. Elohim had raised up many others to surround Abda. And the community continued to grow day by day.

The life is in the blood, Joshua knew.

And it certainly seemed as if not only the blood of Jesus but also the blood of the martyrs was breathing life into the community of the called-out ones.

Chapter 67

BEFORE KINGS

AMAZING REPORTS CONTINUED TO COME IN FROM Suanir and its outlying regions. And the ekklesia in Rhages and in other places throughout the Persian Empire flourished.

On the international front, a man named Nero Claudius Caesar Augustus Germanicus, had recently come to power as the new Roman emperor. And he clearly had a vendetta against the followers of the Way. "Christians," as they were now coming to be called, were being imprisoned and even fed to lions in some places. Many were tortured in various other ways by this Empire that just seemed to go from evil to evil. Crucifixions continued in large numbers. Persecution was definitely being escalated.

Persia was a little further afield, but Roman influence was still felt here. And one day, a detachment of soldiers showed up at Joshua and Ariah's door.

Joshua was being arrested. For crimes against Rome: "for disparaging the divinity of the Emperor and for preaching another kingdom."

He was placed under house arrest. Which meant that he could no longer come and go as he pleased.

At the same time others, and Ariah in particular, were still free to visit him almost any time they liked. He was being held until such a time as Rome could decide what to do with him.

This was inconvenient for sure, but nothing like when he had been imprisoned in the Antonia Fortress in Jerusalem. His surroundings here were almost pleasant.

He was free to read and to write and even to share with his captors the good news of the kingdom for which he was in chains.

Several of his guards became believers.

The last time, he was impatient, wondering why it was taking so long and wondering whether he had been forgotten, wondering when he would be brought out and crucified, but here in this situation, he didn't curse his confinement as he had previously.

He knew that Adonai had a plan.

He had seen Him work things out for His glory time and time again.

"The King of Persia has summoned you," his captor announced one morning. "You are to be taken to the royal palace three days from now."

Joshua couldn't believe his ears.

He had been summoned before the king.

He and others began to pray in earnest for this upcoming meeting.

He remembered Simon saying that Jesus had told the disciples to rejoice when they were persecuted and imprisoned. That they were blessed when so treated. In the company of the prophets of old. That on Jesus's account, they would be brought before governors and kings as witnesses to them and to the nations.

But not to worry, that at that time, they would be given what words they needed to say, "for it will not be you speaking, but the Spirit of your Father speaking through you," Jesus had said.

"Holy Spirit, give me Your words!" Joshua prayed.

He was anxious but not at all afraid.

The day arrived for his audience with the king.

This could easily be his final day.

On earth at least. But...

He was led handcuffed, into the palace.

This was vaguely familiar.

But hundreds of guards, courtiers, and others were here this time.

A man who introduced himself as Ehsan called everyone to order.

Joshua was led to the center of the large room.

"Isa, Jesus Barabbas," Ehsan began, "you have been accused of crimes of treason against the Empire of Rome, and have been called this day to stand before King Vologases Walagash, sovereign of the kingdom of Parthia, to give answer to the questions of who you are, on what authority you are here in Persia, and what message it is that you actually proclaim."

Trumpets played all of a sudden.

Ehsan spoke again.

"His royal highness, King Vologases!"

The Iranian prince, clad in regal robes, entered the room and moved in the direction of the throne.

Everyone bowed deep, touching their faces to the ground.

Everyone that is, except Joshua.

Vologases stared at him.

When Ehsan looked up and saw what had transpired, he reacted almost immediately.

"How dare you refuse to bow to our king, you insolent dog!" he screamed at Joshua.

Every eye in the palace was now on the prisoner.

"Do you not know that our sovereign has the power to take your life?" Ehsan stated, his voice quivering.

Joshua paused.

"He has no power over me other than what is given from above," Joshua said, speaking the same words he had heard Jesus say to Pilate.

He continued calmly.

"I bow to no one, except One alone. To the One you call *Ahura Mazda*, the Wise Lord. The One True Khoda. And to His Son, Isa of Nazareth, the One who came to earth to reveal Him to us, a man attested to us by Khoda with signs and wonders, crucified and raised to life again. Now seated at Ahura's right hand in majesty and power. And to His Holy Spirit, through whom His presence continues to be made manifest in the earth."

The palace was silent.

All eyes went to Vologases.

He was shaking his head. At the same time, Joshua thought he almost saw a slight grin. The king stood and walked over so as to be right next to him.

"You intrigue me, bold one!" he whispered. "You are like few men I have met!"

And then...so that everyone could hear:

"Isa, could you tell us your story, and what it is that you believe?" he said aloud.

He returned to sit upon his throne.

"I am what and who I am because of another man named Isa," Joshua began.

"As to my story, I was born in the small town of Rakkath, in lower Galilee, the second son of devout Jewish parents. My father, Abrahim was a brick maker by trade but also a keen student of the Holy Writings of the Jewish people. He taught all of us, taught me, the ways of Adonai and His call upon His holy people."

"My father was a zealous man and that meant that he attracted the unwelcome attention of this Empire that can countenance no rivals. He was murdered in cold blood for his refusal to submit his thinking to them, even if in almost all other ways he was a conscientious and law-abiding member of society."

"I was barely fifteen years old at the time and my world was turned upside down, never to be the same again. It was a very difficult time."

"A year or so later, I found myself in the wrong place at the right time or the right place at the wrong time…I don't know exactly. But the end result was that I killed a Roman soldier intent on taking advantage of a young and innocent Jewish girl. And so, I became a wanted man, having to flee my home, running for my life."

"My zeal, or maybe more so actually, my anger and hatred, led me to align myself with the band of rebels known as the Qanaim, the Zealous, those jealous for the re-establishment of the Davidic kingdom and the restoration of the Land of Promise to Khoda's holy people."

"And this became my life; the life of Isa, son of Abraham, now known as *Barabbas,* for the next fifteen years. Preaching zeal. Killing all who stood in the way of our ideals. Romans, Herodian Jews, and even Jews who sympathized with the Empire for their own power and prestige."

"And then I met the Man, Isa of Nazareth, on the very day that I was granted my freedom by Pontius Pilate. And I watched this Man die a painful death on a Roman cross when He had done absolutely nothing deserving of such an end."

"I had wondered briefly whether or not He was the One that Adonai had promised, the Messiah sent to deliver the Jewish people."

"But alas, He was dead! He could do no saving or delivering now. I had watched Him die."

"Even so…He came and found me!" Joshua said, his voice rising to a crescendo.

"Risen from the dead, He walked through the walls of the house in which I had confined myself, and called me to Himself. Called me to follow Him."

"Do not fear, Jehoshua ben Abrahim!" He said to me. "I am Isa of Nazareth. I am Elohim's Anointed One. His Son. I came to earth to show people the Father's heart and the way back to Him. I was crucified for the sins of the world and for yours. And I have been vindicated by My Father and have been raised to life even as the prophets of old foretold. I am the Messiah who was to come. And I am calling you to come follow Me. You have a destiny, a calling. You have known it, sensed it, for most of your life. But it is not to kill or to bring about the kingdom of heaven through violence, at least not the kind that you are used to. It is to bring life and healing and restoration to all people. It is time to lay down the ideas of man and embrace the ways of My Father, Yahweh. Our enemies are not flesh and blood, but rather principalities and powers. Do not be afraid! I have overcome them and you will too. I am calling you to be My witness in the power of My Holy Spirit. Most of all, I want you to learn to love once more. I have loved you since the day you were born and even before that and I was right there beside you sitting in the clay on the day that your abba was murdered and your world changed forever. My Father, your Heavenly Father, cried with you then and has every day since. And He is now calling you to Himself. He wants you to be His beloved son."

The palace was completely silent.

"My life has not been the same since. Everything was radically changed that day. *I* was radically changed."

"Every decision that I had made up to that point had been motivated by anger and hatred. And, at the root of it, fear—my own fear that I did not measure up, that I was not significant, not man enough."

"But now, I had met a Man who was completely unlike anyone I had ever met. He was not afraid. He was not angry. He did not hate. He preached love. Even for enemies. And He said that when we love others like that, we show ourselves to be children of our heavenly Father."

"I lost my earthly abba that day when I was fifteen. Jesus introduced me to my heavenly Abba the day that He came to me."

"And then, in Jerusalem that first Pentecost after the crucifixion of Isa of Nazareth, I was baptized with water, but more than that, baptized with His Holy Spirit and fire. I came to live and walk day-by-day in the very real presence and power of Khoda Almighty."

"We see healings, people delivered from demons, the lame walk, the blind see, lepers are cleansed, even the dead are raised back to life again! Adonai had said that He would pour out His Spirit on all flesh, and that we would do even more than Isa had done! We have seen exactly that!"

"Jesus said that when the Spirit was poured out, we would be His witnesses in Jerusalem, and Judea and Samaria, and to the uttermost parts of the earth. It is He who has brought me here to Persia. And I believe that the Parthian kingdom has been uniquely prepared by Ahura Mazda for these good things that I now proclaim."

"A millennium or so ago, your very own prophet, Zarathustra, a man whose origins and life is shrouded in as much mystery as Melchizedek, preached that there is but one Khoda, the Creator of all things. He said that in the battle between good and evil, good will ultimately prevail. He taught that Messiah was coming, that there was a heaven and a hell, and that as responsible human beings, we can choose to honor Him or not, and are held accountable for our choices."

"One of our own nation's greatest and wisest kings, who lived around the same time as Zarathustra, a man named Solomon, said that *'Elohim has set eternity in the human heart'*."

"Who but Ahura Mazda, Lord Creator Supremely Wise, who else would reveal such wonderful things to all men on earth?"

"Was it not He who brought Daniel here to Babylon under Nebuchadnezzar to share with this most powerful king the things of our most Wise Lord? And Daniel and those with him did not bow down to anything other than the One either! Was it not He who delivered Daniel from the mouths of lions when the satraps during King Darius's time were so jealous of Daniel and his connection to Ahura? Was it not He who revealed the things of the end to Daniel during the reign of Cyrus, King of Persia? In one place, Adonai even calls this Persian king 'His servant'!"

"Indeed, Khoda has spoken *in this place* many times."

"He raised up a young girl named Esther, a Jewess who became a Persian queen, during the time of Xerxes to foil the plot of Haman to do harm to the Jews, and led Xerxes to show favor to Esther and her people."

"Was it not He who placed Nehemiah in the capital of Shushan, made him servant to King Artaxerxes, so as to give the king an opportunity to bless him and the prophet Ezra to return to Jerusalem and rebuild the walls and the Temple? Was it not He who in all these things continued to speak and reveal Himself to this great Persian Empire?"

"And then, not that long ago, He, the Ahura Mazda, placed a star here in your eastern skies, to lead some of your very own magi to the place of Messiah's birth, Isa of Nazareth? He is not just our Savior. He is to be Savior of the world!"

"Ahura has given Himself many witnesses in Persia throughout your history, so when He called me here to proclaim the revelation of Himself through Messiah Isa, I did not think it a strange thing at all."

"This is who I am! This is what I proclaim!"

"Messiah Isa of Nazareth, a Man, a God-man, sent from our heavenly Father, to reveal Himself to us. Full of grace and truth. He is the exact representation of Ahura and the image of the invisible Khoda. He was crucified, dead, and buried, but raised to life, vindicated by Khoda Himself. And there is salvation in no one else."

All was quiet.

Vologases stood to his feet.

He was staring intently at Joshua.

Joshua wondered what would happen next.

The sovereign turned to leave.

But he hesitated. And then applauded quietly and slowly.

"I want to hear more," he said finally.

"Another day."

And with that he left the room.

Joshua was led back to his place of incarceration.

His heart full.

Even if he wondered what he had in fact said.

"Thank You, Holy Spirit," he whispered. "Those were most definitely Your words and not mine!"

Chapter 68

UNDER HOUSE ARREST

Joshua continued living under house arrest.

The king called him in several more times.

To hear him. Even to ask questions.

Would he become a believer?

Joshua prayed that he would.

At the same time, he still wondered whether it was possible that one day in the very near future he would be summoned, brought out, but this time, to be crucified.

"Crucify him! Crucify him!"

He had heard those words almost twenty-five years ago now. It was the punishment he had been slated for and should have received, were it not for another Man named Jesus who had somehow taken his place on that occasion, the One who had become his path to freedom.

He knew almost nothing of *the Man* on that first day. Other than rumors and the little that Simon had shared with him. Other than bits and pieces he had heard on the streets.

Now Joshua could honestly say he knew *Him* personally and intimately.

And although they had never really met, in the flesh at least, Joshua supposed that they had met in the way that mattered most.

He smiled to himself.

He had been given more than he had ever imagined he would enjoy. A wife. A family. Even grandchildren. A long and fruitful ministry.

He had received profound purpose and destiny. But most of all, he'd received a relationship with his heavenly Abba.

He was most certainly not looking forward to the suffering that he would have to endure, should that be the way that things were to eventually go. But he actually thought little about that.

Someone had paid *that* price for him.

Someone had been willing to take the cross for him.

Someone he had grown to love.

He felt it would be a small price to pay in return for all that he had been given. In fact, he maybe even looked forward to being able to give that back to the One who had given so much for him.

The first cross would have been deserved.

His only crime these days was being a follower of this other Jesus.

Ariah had visited him yesterday and shared with him part of a letter that the apostle Paul, formerly Saul, at one time a violent persecutor of the ekklesia, had written to the community of the called in Galatia. Someone had brought a copy of the letter to Rhages.

"I have been crucified with Christ," Paul wrote. "And I no longer live, but Christ lives in me. The life I now live in the body, I live by faith in the Son of Elohim, who loved me and gave himself for me."

"We have already been crucified," Ariah said. "All of us! With him!"

In another letter to the ekklesia at Philippi, the same Paul had written, "For me, to live is Christ and to die is gain. If I am to go on living in the body, this will mean fruitful labor for me. Yet what shall I choose? I am torn between the two."

Joshua was indeed torn.

"Whatever happens, Joshua, just know that I love you and have always loved you!" Ariah said.

"You really are the most amazing woman I have ever met and had the joy to know," Joshua replied. "I love you too! So very much!"

Several weeks later, Ariah came to visit again.

"I have a surprise for you," she said.

"But you must close your eyes and hold out your arms."

Joshua obediently closed his eyes. And held out his arms.

A bundle of blankets was placed there.

She brought me blankets, he thought? That was nice of her, but not much of a surprise.

But then, when he was allowed to open his eyes, there was an absolutely beautiful little face peering up out of her wrappings, her little arms breaking free of their confinement and reaching out toward him.

"Meet our grand-daughter, Asenath!" Ariah proudly announced. "And she brought her parents along with her!"

Belonging to Yahweh, Joshua thought.

"How wonderful!"

He looked up to see Khiya and Koumi's smiles. Three others could be seen and heard, three little boys who were pretending to be shy and hiding behind their parents.

"And this is Joshua, and Rahim, and Simon," Koumi said, placing her hand on the head of each one in descending order.

"And they are definitely not as shy as they are pretending to be!"

"Boys, say hi to your Sabba," she said.

Tears filled Joshua's eyes.

Another Joshua in the family. And two others named after their great grandfather and their other grandfather.

How truly wonderful.

Joshua wondered what these children would grow up to become, given the parents that Adonai had given to them, given the heritage they had.

Amazing for sure.

They all embraced each other in turn.

This was almost too good to be true.

Whatever would happen now, Joshua felt that his life was complete.

Still, he hoped he would have much more time.

As a family, they spent the majority of the day just catching up on all that had happened.

"Abba, I would really like to write down your story," Khiya said at one point, somewhat out of the blue. "I think our Abba might be able to use it to bless others! And I for one, just want to hear it all!"

Joshua thought that sounded like a most wonderful idea.

"Maybe…" he said. "I would love to share all of what He has brought me through and done in me with you and others!"

"I love you, Abba," Khiya said, hugging him as they said their goodbye. "And I'll see you tomorrow!"

"I love you too," Joshua said to his chosen son.

That night, as Joshua knelt beside his bed, he concluded his prayer with an, "I love you, Abba!"

He was certain he heard Heaven's reply:

"And I love you too, Joshua my son! More than you could ask, think, or even imagine! My beloved son, with whom I am so very pleased!"

AFTERWORD

Even though Barabbas is mentioned in each of the gospels, he only receives one, or maybe a couple of lines. And as I said at the outset, we actually know little or nothing about him, which makes him ripe for neglect, or for someone like me to fabricate an entire saga about him.

I have enjoyed writing and researching his story, trying inasmuch as possible, to be historically accurate and true to what was and to what I believe could have been. One day I trust, I will know Barabbas's true story. Until then, I offer this as a best guess as to what really happened.

I hope, as you have entered into this redemption story, that Adonai Himself and the Son of God who revealed Him, have touched you as He did me, and as I have suggested He did Barabbas, in a meaningful, profound, life-changing, life-altering way, through His Holy Spirit.

The ancient throng chose Jesus Barabbas. Even though they had been given another option.

What if they had made the other, harder, choice? "Give us Jesus, the one called Christ?"

"Choose you this day whom you will serve," Barabbas's namesake said, "but as for me and my house, we will serve the LORD."

You too have a choice to make. I pray that you choose Jesus. He has clearly chosen you.

Thom

ENDNOTES

1 I believe the Bible to be not only the Word of God but an accurate historical resource as well.

2 Many have suggested this in the past, but for a somewhat recent example, see "Pilate Released Barabbas. Really??" The Bart Ehrman Blog, accessed December 16, 2019, https://ehrmanblog.org/pilate-released-barabbas-really/. Ehrman says, "We have no evidence outside these Gospel accounts that any such person as Barabbas existed." He refers to Barabbas as an, "apparently non-existent person," whose name, in contradistinction to Jesus who is called the Christ, allows the Gospel writers to make what he feels was to them an important point. He says: "And so, in a very poignant way, the story of the release of Barabbas is a story about which kind of 'son of the father' the Jewish people preferred. Do they prefer the one who is a political insurgent, who believed that the solution to Israel's problems was a violent overthrow of the ruling authorities? Or do they prefer the loving 'Son of the Father' who was willing to give his life for others? In these Christian recollections, the Jewish people preferred the murdering insurrectionist to the self-sacrificing savior." Interestingly, Ehrman does feel that the full name, "Jesus Barabbas," is the preferred reading in Matthew 27:17. A more radical example, someone who argues that Jesus Christ never existed as a historical person, is Kenneth Humphreys in "Bar Abbas! Barabbas!" accessed April 5, 2019, https:// www.jesusneverexisted.com/barabbas.html. He holds

that, "The custom of releasing a prisoner, chosen by a crowd at Passover, is palpable nonsense, nowhere attested outside of the gospels and historically bogus. The very existence of Barabbas is blatantly allegorical."

3   CEB, CJB: "Yeshua Bar-Abba," CEV, DLNT, GNT, LEB, MOUNCE, NET, NIV, NRSV, NTE, OJB: "Yeshua Bar-Abba," MSG, TPT, and TLV "Yeshua Bar-Abba."

4   See the footnotes regarding Matthew 27:16-17 in Kurt Aland, Matthew Black, Carlo M. Martini, Bruce M. Metzger, and Allen Wikgren, eds., *Novum Testamentum Graece*, 27th edition (Stuttgart: Deutsche Bibelgesellschaft, 1993), 81.

5   W. Hershey Davis says, "In his [i.e. Origen's] comments on Matt. 24:15 he says that 'In like manner as, according to some, Barabbas was also called Jesus, and yet was a robber, having nothing of Jesus except the name, so there are in my opinion many Christs but only in name.' From these comments it is quite evident that in the MS. which Origen had the name of Barabbas is *Jesus* Barabbas, and that the name *Jesus* before Barabbas was absent from many MSS. known to Origen. His further comments on 27:17 show that he did not absolutely reject the reading *Jesus Barabbas*; yet he disliked the reading, and suggested that the name *Jesus* might be a heretical addition (super-additum) to the text. He also states that in the Scriptures the name Jesus (Joshua) was not borne by both evil and good men as other names (e.g. Judas) but only by good men. He then objected to the reading on the ground that the name *Jesus* could not have been borne by one who was a sinner." W. Hersey Davis, "Origen's Comment on Matthew 27:17," *Review and Expositor* 39, no.1 (January 1942): 65.

6   There is a direct correlation between this shift in Jewish society, documented in many places, and the translation of the Hebrew

Scriptures into Greek known as the Septuagint (LXX) where YHWH was almost always translated "*Kyrios*" meaning "Lord." From this point on, only the high priest could speak the name YHWH and only on the Day of Atonement and within the confines of the Holy of Holies.

7   I owe the majority of this material to Jonathan Price, "Zealots and Sicarii," accessed April 10, 2016, https://jewishvirtual-library.org. This article is no longer to be found at this site but the same article can now be found at https://www.ency-clopedia.com. Another informative resource was Kaufman Kohler, "Zealots," in *The Jewish Encyclopedia: A Descriptive Record of the History, Religion, Literature, and Customs of the Jewish People from the Earliest Times to the Present Day*, ed. Isidore Singer (New York: Funk & Wagnalls Company, 1906), 12:639-643. This resource is now public domain and available on the internet.

CPSIA information can be obtained
at www.ICGtesting.com
Printed in the USA
BVHW030513040620
580682BV00001B/1